Dubh-linn

A Novel of Viking Age Ireland

Book Two of The Norsemen Saga

James L. Nelson

This is a work of fiction. Names, characters, places and incidents either are the product of the author's imagination or are used fictitiously. Any resemblance to actual events, locales, organizations, or persons, living or dead, is entirely coincidental and beyond the intent of either the author or the publisher.

Fore Topsail Press
64 Ash Point Road
Harpswell, Maine, 04079

ISBN: 1484878930
ISBN-13: 9781494878934

DEDICATION

For my beautiful Elizabeth,
my Viking princess,
with the blood of the Norsemen
coursing in her veins.

Dubh-linn: Gaelic place name meaning "Black Pool." The origin of modern-day Dublin

(for other terms, see Glossary page 320)

Prologue

The Saga of Thorgrim Ulfsson

There was a man named Thorgrim Ulfsson, who was called Thorgrim Night Wolf.

He was of no remarkable size, but his strength was great and he was a skilled and much-respected warrior and honored for his skill as a poet. In his younger days he went a-viking with the jarl whom he served, a wealthy man known as Ornolf the Restless.

Through his plundering, Thorgrim became a man of wealth, and married Ornolf's daughter, Hallbera, who was fair and mild-tempered and bore him two strong sons and two daughters. Thorgrim then decided to remain on his farm in Vik in the country of Norway and no longer go a-viking.

Thorgrim Night Wolf prospered as a farmer. He was well liked, and though he was temperate and sparing in speech, and not much given to gaiety, he was a good host and would never be found turning a stranger away from his door, nor denying him a place at table. During the day Thorgrim was kind and good-natured to his men and his slaves, but oftentimes as evening came on he would grow bad-tempered and people were wary of approaching him. It was thought by many that Thorgrim was a shape shifter, and though no one could claim to have ever seen Thorgrim change from a man into another thing, still he became known as Night Wolf.

As the years passed, Ornolf the Restless grew old and fat, but he was still a man of great energy. After Thorgrim's wife, whom Thorgrim loved very much, died in the birthing of their second daughter, Ornolf convinced Thorgrim to go a-viking once more. Thorgrim's oldest son, Odd, had grown to a man and had a farm and a family of his own, and though Odd was strong and clever, Thorgrim did not take him plundering because he thought things would go better for Odd's family if he remained behind.

The younger son was named Harald. Harald was not as clever as Odd, but he was loyal and hardworking, and by the age of fifteen had grown so strong that he came to be known as Harald Broadarm. When Thorgrim went a-viking with Ornolf the Restless, he brought his son Harald to accompany him and learn the ways of men and warriors. This was the year 852 by the Christian calendar, one year after the birth of Harald Halfdansson, who would come to be known as Harald Fairhair, the first king of Norway.

Now, in those days the Norwegians had set up a longphort on the east coast of Ireland at a place which the Irish people called Dubh-linn. It was there that Ornolf decided to sail with his longship *Red Dragon*, not knowing that the Danes had come and driven the Norwegians out and taken the longphort for themselves. On the way to Dubh-linn Ornolf's men plundered a few ships, including one that had aboard it a crown, known to the Irish as the Crown of the Three Kingdoms. It was understood that the king to whom the Crown of the Three Kingdoms was presented should have authority over those kings who were his neighbors. The crown was now to be given to the king at a place called Tara, and that king intended to use the power of the crown to drive the Northmen out of Dubh-linn, but those plans were interrupted when Ornolf and his men plundered the ship and took the crown for themselves.

The loss of the crown caused a great stir among the Irish, and the king at Tara said to his men, "We must stop at nothing to see that the crown is returned to me, so that we might drive these dubh gall from our country." Dubh gall was the word the Irish used for the Danes, and the Norwegians they called fin gall. The king and his men then tried to get the crown back, and this led to many adventures and strife for the Northmen.

Around this time, Olaf the White drove the Danes from Dubh-linn. Ornolf, Thorgrim and those of their men who still lived, joined in the battle and after found a welcome in the longphort. Indeed, Ornolf felt such a welcome that he did not care to leave Dubh-linn or return to his wife, who was well known for her sharp tongue and shrewish ways.

Thorgrim, however, was weary of Ireland and wished for nothing more than to return to his farm in Vik. But the longship which had carried them to Ireland, the *Red Dragon,* had been lost at sea and so Thorgrim set about to find some other means for him and Harald to return to their home.

Here is what happened.

Chapter One

Words could not fell me,
by the fullest means
I, battle-oak, have brought
death's end to many a man,
making my sword's mouth speak.
Gisli Sursson's Saga

The birds of prey lay waiting in the predawn dark, quiet, wings folded. Half a dozen longships, lifting and sinking in the swells coming in from the sea, motionless beyond that, their sails furled and their long yards swung fore and aft. Each held a row of round shields mounted on its rails. A mile beyond their bows, beyond the gracefully curved stems, with dragons and birds worked into the hard oak, was the south coast of Ireland, the cut in the shoreline that formed the closest water approach to the monastery at a place known as Cloyne. The land was just visible, a dark, looming presence in the light of the half-moon directly overhead.

The fleet had come from Dubh-linn, sailing and rowing south then west along the coast. The night before, they had hauled out on a sandy beach a few miles away. In the hours before dawn the men, roused grumbling from sleep, pushed the ships back out into the sea. The night was still, so they used the long oars to drive them down that last stretch of coast until they had reached this place, this spot where they would come ashore and roll through the ringfort, the town and the monastery there. In an hour they intended to own every man, woman and child within three miles, a population who, they hoped, did not yet even know they were there.

The ships ranged in size. The smaller vessels carried twenty or thirty men crammed aboard, while the great, sweeping longships, with rowing stations for forty men, easily held twice that number in their low, sleek, beamy hulls. All told, nearly three hundred warriors sat waiting nervously in the chill of the early morning hours.

It was not the coming fight that made them nervous. Quite the opposite. The thought of bloody battle lifted their spirits, it was the reason they were there. Many of the men, as they brooded on the darkness, turned their thoughts to sheildwalls and sword thrusts and the feel of a battle ax hitting home, and those thoughts provided some comfort to them.

It was the darkness they did not like. The Norsemen hated the dark. If they feared no man alive, they did fear those things that lurked in deep shadow, those things that were not of the world of men, that hunkered down in the hidden places ashore or, worse yet, in the black water beneath their keels. So they sat at their rowing stations and they adjusted their mail and their weapons, and the men from the north waited for the coming of the sun, and the order to take up their oars and pull for the distant shore.

Well aft on the longship known as *Black Raven*, Thorgrim Night Wolf stood looking toward the land, one hand resting on the hilt of his sword. With the other he tugged on the brooch that held the fur cloak clasped around his neck, freeing the metal filigree from his beard. The facial hair was not charcoal black anymore, as it had been in the younger days. A few weeks before he had caught his reflection in a silver chalice, had seen that his beard was now shot through with white, like the last bits of winter snow that cling to the shady places and refuse to melt.

Underfoot he could feel the ship slewing a bit in the swells and he turned to give the man at the steering board an order to shift his helm, but he stopped as he recalled again that this was not his ship, and though he had been given an honored place aft, he had no authority aboard her.

The man who did own the ship, the man who commanded those Northmen who sat at the rowing benches, was Arinbjorn Thoruson, whose fine smile had earned him the name Arinbjorn White-tooth, and he was just visible to Thorgrim at the opposite rail. Thorgrim considered saying something about the way the ship was twisting in the seas, but they did not appear to be in danger of hitting any of the other vessels so Thorgrim kept his own council. He was not one to speak when it was not his business, and often didn't even when it was.

As if sensing that Thorgrim was looking in his direction, Arinbjorn crossed the narrow deck and stood beside him, nodding toward the shore. "What think you, Thorgrim?" he asked, and there was a lightness to his tone, a casual quality that put Thorgrim on edge. "These Irish, will we get a fight out of them?"

"Hard to say with the Irish," Thorgrim replied, choosing his words with care. He had been in Ireland for nearly half a year now, had learned much about the country and the people, and largely despised both. Most of the men who had come from Norway with him and Ornolf the Restless had died in the violence that seemed to trail behind the Crown of the Three Kingdoms like a swarm of bees. Those who survived had been left adrift in an Irish boat made of wood and hide, then were swept up in the great fleet of Olaf the White on his way to take Dubh-linn from the Danes.

"Hard to say," Thorgrim said again. Arinbjorn was just a few feet away, all dark shadow and gray in the moonlight, bulky looking under his fur cape. His teeth seemed to glow. Thorgrim looked away, toward the shoreline. He thought the dawn was coming up, the land more visible now. "Sometimes they will run at the sight of a longship," he elaborated, "sometimes they'll stand and fight. Often it will depend on what their neighbors are doing. Every third Irishman is a king of something, lord of some cow pasture. If they are at war with one another they'll have no men or stomach for a fight with us. If they decide to band together they can field a decent army, put up a real fight."

Arinbjorn was quiet for a moment. "I see," he said at last. "Well, we'll see how things lay soon enough."

Thorgrim's mind went back to the last time he was in that place, standing on the deck of a longship, anticipating a fight. That had been the taking of Dubh-linn and it had involved no great effort in the end. Olaf's force was overwhelming, and Dubh-linn was no longer some outpost barely clinging to the Irish coast, but a genuine settlement, with shopkeepers and brewers and blacksmiths and carpenters and all manner of tradesmen and artisans who did not care a whit for who ran the town as long as they were left alone to earn their living. Those few Danes willing to die to defend Dubh-linn did so quickly, and the rest welcomed the newcomers with a shrug.

Ornolf the Restless and Olaf the White, who had known each other for many years and were great friends, shared a passion for food, drink and women, all of which could be found in abundance in the thriving longphort. Soon Ornolf was proclaiming that the new Dubh-linn was as fine a place as Valhalla was likely to be, without the bother of having to take to the field and spend each day hacking and killing your fellow revelers. Ornolf swore by Odin that he intended to return to Norway as soon as he could. But those claims grew more infrequent with each night spent at the mead hall, until finally, having failed to convince anyone of his sincerity, Ornolf stopped trying to convince himself.

Thorgrim was certain now that it was growing light, and fore and aft men were beginning to move, as if animated by the gray dawn. Thorgrim could make out his son Harald on the fourth oar from the stern, larboard side. The boy had grown since they had sailed from Vik with Ornolf, Harald's grandfather. Grown in many ways. Physically he was twice the young man he had been then. He was certainly as tall as Thorgrim now, perhaps taller. Thorgrim did not like to think on it.

Harald had filled out in the arms and chest as well. He was the kind who could never stand to be idle. If there was work to do, he was the first hand in, and if there was no work to do, he would find some.

In Dubh-linn they had secured lodging with a blacksmith from Trondheim named Jokul and his lovely Irish wife. Of all the craftsmen who had come to Dubh-linn and stayed, the woodworkers and comb makers and leather workers and goldsmiths, it was the blacksmiths who were most in demand, and of them, Jokul was looked on as the best. His home and his shop were larger than most, more accommodating.

Still, the smith had been grudging at first about renting a space to the two men from Vik. Indeed, it was only his wife, Almaith, insisting that they be allowed to stay that swayed him in the end. And that in turn had worried Thorgrim, because he was not sure why she was so eager to have them there, and feared her motives might not be the most pure. That could mean trouble to windward, as he knew all too well, having seen in his lifetime nearly every version of the story of men and women played out before him, and often with himself in a leading role.

In the end, none of those concerns were realized. Thorgrim guessed that it was Almaith's desire for the rent money, or some diversion from the often unpleasant Jokul, that accounted for her insistence that they stay. Harald, for some unfathomable reason, was eager to learn the Irish tongue, and Almaith, a pleasant and patient tutor, set in to teach him the basics of the language. Harald was by nature eager and curious. He began following the smith around, looking for tasks to perform, and soon found Jokul eager to dole them out.

After months of the young man splitting and stacking wood, making repairs to the wattle and timber frame home, pumping bellows at the forge and even learning some crude ironworking, the smith had grown more welcoming in his attitude, and Thorgrim knew he would be loath to see them go. He had tried, in fact, to dissuade them from joining the raiding party of which they were now a part.

Along with Harald's weed-like growth and the near constant work came an appetite that would make any bear shake his head in wonder. But that, too, was well sated in Dubh-linn. As much as the Irish might despise the fin gall, and the dubh gall before them, the longphort was a ready market, a market flowing with plundered gold and silver. Every day, farmers pushed their carts of produce through the high wooden palisade gates, every day sheep herds and swine herds and cow herds drove their beasts along the muddy plank roads to the market. It all seemed to flow into Harald's stomach, and added pounds of muscle to his frame. One of Ornolf's men had recently dubbed him Harald Broadarm, and that name seemed to have stuck.

Thorgrim watched his son work the kinks out of his arms, ready to take up the loom of the oar. He wondered, idly, if the two of them were to come to blows, which might win. Not that such a thing would happen. Thorgrim loved Harald above all things, and would lay down his life for the boy before he would ever raise a hand against him. Still, he wondered.

I have experience and wile on my side, he thought, *even if youth and speed are with Harald.* But of course Thorgrim had been training Harald since he was five, training with shield and sword and battle ax and pike. He had passed on to his son much of his considerable skill with weapons.

A dull light to the east seemed to part the horizon, water and sky, as the sun, with no great enthusiasm, came up at last. A voice came rolling over the swells. "Take up your oars!" It was the voice of Hoskuld Feilan, who was known as Hoskuld Iron-skull, the jarl who owned the longship *Thunder God*, largest of the present fleet, the man commanding the raid on the Irish coast. With those words the long row of sweeps along *Thunder God*'s side rose as one and swept forward in perfect symmetry. With the rowers hidden from view behind the line of bright painted shields, there was, to Thorgrim's eye, something unworldly about it, as if the ship itself had sprung to life.

"To oars! Take up your oars!" Arinbjorn White-tooth shouted. On *Black Raven*'s rowing benches, larboard and starboard, fore and aft, the men pushed down and aft on the thick looms. "Pull together!" Arinbjorn called next and as one the oars came down, the men leaned back, *Black Raven* gathered way. From a sleeping, lethargic thing, the ship came alive, the water swished down her side. Her fabric groaned with the leverage of sweep against oar port, and her motion changed from a dull roll to a determined, forward thrust. Thorgrim felt his spirit surge with the ship under his feet.

He looked out to the east and west as in rapid succession the rest of the fleet gathered way and pulled for shore, spreading out astern of *Thunder God* like men at arms in a swine array. As he shifted his gaze he took a glance at Harald, hoping Harald would not see, not wanting the boy to think he was keeping an eye on him. But Harald was focused on his work, his eyes moving from the man astern of him to the sea and the rig overhead. A good seaman, a sailor's eye. Thorgrim looked toward the shore. To starboard and larboard the rugged country ran down to the water, but right ahead the land seemed to open up in welcome. It was through that gap they would pull, then a few miles up the mouth of a river to their landing place. There was no movement along the shoreline that Thorgrim could see. No one there.

It had been near the end of summer when they first pulled *Red Dragon* up the Liffey River to the longphort of Dubh-linn, late fall when they had returned as part of Olaf the White's fleet. Even if Ornolf had actively tried to secure a ship to return his men to Norway it is likely the winter weather would have closed in before they could have put to sea. But of course Ornolf made virtually no effort at all, and so he and the men with him had spent the winter months in Dubh-linn, the miserable gray, wet winter in the crowded, fetid, mud-choked town of Dubh-linn.

Once it became clear to Thorgrim that Ornolf had little interest in getting himself or his men home, Thorgrim asked and received permission to make other arrangements. Ornolf did not want to see him go, and even less did he want to see his grandson go, but for all his drunken raving Ornolf was not one who was oblivious to the way other men saw the world. He, Ornolf, had talked Thorgrim into going a-viking, mostly against Thorgrim's will. He knew that Thorgrim had come in hopes of dulling the pain of Hallbera's death. When he thought about it, which he did as infrequently as possible, Ornolf suspected that he might have come for the same reason. And Ornolf knew that Thorgrim was ready to go home.

But getting home was another matter. As Thorgrim prowled the quays and the mead hall, and came to know the other warriors and jarls, he soon realized that none would be returning to Norway until their holds were crammed with the legendary wealth of Ireland. There would be more raiding and more plunder before there was a hope of sailing east again. Thorgrim had nothing against raiding and plunder. He had done more of it than any three men were likely to do over a lifetime. But he was not the young man he had been, and he longed for home.

By that time, Thorgrim Night Wolf was well known in Dubh-linn, his reputation as a fighting man set. Stories of past deeds had swirled around the mead hall, the tale of how he had led his men to escape the Danes in Dubh-linn, and fought the armies of the Irish king at Tara. Talk of shape shifting was passed around quietly when Thorgrim was not about.

One night, a month or so after his return to Dubh-linn, three large, drunk and well-armed men had set upon Thorgrim as he left the mead hall. They were looking to make a name for themselves, and were full up with tales of the Night Wolf. The fight had been brief, and had ended very badly for the three men. Had ended, indeed, with each one face down in the mud in various states of dismemberment. Thorgrim met with nothing but polite respect after that.

Thorgrim was aware of these things, and he thought that his reputation would help him secure a place among a ship's company, but he found just the opposite to be true. He was well treated to be sure, men were eager to buy him food and drink, his company, when he was in the proper frame of mind, was sought after, but when it came to joining a ship, there never seemed to be room for another man. It took a month of that before Thorgrim finally understood that no ship's master wanted another man who was also accustomed to command, who might question orders, who might become the focal point for unrest. It was pointless to try to convince anyone that he wanted no more than to take his place in the shieldwall, to do his work, to go home.

In all fairness, Thorgrim had to admit that he would not want a man like himself aboard either.

He had begun contemplating the idea of building a boat that could take him and Harald back to Vik when Arinbjorn White-tooth had sought him out on the quay. "Thorgrim Ulfsson, I hear that you are in hopes of joining a ship," he said.

Thorgrim looked him up and down. Good clothes, silver inlay on the hilt of his sword, silver and gold brooch holding a cape of bear fur. He was a well-made man, and had more the look of a jarl than a farmer or fishermen about him. No, not a jarl. The son of a jarl.

"You hear right," Thorgrim said. His mood, never particularly buoyant, was now all but awash from the constant frustration, disappointment and Ireland's ceaseless, tormenting rain. If it had been later in the day, he would have been unapproachable. But then, if it had been later in the day, he would have secured himself in a place that could not be found.

"I am in need of a man such as you," Arinbjorn said.

"Really? It seems no others are."

"Maybe the others are afraid of the Night Wolf. I am not. I'll welcome any man who can use a sword or a battle ax aboard my ship."

Thorgrim had only one condition, and that was that Harald be welcome aboard as well, and Arinbjorn agreed to that with enthusiasm. And so, two weeks later, Thorgrim Night Wolf found himself closing with the Irish coastline, ready to vault over the side of a longship into the shallow water, ready to push up a narrow path and fall on the unsuspecting people of the ringfort and the monastery supposed to be just beyond the high banks of the shoreline.

Black Raven's stern rose up, just a bit, as the swell from the sea passed under the keel, then down it went as the bow came up in turn. There was land on either side of them now as they entered the wide estuary, and the ocean rollers gave way to flatter water. The sun was up, the sky gray but without rain, the shore a muted stretch of green and brown, the longships things of beauty as they swept forward with gathering momentum.

"Look, there!" Arinbjorn said. He was pointing beyond the starboard bow. Thorgrim followed his arm. There were men standing on the low ridge of land that bordered the water. They were just visible against the gray sky, four or five of them.

"Sheep herds, you think?" Arinbjorn asked. "Fisherman, perhaps?"

"Perhaps…" Thorgrim said, with no conviction. And just as the word left his mouth, three more appeared, mounted on the pathetic little beasts that the Irish called horses. They seemed to be watching the approaching ships – indeed, what else would they be looking at? Then they whirled around and disappeared from sight.

Very well, thought Thorgrim, *we still have plenty of advantages on our side. Surprise is just not one of them.*

Chapter Two

It is rare to find one to trust
amongst the men who dwell
beneath Odin's gallows
for the dark-minded destroyer of kin
swaps his brother's death for treasure
Egil's Saga

The church that stood within the protective circle of the ringfort, the ringfort that surrounded Tara, the seat of the high king of Brega and some said of all Ireland, was nothing terribly remarkable, Tara and Ireland being as they were on the fringes of the civilized world. It was timber framed, rectangular, of no great size. But the high-peaked roof was made up of new thatch, the long dried reeds intricately braided and twisted around the peak and eaves. The walls, wattle-made, were smooth and whitewashed until they seemed brilliant on those remarkable and few days when the sun shone. The windows sported glass panes.

Inside it was tidy, scrubbed and swept from tabernacle to vestibule. It looked as good as it was going to look, which was only proper, because on that day, the same day that Thorgrim Night Wolf and Harald Thorgrimson were preparing for a bloody fight on Irish soil, a royal wedding would be taking place.

Had it been summer, the rafters and beams and the altar deep in the interior would have been brilliant with bursts of colorful wildflowers - bindweed, pink willowherb, yellow marsh ragwort and little robin – made up in raucous bouquets. The sun might even have been shining in blue skies, the windows and doors of the church open and sweet warm air blowing through.

But it was not that time of the year. It was early spring and the skies were a gray that sometimes bordered on black and the rain was pouring down. The church was draped in swathes of colorful cloth, but that was a poor substitute for the flowers. The windows and doors were shut against the driving rain. The gloom of the church's interior was dispelled at intervals by torches and candles, but still much of the space was lost in deep shadow, despite it not being quite noon. The stone floor was already slick with mud, and that just from the abbot and the women of the court getting the place ready for the joyous occasion.

In command of the ceremony, overseeing preparations like a king at the head of an army, Morrigan nic Conaing whisked around the church, taking care not to slip on the glistening floor. She paused by the altar, looked down the length of the aisle and frowned. By the time all the guests had filed in, the mud would make that aisle genuinely treacherous. The bride might well slip and come crashing to the stone floor.

Hmm...Morrigan considered the possibility. *Would that be a bad thing?* There were certain aspects of such an accident that might recommend it. But it was her brother, Flann mac Conaing, who would be giving the bride away, walking her down the aisle. If the bride went down, she might take him with her. It would do little to bolster his position at Tara to have him flailing on the muddy floor in a tangle with some pathetic tart in a near-white dress.

"You there, Brendan," she snapped at a slave who was scraping wax drippings from the floor.

"Mistress?" he said, his tone properly cowed.

"See there are fresh rushes to lay along the aisle here. See that they are put down just before the guests take their places."

"Yes, ma'am." That was all Morrigan wanted to hear.

The bride was Brigit nic Máel Sechnaill, daughter of Máel Sechnaill mac Ruanaid, late high king of Tara, who had been cut down while fighting one of the many minor squabbles for power in which the numerous kings of Ireland were always engaged. For all the mourning at Máel's death, the wailing and gnashing of teeth, Morrigan knew him for what he really was, a vicious, brutal man. She was certain his wickedness had not escaped the attention of her Lord, was certain that even before his body hit the sod, God had plunged Máel's soul down into the depths of hell.

His enemy on the field that day had been Cormac ua Ruairc, king of Gailenga, brother to Brigit's late husband. The loyalties, the enmities, the intrigues of Ireland were like the Northmen's carvings of mythical beasts, all interwoven and twisted around and around, endlessly complicated.

Cormac had lost the day, and for his efforts to usurp the power of the high king, Lord of Brega, he had been tied to a stake and disemboweled before the remnants of his army. On the positive side, it made Cormac's surviving troops welcome the chattel slavery that would now be their station in life.

How Máel Sechnaill had been killed, no one knew. In the madness of the battle, no one had seen him fall. It was not until the men from Gailenga had called for quarter, had thrown down their arms, that the high king had been found, mud-spattered, wide-eyed, a great rent from a sword thrust in his neck.

Morrigan ran her critical eyes around the church once more, frowned at the tall candles burning on either side of the altar. One was ten inches shorter than the other. It would certainly look better if they were the same height, but was it worth the expense of getting two new ones? If she left it, would it appear as if she did not care about Brigit's wedding? In point of fact she did care. At present she thought of little besides Brigit and what might happen as a result of this marriage. She cared so much it made her wild with fury. She was like a wineskin, stretched to bursting with anger, but containing it, keeping it all inside.

The candles were fine as they were.

Morrigan heard a door open and the flames in the various candles swayed, guttered, then came to attention again as the door closed. Donnel swept into the church, his cloak hanging heavy and dripping off his shoulders, his shoes and leggings brown and glistening with mud.

Donnel and his brother Patrick were sheep herders, or had been sheep herders, when they had come upon the young nobleman who was carrying the Crown of the Three Kingdoms to Tara, from whom the Northmen had stolen it. The sheep herders had brought the man to see Máel Sechnaill, and they liked what they saw of Tara. And Morrigan liked what she saw of them; young, strong and smart, and they were eager enough to never herd sheep again that they would do whatever was asked of them.

"Donnel," Morrigan said. "Are you just now back?"

"Yes, ma'am," Donnel said, giving a shallow bow, like a wealthy bishop genuflecting. "I come direct to see you, ma'am."

Morrigan nodded her approval. "Cloyne?"

"Fair warned this week or more."

"Clondalkin?" Morrigan asked.

"Clondalkin as well, if your men in Dubh-lin are to be trusted at all."

"Do you trust them?"

"I do, ma'am. They've too much to lose, and naught to gain. Patrick feels the same."

Morrigan nodded. These young men were learning the rules of the game, learning them fast. Information. Knowledge. That was what she had learned from that bastard Máel Sechnaill. The late high king had been sure to know everything that went on in his kingdom.

Well, nearly everything.

"You've made a good job of it, Donnel. Now, go and dry yourself, and eat and rest. I've more need of you, and I won't have you laid low."

Morrigan did indeed have need of Donnel. And Patrick. And all the men she had working in the shadows. Morrigan's brother, Flann mac Conaing, had taken command at Tara on the death of Máel Sechnaill mac

Ruanaid. Flann had his following among the minor kings, the *rí túaithe*, who owed their allegiance to the high king at Tara. Flann was part of Máel Sechnaill's *derbfine*, his family going back four generations. They were, in fact, second cousins, and that was enough under Irish law to give Flann a legitimate claim to the throne.

But just because Flann had a claim to the throne, and was sitting on it now, did not mean it was his. He was not the *tánaise ríg*, the heir apparent. If Brigit gave birth to a son, grandson of Máel Sechnaill, there was every chance that the little bastard might be looked on as the *tánaise ríg*, and Flann – and Morrigan – would be out as soon as Brigit could arrange it. That could not happen.

Despite being of the royal line, Morrigan had been taken captive by the dubh gall years before, had ended up as a thrall in Dubh-linn. She had suffered years of humiliation; raped, beaten, starved. And when she had the means to escape, word had come that Máel Sechnaill wished her to remain, so that she might keep an eye on the Norsemen in Dubh-linn, and keep Tara informed of what they were about. Years more of suffering were hers because of that, years of terror and degradation, until at last she had helped Thorgrim Night Wolf and his band escape from the Danes, and had fled the city with them.

No. After all that, after seeing her brother rise to hold the throne at Tara, with the Crown of the Three Kingdoms in his possession, after enjoying the exalted position that his place gave her, she would not be pushed aside by some empty-headed little whore. And from her place at Tara Morrigan would quench that red-hot ember that burned in her, that hatred for all the heathen pigs who came across the sea in their longships and defiled her Ireland. If there was one thing she had learned from the bastard Máel Sechnaill, it was how power was gained and kept. And she had not been idle, not idle at all.

"Thank you, ma'am," Donnel said. He made another shallow, awkward bow, an imitation of the courtly manner which had been utterly foreign to him less than a year before, turned and was gone.

"Very well!" Morrigan clapped her hands loudly to get the attention of the servants and slaves working at their various tasks. "It is near time, finish up and be quick about it." It had been half an hour at least since the Angelus bells had chimed, and the monks who lived in the monastery within Tara's ringfort would be finishing their prayers and turning their attention to the nuptial ceremony.

The sound of the rain outside grew suddenly louder, and a blast of wet, cold wind wrapped around Morrigan as the main door to the church opened and Father Finnian came in, pushing the door closed against the storm. A cloud of dried rushes lifted in the wind and scattered along the floor of the nave.

"Father Finnian," Morrigan said, bowing her head in a respectful manner.

"Morrigan." Finnian lifted his hand and made the sign of the cross toward Morrigan, and Morrigan bowed deeper and crossed herself in thanks for the blessing.

Of course she would have asked him *to perform this atrocity*, Morrigan thought. Morrigan was nothing if not true to her faith. It had sustained her during her years of captivity. She had spent hours meditating on the sufferings of Christ and of beloved Saint Patrick, he also a slave. It was one of the few things that had eased the agony of her ordeal.

She loved all of the priests and brothers of the monastery. They were good men, simple men, for all their learning, steady and devout. But Father Finnian was different. He was an enigma. He was not much given to talk, for one thing. This set him apart from the others, who seemed to chatter away ceaselessly, as if to exercise their gratitude at not having had to take a vow of silence. Nor did Father Finnian show much deference to Morrigan's new status. The others, unsure how the power struggle would shake out, sought to win the good graces of all, but Finnian took another tack, and seemed not to care about the good graces of any.

That was not to say Finnian was in any way disrespectful. He was not. Reserved. That was how he was best described. Reserved. He was not old, in his thirties, perhaps, and even the tonsure could not detract from his remarkably handsome face; nor could the loose brown robes of his calling entirely disguise a strong and athletic frame. Ireland was a land of abundance, and the monks ate well, and on some it showed. But not Father Finnian.

Morrigan could not help but find him appealing. She had had dreams about him, unbidden nocturnal visions, and that disturbed her profoundly. In confession she could not bring herself to speak of her attraction - the word lust had come to mind, and she recoiled at the thought – and her failure to confess left the sin hanging and unforgiven.

"Is there anything more I can do, Father Finnian?" Morrigan asked. The monk looked around the church, blue eyes taking in the fresh rushes on the floor, the swathes of bright colored cloth, the candles adorning the alter. He nodded, and his lips turned up in just a hint of a smile.

"No, child, it appears you have seen to everything. You know, this church and all of Tara would be swallowed up if you were not here to look after it." The words were kind, but the tone was no more obsequious than a comment about the weather.

"Well," Morrigan said, "it seems to have stood for all the years I was a slave to the dubh gall," the words coming out more bitter by far than she had intended. She felt her face flush, but Father Finnian just nodded, with that look of calm understanding.

"It stood, child, but it did not stand strong."

Finnian was dressed in his white vestments now, not the course brown robe in which he was most often seen. Of the many men in the order (and it was one of the most populous in Ireland, in no small part because of the protection that the ringfort of Tara offered against the ceaseless ravages of the Norsemen) Father Finnian was one of the few ordained to the priesthood, thus one of the few who could perform the sacrament of marriage. The hem of the garments were wet and plastered with mud and it was everything Morrigan could do to not snatch them up and try to rub them clean.

Then, from above their heads, the bells of the church began to ring, calling those who had been waiting, the retinue of Tara, the *rí túaithe*, anyone of any significance within twenty miles, to the wedding of Brigit nic Máel Sechnaill, daughter of the late and greatly mourned Máel Sechnaill mac Ruanaid.

Father Finnian turned to Morrigan. "The time is here," he said.

Indeed, Morrigan thought.

Chapter Three

There are ax-ages, sword-ages-
Shields are cleft in twain, -
There are wind-ages, wolf-ages,
Ere the world falls dead.
The Fooling of Gylfe

Thorgrim Night Wolf was tired.

He was tired of the voyaging, tired of the thousand concerns that were the lot of any leader of men, weary of consideration. But for all that, he could not deny the stirring in his blood when he heard the bow of *Thunder God* scrape up on the beach, leading the other ships in.

Starboard and larboard, the men aboard *Black Raven* gave one last pull, and as the momentum carried the ship the last fifty feet to the beach, Arinbjorn called out, "Ship oars!" As one, the long sweeps came inboard and the oarsmen held them straight up. Thorgrim tried and failed not to glance in Harald's direction, but the boy was handling his oar as well as any of the more experienced men.

A raid. Tired as he was, he loved this. It reminded him that he was still alive. And he knew that if, in an hour's time, that was no longer true, then he would die the way a man was supposed to die.

"Who is that fellow?" Thorgrim asked Arinbjorn as the *Black Raven* closed fast with the beach. Up near the bow, one of the ship's company was whirling around, practically spinning where he stood. He wore only leggings, no mail, no shirt, no helmet to cover the wild mop of hair. His beard thrust out in various directions like a shrub that is beyond control. He held a short sword in his left hand, a battle ax in his right. He was thin, and had he been clothed he might have seemed weak and emaciated, but stripped to the waist his muscles stood out like the gnarled roots of a tree.

"Starri Deathless," Arinbjorn said. "He's a berserker. Leads a band of berserkers."

Thorgrim nodded. He could see at first glance that Starri was a berserker, a member of that cult of warriors who went mad at the prospect of battle. They plunged into a fight with a ferocity that was ordained by the gods, a blood-lust beyond even what the Norsemen considered normal. Thorgrim had fought alongside berserkers before and he recognized the signs, the disdain for armor, the frantic energy in those moments before the fight.

"I hadn't noticed him until now," Thorgrim said.

"He keeps to himself most of the time. In a fight, he's hard not to notice."

And then the *Black Raven* ran up on the sand and Thorgrim stumbled a little at the abrupt stop. The men leapt up, the oars were carried forward and stacked on the gallows amidships, and Thorgrim could feel his heart beat faster in his chest. He reveled at the thump of shields being lifted from their resting place on the gunnels, the odd metallic swish of mail shirts as the men vaulted over the low sides of the ship. They splashed into the surf and grabbed hold of the rails and pulled with a will. The shallow vessel came up on the sand. Long mooring lines were run up the beach to hold it in place.

Harald looked over at Thorgrim, unsure if, at his age, he could join the others without his father's say so. But Thorgrim gave the faintest of nods and Harald was off like an arrow, racing forward and then flinging himself over the side into the shallow water. He wore an iron helmet and a mail shirt, a shield on his left arm and a battle ax in his right hand. To Thorgrim he still looked like the little boy he once was, running around the farm in Vik with his play armor and wooden ax.

Harald's helmet, mail and weapons, like Thorgrim's, had been borrowed from Arinbjorn before they put to sea. For all the cattle and land and buildings and slaves Thorgrim owned back in Vik, in Ireland he was nearly destitute, having lost everything in his fighting with the Irish. The only possession he had was, happily, his most prized; his sword, Iron-tooth, taken from him by the Danes and returned (he still did not know how) by the thrall he knew as Morrigan.

At last it was only him and Arinbjorn aboard and they went forward to a place where the ship had been pulled up on the sand. Thorgrim put a foot on the gunnel, stood and dropped to the beach, Arinbjorn behind him. The last of the fleet was coming ashore. The narrow strip of sand, with the sea on one edge and tall, scrubby cliffs on the other, was filling with the men who had come to fight.

Thorgrim straightened and found himself standing beside Starri Deathless, who was still whirling around, and Thorgrim had to step back quick to avoid catching Starri's battle ax in the jaw. And in that instant their eyes met and Starri froze, just stopped, as if he was turned to stone, and held Thorgrim's gaze. Starri squinted and cocked his head, as if trying to get a closer look. Thorgrim held his eyes, not sure of the meaning of this, unwilling to look away. He would not be stared down, not by anyone, not even a berserker. Especially not a berserker, who, when not needed for the fighting was generally not considered fit for the company of men.

But the look in Starri's eyes held no threat or challenge or anything that smacked of hostility. Thorgrim could not imagine what was going on in the man's mind. Then Starri spoke, and his voice was calm. "Pray, what is your name?"

"Thorgrim. Thorgrim Ulfsson, of Vik."

"But they call you something else, do they not?"

"They call me Thorgrim Night Wolf."

"Yes, yes. The night wolf. You are the night wolf, and you are favored by the gods." And then Starri nodded and turned away and ambled off, as if Thorgrim had drained the madness from him.

"Odd duck," Arinbjorn said.

"It's who they are," Thorgrim said.

"Here," Arinbjorn nodded up the beach. "Hoskuld Iron-skull is calling the leaders together. Join me."

Thorgrim hesitated. "I am not a jarl, or the owner of any ship. I lead no men. I have no business at a gathering such as that."

"Nonsense! A man such as Thorgrim Night Wolf? Your council would always be welcome. Come with me." So Thorgrim followed Arinbjorn White-tooth up the beach to where the men who commanded the ships of the fleet were gathered around Hoskuld Iron-skull.

"You saw the riders on the ridge, I have no doubt," Iron-skull was saying as they joined the circle. "They'll be ready, waiting for us. We do not know how many." Hoskuld was a big man, filling out with age, but he still exuded power in his bearing and his voice. He wore mail, finely wrought, a helmet that would have gleamed if the sun had been shining, and around his shoulders a cloak made of some fine fur. Ermine, perhaps. He was a wealthy and powerful jarl, and everything about him reflected that fact.

"There's a tower at Cloyne," one of the other jarls offered, "maybe tall enough to have seen us at first light."

"A tower?" Arinbjorn said. "I was never told of any tower."

Hrolleif the Stout, who owned the ship *Serpent* and whose face was all but lost in his beard, shrugged as if it did not matter, and Thorgrim silently seconded the gesture. It did not matter.

But jarls would talk, and each would be heard, so the conversation went back and forth for some minutes more. Bolli Thorvaldsson, a minor jarl from the south of Norway, owner of *Odin's Eye*, the smallest ship in the fleet, favored the swiftest possible advance. Arinbjorn offered his own suggestion. "Let us take a third of our men, circle around to the south. If they are waiting for us in numbers, then the chief of our men will attack face on, and once engaged the third will attack from the side."

There was silence at that. Some nodded, but not with any great enthusiasm. Hrolleif spit on the sand, then wiped away the part that hung up in his beard. "Too fancy. Too fancy by half, I say," Hrolleif said. "Right at them, that's the way."

"Thorgrim Night Wolf?" Hoskuld Iron-skull asked, catching Thorgrim off guard. "You have spent some time now in this cursed country, what do you say?"

Thorgrim thought for a second. He was with Hrolleif in spirit, but he was serving at the pleasure of Arinbjorn White-tooth. Arinbjorn was no fool, and his idea was not necessarily wrong. There was no shame in thinking things through or trying to outwit your enemy. Yet….

"The Irish will not have mail, or few will," Thorgrim said at length, "and they will not have battle axes. Some are mounted on creatures they call horses, but if any of you mistook them for swine it would be no wonder." Some of the others smiled at that, some nodded. "I like what Arinbjorn suggests, but I think the biggest threat from the Irish are sheer numbers, in which case I would not care to have our company divided."

There followed a brief and disorderly discussion, with nearly all speaking at once, but it was clear that a great majority agreed with Thorgrim, and they would take that course. "That ridge is what we must worry about the most," said one of the men whom Thorgrim did not know. He pointed with his chin to the high ground that bordered the beach, the narrow cut of a trail that led through the scrub. "We can't go but two or three abreast up that trail. If these Irish know anything, they'll hit us there, butcher us as we come on."

Hoskuld Iron-skull closed the discussion. "That is why the gods give us berserkers," he said.

Chapter Four

We sailed our ships to any shore
that offered the best hope of booty;
we feared no fellow on earth,
we were fit, we fought in the battle fleet.
Saga of Arrow-Odd

Harald Thorgrimson's helmet slipped forward as he ran, despite the chin strap. The cursed thing covered his eyes for an instant, until he pushed it back into place. But now his vision was blurred by the sweat that ran liberally from under the padding despite the cool, damp weather. Still, he kept the helmet in place. He knew his father would be angry if he discarded it, and in some unexplored corner of his mind he was happy for the protection it offered as he raced into battle.

Just ahead of him, on the narrow path running up the sandy dunes from the beach, hemmed in by tangled shrubs, charged Starri Deathless and his berserker band. Behind Starri was that company's second in command, if berserkers could have such a thing, a Swede named Nordwall the Short. Starri and Nordwall were as opposite as two men could be. Where Starri was tall and wiry and constantly in motion, Nordwall was short and broad, a powerfully built man who tended to remain motionless, his eyes alone constantly roaming. He moved only when he had good reason to do so, and when he did, his actions were explosive.

One could not say that Starri was *leading* the attack, since he was utterly oblivious to the men behind him. He was, rather, flinging himself up the trail, his only thought to get at the enemy.

Harald was not pleased about having to advance in the wake of the berserkers. He had wanted very much to lead the attack himself, to be first up the trail, but Hoskuld Iron-skull had said no, the berserkers would lead, and that was an end to it. Harold was more than a bit put out by that. The fact that he was most likely the least experienced warrior there did not even occur to him.

Berserkers…. Damned madmen…. Harald thought as he pushed up the trail as fast as he could. He might not have had the frantic energy of the others, Starri, Nordwall and the half dozen in the van, but he was the youngest of all the ships' companies, and had the legs and the lungs on the rest. So, if he had to trail behind the berserkers, at least he would be the first among those who were not entirely insane.

Father…he'll be gasping for breath by this point, Harald thought with no small measure of satisfaction, but those thoughts were interrupted by the swishing sound of an arrow passing close by. He pushed his helmet back again, looked up as he ran, looked up in time to see a bowman on the ridge one hundred feet away. He wore a rough, green tunic, a leather helmet. He had his arrow knocked and drawn full length.

Harald's reflex was to duck, to swerve out of line, and he actually took a step to the right before he corrected himself with an oath and charged straight on. The bowman let the arrow fly - Harald could see it streaking down the hill toward him. How many times had he himself let fly an arrow and watched it fly away? And now here was one flying at him. There was time only to feel a surge of panic. His mind was wiped clean of thought, he could think of nothing to do but charge on. Then the man to his right leapt sideways to avoid a tangle of brush, and the move put him straight in the path of the three foot shaft.

The arrow's impact stopped the berserker's forward motion and sent him reeling back. The wicked metal tip erupted from the man's back in a welter of blood that felt to Harald like warm spray. Now Harald did leap aside to avoid the falling, writhing man. Spared, for the moment, Harald felt his panic turn to shame, and vague thoughts of Thorgrim and what he might think jumbled in his mind and solidified into anger and determination. He looked up as he ran, adjusted his helmet, raised his battle ax and let a wild shout rise from his lungs.

There were more bowmen on the ridgeline, half a dozen, and they let fly at the onrushing Norsemen. Harald could hear the swish of the arrows, all but lost in the growing shouts, the screams and animal howls of the berserkers as they covered the last fifty feet up the trail. Starri Deathless had an arrow through his upper arm, the head passed clean through, the shaft lodged in his muscle like it was some sort of decoration, but he gave no sign that he was even aware of it. He was howling like a wolf, his ax and short sword held overhead, his bare chest exposed as if making a target for the bowmen, but rather than firing, Harald could see they were backing away as the berserkers closed with them.

Starri was up and over the edge of the high ground and lost to sight, Nordwall at his heels, the others crowding behind and Harald pushing hard to keep up. All his youth and strength were not enough to allow him to keep pace with the unworldly energy of the berserkers as they raced into a fight. He adjusted his helmet and glanced over his shoulder. The next man was four of five paces behind, another right behind him, and the rest of the Northmen spread out along the trail, legs working hard in the sandy soil, a long line of bright colored shields and polished weapons coming up behind. He could not see his father, but knew he would be coming on as fast as his old legs could carry him. Harald could not recall exactly how old his father was, but he had to be in his fourth decade at least, and the years were starting to tell.

And then Harald was up over the ridge himself, his soft leather shoes digging in, pushing him on, up onto the flat ground and into a scene of madness. The Irish had made a shield wall of sorts, and the bowmen were retreating behind it, firing as they went, and the berserkers were flinging themselves in disordered array at the defense. Harald slowed for a second, taking it in, looking for the most advantageous point to add his weight to the fight. Beyond the struggling men, two hundred yards back, the land dipped down into a low spot, hidden by the hill on which they stood, then rose up beyond that and rolled away in fields that seemed dull green in the overcast, with patches of trees dotting the countryside, and a brown scar of a road no doubt leading back to the town of Cloyne.

Starri Deathless was flailing at the shieldwall with short sword and battle ax, his arms moving like tree branches whipping wildly in a storm. Splinters flew from the shields held up to fend him off, sprays of blood shot through the air. Beside him, Nordwall the Short hacked at the defenders, swinging down at the heads of the men in the shieldwall, wrenching his weapon free, then an upward swing from below. To Harald, all of Ireland seemed to contract down to that one flat hill top, and there was nothing but the struggling men, no sound but the shrieks of the wounded, the screams of the enraged.

Harald could see the left wing of the shieldwall starting to bend forward, turning like an arm to envelope the berserkers, who were too inflamed to notice. In a moment the Northmen would be fighting an enemy in front and behind.

There, there, there...the word churned in his mind and he charged forward, battle ax raised, leading with his shield, in just the manner Thorgrim had taught him with wooden toys on the farm. A shout came from his gut, burst from his mouth, rose up and up into a wolf's howl. He saw the men at the extreme edge of the shield wall look up, saw moustaches, beards, looks of shocked surprise and then he was on them, slamming into the nearest of the Irish defenders. He felt the shock reverberate through the boss of his shield. The Irishman stumbled, Harald's battle ax came down, came down with such force and momentum that the weapon was not slowed in the least by its impact with the man's head, but instead passed clean through and struck the back of his shield.

The man was dead and of no concern to Harald, so Harald let him fall away. He wrenched his ax free of the shield and swung it back, and on the backswing caught a sword slashing at him from behind the shieldwall. The man who had swung the sword was knocked off balance by the move and Harald drove his shield into him, sending him staggering back. Harald raised his ax, but - by luck or design - the man had stumbled beyond the reach of the three-foot weapon.

Harald was pivoting right when he sensed men around him, and then more of the Vikings who had pushed up the path at his heels flung themselves into the fight. On his left hand Harald had a glimpse of a yellow shield with some sort of red design on it. He looked to his right, took his eyes from the enemy in front, and even as he did, he heard his father's voice in his mind commanding, *keep your eyes on the fight!*

Just as the words came to him he was struck in the side of the head by something, some weapon that made his helmet ring and knocked him off balance. Then the helmet slipped down over his eyes, blinding him, completing his humiliation.

With hands encumbered by sword and shield he tried to push the helmet back. He clenched the muscles in his stomach, bracing for the sword thrust through the mail, through his gut. Images swirled in his mind of his body sprawled on the field, dead, helmet over his eyes, the Valkyries laughing as they passed him by…*No one goes to Valhalla who dies so stupid!*

And then another blow to the head, from the other side, and the helmet flew clean off. Harald had a sensation like swimming in the sea back in Vik, coming up from the silent depths of the fiord, breaking through the surface of the water into the bright light. He was free of the helmet, his vision was clear, and with a shout he leapt forward, ax over his head, his arm tensed and ready for a mighty swing like the arm of a trebuchet.

Harald's ax came down. The blade struck the edge of an upraised shield and shattered it and the ax lodged in what was left of the wood. The man holding the shield thrust his sword at Harald's throat, but Harald knocked it aside with his own shield. He jerked the handle of the ax, but could not get it free.

The shieldwall was starting to collapse. It took considerable courage and discipline to remain locked shoulder to shoulder in the face of a determined enemy, and that was more than the part-time soldiers defending Cloyne could muster. One by one they began to break away, leaving gaps in the line through which the berserkers flung themselves with their inhuman fury, weapons singing, as the other Northmen, just as determined, struck the line on the flanks.

Harald and the man he was fighting were caught in a weird dance, Harald trying to yank his ax free, the Irishman trying to regain control of his shield as he thrust his sword at Harald and Harald knocked the blade away.

Enough, Harald thought. He released the ax, which threw the Irishman off balance and Harald, reverting to the most ancient weapon of all, thrust his fist over the edge of the shattered shield and smashed it into the man's face. The blow would not kill him, but Harald felt the Irishman's nose collapse under his fist before the man whirled around and fell to the wet grass.

There were weapons scattered on the field now, dropped by the wounded or the dead, or discarded as a prelude to flight. Harald, his eyes locked on the men before him, reached down and snatched up a sword, and even as he straightened, the shieldwall collapsed. As if on some signal that could be heard only by the Irish, the men sent to defend Cloyne backed away, turned, and fled north, turned their backs on the raiders as they raced for what they hoped would be safety.

Up and down the line Harald heard the shouts of victory, the outraged screams of the berserkers who wished their enemy to fight to the death. The Northmen rolled forward, building speed in pursuit, a pell-mell, disorganized chase based on no plan beyond catching the fleeing men and finishing them off, stopping them before they could make another bloody stand.

Harald felt he was under no orders now to allow the berserkers to take the lead, so he dug in hard as he ran, pushing to be the first to catch up with the Irish in their flight. He could hear voices behind him, the sharp bark of orders, could pick out the sound of Hoskuld Iron-skull's voice and even that of his own father.

"Halt! Halt! Halt!" The words finally registered with Harald. *Halt?* With complete victory right before them? Harald pressed on, determined to ignore them. *Old men, too timid*, he thought.

Ahead of him he could see the Irishmen disappear over the crest of the small hill on which they had been fighting, their retreat turned to a route as they threw weapons and shields away. Even loaded down as he was with shield, sword and mail, Harald felt sure he could overtake them, and then they would be defenseless. He pressed on hard, the edge of the flat hilltop just yards away.

And then he reached it, and the land sloped sharp away, and Harald put his foot down in front of him and skidded to a stop. In the low place between that hill and the next, drawn up in a line several hundred feet long, was the real shieldwall, the real defense of Cloyne, and not a decoy which Harald now understood the first one had been. The Irish had hoped the Norsemen would do just what Harald had done, charge mindlessly after the retreating men and right into the arms of the real army.

Maybe the old men are not such fools, Harald thought, not for the first time.

The Irishmen below stood locked shield to shield, and behind them, archers stood with arrows knocked. The flanks of the shieldwall were anchored by mounted warriors with lances. Even young Harald, raw and inexperienced as he was, could see that these men would not be so easily brushed aside.

Chapter Five

Harsh was the rift
that the wave hewed
in the wall
of my father's kin.
Egil's Saga

Brigit nic Máel Sechnaill, the new bride, the lovely young woman around whom the events of that festive wedding day revolved, sat all but ignored at the head table in the great hall of Tara. She felt the smile that was plastered to her face slipping away and she forced it back on, in the off chance that someone was looking at her. She reached for her goblet of wine and took a deep gulp. She hoped it would ease the memories of the morning past, and the anticipation of the night to come.

The great hall was one of the features that set Tara apart from the other, less substantial royal residences within its sphere of influence. That spacious gathering place, scene of coronations, weddings, feasts, preparations for battle, made Tara more than just another seat of power situated within the confines of a ring fort, a smattering of round wattle and daub homes, albeit bigger than most. The hall was timber framed, heavy built, like the church, but twice its size. It was here that the local *rí túaithe* were wont to gather, summoned to councils several times a year, or when there was some threat to their region and they and their men were called up for military service.

In either case, such gatherings turned invariably into raucous bacchanals. It was through copious food and strong drink, doled out under the high-beamed roof of the great hall, as much as through military strength or carefully arranged marriages, that the kings of Tara cemented their power.

Brigit was certainly no stranger to such things. Indeed, she had endured dozens of them, but this was the first at which she was ostensibly the center of attention. Her previous wedding had been held at Gailenga, on the Leinster borderland, at the home of her husband, Donnchad Ua Ruairc. In the presence of the high king, Máel Sechnaill mac Ruanaid, and on Donnchad's express orders, the *rí túaithe* who gathered for the royal wedding had all been on their best behavior.

This time, absent the intimidating presence of Máel Sechnaill, and with one of their own the bride-groom, the minor kings felt no such restraint. The space was loud with shouting, laughter, arguments. At the far end of the hall a huge fire burned in the hearth, warming the already warm room and filling it with a weird, undulating light.

Sitting beside Brigit at the center of the head table, as poorly behaved as any of the *rí túaithe*, actually worse than most, was the groom, Conlaed uí Chennselaigh, a minor king from Ardsallagh, which was a minor kingdom to the northwest of Tara. Brigit watched him chew – not a pleasant sight - then ducked aside as he hurled a chicken bone at one of the *rí túaithe* seated at the long table down the center of the hall. The bone bounced off the head of the intended target and the man looked up, furious, but then on seeing who had thrown it he laughed, a great guttural laugh, and Conlaed joined him.

Oh, Dear God in Heaven, preserve me, Brigit prayed. But of all the *rí túaithe* Conlaed uí Chennselaigh was not the most objectionable, and indeed he had a number of attributes in his favor. He was young, certainly no more than ten years senior to Brigit, who was herself eighteen. He was good looking in a thick, muscular sort of way. His hair was blond and his eyes blue, which was important for Brigit's purposes, and he was far too dim-witted to try anything as ill-considered as exercising any real authority. Indeed, he was too dim-witted to even wonder why the beautiful daughter of Máel Sechnaill mac Ruanaid, the most sought-after woman in Brega, would show this sudden interest in him.

Brigit sighed, softly, as she watched her husband wipe mead from his chin with the sleeve of his tunic. It was her own weakness and stupidity, she knew, along with some damned bad luck, that had brought her to this place. But she was the daughter of Máel Sechnaill mac Ruanaid, descended from a long line of tough, sometimes brutal kings of Brega, men who did what they needed to do and did not agonize over it, and she would do the same. The past three months had been very instructive to Brigit. The scales had fallen from her eyes.

And so she had taken uí Chennselaigh for husband. He was one of the only men she could count on. She could count on him to spend his days in hunting and drinking and gaming and silently blessing his good fortune. She could count on him to avoid any sort of official duties or responsibility, to actually be grateful to her for her willingness to oversee the running of Tara and the lands that fell under its influence. She could count on the men at arms under his command and the lands of his kingdom to now be hers.

Conlaed would not involve himself in the struggle for power that Brigit could see coming between herself, Flann mac Conaing, and his sister Morrigan.

This fight for control of the Kingdom of Brega would have been hard fought in any event, but now with the Crown of the Three Kingdoms sent to Tara, the stakes were higher by far. The crown was an ancient thing, how old no one knew, but it was rumored to have been crafted by the druids before the coming of the new faith. It was now held by the abbot of Glendalough, and it had not left that place in living memory. But ancient law decreed that the *rí ruirech*, the high king who was given the crown would be *rí ruirech* not just of Brega or Leinster or Mide, but of all three, until such time as the abbot called for the crown's return.

The Crown was to be given out only when there was a grave threat to the land. And there was. The spreading stain of *fin gall*, the white strangers, the Norsemen in Dubh-lin. They needed to be eradicated, stamped out like vermin before they became too numerous to defeat. The *fin gall* could not be driven back into the sea if the three kingdoms were making war on one another. The Northmen were powerful, and only united could the Irish counter that threat. That was the purpose of the Crown. That was what Brigit would do. Once she had given birth to the *tánaise ríg*, the heir apparent, and through him solidified her own rule over the seat of the high king.

"A toast! A toast!" Flann mac Conaing stood, three places down from Brigit, and raised his goblet. Flann had given Brigit away in the absence of her father. She had allowed him to do so, despite her suspicion that her father had actually been killed by Flann in the confusion of battle.

"I give you Conlaed uí Chennselaigh of Ardsallagh, and Brigit nic Máel Sechnaill," Flann shouted over the roar of the hall, which dimmed only a bit with his calling for the toast, "who I this day had the honor of giving away as bride!"

You'd like to give me away, wouldn't you, you traitorous bastard, Brigit thought as she smiled down at the several hundred or so drunken revelers. *Like to give me to the devil, I shouldn't doubt.* But now was the time for unity, or the appearance of it, until Brigit was ready to make her move.

A cheer rose up from the crowd in the hall, shouting, thumping of fists and cups on the table. With all the drink that had gone down their throats they would have cheered one of the ubiquitous hounds defecating on the floor. "May the happy couple live long, fruitful and joyous lives!" Flann concluded.

And may they rule with wisdom over Tara and the Three Kingdoms, Brigit added silently, certain that Flann would add no sentiment of that kind. Flann raised his goblet, the others in the hall did as well, and they drank deep. And that was all Brigit could endure. She turned to Conlaed to make her excuses when another voice filled the hall. Now it was Father Finnian standing, still dressed in the white vestments he had worn while performing the sacrament of marriage. Finnian had been asked to sit at the head table while his fellow brothers sat elbow to elbow with the *rí túaithe,* sharing with them their enthusiasm for food and drink.

Now he was standing, arms raised. "A blessing on the couple!" he called, and this time the noise in the great hall quickly tapered off to just a few voices, until those people caught on that they were the only ones still causing a ruckus and so dropped off into an embarrassed silence.

"May the blessings of the Holy Trinity, Father, Son and Holy Spirit, shine down on this couple, and may their union be a means by which the Most High brings peace to our troubled land. May their union be fruitful, and may their spirits, united with our Lord Jesus, calm the troubled waters of Tara and the Three Kingdoms and bring everlasting peace and unity to our land." His voice was clear and loud, his tone both subservient and commanding, a neat trick. Throughout the hall the *rí túaithe* muttered their "amen"s with an enthusiasm, or lack thereof, that was in proportion to their loyalty to Flann mac Conaing.

Morrigan will not care for that blessing, Brigit thought. She looked around the room. Morrigan had been at the head table, by her brother, but now she was gone.

Morrigan. She was the one, Brigit suspected, who was the ambition behind Flann. For years Flann mac Conaing had served her father loyally and well, while Morrigan had suffered in unimaginable ways at the hands of the *dubh gall.* Now she seemed eager to make up for those years. She had seen a path to power, and to the wealth of Tara, and she had eagerly pursued it, and she had taken her brother along with her. Like Brigit, she needed a man to be the face of the power she wielded.

It took less than a minute after Father Finnian finished his blessing before the noise in the great hall built back to its previous level. Brigit turned to her husband and tugged on his sleeve, then tugged harder until she had his attention. "I am very tired," she said. She spoke loud but he still had to lean in to hear her. "I am going to go to bed."

Conlaed nodded and smiled, his mouth full of food. "Will you remain here long?" Brigit asked, and Conlaed shook his head. "Very well. Good night, husband," Brigit said. She stood and stepped down from the raised floor on which the head table stood, and the crowd in the hall banged the tables and cheered in appreciation of her. There was an undercurrent to their enthusiasm which she did not think was quite appropriate, but she ignored it, and them, and she sailed out of the hall. Had Máel Sechnaill still been alive, or Donnchad, any man who treated her with such disrespect would have seen his guts spilled out on the floor. But they were dead, and Brigit had only herself as lord and protector.

As she moved to the door she heard a voice behind her. "Brigit? Brigit, dear, are you off to your chambers, then?" Father Finnian had also slipped away and come after her.

"Yes, Father Finnian," she said. "I'm very tired."

"May I see you to your door?"

"I would be grateful."

Father Finnian pushed open the heavy oak door and they stepped from the loud and suffocating great hall into a night that was dark and cool, still wet from the rain that had fallen earlier. There were frogs and insects filling the night with sound, but they sounded quiet and muted after the noise of the wedding celebration.

The two of them walked across the muddy grounds of the ringfort, toward the royal residence. This, like the church and the great hall, was something that set Tara apart from the seats of the minor kings. The homes of those lesser nobles tended to be roundhouses, wood structures with conical thatched roofs, larger versions of the cottages that most Irish occupied. But not that of the high king of Tara. Tara's royal house, like the great hall, was timber framed, wattle and daub, a great rectangular building with a high thatched roof and a multitude of private chambers, an imposing and intimidating edifice by Irish standards.

Brigit had always occupied a chamber in that house, but with the death of her father she had moved into the royal chamber, the largest room in the largest house. She had wondered before she did if Flann and Morrigan would try to claim it for themselves, but they were clever enough to avoid so brazen a grab for power.

"Thank you, Father Finnian, for that fine blessing," Brigit said, as much to break the silence as anything.

"You are welcome, child." They walked a few more paces, the muddy ground pulling at their shoes. Then Finnian added, "Tara could use a few blessings these days. I ask them of the Lord, and hope it is His will to provide."

"We could use blessings," Brigit echoed. She liked Finnian. There was a strength about him, and a calm that she did not often see in the monks who made the monastery at Tara their home. He had only been there a year or so, but he had a presence that made it seem as if he had always been a part of the royal household. And he was attractive as well. Brigit could think of nothing nobler than a man following a call to the priesthood, but she could not help but regret that a man such as Finnian had removed himself from the pool of potential husbands.

What a waste... she concluded.

"It was a fine ceremony, dear, did you not think so?" Finnian said. His voice was soft like the night.

"Yes. Thank you again for the sacrament."

Finnian made a gesture of dismissal. "My poor part was the least of it. I was pleased to see the effort Morrigan put into the celebrations. Nearly all of the local *rí túaithe* were here to celebrate."

"Nearly," Brigit said, though Finnian seemed to take that as a better thing than she did. He was a hard one to read. He often acted as if there was not a problem or conflict in the world, though Brigit was quite certain he was not as naive as that. "I was sorry to miss Ruarc mac Brain," she added. "The Uí Dúnchada had no representative here."

"I had word that Ruarc's wife is very ill. He would not wish to leave her side. Did Morrigan not tell you? I feel sure I told her. He's a good man, Ruarc."

"He would be a good ally. He commands many men-at-arms and foot soldiers as well. With the Uí Dúnchada of Leinster and the house of Máel Sechnaill together we might stand a chance against these fin gall. Drive them into the sea, perhaps."

And Morrigan would certainly prefer I think he was ignoring me, she thought.

Finnian gave her a curious look. "What?" she said. "Have I said something wrong?"

"Not at all, not at all," Finnian said and smiled. "I am just marveling at how you speak more like a ruler on her throne than a bride on her wedding night."

"I have been a bride before, Father," she said. "I have never before been a ruler."

They walked on in silence to the door to the main house. Brigit wondered what Finnian might say, if there was some motive to his walking her across the compound, beyond seeing to her protection. But he only bowed and said, "I wish you good night, Queen Brigit."

"Thank you, Father Finnian. And a good night to you." Finnian straightened, nodded, and walked off.

Queen Brigit… No one had ever called her that before, nor was it clear that she would hold that title. *What did he mean by that? Did he mean to signal his support of me?* She frowned and pushed her way through the heavy oak door of the royal house and into the smoky, dim interior.

The passageway between the various walled off rooms was lit with a few candles, the light of which was further obscured by the lanterns that held them, but Brigit needed no light at all to find her way. She pushed open the door of her bed chamber and almost sighed out loud, relieved to have reached that sanctuary, that haven of peace. All day she had been dreading the night, the marital bed, and what she imagined would be the rough and clumsy attention of her husband. But now she was quite certain she had gained a reprieve, and that Conlaed would be spending the night on the floor of the great hall, wherever he happened to collapse.

A fire was burning low in the hearth, and the room had a warm glow, the far reaches all but lost in shadow. Brigit didn't see the figure sitting in the chair beyond the bed, did not recognize it as a person, but when that person stood she jumped and gasped. She took a step back. Her hand reached out, instinctively looking for a weapon.

"Brigit..." The figure came closer, and Brigit recognized the form, the voice, but recognition did not bring much relief.

"Morrigan..."

Morrigan stepped into the light of the low fire, which gave a reddish hue to her pale skin, her light brown hair. She was a small woman, and pretty, despite all that she had suffered. In the fire's light Brigit noticed the tiny lines around Morrigan's mouth and at the corner of her eyes. There was a hardness in her eyes, no expression on her face. She might have been carved out of ivory. "Congratulations on your nuptials," she said.

"Thank you."

They stood silent for a moment, like swordsmen, each waiting for the other to make the first move.

"I have the means, you know, to help you out of your troubles," Morrigan said at last.

"What troubles?" Brigit asked, and heard the false note in her voice.

Morrigan smiled. "Please. Even so great a fool as Conlaed uí Chennselaigh can count to nine. When the baby comes, it will take no great figuring for him and everyone else at Tara to know it is not his."

A dozen responses swirled through Brigit's head. Argument, denial, feigned bewilderment, but she could see that each was pointless. Morrigan knew. Somehow, Morrigan knew, and what Brigit had thought a profound secret, Morrigan could now use as a bludgeon.

The birth of her child seven months or so from her wedding date was a problem she had long seen coming, even with her hurried courtship and marriage. She had already considered various solutions – claim the baby had come early, or that she had lain with Conlaed before their marriage. But each of these depended on Conlaed's cooperation, which was not at all certain.

"I have certain herbs, you know," Morrigan continued in a low and conspiratorial voice, "that will make you lose the baby. It will be as if this never happened."

Brigit studied Morrigan's face. Morrigan was skilled in those arts. She knew the use of herbs, roots, berries and other medicines. She could heal and she could kill. Indeed, this very solution had crossed Brigit's mind. Doing so, however, would have meant admitting her condition to Morrigan, and that she would not do. But Morrigan already knew, and was offering a way out....

"Brigit," Morrigan said, "I don't want to see you disgraced. Let me help." And with those words, all the uncertainly, all the doubt in Brigit's mind shed away like a thin layer of ice, and under it, something steely and hard. Morrigan had no desire to help. At least not to help Brigit.

"Get out of my chambers," Brigit said, and she was surprised to hear the voice of Máel Sechnaill coming from her throat.

"Don't be a fool," Morrigan said. "You'll be shunned, you'll be called a whore."

"Out."

"Do you think the bastard son of some *fin gall* swine will ever be considered the *tánaise ríg*? Do you think his whore of a mother will ever be called 'queen'?"

To that Brigit did not respond. She and Morrigan held one another's eyes, and their fury burned like the bonfires of the ancient druids. Then with a swirl of her cloak, Morrigan left the chambers.

For a long time, Brigit stared after her, looked unseeing in the direction Morrigan had gone, while her mind went over and over what had just played out. She was happy. She was happy she had not stumbled into any trap that Morrigan was laying, happy that the life would continue to grow in her.

But that decision, like any she made, carried its own dangers with it. She was happy. And she was alone, and she was very afraid.

Chapter Six

I have wielded a blood-stained sword
and howling spear; the bird
of carrion followed me
when the Vikings pressed forth…
Egil's Saga

The Norsemen drew up on the ridge and considered the Irish shieldwall before them, the horsemen on the flanks. Even the berserkers had stopped short at the sight of so extensive and organized a defense. And now the two sides stood, looking at one another. The Irish archers in the distance tried their best to inflict some injury, their arrows flying overhead or thudding into the dirt at the Northmen's feet. On occasion a spent arrow would impale itself unenthusiastically on someone's shield, but the Vikings paid scant attention.

They were gathered in loose groups around their standard bearers, each to the ship in which they sailed, the master whom they served. Some were standing, some sitting. Wineskins were passed from hand to hand. In the field between the armies a nightingale sang, and another responded, an odd, incongruous sound.

Once again, the leaders of the various bands gathered together to determine the best course.

"I do not care for the mounted warriors," Arinbjorn said. "We could break the shieldwall and send them running, but those on horseback can move too fast for us to stop."

The others nodded, faces grim. The horses gave the Irish a mobility the Norse did not have. And that was not all. *If they have horses, then they are not just a bunch of hapless farmers,* Thorgrim thought. *If they have horses, then they are trained and well-equipped fighting men.* He was not sure if that had occurred to the others, but he was not one to offer advice that had not been requested.

"Sure all these damned men did not come from Cloyne," Hoskuld Iron-skull spat, echoing the frustration of the others.

"There is the tower," Arinbjorn offered. "Thorgrim, what think you?"

"This is not because of the tower," Thorgrim said. "They could have had a few hour's warning from the tower, no more. These men gathered long before that." That observation was met with more nodding among the assembled leaders.

"Hear him," said Starri Deathless, who for some reason was hanging on the fringes of the council, though he had no business there. No one was going to ask the advice of a berserker; even their presence was barely tolerated when they were not required for the hard fighting. The blood on Starri's chest and arms and in his hair was drying into a dark brown crust and making him appear even more mad than usual.

"Well, if the Irish won't do anything, then we must," said Hoskuld. "We can't stand here until we all grow roots." Again there was a grumbled agreement among the other men.

Thorgrim's sword was still in his hand and he raised it, intending to point toward what he perceived as a weak point in the enemy's shieldwall. In that same instance, on the far side of the line of Irishmen, an unseen archer let fly at the massed group of men on the ridge. 'There…" Thorgrim said when he felt Iron-tooth jerk in his hand, heard a strange clang and screech of metal on metal. He was uncertain at first what had happened. He looked along the blade of his weapon.

To his surprise he found that the iron arrowhead had hit the sword's edge and split in the middle, and now held Iron-tooth lodged in its grip. The arrow, still quivering from its abrupt stop, had been flying directly at his neck, and would surely have pierced his throat if it had not split itself on the sword.

In the many fights, great and small, in which Thorgrim had taken part, he had seen many odd things, many that defied explanation. He had seen dead men without a mark on them, and others who had been left for dead, mangled beyond recognition, who lived for years after. He had seen arrows and spears embed themselves in a thousand odd ways. Once, two arrows had lodged themselves on either side of a leather helmet he was wearing, making the helmet appear to be mounted with horns, as Odin was often depicted in amulets. Another time a spear passed between his legs so high up he could feel the shaft sliding along his crotch, but it did him no harm at all.

But for all that, Thorgrim had never seen anything quite as unique as that arrowhead split on his blade. The chances of such a thing happening seemed unimaginable to him.

"Look at this, here," said Hrolleif the Stout, who had seen what had happened. The others gathered around, looked and nodded their amazement. But they, like Thorgrim, had seen their share of amazing sights, and they were practical men, not much given to flights of imagination. They agreed that it was an extraordinary thing, and then all turned back to the problem at hand.

All, that is, but Starri Deathless. As the others moved aside, there was Starri, looking with wide eyes, mouth open, at the arrow embedded on Iron-tooth's blade. He made as if to speak, uttered a few sounds, and pointed at the arrow. Thorgrim, slightly embarrassed by the attention, looked from Starri's finger to the arrow and back to Starri's blood-smeared face.

"Thorgrim," Starri said at last. "Thorgrim Night Wolf, you are surely blessed by the gods."

Thorgrim smiled and looked at the arrow as if noticing it for the first time. "These things happen, Starri. Sure you've seen your share of such things." Then, as if to emphasis the commonplace nature of the thing, Thorgrim pulled the split arrowhead off the blade and tossed it aside.

"No, I've not seen such," Starri said. "Not like that."

If Starri meant to elaborate, he never had the chance. Suddenly, like an unexpected clap of thunder, a cheer went up from the Irish ranks and the shieldwall rolled forward like a solid thing.

"To arms! To arms!" Hoskuld shouted. The men huddled in conference scattered, each racing back to his own men, each shouting as he did for the Norsemen to take up arms. But the men needed no encouragement. Those who a moment before had been sprawled on the cool grass, half asleep, were now on their feet with shields in their left hands, swords, battle axes or spears in their right. They ran forward and took up their place in the shieldwall the leaders were forming.

Arinbjorn and Thorgrim ran along the edge of the hill to where the men of the *Black Raven* were getting to their feet. Thorgrim searched the faces for Harald, saw him midway down the hastily organized line. His helmet was gone, which did not please Thorgrim, but Harald took his place with the others like a man accustomed to battle.

Thorgrim turned and nearly collided with Starri Deathless, who had apparently followed on Thorgrim's heels, with Nordwall the Short and the other berserkers behind him. "We're with you," Starri said. "Any man so blessed by the gods, we'll stand with him."

There was no time for a reply. The Irish shieldwall, like a wave that first starts breaking far from shore, crashed into the Norsemen's half-formed defense. Thorgrim felt a shudder along the line, heard the clash of hundreds of shields on shields, the cumulative shout of Irishman and Norseman suddenly tangled in battle. The raiders were pushed back a step. The first scream of agony rolled down the line and was cut short.

"Meet them! Hold steady!" Arinbjorn shouted. He had taken a place in the shieldwall, on the far left flank, but there had been no time for Thorgrim to lock shields with the others, and now he stood a few feet back, looking at the fighting men but not engaged himself. Beside him, Starri, Nordwall and the others looked frantically around as it dawned on them that there was a battle taking place and yet their weapons hung limp in their hands. Starri shrieked, raced for the line of struggling men, the vow to stand with Thorgrim becoming more of a metaphorical concept.

What happened next, Thorgrim could never quite explain. Starri came up behind the nearest of the Black Ravens and seemed to vault clear over the man. Perhaps he put a foot in the small of his back, Thorgrim never saw, but from Thorgrim's point of view Starri seemed to leap or even fly over the line of men, coming down feet first, battle ax swinging, on the far side of the shieldwall.

He disappeared from Thorgrim's view, and Thorgrim figured that was the last he would ever see of Starri Deathless, that in the wake of the battle they would find the hacked up remains of what had once been that half wild man. Maybe. More likely the pieces would not be big enough to name. Thorgrim pushed thoughts of Starri aside.

The Irish were driving them back, one grudging step at a time. Thorgrim could see the men's soft leather shoes digging into the Irish sod as the Norsemen tried to hold the line in check, could see the axes and spears and swords rising up above the helmeted heads, flashing dull in the muted daylight. This was a view he had never had before. Always, he had stood his place in the shieldwall, or led from the front of a swine array charging an enemy. This place – behind the line, able to see nearly all the line of men with a turn of the head – this was something new.

And from that vantage he could see dangers that would not be clear to someone standing in the shieldwall, someone thinking only of the five square feet of ground on which he stood, and the men with whom he was fighting for command of that small plot. Thorgrim could see the riders on the flanks, see their stubby horses prancing and stamping. Those well-armed men, stationed behind the shieldwall, had used the mobility their horses could provide to race around the ends of the line. Thorgrim could see them sliding down from their mounts, readying themselves to come at the rear of the line, to sweep around from either side and catch the Northmen from behind. And that would be an end to it.

"Back!" Thorgrim shouted. He raced down the line, shouting as he did. "Back! Take a step back! Easy now, step back!"

He had no authority to give orders even to the men of the *Black Raven*, never mind the entire Viking army, but he could see disaster looming and knew there was no time for a proper chain of command.

"Back now, back, back!" And the Northmen listened, they took a step back, and then another. Disciplined steps, not a panic-edged retreat, not the kind of retreat that would devolve into a route, they continued to move back over the wet grass, reacting to the steady authority of Thorgrim's voice.

A cheer went up along the Irish lines as the defenders sensed their enemies giving way. But it was premature, Thorgrim could see that, because now, as he had intended, the left and right flanks of the Norse shieldwall were backed up to the steep ridge that dropped away to the beach below, and the experienced troops to the left and right, greatest threat to the Norsemen, could no longer get behind them. Their flanks were anchored to the cliffs, and there they stood.

What had started as a clever ploy and well executed attack by the Irish line had devolved now to no more than brutal, one-on-one butchery as the men in the shieldwall hacked and slashed at the men facing them. They screamed, cursed, bled, died on that stretch of grass. Thorgrim could see one of the Black Ravens, dead, his head nearly severed, yet still standing in the shieldwall, his body jammed tight by the men to his left and right.

Thorgrim adjusted his grip on Iron-tooth, looked for a spot where he could get into the fighting. He had no notion of how this would end. Perhaps they would stand there, Norsemen and Irish, face to face, until there was but one man left alive and his side would be called the winner of the day.

The sound of the battle was a roar, like surf, punctuated here and there by shrieks, shouts, curses, horrific sounds. And then, suddenly, a new sound, a commotion, a swirling of noise from the shieldwall at Thorgrim's left. Screams, shouts, a note that Thorgrim recognized. It was panic.

Who? Thorgrim thought and at that moment a great rent appeared in the Irish line, men knocked aside, the unbroken row of shields broken now, and in the gap stood a horrid and unworldly creature, skin blood red, white teeth flashing, hair standing at wild angles. It was screaming and wielding an ax, swinging it in great arcs. Thorgrim gasped and felt a stab of panic like a dagger point. There was nothing left in the world that could frighten him, but this thing was not of the world, that much he could see.

Then the thing looked at him, their eyes met, and the thing screamed "Night Wolf!" and Thorgrim realized he was wrong, the thing was indeed of this world, it was Starri Deathless who had hacked his way through the line from behind. And had given the Northmen a way to victory. Because a shieldwall was a hard thing to break, but once broken was nearly impossible to put to right.

"You men! Here! To me! To me!" Thorgrim shouted to the men at the far end of the shieldwall. He could pull men from the flanks, he knew, and not destroy the integrity of the defense. But he did not wait to see if they would follow. Rather he raised Iron-tooth and charged forward, charged for Starri, for the gap in the line. He burst through, found himself looking down the length of the Irish shieldwall, the man before him too occupied with the Norseman he was fighting to even see Thorgrim there, and with a vicious thrust Iron-tooth claimed his first victim of the fight.

A short Irish sword came slashing down, the man wielding it lost in the press, but Thorgrim turned it easily, then cut sideways and felt his blade bite, felt the man he struck go down. The wicked point of a spear embedded itself in his shield and he jerked the shield to the left, pulling the man wielding it off balance. Thorgrim had a glimpse of wide eyes, a dark moustache, and then Iron-tooth slid through the man's ribs and with a shriek he was down, the scream choking in a welter of blood.

Someone backed into Thorgrim and Thorgrim started to wheel, to meet this threat, while keeping his eyes ahead as well. From the corner of his eye he could see Starri's lanky arm, could see that his skin was not red, but rather it was bathed in blood. It was Starri who had backed into him, and so they stood, back to back, weapons flailing as the Irish struggled to kill them both, to patch up the rent in the shield wall, to push the raiders back into the sea.

They might have done so, too, but just then a great shouting came from Thorgrim's left and he had a glimpse of the massive bulk of Hoskuld Iron-skull, more bear than man, racing toward the gap in the line, a trail of men behind him. They broke right and left, slammed into the ragged edge of the torn shieldwall, began rolling up the length of struggling men.

Thorgrim took his eyes from the fight to watch Hoskuld plunge into the attack, and for that second's lapse of attention received a sword thrust in the chest. The point pierced his mail and he felt the blade's edge run along his flesh, but he swung his shield hard and caught the sword and knocked it away. He felt the blade slice him again as the edge of his shield slammed it aside. He counterthrust, plunging Iron-tooth through his attacker's green tunic, twisting the blade, jerking it free.

The Irish shieldwall was crumbling. Men who just moments before had been so sure of victory now saw their tight defense collapse as more and more of the Northmen poured into the gap that Starri Deathless had cut in the line and Thorgrim Night Wolf had stepped in to widen. The Irish began to fall back, one step, then two, then the men toward the back of the shield wall, those far enough from the fight that they could risk turning their back on the enemy did so, racing back across the ground they had won, racing for the dubious protection of the monastery at Cloyne.

That was an end to it. Any man on that field who had seen combat before knew that once the running began it would not stop, and even to those who had not seen combat, that much was clear. The Irish fled down the road, tossing weapons aside. The wounded limped after them, only to be cut down by the Northmen if they were far gone in their wounds, or knocked on the head if they were still healthy enough for the slave market.

The Norse army charged after them. They waved their weapons and shouted and beat their shields and raced after the fleeing Irish for a good quarter mile before they were all doubled over, heaving for breath, spent and beaten like borrowed mules. They had won, but the fight was out of them. The killing was done. For that day, at least.

Chapter Seven

Once more I have told my dream
to the makers of arrow-floods.
They will surely feel
my weapons bite their armor
if rage comes upon me now.
Gili Sursson's Saga

Harald's tongue was hanging out of his mouth and his eyes were wide, but he seemed not to notice, so intense was his concentration. Thorgrim was sitting on the ground and leaning back on his hands and looking down at him. He might have laughed if the pain had not been so great and his mood so foul, and growing more so as the sun edged toward the horizon.

In his right hand, Harald gripped a needle threaded with a sinew thread. With his left hand he tried to pinch together the edges of skin on Thorgrim's lacerated chest. Harald's fingers were slick with blood, and the skin was slick with blood, the edges lost in the red mess, and finally Harald simply gripped as hard as he could and drove the needle through the torn flesh. Thorgrim made no comment.

The needle pierced the skin, adding a sharp pain as a counterpoint to the dull ache of the double wound, a laceration where the sword went in through Thorgrim's mail, and another when it came out. As Harald pulled the sinew taut, Thorgrim dug into the sod with his fingers, but his face showed no reaction and he did not make a sound.

"I'm sorry, father," Harald said. "Did that hurt?"

"No," Thorgrim said, and at the same time Starri Deathless, sitting nearby, said, "Of course it hurt." But it was just an observation, no more. By his tone Starri might have been commenting on the weather.

To no one's surprise, the berserkers had chased the Irish further than any of the other warriors had, but they too were blown and exhausted and could only run so far. In truth, in the wake of a battle, when the fighting madness passed, the berserkers were often the most wasted of all the men. After the Irish had fled, Thorgrim found Starri sitting cross legged amid a heap of bodies, hunched over and crying bitterly.

For a long moment Thorgrim had just stood there, not sure what to say, but understanding somehow that his presence was wanted and appreciated. At length Thorgrim said, "What is it that grieves you, Starri? Was one of your fellows killed?"

"No, no," Starri said, his words broken by his sobbing, "well, yes, some were. Damned sons of whores…"

Starri looked up at Thorgrim. His tears had made white tracks through the brown, dried blood on his face, and Thorgrim thought, *I would not have guessed this man could look more bizarre, and yet here he is…*

"Yes, some were killed," Starri continued, "Hadd and Frodi. Alf was still here when last I saw him, but he will not be long. And here I am…here I am…still in this cursed world, even as the Valkyries lift my fellows from the field!"

"You're sobbing…" Thorgrim said, looking for the words, "because you were not killed?"

"Of course, Night Wolf! What man could do anything but curse the fate that keeps him in this world and denies him the pleasures of Valhalla!"

Thorgrim nodded. He was not sure what to say. There was not a man there, himself included, who did not believe with utter conviction that a glorious death on the field of battle would bring him to an even more glorious life in Odin's Valhalla. And yet, how many of those held a belief so strong that they would weep to find themselves still alive? Many of those who lay strewn and bloody on the field, if given the choice, would likely have put off the journey to the afterlife for a few more years.

And you, Thorgrim Night Wolf? Thorgrim asked himself. When his wife had died, most of the joy of this world had gone with her. Thorgrim did not want to die, but he was indifferent about living. And that made him nearly as dangerous a man as Starri Deathless.

Reflexively, Thorgrim glanced over to where one of his shipmates from the *Black Raven* was binding a cut on Harald's arm. When the fighting had stopped, Thorgrim had immediately sought out his son. Harald was red faced, splattered with gore, jubilant from the fight. The cut on his arm, more of a tear from the point of spear, was an ugly, jagged wound, but not deep, and it had already stopped bleeding by the time Thorgrim had found the boy. Harald did not even know the wound was there until Thorgrim had mentioned it.

So what of Harald? Thorgrim loved all his children, but he and Harald had been a-viking for nearly a year now, and that changed things. Thorgrim might have been indifferent about his own life, indifferent about the lives of all the men with whom he sailed, but he was not indifferent about Harald.

He was not ready to leave Harald alone in the world. The boy was growing up. But he was not grown.

It was that attitude, the need to help Harald to manhood, which led to Thorgrim's sitting on the grass and enduring his son's painful ministrations. Stitching wounds was a skill that every warrior needed to possess, and practice was not so easily come by, because no one was going to ask a man to stitch him up who was unpracticed in the art. So Thorgrim insisted that Harald get some practice on the two wounds he had earned in the fight. Harald agreed, but with no enthusiasm. Indeed, he showed more trepidation, his hands literally trembling, than Thorgrim had ever seen him display before battle.

"All right…there." Harald pulled out his knife and cut the bitter end of the sinew. "Done."

"Good job, son," Thorgrim said, with all the enthusiasm he could muster. Thorgrim could have done a better job if he had done it himself, and it likely would have been less painful, but he was nonetheless proud of his boy, even if he could not bring himself to say more. It was just the evening, and the foul mood was setting in on him. He called it the black mood, and men knew to keep clear of him when he was wrapped up in it. It did not come every night, but often enough, and generally in the wake of fighting. It did not always lead to wolf dreams, but it did that often enough as well. In the black mood, Thorgrim was not just unfit company, he was dangerous company. The black mood had earned him the name of Night Wolf.

Starri glanced over. "That's quite a scar you'll get from that, Thorgrim," he observed. Starri was looking better than he had after the battle. Once he had composed himself, choked down his grief at being still alive, he and his fellows had gone down to the water and plunged in, washing the blood and madness from them. They had combed their hair and pulled on tunics and looked as much like normal humans as they ever could.

A few of the berserkers had died, as Starri said, but most had not. Nordwall the Short had come away with a few vicious wounds, but nothing likely to end his life. The rest were in much the same condition. It was a wonder to Thorgrim how anyone could go into battle with such utter disregard for their lives and come out with no more than a few scratches. Perhaps that was the trick.

Thorgrim pushed himself to a sitting position and then stood. The pain in his wound was excruciating and he feared he had ripped it open again, but looking down he could see that, inelegant as Harald's work was, it was at least sound. Thorgrim grabbed up his tunic, which was crumpled on the grass, and pulled it over his head, the loose garment happily not requiring a great range of motion to slip on. Harald stood as well, unsure whether or not to help. He offered an arm, withdrew it.

"Forgive me, Harald, I think I'll walk a pace," Thorgrim said. Harald nodded. The boy knew what he meant. As the sun plunged beyond the horizon, it would come that time of the evening when Thorgrim would not be fit company for men.

Soon the leaders of the various longships would gather again to discuss what was to be done next. They had encountered far more armed men than they had anticipated, and now those men were entrenched in the ringfort that encircled Cloyne. Did the raiders have men enough to take the fort? Was it worth the effort and the carnage? Or should they just take to their ships and fall on another, less prepared town? All crucial questions, and Thorgrim did not care the worth of a rat's ass about any of it.

He moved off across the field with the evening dark spreading over the hills, past the clumps of men sparking cooking fires or collapsed in exhaustion or tending to their wounded or moaning their lives away. He walked clear of them all, toward the distant town of Cloyne where he could see a few fires already burning. He sat, cross-legged, staring out toward the town. He was not alone, he realized; he sensed a presence behind. He turned to see Starri Deathless sit in the grass as well, fifteen feet away. Starri did not speak, he did not look at Thorgrim. He just sat.

Normally, Thorgrim would not tolerate the near presence of another when the black mood was on him. Sure, at times he might find himself on shipboard, or crowded in a small house in foul weather, and at those time there would be men near, but they would keep their distance, and that made it tolerable. Never, never had someone deliberately tried to keep company with Thorgrim at such a time.

But somehow Starri, he found, was like a seamless piece of the whole thing, his presence neither an irritant nor a comfort, like an evening when the temperature is perfectly moderate, as if there was no temperature at all. Thorgrim turned away without a word and looked back into the distance and the fading light.

The gray evening yielded slowly to dark night, and Thorgrim sat and stared out into the distance, and then into the blackness, which was punctuated by only a few bright and undulating spots of light, camp fires or torches in the far off town. He felt the blackness welling up in him. His thoughts were an incoherent jumble, there were no words in his head, at least none in any language known to man, no motion in his body; he was all mood and feeling and instinct.

And then, sometime later, though he had no sense of time passing, he was running, moving swiftly along the grassy hills, keeping to the dark places. He felt strong and lithe. The wound in his chest gave him no pain. The monastery of Cloyne was ahead, and the little town that clustered around it. The air was rich with smells he had not noticed before; hearth fires, cooked meat, men and women (he could differentiate the smells now), fresh turned earth, moldering straw on the dirt floors of the home. Fear.

He came in closer, not afraid, he had no fear, but wary of the places where men lived. The night was overcast, but not black. The dirt walls of the ring fort were near, blocking out the dull light overhead. The walls were crowned with a fringe of sharpened pikes shaped from small trees, making an overhang on which an attacking army would be caught up and slaughtered as they went over the wall. The dark tower rose up from the unseen monastery like some mythical giant, keeping its ceaseless watch over the countryside.

There were voices coming from the ringfort now. The words made no sense, but he could feel the tones. There was anger, and more fear. There were men moving, a lot of men. He could smell horses and hear their hooves on the soft ground. He could hear weapons clattering. A worn, bare patch of ground that might have been construed as a road circled the walls. Thorgrim steered clear of that, and instead slipped into a shallow gully that paralleled the ringfort and there he moved silently through the shadows.

At length he came to a place where he could see the regular walls of the ringfort broken by massive wooden doors, twenty feet wide, as high as the walls and just as impenetrable. On either side of the doors, standing atop the walls, were armed men with torches, and fires burning on the ground leading up to the gate, so that no one, not even Thorgrim Night Wolf, could approach unseen.

And as he watched, the gate swung open and a column of men emerged, moving in some semblance of regular order. Thorgrim tensed, moved farther back into the shadow. Voices called out and others replied and Thorgrim could sense the anger in the strange words. This meant something, this was important, these armed men sallying out from the ringfort, but he did not know what it signified.

The marching men made no sound, and they carried no torches or light of any kind and they came through the gate to the road along the fort's walls. Two men on horseback led the way. The horses shook their heads and one whinnied, sensing Thorgrim near, but its rider gave it a reassuring pat and Thorgrim remained motionless and horse and rider moved past.

The riders swung off to the north and soon were lost in the dark and the rest of the men followed behind. It took some minutes for them all to make their way out, marching with shields on arms and spears held over shoulders. And then the big doors were swung closed behind, slamming shut with a sound that suggested strength and finality. Thorgrim kept to the low place and followed behind the marching column. The sea was south of them, he could smell it, a constant backdrop behind all the other, more ephemeral smells, but these men were not going in the direction of the sea. They were going in another direction entirely.

Thorgrim followed, hidden by shadow along his track. The men marched, some limping hard with wounds suffered from the day's fighting. The smells were pungent. Sweat and wool, leather, iron, horses. Anxious eyes glanced out into the dark. But they did not break their stride.

Beyond the gate the column swung off, following a wide, rutted track, the chief road connecting Cloyne to the lands to the north. Thorgrim crouched and watched and then something else caught his attention. Two figures were moving along the edge of the ringfort, also watching the column marching off. They were not hiding; one was even carrying a torch. They paused for a moment, then turned toward the wall of the fort, a seemingly unbroken expanse of earth,

The two men stopped and one banged against the wall with the hilt of his sword, the sound of iron on wood, not earth. He banged twice in rapid succession, paused, then once again. A small door, all but invisible in the wall, opened and a weak light spilled out. The two men ducked through, the door closed, and Thorgrim Night Wolf awoke.

Chapter Eight

I've ended up the same way as the wolves –
they devoured one another,
and didn't notice until they got down to the tail.
The Saga of the Confederates

Starri Deathless was still there. He was seated just as he had been when Thorgrim turned his back on the man, before Thorgrim fell asleep or lapsed into his wolf dream or whatever it was that he did. He himself did not know, had never known. One minute he was there, another he was elsewhere. The wound in his chest throbbed with pain.

"You're back," Starri said in his conversational tone. Outside of battle, nothing seemed to move Starri to excitement.

"Was I…" Thorgrim looked around. Overcast night, a dull light from above, points of light from the distant fort. He was back from a wolf dream. He did not think any man had ever sat as Starri Deathless had at his side during a wolf dream.

"Was I…here?" Thorgrim asked. The wolf dreams let him see things, understand things, but he did not know how. If he was looking for some clarity, however, he was asking the wrong man. Starri just shrugged. "Whether Thorgrim was here or not, I could not say. But the Night Wolf, I think, was afield."

They sat in silence for a moment and Thorgrim looked out toward distant Cloyne. He felt an odd sense of peace, not the way he generally felt returning from a wolf dream. He wondered if Starri Deathless was the cause of that, if the man had some magic about him, something not of this world.

"What did you see?" Starri asked in a soft voice.

Thorgrim ran back over the dream-like images in his head. "They left. The men-at-arms at Cloyne. They left. They marched north."

Silence. "Why would they do that?" Starri asked.

Silence. "I don't know. But I don't think all those men were from that one place. Perhaps they reckoned they've done enough for Cloyne, and are going off to protect their own homes."

Thorgrim looked at Starri and Starri nodded slowly. "That would stand to reason," he said. Thorgrim let the memory of the wolf dream swirl around in his head. He frowned, looked away, looked back as another image began to materialize. The more he thought on it, the more vivid it became, and the more he understood its importance.

"What is it?" Starri asked.

"I saw something else," Thorgrim said.

Arinbjorn White-tooth was asleep. It had been a long day, beginning in the pre-dawn hours, as the longships readied for the attack, and stretching on through some hard fighting. Arinbjorn's sword had been well-bloodied, no one could accuse him of not being in the thick of it. Thorgrim, he had noticed, had not even joined the shieldwall during the fight.

He had drifted off to sleep with thoughts of Thorgrim playing out to the last. Whatever part the Night Wolf had taken in the battle had apparently been admirable. Arinbjorn heard men talking of it. The last Arinbjorn had seen of Thorgrim, as the Irish had pressed home their attack, he had been hanging back, behind the shieldwall, and that would not do. Then, seconds later, the Irish were on them and Arinbjorn had been too locked up in his own fight to notice what Thorgrim was doing.

But Thorgrim had acquitted himself well, apparently, which was good, because they were linked now in the minds of the men of the *Black Raven* and the others: Arinbjorn and Thorgrim. Arinbjorn had taken a risk, a carefully calculated risk, asking Thorgrim to join his company. He had done it to enhance his own status by association with the man from Vik. Thorgrim's reputation was spreading in Dubh-linn, and Arinbjorn hoped to get some of that bright light to reflect on him.

It could have gone the other way – Thorgrim could have let Arinbjorn down, or worse, outshone him. But thus far it seemed to be playing out as hoped. Arinbjorn the leader and Thorgrim his hirdsman. Which was not exactly the case. To say Thorgrim was a hirdsman was to suggest he was a permanent part of Arinbjorn hird, his private force of warriors. And Thorgrim was not that. Thorgrim was part of the félag, the fellowship of men who had signed aboard the *Black Raven* for this voyage. They owed allegiance to Arinbjorn, and to one another, for the time that voyage lasted, and no more. But that still meant that any glory Thorgrim accrued would be shared by Arinbjorn.

And so Arinbjorn did not just sleep, he slept well. Nothing had occurred on that day of battle to trouble his mind and disturb his rest, and his circumstances were comfortable enough. Unlike many of the

Northmen, who were asleep on the damp ground wrapped in furs, Arinbjorn was lying on a portable bed, the posts of which were carved into the heads of leering beasts. That and his armor and weapons and sea chest were housed under a red and white striped marquee which his slaves had hauled up from the *Black Raven* once he was certain the Irish were gone for good.

In the dream he was having, Arinbjorn was arguing with someone, and then a second person joined in, and though the words were not very distinct, and the topic of the argument (it might have been a negotiation as well) was not clear, Arinbjorn was winning handily, turning each of their rhetorical thrusts away. He had a sense of euphoria and triumph. And then, suddenly, he was no longer winning. His arguments were collapsing, he was tongue-tied, he could see the grins on the faces of the men with whom he was debating. The euphoria turned to panic.

He woke with a gasp and looked around the marquee, dimly lit with a single candle he kept burning all night. He realized there were voices outside the flap. One was Hrafn Troll, the man assigned to stand guard for the night watch. Arinbjorn recognized the second as the gravelly voice of Thorgrim Ulfsson, who apparently wished to speak with him and was apparently meeting some resistance from Hrafn, as was proper for a guard.

"Hrafn!" Arinbjorn called. "It's all right. Thorgrim may have leave to enter." Arinbjorn heard a grunt, feet shuffling, and Thorgrim stepped into the marquee. He looked irritated.

"Thorgrim! Forgive me." Arinbjorn stood and held out his hand and Thorgrim took it. "Hrafn was only doing his duty, you know. I should have told him you always have leave to speak to me."

Thorgrim grunted. "Not sure why a guard is needed. You're surrounded by three hundred of your fellows."

"A man has enemies, you know," Arinbjorn said, "even among his friends." It was a well-practiced answer. "Sit, please," he added, gesturing toward a camp stool.

Thorgrim sat, cast an eye around the interior of the marquee as if he had never seen its like before. Arinbjorn sat on the edge of the bed. Thorgrim cleared his throat. He was clearly having difficulty finding the words. That was not like him. He usually doled out his words sparingly, but with a confident authority. Arinbjorn waited.

"Here's the truth, Arinbjorn," he said at last. "I have these dreams, have since I first came to manhood, and I can see things in the dreams. Tonight I had such a dream, and I saw that the men-at-arms at Cloyne left. They marched off north, leaving the town all but undefended."

Arinbjorn nodded and thought about the words. "These are just dreams, you say? I've heard tell of this. Take no offense, please, but men talk of you. They talk of the Night Wolf."

"Dreams, yes…I don't know," Thorgrim snapped, his tone seeming to be harsher than he intended. He swallowed, began again. "I don't know if they are dreams, or what they are. The point is, what I see is the truth, and I saw the men leave Cloyne. We should attack the ringfort now, the whole army. It would be entirely a surprise, and we would take them with ease."

"The men may be gone, but the walls are still there."

"That's something else I saw. Another way in, a secret door. I think I could get them to open it. Me and a dozen picked men. We could go in through the door and open the main gate, let the rest in."

"That's madness! You'd be killed for certain."

"Not if we were fast, and the rest of the army was distracting them. And if I had the right dozen men."

Arinbjorn stared through the flap of the tent, out into the dark, and thought. Thorgrim may command respect, but he commanded no men, no ship. He had no real authority. It was up to him, Arinbjorn, to act or not.

"Obviously, Thorgrim, I cannot order the army to do anything," he said. "For this voyage we have sworn allegiance to Hoskuld Iron-skull."

"Oh course. But if you wake Iron-skull and the others, explain the situation, they will follow your advice. I will speak with them, if you wish."

Arinbjorn considered all the implications of what Thorgrim was saying, all the possible ways that this thing could play out. If Thorgrim was right, and Arinbjorn spearheaded it, then he was a hero. If Thorgrim was wrong, Arinbjorn would be leading the army to destruction. Humiliation at best, death at worst.

Was Thorgrim to be trusted? The man clearly believed what he said, but even he did not know where this came from, if it was a dream, a vision from the gods, what it was. A weak twig on which to hang the fate of an army.

"No, Thorgrim, forgive me, but I cannot support this." Arinbjorn held up his hand to silence Thorgrim's protest. "I believe you. I do. Personally. But it is too much to ask Hoskuld Iron-skull and the others to risk everything on your…dream."

Thorgrim looked into his eyes. He did not say anything. Arinbjorn found it particularly disconcerting.

"You understand, I'm sure," Arinbjorn said, as much to break the silence as anything. "The jarls will meet in the morning, reckon on what to do. You are welcome to speak then. But I must insist this idea of yours wait until morning." It occurred to Arinbjorn that the others might embrace this plan, and it might succeed, and then he would appear a weak fool for thinking otherwise. Better to let it die here.

For a long moment Thorgrim remained on the stool, seemingly unsure as to whether he should say anything else. Finally he stood. "Very well, then, Arinbjorn," he said, and there was no discernable tone to his voice, no anger, bitterness, relief, just the words. "Until morning." He swept out of the marquee, leaving the flame of the candle dancing in the air he disturbed.

Chapter Nine

The Helm of Fear hideth no one
when bold men bare their swords;
when many are met to match their strength,
'twill be found that foremost is no one.
The Lay of Fáfnir

Dawn was still several hours away as the small band, a dozen or so men, moved through the low places, the places lost in the moon's shadow, working their way closer to the walls of Cloyne's ringfort. Thorgrim led the way. Behind him, Starri Deathless moved on long stork legs and Harald, shorter and broader, followed close behind. Harald, Thorgrim could tell, was vying with Starri to be next in line, a contest of which Starri was completely oblivious.

For Thorgrim, the decision had been made the second he had stepped from Arinbjorn's marquee. He could not go over Arinbjorn's head to Hoskuld Iron-skull, that would not be right, but Arinbjorn did not have the authority to stop him from going to Cloyne if he so chose, and taking anyone with him who wished to volunteer.

"The berserkers are with you, have no doubt of that," Starri said when Thorgrim explained what he had in mind. And they were - assembled within ten minutes, weapons ready, hopping from foot to foot, their faces wearing the same expression as a dog waiting for the command to fetch. It occurred to Thorgrim that perhaps the berserkers were not the best men to have on a mission that required stealth, but there was nothing for it. They were the only ones on whom he could call, and only because Starri seemed to have attached himself to him.

Thorgrim had roused Harald as well, who had more difficulty coming awake than the berserkers had, but once he understood why he was being disturbed he was up and ready in minutes. They moved off quietly through the night.

Thorgrim had a plan, or at least an idea that might rise to the level of a plan; get through the hidden door, keep their presence a secret as long as they could, open the main gate and keep it open. Once the doors swung open, it would be chaos in the ringfort, and that chaos, Thorgrim hoped, would attract the attention of the Northmen.

He had tried explaining it to the berserkers, but they had become bored and impatient half way through the explanation. They did not care about such fine things as plans.

Crouching low the band followed the edge of the hill, keeping below the low crest that hid them from the men on the ringfort's wall. A flickering glow told Thorgrim where the watch fires were burning near the main gate and he skirted past that place, then moved to the edge of the hill, Starri on one side, Harald on the other.

"There, just beyond where the light of the fires reach, we'll cross one by one to the wall of the fort," Thorgrim explained.

"So close to the fires? Why not circle around to the north side of the wall, far from the light?" Harald asked.

"Because the guards on the walls there will have eyes accustomed to the dark. Here, the fires reveal anyone advancing against the gate, but make it harder for the men to see things moving in shadow."

The men ducked below the crest of the hill again and moved on, another five rods, and Thorgrim held them up again.

"I'll go…" Starri said, a little too loud and a little too eager. Harald began to protest but Thorgrim held up a hand.

"I'll go," Thorgrim said. "Harald next. Then, Starri, you send your men one at a time. You come last." He did not wait for objections. He half crawled to the top of the high ground, paused and then moved down the hill, the wet grass soaking his soft leather shoes. His left hand clenched the grip of his shield and he was careful to keep it clear of Iron-tooth's pommel, where it might knock and give an alarm.

The grass faded to packed earth as he reached the cleared area that surrounded the ringfort, just as he had seen in the wolf dream. The watch fires were bright and he was careful not to look into them. He scurried across the open space, tensed, ready for the sound of discovery, but the blinding light from the fires, the crackling of the wood, the sounds of the night, the late hour when vigilance was relaxed, hid him from anyone who might be watching.

He pressed up against the dirt wall that surrounded the village of Cloyne, let his breath settle, looked back in the direction he had come. Harald was already moving across the open space. He, too, made it undetected and pressed his back to the damp earth wall as Thorgrim watched the squat shape of Nordwall the Short move toward them through the dark.

Thorgrim smiled to himself and shook his head, the irony of all this coming to him unbidden. *Why am I taking part in this stupid, reckless raid?* he asked himself. He knew the answer. *So I can be done with stupid, reckless raiding.*

He had all the wealth a man could ever want, at home, in Vik. He had done all the adventuring a man could crave. He was done. But Arinbjorn was the only means he had been able to find to get him and Harald back to Vik, and Arinbjorn would not go home until he had met with sufficient success on this voyage.

Here I want nothing but to give this up and go home, Thorgrim thought, *but to find the means to give it up I must do yet more. So let us get on with it.*

Starri came fast across the open space and pressed himself against the wall. Thorgrim leaned over and looked at him and in the dark he saw Starri nod. All were across. Starri's movements were taking on a weird, jerky, frenetic quality. The berserker was waking up.

Thorgrim put his hand on Iron-tooth's grip, then realized that was not the weapon he wanted. He reached around and drew the long dagger that hung on his right hip, then moved forward, keeping close to the wall, his shield bumping it on occasion. He was confident they could not be seen now – it was very dark in the shadows of the ringfort, and any guard would have to lean far over to look down at them. Whoever was left in Cloyne would be looking for threats coming across the open space, not moving along the base of the wall.

They circled around the edge of the ringfort, one hundred rods, two hundred rods. Thorgrim tried to judge where the door might be, but he was looking at things from a very different perspective now. They were moving through blackness, the world invisible beyond the great looming wall. And then Thorgrim's hand felt the edge of a heavy wood frame and he slowed up and the others slowed to a stop. He ran his hand over the face of the door and slowly it began to materialize in the dark. They were there.

Thorgrim handed his shield to Harald and took a new grip on his dagger. He cocked his arm and banged the hilt of the weapon on the door, two hard raps, a pause, a third rap, just as he had heard the man do in his wolf dream. He waited. No sound. Then a slight shuffling of feet behind him, the berserkers eager to get at it. No sound. Frogs somewhere out in the dark. Then the muffled creak of a latch being lifted on the far side of the door, the grinding of hinges as the door swung in.

Thorgrim stepped into the door frame and came face to face with the guard who had opened the door. The man looked annoyed, sleepy, until the instant that he realized Thorgrim was no Irishman. Thorgrim could see it all play across his face - surprise, confusion, anger, fear - in the few seconds it took to grab a handful of the man's tunic in his left hand, jerk him out the door, and with an arcing backhand stroke of his right hand cut the man's throat and drop him, kicking and silent, to the dirt.

Harald held Thorgrim's shield out for him. Thorgrim took the grip in his left hand and pushed the heavy wooden door open the rest of the way. There would be another guard, of that Thorgrim was certain. And sure enough, he was there, getting up from a small bench, that same look of sleepy annoyance on his face. Thorgrim slammed him hard in the head with his shield and stepped over him as he fell in a heap and Harald, coming behind, finished him the way Thorgrim had done the first.

They were in. Thorgrim moved along the wall, keeping to the shadows as much as he could, his eyes searching the little settlement enclosed by the ringfort. Cloyne. In the dull light of the moon, blanketed by the overcast, he could see the tower looming over the town, and he wondered if the people were already in there, if they had climbed to the imagined safety of that place, had drawn up the ladders through the high doors once the men-of-war had marched away. All of Cloyne might be there, as far as he could tell. He had encountered only two Irishmen so far, and now they were both dead.

He moved on, quickly and carefully, his feet making no noise. He could hear an odd sound, a gnawing sort of sound, like a mouse or a rat, but louder, and it seemed to be keeping pace with him. He stopped and looked back. Nordwall the Short was chewing on the edge of his shield, trying to hold himself in check. He could see some of the other berserkers also seemed to be having a hard time keeping control of themselves. Harald had noticed it, and he gave Thorgrim a look as if to say, *I'm not sure what to do with these people….*

"Steady, men, steady, a little further," Thorgrim said in as loud a whisper as he dared and pressed on. He could see armed men walking slowly along the top of the wall, twenty feet above their heads, but those men were looking out into the dark, not into the confines of the town. There would be no reason to look into the town.

The Northmen moved fast. Thorgrim almost fell over a rail fence marking the edge of someone's property. A couple hundred feet from the wall he could just make out a round wooden building, some farmer's cottage, capped with a conical roof of thatch. He stopped and got his bearings again. From his vantage he could see maybe ten similar houses, each sitting on its little plot of land. The diameter of the ringfort was perhaps a quarter of a mile, and Thorgrim guessed there were two or three dozen or so buildings within the confines of the walls, including the tall wood frame church which he could now see to the right of the tower.

A wide road ran through the center of the walled town, and Thorgrim debated whether they should take it, just walk right down the middle of it like they belonged. Sometimes the open was the best place to hide. But no, he did not like those chances. Instead he climbed over the rail fence and dropped to the other side. The impact of hitting the ground pulled at his fresh wound and caused a stab of pain to shoot through his chest. He could hear the others follow as he moved on.

Another fence. They were over it and plunging forward when Thorgrim heard the sound he most feared, a sound for which he had been bracing himself since they left the small door and the dead guard behind. It started as a low growl, a menacing sound, too low to cause concern, but quickly grew louder.

"Damn it!" Thorgrim said in a sharp whisper. In one fluid motion he sheathed his dagger and drew Iron-tooth, and just as the blade cleared the sheath the growling turned into a full-throated barking, the kind of barking that announced unequivocally that there was danger near.

I hope this damned cur is tied up, he thought as he pushed quickly on. But the damned cur was not. From the direction of the cottage the animal came charging at the men, a dark shape, its bared teeth visible in the night. It went airborne ten feet from one of the berserkers, a man named Jokul, leaping for the intruder's throat, and for its trouble was skewered in mid-flight by Jokul's sword and flung aside.

The creature's enthusiastic barking, however, had been enough to inspire the neighboring dogs. The noise was taken up from the houses flanking the little cottage, and then from further and further within the village, a great cacophony of barking and yelping until it seemed as if every dog in the Western World was howling away.

"How many…damned…damned dogs do these…damned Irish have?" Starri spluttered.

"Come on, time to move," Thorgrim said, speaking out loud, because the time for stealth had passed. He leapt the near fence and raced across the yard and over the next. He could hear voices now, human shouts above the dogs, and he could see torches flaring up around the compound.

Thorgrim could see the main gate ahead, outlined by the fires that burned on the other side. His wound was a searing pain and he could feel fresh blood running down the inside of his tunic. He had left his mail behind, as had Harald, because the Irish did not wear mail and the telltale metallic rustle might have given them away. And as he ran, and as his breath became more labored, he did not miss it.

"Watch for the dogs!" he shouted over his shoulder. "They'll release the dogs!" The Irish knew only that there were invaders among them – they did not know how many and they apparently did not yet know where they were. Rather than try to organize a defense, he guessed they would just let the dogs go, let the dogs find the enemy and bring them to ground. It was what he would do.

They were fifty feet from the main gate, crossing open ground now, no fences, when the men on the wall saw them at last. Thorgrim did not understand the Irish words, but he understood the frantic shouts, the pointed fingers, the arrows knocked in bow strings.

Thirty feet and Thorgrim finally saw the dogs. There were a dozen at least, coming from different directions, running flat out and barking and snapping as they converged with Thorgrim and his men.

Thor's hammer! He did not want to stop until they reached the main gate and forced it open. There was no chance of help from the others until that happened. And they could not let the men-at-arms get between them and the gate. But if they kept on running, the dogs would tear them apart.

"Shield wall! Shield wall!" he shouted and skidded to a stop. He held his shield up as the first of the dogs leapt at him, spittle flying from its mouth, teeth bared. He met the dog with his shield and sent him sprawling back, slashed at another. He hoped the men would form some kind of defense, maybe they could back down to the gate, keeping a united front to the dogs.

From his left another dog came out of the dark. Thorgrim never saw it until the animal's wicked teeth sank deep into the muscles of his upper arm. He shouted in agony, tried to slash at the beast with his sword but he could not reach around his shield with the blade. Another leapt at him from the right, but its vicious bark collapsed into a howl and a whine as a sword, Harald's sword, met it in midair and knocked it aside. Harald stepped to the left and drove his sword through the dog on Thorgrim's arm, drove it again, hacked at the dog until at last it let go and dropped away.

Father and son turned together to face the next, but Starri was in front of them, ax in one hand, short sword in another, flailing at the four legged attackers and Thorgrim realized that the terrible howling he had heard, which he had taken for the pack leader, was in fact Starri Deathless. The other berserkers were with him. Nordwall had a dog clinging to his arm, whipping back and forth as the Swede worked his ax, and the short man seemed not to even notice.

Jokul and a man Thorgrim did not know were back to back and surrounded by howling, snapping dogs looking for a way past the men's lightning-fast blades. One dog lay still, two more were limping off. Thorgrim wondered if Cloyne just might be running out of dogs when he saw Jokul jerk back, twist, swinging his sword wildly, then collapse, the shaft of an arrow jutting from his back. The dogs were on him in an instant, tearing at his flesh. Thorgrim wheeled around. The guards were gathered on the wall above, and several were bringing bows to bear.

"Come on! To the gate!" The archers were a threat much greater than the dogs. "Starri, get your men back, back to the wall!" He gave the order but he was not at all sure the berserkers were conscious enough of their surroundings to obey. All around them the dogs were growling and barking and hunching down for a leap, but they were holding back, not flinging themselves at the Northmen. Thorgrim realized that the berserkers were more vicious and wild even than the pack of dogs, and the dogs sensed as much.

This was the moment. "Harald, with me!" Thorgrim shouted and ran on, closing with the big wooden doors that could welcome the world into Cloyne, or hold it at bay. An arrow stabbed into the ground at his feet and he nearly stumbled over it as he ran. Starri and the berserkers formed a sort of rear guard, holding the circling dogs back.

Thorgrim could make out the heavy cross piece that held the big doors closed and he figured he and Harald would be enough to lift it out. Ten feet to the doors and three men burst out of the shadows at the far side, swords in hand, racing to meet them.

The first came at Thorgrim, sword held high, and Thorgrim could see the wild swing coming. He held his shield to one side, sword to the other, opened himself up, inviting the clumsy stroke, and as it came he raised the shield and turned the blade aside and thrust for the man's exposed chest.

And that would have been the end of it, but the Irishman to his right chopped down at Thorgrim's blade, an awkward move, but effective, knocking Iron-tooth's point to the dirt. He tried to follow up with a slash at Thorgrim's head, a mistake, as Thorgrim caught the man's blade with his shield, stepped in and drove his heel down on the man's knee. He felt the give of the bone, heard the crack and the shriek at the same moment.

He turned his attention back to the first man. Beyond him he caught a glimpse of Harald trading blows with the third man. The Irishman knew his business, and even six months earlier Harald would have been no match for him, but Harald was not the same young man now. His sword and shield worked together as they fended off the Irishman's sword and short sword, the blades glinting in the torch light.

No time for this, Thorgrim thought. The man he was facing was the poorest swordsman of the three and Thorgrim did not waste time; a parry of his blade, catch the counter attack with his shield and he ended it there, then stepped over the man and drove his sword through the neck of the one Harald was fighting, ignoring Harald's disapproving expression.

"The gate!" Thorgrim shouted. He looked behind. The berserkers were fully engaged with the dogs and with the armed men who were now cautiously advancing on the invading force, finally realizing, perhaps, how few in number they were. Another of Starri's men lay dead, and another was kicking and thrashing and clawing at an arrow that was run through his gut.

He set his hands on the bar. "Help me with this!" he shouted and Harald grabbed on and they heaved together and the heavy oak beam lifted up from the iron holders. They tossed it aside and put their shoulders to the heavy doors. It was chaos within the confines of the ringfort now; men were shouting, the dogs were howling, the bells in the church had begun ringing out their warning and call to arms. That was good. That was the plan. Noise and confusion within the walls would serve as a clarion call to the others still in camp.

Thorgrim and Harald pushed together. The heavy doors resisted at first, but as they began to swing they gathered momentum, swinging faster, until finally they were full open, Cloyne's defenses gone, the way clear for the Norsemen to pour into the fort. And beyond the gaping doors only darkness, quiet, not the least sign of life, nothing at all to suggest that anyone would be coming soon. Or ever.

Chapter Ten

My foes sought me out,
swinging their swords
but I did not fall then.
I was outnumbered,
yet I fed the raven's maw.
Gisli Sursson's Saga

For the second time that night, Arinbjorn White-tooth was awakened from a sound sleep, and he was not happy about it.

"Hrafn! What in the name of Odin is it now?" he snapped as soon as he understood that he was no longer dreaming.

"I don't know," Hrafn said. "Something. Something is happening."

All-Father save me from these damned fools, Arinbjorn thought as he kicked the furs off and climbed out of his portable bed. He pushed past Hrafn and through the marquee's flap and into the night. It was cool and damp and dark, but there was an edge of excitement in the air. It took Arinbjorn a moment to get his bearings and understand the cause of it. Bells. There were bells ringing out from the direction of Cloyne. He turned toward the sound. Now he could hear shouting far off, and could see pinpoints of light as men with torches ran in various directions, like sparks floating off a fire.

Damn it!

"Hrafn!" Arinbjorn shouted, louder than was necessary. "Is Thorgrim in camp? Go find out, and be damned quick about it!"

The guard ran off and Arinbjorn continued to stare in the direction of Cloyne. All around him he could see men climbing out from under bedding, grabbing up weapons, staring off in the same direction that he was. He could hear the murmur of speculation.

Hrafn was back quick, though he could not have been quick enough for Arinbjorn. "Thorgrim and his son are gone. So are Starri and his band of lunatics. Thorodd saw them heading out, maybe an hour ago, but he doesn't know where they went."

I bloody do, Arinbjorn thought. *Damn him!* Arinbjorn was angry because now he had to make a decision, and that decision could have far-reaching consequences for the only thing he cared about, which was himself. It was a decision that required a huge gamble, and if it went against him, it could be very bad.

But Arinbjorn was a wealthy and powerful jarl, and he had not become such by agonizing and vacillating. "Call up the men," he snapped at Hrafn. "To arms, we are going into battle."

Hrafn was smart enough to not ask questions, and as he hurried off to obey, Arinbjorn hurried off to seek out Hoskuld Iron-skull and the others. He found them, as he imagined he would, near Iron-skull's camp, the commanders of the various ships gathered and staring out into the dark, trying to guess what might be going on.

"Arinbjorn!" Hoskuld said as he approached. "I was going to send for you. What do you make of this?" He pointed with his long beard toward the distant town of Cloyne.

"This was my doing," Arinbjorn explained. "I thought to have some of my men make their way into the town, secretly, open the gates, let the rest of us in. I asked for volunteers. Thorgrim and the berserkers, they stepped forward. It seems they are discovered."

Hrolleif of the ship *Serpent* made a noise. "Were you going to tell any of us about this? This sort of thing works better if people actually know it's happening."

"The idea came to me in a dream, a gift from the gods, I should think. No time for councils and such. I judged that I should act," Arinbjorn explained. "I was going to alert you just now, rouse the men and prepare them to advance. My men are arming as we speak. We should have had time to prepare, but Thorgrim has mistimed it. He was not supposed to make for the gate for another hour."

Hrolleif grunted. The others made various sounds. Hoskuld Iron-skull said, "I reckon you should have told us, at least, even if you kept the men out of it."

"I should have, and I apologize, but in truth the idea came to me just an hour or so past. Sometimes the bold move is the right move." It was a good response, he knew. Part contrition, part challenge, daring any of them to find fault with his boldness, or suggest that they themselves would have been more cautious.

"In any event," Hoskuld Iron-skull said, "It looks like Thorgrim could use some help. Let us get our men under arms and moving. Quickly now."

The leaders broke like a flock of birds startled into flight, each hurrying back to their part of the camp, bellowing orders as they went. There was no call for stealth now. All of Cloyne was up in arms, it seemed to be madness there, and every one of the Norsemen was eager to get in on it.

By the time Arinbjorn returned to his camp his men were awake and armed and his slaves were standing ready with his mail, helmet, shield and sword. He donned his gear quickly and led his men forward to where the rest of the army was forming a rude line facing Cloyne. The noise from the distant town seemed even louder now, and Arinbjorn could pick out the sharp bark of dogs among the other sounds.

Hoskuld Iron-skull strode in front of the line, his sword held high. "Let us hurry now, to the aid of our brave brethren. If the gods are with them, then we will find the gates of Cloyne open to us! Let us make a noise as we advance that will make these Irish whore's sons crap themselves just to hear!" With that he turned and advanced toward Cloyne, his momentum and the roar in his throat building as he lumbered forward, the Norse army following behind.

Arinbjorn hurried with the rest, but his mind was elsewhere. This whole thing could still work in his favor, or not, and it depended on whether the attack was a success, on whether he got credit for the plan, on whether Thorgrim told the others about their disagreement earlier.

Thorgrim may be dead, Arinbjorn thought as he picked up his pace, and the thought calmed him. *The gate open and Thorgrim dead...* If the gods were still favoring Arinbjorn White-tooth.

The main gate was indeed open. That part had been relatively easy. Save for the three guards who tried to stop them, and died in the process, Thorgrim and Harald had swung the big doors wide apart with no opposition. But that was where their luck had ended.

There was no sign of the others launching an attack against the town. There was every indication that the men of Cloyne realized they were not facing a numerous enemy, and that even with most of the men-at-arms having marched off they still greatly outnumbered the band who had managed to get inside the walls.

Thorgrim's back was pressed against the door. Across the twenty foot gap he could see Harald pushed hard against the other. One side of the boy was lit up yellow in the light of the watch fires burning at the entranceway, the other in deep shadow.

Now what, now what? Thorgrim asked himself. Keep his men alive, keep the gate open, until the others came, and if the others did not come then get out of there as fast as they could.

Something brushed past Thorgrim's shoulder and in the same instant he felt the jar of an arrow embedding itself in the back of his shield. He turned and looked up. There were archers on the wall above. Thorgrim could not imagine how the man had missed from that distance, but he would not give the next one so easy a target. He pushed off from the door and waved his sword at Harald.

"Come on! Come on!" he shouted and as he did he saw an arrow streak over his head and drive into the thick oak door against which Harald stood. The shaft quivered from the impact, a foot from Harald's face. Harald needed no further prompting to move.

They ran back into the ringfort where Starri and his berserkers were formed in a semi-circle defensive line, holding off the men and dogs that were throwing themselves at them. There was little organization to the Irishmen's attack, which worked to the Northmen's advantage, but the Irish had numbers on their side, and numbers would win in the end. No more than a dozen men had come with Thorgrim, and there were fewer now. It was the berserkers' manic ferocity alone which was holding the Irish at bay; absent that they would have all been dead by then.

Thorgrim charged the line, swinging his sword at the Irishmen who were working their way around the left flank. "Starri!" he shouted. "Get your men moving back! Back!" If they could get their backs to a wall, or get through the gate, they might have a better chance of holding off the rest.

To Thorgrim's surprise, Starri Deathless heard him and shouted the order, stepping back as he did, then stepping back again. A roar went up from the Irish as they sensed that the handful of Northmen were about to break. Again they pressed the attack against the berserkers and again were driven back by the wildly swinging blades of sword and battle ax.

Another step back. An arrow swished past and caught Nordwall the Short in the shoulder, spinning him around with a shout of agony. Thorgrim looked over his shoulder. The archers on the walls behind had found new targets.

Where is Harald? Thorgrim looked anxiously around. He had thought the boy was with him. If they were going to die here, then he would want them to die together.

From out of the dark came a shriek, a terrible sound, at once frightening and triumphant, a shout like Thorgrim had never heard, and yet one with a tone oddly familiar. Heads turned. A heavy cart came rolling into the light from the fires outside the gate, careening toward the Irish who were attacking Starri's men, jouncing along backwards at a crazy speed. A pile of hay heaped onto the cart threatened to topple over as it bounced and jolted. And then Thorgrim saw Harald, holding the shafts, pushing the cart like some two-legged draft horse. There was a wild look on his face, and his mouth was open in shouting.

The shear surprise of the thing stopped the fighting dead. Norse and Irish paused in mid-swing of their weapons to look at this odd sight. And as they watched, the cart, moving faster with every one of Harald's powerful steps, slammed into the crowd of Irishmen, knocking them down like saplings in a hurricane and sending the rest leaping out of the way.

"Grab the cart! Grab hold of it!" Thorgrim shouted, sheathing Iron-tooth and taking hold of the wagon's rough wooden sides. Here was a rolling defense, a mobile fortification. The berserkers grabbed hold as well, checking the forward momentum as Harald held the shafts and dug in his heels.

Thorgrim waved his arm, gestured toward the open gate. "This way, this way, pull the wagon along!" Willing hands grabbed hold and shoved the wagon around until it was pointing in the new direction, then ran along either side, driving the vehicle over the hard packed ground. They were just passing through the gates when Thorgrim shouted for them to stop, and again the momentum of the wagon was checked.

"Turn it sideways and push it over!" he ordered and the heavy, rough cart was shoved around until it stood sideways in the open gate. In the flickering light of the fires the Northmen could see that the Irishmen had recovered from the shock, had gathered again and were advancing cautiously toward the wagon.

The Northmen were on the other side of the wagon now, their backs to the open countryside through the gate, and they heaved, grunting and straining, as they lifted the side of the wagon off the ground. Nordwall stood beside Thorgrim, the arrow jutting from his shoulder, but he pushed with a will, as if he was fresh as the morning dew.

Odin, All-father, does anything stop these people? Thorgrim thought.

The cart lifted, balanced for a second on its two starboard wheels, then toppled over on its side, spilling the load of hay through the open gates. Arrows thudded into the wood where the hay had been piled, but the archers on the walls could not reach the handful of men huddled behind the wagon. Thorgrim peered over the edge of the temporary defense. The Irish were still coming on, swords and shields in hand. They were moving slowly, bracing for the next surprise, but they were not hesitating in their advance. And there were a lot of them.

"They'll rush us, any minute now," Thorgrim warned, and no sooner had he said that then he heard a shout raised from beyond the wagon, an Irish battle cry, and the sound of dozens of feet moving fast toward them. And in the same instant, another battle cry, a single voice from behind. Thorgrim turned to see Harald running toward the wagon from the watch fires beyond the gate. In his hand he held a thick tree branch, the end flaming like a torch, which he must have pulled from one of the fires burning behind them.

Harald charged at the wagon from one side as the Irish charged from the other. With a shout, Harald vaulted up onto the side of the overturned cart, flaming branch in hand. Thorgrim opened his mouth to order him down when Harald flung the branch into the mound of hay that lay between the cart and the advancing enemy. The hay made a rushing sound as it burst into flames, a great wall of fire separating Norsemen from Irishmen. Thorgrim could see the Irish shielding their faces from the heat and the brilliant light, backing away from the conflagration.

Thorgrim smiled and shook his head. The boy had shown more initiative and creativity in the past hour than Thorgrim would have guessed he had in him. It would be a shame if they all died in the next few minutes.

He looked over his shoulder, past the flames of the watch fires, into the dark countryside. Harald's trick would hold the Irish off for a few moments more, but once the flames died the men of Cloyne would overrun the makeshift defense. There would be no keeping them at bay. And he, Thorgrim, could not let the others die for his own ill-conceived plan. He would hold the Irish back for as long as he could, let his men race off into the night. He did not think the Irish would follow them toward the Northmen's camp. The hard part, he knew, would be convincing the others to leave him.

That decision made, Thorgrim started to turn back toward the enemy advancing from the ringfort when his eye caught a movement out in the dark. His first thought was that more Irishmen had come out of the secret door, circled around behind them, and now he and his men would be trapped between the two forces. He squinted, trying to see past the watch fires. There was definitely something moving, coming toward them.

He adjusted his grip on sword and shield. And then, for the second time that day, he saw the great mass of Hoskuld Iron-skull charging into battle, a screaming horde of Vikings at his back.

Chapter Eleven

To put bolster on bench
shall my bride now with me
make haste homeward;
a hasty match this to many will seem
they'll not rob me my rest at home.
The Lay of Alvís

From the back of his horse, Conlaed uí Chennselaigh could see the spire of the church, the high peaked roof of the great hall, and the walls of the ringfort surrounding Tara slowly rise above the green hill up which he was riding. He half stood in the saddle, letting his strong legs absorb the shock of the horse's footfalls, and marveled at the sight. His home. His new home. He was still not entirely sure how that had happened.

On either side of him, half a length back and trailing behind, were more than a dozen of the *rí túaithe*, those who had stayed on after the wedding and the subsequent feast. Most of the minor kings who had come for the ceremony had left the following day, returning to their own holdings to attend to their usual business: overseeing farms, collecting rents, crushing familial plots against their rule. But the younger men, those with whom Conlaed uí Chennselaigh had long associated, did not leave. They were having far too good a time to go home.

Here, laid before them, was all the luxury of Tara, the free food, free drink, fine hunting, and a tolerable abundance of women. And it was all under the authority of one of their own, one who had somehow managed to get himself elevated to a place where this was his to command.

Conlaed was not, of course, *rí ruirech*, the high king. Even he was not so deluded as to think that. The line of succession was very much in flux. But even if the limits of Conlaed's authority were not clear, he found that his rule certainly extended as far as the kitchen, the beer and wine stores, and the stables, and that was enough for him and for the young nobles gathered there. In truth, he did not wish for any more responsibility than that of leading these men, once his fellows, now his subjects of sorts, in their daily hunts. The thought of actually ruling a kingdom such as Tara frightened him.

Tara. He looked up again at the walls and the rooftops that were revealing themselves from behind the hill. Some unseen guard was swinging open the big main gate so that the hunting party could enter the ringfort without breaking stride and thunder impressively down the wide main road to the stables. And when they did, Conlaed uí Chennselaigh would lead them. No one rode in front of him. No one would presume to do so. Only the yipping, frenetic hounds had the audacity to race ahead of Conlaed's horse.

Thoughts of Tara invariably brought thoughts of Brigit to Conlaed's mind, and with those thoughts, a flush of guilt. In truth, he had not spent much time with her since their betrothal. His days had been spent in riding and hunting, and as the sun set he and the others would return, muddy, tired and boisterous, to yet another feast in the great hall. And regardless of whatever Conlaed had intended on waking that morning, whatever firm resolutions he made through the pounding in his skull, by nightfall he was once again passed out on the floor or slumped over a table, where he remained for the night. And so it had been, for an entire week.

Tonight I shall not drink so much, no, not so much, he thought. He could feel the sweat run down his cheeks despite the cool of the early spring. His nose was filled with the smell of horse and dog and leather and unwashed men and wet grass. *Tonight I will…*

He did not finish the thought, because even thinking what he was about to think was too humiliating, even in the relative privacy of his own head. He had not yet consummated his marriage, lain with his new bride, made the beast with two backs, whatever one wished to call it. It was not that he did not want to. Brigit was the most sought after woman in Ireland, her beauty was exceptional, unmatched in the kingdom. And Conlaed was certainly not the type of man who shunned the company of women.

It's the drink, and the company of these fellows…. He did not let his thoughts go further down the path than that, leaving the real truth as a vague and unexplored mass of impressions, like a distant mountain, half lost in the mist, which Conlaed would not dare climb. The real truth was that he was afraid of her. She was so beautiful. So much more clever than he was, a fact that he had only come to appreciate right before their wedding day.

If Conlaed had climbed any further up that mountain of doubt he would come to the most daunting of all cliffs. Brigit was not a virgin. She had been married before, to Donnchad Ua Ruairc, no less, a man who had had the balls to rebel against Máel Sechnaill mac Ruanaid, Brigit's father. That was a thing Conlaed would never have dared do, even if he was ambitious enough to consider it.

Instead, he had fought for Máel Sechnaill. He had watched Donnchad meet his death at Máel's hands without the least trace of fear, and give no more than a sharp intake of breath as he had been disemboweled. Deep in the rarely explored parts of his mind, Conlaed reasoned that any man so terrifically brave must have also performed heroic feats in bed. He wondered how he could ever be the match of such a man, and the answer made him sick with anxiety.

The main gate of Tara swung full open just as the hunting party reached it. They passed through at full gallop, and neither Conlaed nor the *rí túaithe* bothered to acknowledge the guards who struggled with the heavy doors. Rather, they pounded down the main road that cut through the center of the ringfort, heading for the stables, leaving it to anyone in their way to get clear before they were trampled.

At the stables they reined their horses in with a great flourish that would have produced a cloud of dust on those few days when the ground was dry enough to produce dust. Conlaed was grinning now. The slight discomfort he had felt on seeing Tara again was gone with the thrill of their most excellent and dramatic entry into the seat of the high king, the anticipation of the food and drink waiting in the great hall, and the flush from all the food and drink he had already consumed that day.

He swung down off his horse as the groom took up the reins and tried to calm the excited animal. One of his companions handed him a wine skin and Conlaed squirted a stream into his mouth and wiped the run-off from his chin with the sleeve of his tunic. His hands were red and crusted with the blood of the third deer they had run to ground that morning. An excellent day so far.

Laughing, shouting, quarreling in the happy way of men, Conlaed uí Chennselaigh and the *rí túaithe* turned their backs on the stables, walked past the head groom's small hut, past the more substantial building that housed the priests, and around the front of the church, which was not their destination, but rather an obstacle between themselves and the great hall. They were just stepping past when the church's big oak door creaked and swung open. The men picked up their pace for fear of being waylaid by some tedious cleric.

"Conlaed?" It was a feminine voice and Conlaed was seized with panic that it might be Brigit, but he put on a brave face and smiled as he turned. But it was not Brigit, rather, it was Morrigan nic Conaing, the sister of Flann. As far as Conlaed could divine, Flann wielded the real authority at Tara, though Morrigan seemed to have considerable influence as well. It was all very confusing.

"Morrigan! How fare you?" Conlaed asked brightly.

"I am well, thank you. Might I have a word with you? In private?"

"Ah, of course, of course..." Conlaed was not sure where this might be heading. Morrigan had always been very kind to him, very helpful, even deferential. Still, she made him nervous, and he was not sure why.

There is something wicked about this place... he thought, no doubt all part of the intrigue that surrounded the court of the high king. He considered moving himself and Brigit to his own home at Ardsallagh, saying to hell with Tara. But that would no doubt lead to a fight with Brigit, and that thought made him nervous as well.

"You fellows go on, I'll catch up," Conlaed called and the rest moved on in their boisterous way as Morrigan led Conlaed into the narthex of the church. They were all alone. Conlaed closed the oak door and Morrigan turned and looked at him.

"Are you settling in well?" she asked at last. "Are you finding Tara to your liking?"

Conlaed nodded, trying to divine any hidden meaning to the question, though he knew he often had trouble divining even the explicit meaning of a question. "Tara is fine. A fine place. Yes, I am enjoying it very much."

Morrigan smiled, and it seemed a genuine smile. "Yes, I had thought so." She chuckled. "Yes, I can see you are settling right in."

Conlaed smiled and chuckled as well, then asked, "How do you mean?"

"Well..." Morrigan seemed to be looking for the words. "Let me just be the first...I hope the first...to congratulate you."

"On...my marriage?"

"No. I don't suppose I'm the first to do that. On...your heir."

Conlaed touched his head. "My hair?"

"No, your heir. Your son. Or at least I pray it's a son. On the baby that your wife carries."

Conlaed squinted at her and shook his head. "Baby...? You think Brigit is with child?"

"Sure Brigit is with child. Has she not told you?"

"I...how do you know this?"

"Forgive me, Conlaed, if you had intended to keep it a secret. I'll say nothing. But a woman knows such things. Brigit is so thin. She shows already."

Conlaed looked away, into the dark interior of the church. He knew little of offspring and such, except with horses and dogs, but he was pretty sure that a woman would not show after just a week. He tried to recall how things had run during the various pregnancies of his various sisters.

And then he remembered. She should not be showing at all. She should not be with child, because he and Brigit had not.... And then he understood.

"You are certain of this?" he asked, and his words came out in a low and menacing growl, but Morrigan seemed not to notice.

"Oh, yes, I am certain. No doubt she was waiting for just the right moment to give you the happy news. And now I've spoiled it." She reached up and stroked his cheek, rough from three days' growth of beard. "Please do not tell her I gave her secret away."

After Morrigan left, Conlaed stood for some time in the narthex, looking at nothing, trying to think. Had she cuckolded him while he and his fellows were hunting? Would she really show after a week? Or might she have been pregnant when they married?

Finally he pushed the big door open and stepped out. The sun had set in the gray sky and it was nearly full on night as he crossed to the great hall and made his way inside. The smell of the cool evening air was lost to that of a peat fire and roasting venison and the various torches burning in sconces in the walls, and the quiet was blown away by the shouting and laughter of the *rí túaithe.* Conlaed took his place at the head of the table, grabbed up his goblet and drank deep. He was scowling and silent, but none of the others seemed to notice, and the festivities went on as if he was not even there.

Food was set in front of him, but he had no appetite. Wine, mead, beer was passed his way, and that he did take, swallowing down any fermented thing placed before him. The roaring of the *rí túaithe* became a solid and unintelligible noise, like a heavy surf, pounding and receding, and Conlaed paid it no mind as he lost himself in his thoughts and his drink.

The bitch would never show after a week, no... he concluded. Was she showing? He had never seen her naked. *Bloody coward, bloody weak, pathetic...* Had she been with child when they were married? Then why marry him? What of the father?

Bloody whore...make me look the fool...does she think me not man enough to rut with her? With each swallow, with each moment, his anger and confusion grew. And then another thought came to him, shot out of the dark like a bolt of lightning.

What if she was with child when we wed, and she married me just to make others believe the bastard was not a bastard? With that thought, the lightning spread until the whole puzzle was illuminated, lit up bright. All the disparate and scattered bits of his scattered thoughts suddenly fell into perfect order.

Conlaed pounded the table and shot to his feet. "Traitorous bitch!" he shouted, so loud the other men at the table suddenly looked up at him. They were silent, just for a beat, and then one shouted, "Do you mean Aidan, here?" and the rest roared with laughter.

"Bitch!" Conlaed shouted again and he grabbed the edge of the table and flung it over, spilling food and drink on the hard-packed dirt floor, sending half the men leaping clear as it fell. The *rí túaithe* were bent double with laughter, hardly able to speak.

He turned on his heel and staggered purposefully for the door. *Find out if she's with child, find out who…the bloody…who…* Behind him, the laughter and shouting of the men of the hunting party did not diminish a bit. No one made a move to follow Conlaed uí Chennselaigh from the room, no one asked him to where he was bound.

Chapter Twelve

When we parted, flaxen goddess,
my ears rang with a sound
from my blood-hall's realm.
Gisli Sursson's Saga

Through the thick walls, tapestry-covered, through the shuttered windows of the royal household, Brigit had heard the shouting of the guards, the creaking of the main gate swinging open as Conlaed and his hunting party returned. She had felt as much as heard them go by, the pounding of their horses' hooves setting up a faint vibration in the floor and walls. And then, nothing.

It had been that way for a week, every night since her wedding. Alone in her dim-lit room she braced herself for the possibility that Conlaed uí Chennselaigh, her husband, would make an appearance in her bed chamber. *Their* bed chamber.

That possibility created a great stew of emotions in her mind. Fear was one, maybe the most prominent one. Hope. She had lured Conlaed into marriage for the express purpose of quickly consummating it and giving legitimacy to her child. Luring Conlaed with the tacit promise of wealth and sex had been about as difficult as luring a ravenous wolf with a slab of raw meat, which made her present situation all that more inexplicable. But if he would not cooperate with regard to consummating, then she had made a terrible mistake.

Anticipation? Yes, she felt a bit of that. Brigit was not adverse to the attentions of men. It was what had put her in that awkward situation to begin with. In the end she looked on Conlaed's appearing in her bed chamber the same way she might look on a visit to the barber surgeon to have a tooth out – as a thing to be dreaded but which could not be avoided, with a faint hope it might not be as bad as she thought, and the near certainty her situation would be much improved when it was over.

She ate alone in her bed chamber as she had for all the past nights, and listened for the sound of his approach, but there was nothing. The night was still, the quiet punctuated occasionally by a barking dog or a muted laugh or shout from the great hall. She worked at her embroidery by the gutting light of a candle until her eyes began to shut of their own accord, then she set the work down on a table and sighed. She was wearing a fine white linen leine that gently hugged her body and featured a neckline that plunged down to reveal the tops of her breasts. It had made her feel desirable when she put it on, but now it made her feel foolish.

Certain at last that Conlaed would not be making an appearance any time soon, if ever, Brigit stood, stretched, then climbed into bed and pulled the heavy blankets and furs over her. She could not imagine what the problem was. She was showing just a bit, but she did not think enough that Conlaed would notice. Every man had always reckoned her a great beauty, and she was sure she was not so changed as to alter that.

She had heard that there were some men who preferred the company of other men, not just in fellowship but also in what would normally be a woman's office. The idea seemed unfathomable to Brigit, and she was not even sure how it would work, but she was beginning to wonder if Conlaed was such. And so her mind turned to thoughts of how she might now rid herself of this problem.

For some time she lay awake, staring into the dark, her mind racing with thoughts of her predicament, and paths that would lead her out of it, and lead her son, if such he was, onto the throne of Tara, preferably with the Crown of the Three Kingdoms on his head. She thought of Harald, his young, perfectly sculpted body, the ease with which he had killed the men who had tried to do unspeakable things to her. She could see his long, blond hair, the voluptuous curve of the muscles in his arms.

At some point, in the dark hours, she drifted off to sleep and her sleep was sound, her body compressed under the pile of bed clothes. She dreamed an elaborate dream of being chased by some unseen thing, racing for the door of the church, slamming the door against the approaching menace, and then she was awake, her eyes open, staring out into the dark.

What was that? she thought. Had the slamming door been just in her dream, or had the dream incorporated the real sound? She cocked her head and now she could hear fumbling in the passageway outside the bed chamber, and she thought she heard a low, muttering voice. Conlaed, come at last? If so, he was likely too drunk to do her any good.

She sat up and looked toward the door, but there was no light at all in the bed chamber, and she could see nothing. She heard a hand on the latch. The door swung open and the faint light of a candle spilled into the room. Conlaed was holding the candle, and he was not a pretty sight.

"Conlaed..." Brigit called out hopefully. "Husband...?" She pushed the bed clothes off her legs and swung her legs off the bed. Conlaed closed the door behind him.

"Stand up," Conlaed growled and he took a step across the room and set the candleholder on the table. Brigit stood. They looked at one another. Brigit could see that Conlaed was drunk, quite drunk. He swayed a bit as he stood and his head was cocked forward. He was scowling. His brows were crushed together.

"What is it, husband?" Brigit said. She spoke softly, soothingly, as she would to a dangerous animal from which she could not escape. She was afraid.

"Disrobe," Conlaed said.

Brigit's hand went to the neckline of her leine, but she hesitated. Did he mean to bed her like this? She had prepared herself for any number of unpleasant situations, but this was beyond what she was ready for. "Why?" she asked. "What do you mean to do?"

Conlaed took a step forward, the motion pure menace. "I said disrobe!" Three words, rising in volume until the last syllable was a full shout. Brigit pulled the neckline of her leine closed.

"Husband, you are in your cups," Brigit said, still in her soothing tone. "Come to bed."

Conlaed took another step. "Are you with child?" he demanded. Brigit sucked in her breath. The question was like a punch in the gut and she had not seen it coming.

"How could you think...how could that be?" she stammered.

Morrigan, you hellish witch, she thought.

Conlaed took another step toward her. His hand came around in a great arc. The swing was slow and clumsy and Brigit saw it coming, but she was paralyzed by the shock of the thing and could not move. Conlaed's open hand hit her on the side of the head and sent her staggering, knocked her right off her feet. The flame of the candle seemed to separate into two, three flames, the room whirled, and the concussion of the blow shuddered through her skull as she fell across the bed.

She pushed herself up on her elbows, pushed the hair from her face. Conlaed was standing over her, his open hand now clenched in a fist. "You whore! You damnable whore! I asked you if you were with child!" His arm shot out and he grabbed a handful of her leine and jerked her to her feet. Conlaed may have been stupid, but he was a man of great physical strength, and he could jerk her around like one of the cloth dolls she had played with as a girl.

Their faces were no more than a foot apart and Brigit could see the unchecked fury in Conlaed's eyes. But in the few seconds it had taken for him to pull her to her feet, Brigit had passed from fear to shock to her own level of fury. She was not a cloth doll. She was not bloody meat to be thrown to the dogs. She was Brigit nic Máel Sechnaill, daughter of Máel Sechnaill mac Ruanaid, the high king of Tara.

"Go to hell, you pathetic pile of horse shit," she said, her voice no more than a growl. She raised her hand in a fist and when Conlaed's glance shifted in that direction she kicked him hard in the crotch. It was a solid blow, but the aim was off, and when Conlaed released his grip and doubled over it was as much from instinct as pain.

Still, it was enough. Brigit shoved him and raced off to her left, to where she would have fighting room. Conlaed roared, straightened, plunged after her. Brigit grabbed a wide, shallow wash basin on a table by the wall and whirled around just as Conlaed closed with her. The water from the basin hit Conlaed first and then the earth ware bowl smashed against his face.

"Whore!" Conlaed shouted and grabbed at her, but she was past his grip and heading for the other side of the room. An iron candle holder, a tall one, floor standing, was near the head of the bed and Brigit managed to grab it with two hands like a broadsword and swing it around as she turned. Had Conlaed been a foot further behind, the base would have taken him in the head and ended it there, but he was faster than that, right on Brigit's heels, and the stand bounced against his shoulder, knocking Brigit off balance.

In that instant Conlaed was on her. His two powerful hands grabbed her neck, thumbs pressing into her throat and squeezing hard. Brigit felt her eyes bulge, her hands flail and claw at Conlaed's face, but his grip did not falter, his expression of pure hatred did not change, and he squeezed harder still.

The room began to swirl, the pain in her throat was excruciating, as if he was crushing the bones in her neck. She clawed at him, slashed at him with her nails, kicked his shins. She felt the consciousness draining from her, but still she fought. Her hand fell on something at Conlaed's side, the hilt of his hunting dagger. With never an organized thought she drew it free, cocked her elbow and drove the needle blade into Conlaed's stomach.

The effect was instantaneous. His hands fell from her throat, grabbed at the dagger, but Brigit pulled the blade free before Conlaed could touch it. They staggered away from each other, Conlaed bent in the middle, hands clamped on the wound, Brigit reeling and gasping. Conlaed's mouth was open, his eyes wide. She could see the dark blood running over his fingers.

Their eyes met, and Brigit felt her own blood rise, the blood of generations of Irish kings coursing through her, and she felt her fury far beyond anything she could have imagined. This lowly piece of garbage had struck her? Her? Brigit nic Máel Sechnaill?

"You son of a bitch!" she screamed and stepped forward and drove the dagger into Conlaed guts one more time. He made a gasping, gurgling sound. His eyes bulged. Brigit grabbed his hair and pulled him upright and stabbed him again. He tried to double up but she would not let him. Instead she held him up by a handful of his hair, looked into his eyes, made sure he was looking into hers, and then with a great arching slash of the dagger opened up his throat with a cut so deep she felt the blade bounce off bone.

Blood sprayed from the wound, showered her, but she did not flinch from this baptism, did not move; she just watched at Conlaed flailed his arms and blood erupted from the gash. Then she shoved him aside, let him drop to the floor and kick out the last thirty seconds of his insubstantial life.

Brigit watched him die. She felt nothing. The fury began to ebb and her hands began to tremble, not with fear or disgust or remorse, but with the excess of energy still coursing through her. She tried to drop the dagger on Conlaed's now still body but already the blood had congealed enough that it stuck to her skin and she had to use her left hand to peel it free. She sat down on her bed, stared vaguely at the inert form lying on the floor.

Now what? she wondered.

Chapter Thirteen

As I fall asleep, she appears,
and comes to me besmeared
hideously in human blood,
and washes me in gory flood.
Gisli Sursson's Saga

For a long time, Brigit sat on the edge of her bed. Her eyes were fixed on the body of her late husband, lying in its back, arms flung out at the sides.

Eighteen years old and twice a widow, she mused. *A dangerous business, marrying into this family.*

She heard the sound of doors opening, furtive steps outside the bed chamber. The loud and violent altercation had attracted the attention of others in the household, but none had actually dared to knock on the door and ask if all was well. And then it had grown quiet in the royal bed chamber, which was excuse enough for the others to slink back to their own rooms and avoid any involvement in the dispute. Or so Brigit guessed. In any event, no one knocked on the door.

She wondered if Morrigan had been there, outside the door. She could just picture the look of satisfaction on her face, well hidden beneath an expression of terrible concern.

Brigit's thoughts kept wandering away, then slinking back again, as she sat watching Conlaed by the light of the candle, bleeding out on the floor. *Such a lot of blood*, she thought. More than she would have guessed. It made a dark pool around him, growing wider and wider, and then finally it stopped.

What shall I do now, what, what? The trembling in her hands subsided and her thoughts became more ordered. She could not remain at Tara. It was the only home she had ever known, save for her brief first marriage, but it was no longer safe for her there. Maybe if she had just stabbed Conlaed once, she could argue that she had done so just to save her own life. She knew she would have bruises on her cheek and neck to prove her story. But she had made a real mess of him, had flayed him the way her father would have done, had given in to a deeper rage than she would have ever guessed was there. And that would be hard to explain.

And even if she could explain that away, the people to whom she would be explaining it were not her friends. Flann mac Conaing was on the throne of the high king and Morrigan, who was no doubt behind the night's events, was pulling his strings.

Flann's rule may have been a temporary arrangement, ostensibly, but Brigit had no doubt that Morrigan intended to make it permanent, with the Crown of the Three Kingdoms as an added enticement. There were some at Tara still loyal to Brigit and the memory of Máel Sechnaill mac Ruanaid, but most, seeing which way the wind was blowing, were now in Flann and Morrigan's camp.

The only other faction wielding power at Tara was the *rí túaithe* and the handful of men-at-arms they had with them, and they were not likely to defend the woman who had gutted their benefactor like a trout.

At length she stood, a deliberate and determined motion. "I have to go," she said softly. But where? And with whom? She had to leave Tara but she could not go wandering the roads alone. In her mind she took inventory of all the men at Tara who might help her, and one after another she rejected each.

Then she stopped. A faint smile came to her lips. *Yes, yes, there is one...* She looked down at her leine. The blood had mostly dried, turning big patches of the white linen stiff and brown. She thought about changing, but decided against it. The bloody cloth created just the right effect. She crossed to the window, opened the shutters a crack and peeked out. The night remained quiet, and she could see no one moving in any direction.

She turned and took one last look at her bed chamber, then prepared to step up and through the window when another idea came to her. She moved swiftly across the room and snatched up the candle, which by some miracle had remained upright and burning during her fight with Conlaed. She looked around the familiar room in the dim, familiar light.

The bedclothes, she thought. *And the tapestries.* She gripped the corner of the tapestry nearest her and flipped the corner onto the bed. She tossed the heavy furs onto the floor, leaving only the wool and linen blankets on the straw-filled mattress. She set the candle on the floor and moved it toward the bed until the flame licked at the corner of one of the blankets. The fire sputtered and danced and then caught the cloth and began climbing up the blanket, up the bed, spreading and consuming more and more of the bed clothes. The room was growing brighter as Brigit pushed open the shutters just wide enough for her to get through, dropped to the ground outside and pushed the shutters closed behind her.

Brigit hurried across the open space in which the royal residence sat, the cool dirt and mud pulling at her bare feet. She paused once to turn and look back. She could see just the thinnest sliver of light where the shutters to her bedchamber were imperfectly closed, but other than that there was no sign from the outside of the building of the fire burning within. The walls were thick built out of daub, a mixture of dirt and clay and straw, and she hoped it would take some time before the flames spread enough to be noticed.

She left the royal home behind and hurried toward the looming dark shape of the church, one hundred yards away. Further off she could see the great hall, with light still spilling from the windows, but all was quiet there as well. She pictured the *rí túaithe* dead drunk and sprawled out on the floor like her husband, though presumably not in pools of their own blood. Their vomit, perhaps.

She moved along the north side of the church, just feet from the rough stone wall, and still there was no sign that she had been seen, no sound of an alarm. At the front of the monastery she stopped. It was too dark to see the latch, so she ran her hands over walls, over the oak doors, until she felt the cool iron mechanism. She fumbled with it for a moment until she heard a sharp click that sounded preternaturally loud in the night. She sucked in her breath. The heavy door swung in, just an inch, and thankfully made no further noise. Brigit pushed it a few inches more, enough to let her through, and squeezed inside. She left the door ajar, for fear it would creak in closing.

For a minute she just stood and let her eyes adjust. It had been dark enough outside, but it was darker still inside the monastery building. Soon the blackness began to resolve itself into forms – a hallway, a series of doors, a wooden chest against a wall. Before her father's death she had served as head of all households at Tara. As such, she had on occasion inspected the work of the servants and slaves who had been sent to clean the brothers' quarters, so she knew which door she needed. She hoped the arrangement of the rooms had not changed since she had last been there.

Brigit took a careful step, then another. She began to move down the hall, running her hand along the wall, counting the doors as she passed. She felt no panic, no fear, just a determination to do what she needed to do, and that surprised her. So much in the past few months had surprised her, but nothing so much as these new insights into herself.

Three, four, five… She could hear thick snoring sounds from behind the doors, the well-fed monks and priests of Tara taking their rest. *Six, seven, eight…* Her shin slammed into some dark object she had not seen. She stumbled, and whatever she had hit made a scraping noise on the floor. A curse ran through her mind and she paused and listened, but the noise seemed not to have alerted anyone.

She moved on. Another door, and then she was there. She paused for a moment. She was too calm. She stirred up images in her head of Conlaed slapping her across the face, of his hands crushing her throat, and she felt the anger and the fear rising again. She thought of her father lying in wake and tears welled up in her eyes. She grabbed the wooden latch on the door, lifted it, and slipped inside.

The cell was darker even than the hall. Brigit could sense his presence, but she could see nothing. She took a tentative step deeper into the room, hands in front of her. And then from out of the dark came the soft voice of Father Finnian.

"Brigit? Brigit, dear, is that you?"

"Father Finnian! Oh, Father Finnian!" She said the words softly, with a tone of desperation and a stifled sob. Despite the darkness she could see him now, a darker shape just a few feet from her. He was not in his bed, as she had expected. She hoped he was dressed.

"By our Blessed Mother, girl, whatever has happened?" he asked, but rather than answer Brigit flung herself at the priest, arms open. She felt her face press against the coarse wool of his robe, felt his strong arms wrap around her. He held her, and did not ask for further explanation.

She pressed herself against him and sobbed all but noiselessly into his robe, as the emotions she had manufactured a moment before were overwhelmed by the genuine thing. All the terror and the loss and the agony of the past hour, the past week, the months since the Crown of the Three Kingdoms and the fin gall had both come to Tara and ripped her life apart like a knife through thin cloth, it all flowed from her eyes now and soaked into the dark brown cloth of Finnian's robe.

Brigit had a sense for time passing, but no notion of how much had passed. As she cried herself out she recalled that time was short, that this catharsis was a luxury she could not afford. She pushed herself away from Finnian, not enough to break his hold on her, just enough for her to look up into his face, which she could now discern, inches away.

"My husband…" she began, choked up, swallowed, and began again. "My husband…tried to kill me…."

"Oh, you poor dear thing," Finnian said. He sounded concerned, but not surprised. "Are you hurt, at all?"

"Yes…I'm…. I'm hurt, some. Not so bad. Conlaed…I killed him. He was choking me, I pulled his dagger from his belt…"

She felt Finnian's right hand lift off her back and she knew he was making the sign of the cross on himself. "You're sure, girl? You're sure he's dead?"

"Yes." She pushed further away from him, so that she was looking into his eyes, and his arms were no longer wrapped around her. When she spoke, her voice sounded more determined than afraid. "I have to leave Tara. I have to go now."

She could see Finnian shaking his head. "Why do you have to do that? Sure if Conlaed was trying to kill you, there'll be no harm come to you for what you've done."

"They'll see me burn at the stake for this. Morrigan, Flann. You know they are only looking for a reason to be rid of me."

Finnian was quiet. He said nothing in response. Because, Brigit was sure, he knew she was right. She waited for the obvious questions. *Do you mean for me to go with you? You expect me to help in this?* But those questions did not come because Finnian apparently knew the answers already. Instead he asked, "But how will we ever get unseen out of Tara? There are guards at every gate, every way in or out."

Then, from out in the night, came a muffled cry, an unintelligible shout. They paused and were quiet and heard another shout, clearer this time.

"Fire! Fire!"

They stood silent in Finnian's cell and listened. It was as if the night outside had exploded. Shouting from every quarter, feet running, and soon the sound of the church bells ringing an uncoordinated and frantic toll.

"We'll leave now," Brigit said, speaking louder than she had yet done. "We'll leave this instant. No one will see us go."

Chapter Fourteen

[Ireland] flows with milk and honey,
There is no shortage of wine, fish and birds
And it is remarkable for its deer and goats…
Breda, 8th Century

D*ubh-linn…the gods play with me…* Thorgrim Night Wolf stood at the bow of the *Black Raven* and indulged in rare and uncharacteristic self-pity. He knew it was like some exotic and expensive treat, delicious in small amounts, but something a man could soon become over fond of. And when that happened, it would be the end of him.

But at that moment, with the light mist falling, with all they had endured for the past weeks and the little they had to show for it, with the accursed Dubh-linn opening up before them as the Ravens swept the ship up the River Liffey, Thorgrim decided the time was right for a taste.

All this to get back to Vik, and again I am returning to Dubh-linn…

Not that it was at all a surprise. He had known from the outset that they would be returning to the longphort. It was what Arinbjorn had promised on Thorgrim's agreeing to sail with him. They would join Hoskuld Iron-skull's raid, return to Dubh-linn to sell what plunder they wished to sell there, then sail for Norway. But in the mood that Thorgrim found himself, reason played no part.

The longphort of Dubh-linn laid spread out on the banks of the river and climbing up the low hills that ran up from the water. There were dozens of houses and outbuildings. Squat, square little structures, some plank built in the Norse style, some wattle and daub, built shoulder to shoulder, each with its neat peak of thatch, each plot of land framed by wattle fences that sliced up the brown, trampled earth into somewhat regular spaces. A thin column of smoke rose from each of the houses, rose in the still air and mixed into a wispy cloud that hung over the town and reached Thorgrim's nose even from that distance. The sky was gray, the river was gray, and it gave the entire town a gray aspect, as if color was as scarce as sunshine in that country.

A dozen ships were pulled up on the muddy banks or tied to the few wharves built out from the shore, the sleek longships that carried the raiders and the beamy knarrs that carried the tons of cargo that flowed in ever greater amounts to and from the Irish port. It put Thorgrim in mind of the great Danish trading center of Hedeby, and the way it was growing he imagined it would soon rival Hedeby in importance. Beyond the houses and workshops, holding it all in like a belt drawn too tight, a broad earthen wall topped by a post and wattle fence separated the Norse town from the country beyond. Ireland, furious at this invasion, but in its chaotic state helpless to stop it.

Across the water Thorgrim could hear the occasional ring of a hammer, the thud of something heavy dropping into place, the shouts of men engaged in some unseen work. The people of Dubh-linn were not just men gone a-viking. They were blacksmiths and carpenters and shipbuilders and jewelers and merchants, and it seemed to Thorgrim that their numbers had increased just in the short time he had been gone. They had their homes, they had their wives, Norse or Irish. They were there to stay.

Not me…not me…

The raid on Cloyne had not been a great success, but neither had it been an absolute failure. Once Hoskuld Iron-skull had led the rest through the gates that Thorgrim and his band had opened, all resistance disappeared like smoke in the wind. The town's defenders, the swifter ones, fled to the tower, scrambled up the ladder and pulled it up behind them, leaving the rest to throw their arms aside and beg for quarter, which was generally granted, since they were young men, fit enough to take up arms, and not too swift of foot, and therefore having great potential for the slave market.

With the bulk of the population sequestered in the tower, the raiders had taken their time in plundering the town. They found food stores, livestock, a few trinkets, more unlucky Irish who would be heading for the slave markets. They did not find much else. Even in the monastery, even in the church, they found only a few bits of silver, a chalice, a few small plates, nothing of great quantity or quality.

"I agree with you, Thorgrim," Hoskuld had said as they watched their men pull the interior of the church apart. "These people, they knew for some time we were coming. They have hidden everything of value." Hoskuld had already tried extracting information from some of the prisoners, and he could be very persuasive, but in the end he concluded that they were genuinely ignorant. Thorgrim agreed. Peasants, in his experience, would only endure so much to protect the wealth of their lords and masters, and that threshold was pretty low.

Thorgrim pulled his eyes from the depressing sight of Dubh-linn, with which they were rapidly closing, and looked over the other ships of the raiding voyage, *Thunder God, Serpent* and the rest, each pulling with a steady rhythm up the river. They had their yards swung fore and aft and lowered, and the menacing carved heads that had adorned their stems were removed so as not to frighten any spirits of the land that might be inclined to be helpful. If such there were, Thorgrim guessed they had been brought from the Norsemen's homelands. There was nothing native to Ireland that would welcome the men from the North.

He continued to turn, scanning the ships, fully aware that this was only an excuse to glance aft at Harald and see how the boy was doing. He was at his place, fourth oar from the stern, larboard side. From behind he looked much like the others, a bit shorter, perhaps. Only the shock of long yellow hair, bound loosely by a piece of string, gave his identity away.

"He's fine, you know." Starri Deathless made this observation without looking up. He was seated on the planks which made up the foredeck on which Thorgrim stood. He was sharpening a two edged dagger to an absurd level of perfection. He worked at the blade with a whetstone, then tried the edge on the hair of his left arm. Thorgrim could see a series of bare patches where previous tests had shaved him clean, but Starri just frowned and applied the whetstone again.

"The men reckon Harald has your luck," Starri continued. "They like him. Thorgrim Night Wolf's luck without any of his miserable attitude."

"'Miserable attitude,' is it? That's something, coming from the likes of you."

Starri made no reply to that, just smiled and continued to fiddle with his knife. If Harald's reputation was much raised among Arinbjorn's men, it was thanks both to his bold deeds and Starri's relentless recounting of them. Proud as he was of his son, Thorgrim did not think it was his place to brag about him. Bragging about the exploits of one's children, he figured, was nearly as bad as bragging about one's own exploits, and he recoiled from the thought of doing that. But Starri felt no such hesitation.

After the fight, Thorgrim had found the berserker by the gate, slumped against the hay wagon. He thought the man had finally won his voyage to Valhalla, but no, Starri was still alive and unharmed. He had collapsed to the ground in despair, and as soon as Thorgrim asked him if he was unhurt he wailed that he was fine and began weeping bitterly at the injustice of it all.

Once the anguish of surviving the fight had passed, Starri was quick to sing Harald's praises, relating to anyone who would listen the incident with the hay wagon and the fire at the gate. Thorgrim discovered that Starri could tell a story well, and even behave in something approaching a civilized manner when he was not in a bloodletting rage. The berserker went so far as to compose some verses, which he recited in the evenings, and though he was no skald, they were not bad, and were much enjoyed. Harald blushed and stammered throughout, and genuinely did not know how to respond to praise, which in Thorgrim's mind was a mark of true humility, the right kind of humility, a warrior's humility, and it made him prouder still.

Thorgrim's first encounter with Arinbjorn White-tooth after the fighting had ended was odder even than his meeting with Starri. Arinbjorn had seen him first, called out his name, and when Thorgrim turned Arinbjorn approached with arms outstretched and his well-known smile on his face. "Thorgrim Night Wolf!" he shouted, embracing Thorgrim enthusiastically while Thorgrim took a tentative stab at returning the affection.

"The gods smile on you still!" Arinbjorn continued. "You have won the day for us! I made the right choice in asking you to join me on this voyage, there can be no doubt of it! The truth of that is on every man's tongue."

Thorgrim pulled away and just nodded. Words were not his weapon of choice and he was not sure what to say. There was a false note in Arinbjorn's words, of course. Thorgrim had ignored the man's orders, had gone into Cloyne despite him, though only the two of them knew it. But there was a deeper subtlety to what Arinbjorn was saying. The words, the tone, had a conspiratorial quality, as if suggesting that the raid had been their mutual plan all along, or at least that the others should be made to believe as much.

"The gods have been good to us all, Arinbjorn," Thorgrim said at last, no trace of rancor or condemnation in his voice. He could all but see the relief on Arinbjorn's face. But why should he say anything else? Arinbjorn might plume himself with feathers he did not earn, but it did no harm to Thorgrim and his men. Everyone in the camp knew who it was who opened the gates of Cloyne, and who had remained in their tent. Thorgrim would not suffer a blow from another man, a blow to his person or his reputation, but Arinbjorn's silliness did not amount to so grave an injury.

"The gods bless us, but you have helped them along," Arinbjorn continued, his enthusiasm not abated. "When the loot is divided up, and the *Black Raven*'s share given out, you and your son shall have three shares. And the others with you shall have two shares."

"That's very generous," Thorgrim said, "but it is not necessary."

But Arinbjorn insisted, and so Thorgrim agreed. He could see that Arinbjorn was looking to purchase silence, which he would have had for free, but the fact was that Thorgrim still needed Arinbjorn. Thorgrim did not think the prospect of finding a ship to Vik had improved any in the few weeks they had been gone. Arinbjorn White-tooth was still the best, and perhaps only chance that he and Harald had of making their way home.

Starri Deathless stood up from the foredeck and slipped his dagger into his sheath. It was a simple move, but when done by Starri it took on a poetic quality. Powerful, sinewy and lithe, the man seemed to float up from the deck as much as stand, like a bird unfolding its wings and taking flight. One second he was down, the next he was up. Thorgrim had never been able to move like that, and it had been years since he could even come close. He wondered how old Starri was. Not young. Thirty summers gone, at least. Maybe forty, fifty. You could not tell with a man like Starri.

"What in the name of Thor is around your neck?" Thorgrim asked, noticing the trinket for the first time, bound by a leather thong and hanging against Starri's thin chest. Starri took it up between two fingers, examined if as if seeing it for the first time.

"Your arrowhead," he said.

Thorgrim took it from his fingers and examined it closer. It was not his arrowhead, strictly speaking, but some Irishman's arrowhead, the arrowhead that had split itself against Iron-tooth's blade. "Why do you have that?" Thorgrim asked.

"Why do you not? A sign of the gods' respect? Odin may just as well have leaned down and kissed you on the head, and you toss it away like so much garbage. But I snatched it up as soon as you did. Picking up your scraps, like a dog under the table." There was no malice in his tone. He was just explaining how things were. Indeed, Thorgrim was often surprised by Starri's generally even temper, what with his being a berserker and all. Maybe the occasional berserker rage purged madness from his system, like a good thunderstorm driving the heat away.

Hoskuld Iron-skull's *Thunder God* was the first of the longships to reach the muddy place where the vessels would beach. The bow ran up onto the shore, the way was checked, and the men leapt over the low sides and grabbed hold of the gunnels, running the shallow draft ship further up on shore, with Hoskuld standing like some fur-covered monument on the deck aft.

Sea Dragon was next, then *Serpent* and *Eagle's Sword* and then *Black Raven.* Thorgrim staggered a bit as the bow touched and the way came off. He looked aft. Harald, of course, was the first to his feet, the first to have his sweep stowed away. Their eyes met. Harald grinned, and then with the ease of youth he vaulted over the side and landed up to his waist in the river.

The rest of the crew followed, going over the low rail as if they were abandoning the ship is a great panic. Thorgrim, taking advantage of his status as a wealthy and powerful, if temporarily displaced, leader of men, chose to remain dry, as did Starri, who, as a recognized madman, felt free to do pretty much whatever he wished.

One of the *Black Raven*'s men came forward, a length of braided walrus hide rope in his hand. Thorgrim stepped aside as he tossed the bitter end to the others in the water and made the inboard end fast. Thorgrim looked aft. Other than the man with the bow line, Arinbjorn and the helmsmen were the only others still aboard, and he knew he could ignore the jarl no longer. He walked aft between the rows of sea chests, larboard and starboard, that made up the rower's benches. The decking underfoot was set into notches in the ribs but not secured, making it easier to take up and gain access to the bilges for storage, or for bailing, and every few feet Thorgrim could feel a board move as he stepped on it.

"Arinbjorn, I congratulate you on a safe return, a profitable voyage," Thorgrim said, stepping up to the jarl and extending a hand. Arinbjorn took it gratefully. On either side, the men of the *Black Raven* gripped the gunnels and cursed the mud and hauled the elegant ship up onto the river bank.

"And you, Thorgrim Night Wolf. You have my sincerest thanks for all you have done this voyage." The words sounded sincere, and Thorgrim guessed they were. Arinbjorn was no doubt genuinely grateful to be back, with his ship, men and reputation pretty much intact, and him somewhat wealthier for his trouble.

"As to profit, yes, it will be somewhat profitable, I should think," Arinbjorn was still talking. "We'll see what price these slaves will fetch us, what miserable scraps of plunder we managed to find. I'll see your share, and Harald's, brought to you once it is all reckoned up."

"Thank you. We are both grateful for the chance you've given us," Thorgrim said, but Arinbjorn waved the words off with his hand. "There is the matter as well," Thorgrim continued, "of returning to Norway? I'm sure I made no secret of my eagerness to get back to my farm at Vik."

"Yes, yes, of course!" Arinbjorn said enthusiastically. "Back to Norway, that is still my intention. I have a wife and children, you know, and I miss them terribly. Once we have this business settled up, then we shall speak of returning home." He smiled broadly, took Thorgrim's hand again and with his other hand slapped Thorgrim in a companionable way on the shoulder.

"Thank you, Arinbjorn, I am much relieved," Thorgrim said, but in fact he was not relieved. He was, in fact, sick with despair. Because he had no choice, as far as he could see, but to put his hopes in Arinbjorn White-tooth, and Arinbjorn White-tooth had the sincerity of a snake.

Chapter Fifteen

Night is now, now shall we fare
over moist mountains…
scatheless we both shall 'scape their might
The Lay of Skírnir

It had been just minutes, five minutes perhaps, maybe less, between the moment that Brigit and Father Finnian had first heard the words, "Fire!" and the moment they emerged from the monastery into the night, but in those brief minutes it seemed the whole world had changed, like the End Times had come.

Fire… There were few words that struck such immediate terror because there were few forces that could deliver destruction so quickly and completely. A devastating storm would be seen hours before its arrival. Even an enemy striking as swiftly as it was able would be discovered well before the first arrow flew. But fire? Its approach was silent and unseen, and by the time it was discovered it might well have a grip that could not be shaken.

And that was the case with the royal household. Brigit, of course, had been the first at Tara to see the fire, Finnian the last. As the brothers flung open the doors to their cells and pounded down the dark hall, summoned by the call of "Fire!" as surely as any call to prayer, Finnian had pulled one of his brown robes from a chest at the foot of his cot and helped Brigit slip it over her head. He bunched the cloth at the waist so it would not drag on the ground and tied it in place with a waist cord.

Brigit raised her arms and let him adjust the robe. His hands were strong and dexterous and he worked with no hesitation, none of the awkwardness men often displayed in such situations. His confidence gave Brigit hope.

By the time Finnian finished with the robe and opened the door of his cell to peer out into the hall, moving cautiously, with Brigit standing well back in the shadows, the monastery was deserted, all its occupants gone to help or to watch, as was their wont.

"Come along," he said and Brigit followed. They moved quietly down the hall. The door at the end had been left open and the light from the fire was finding its way inside, which made the going much easier. They paused by the front door and Finnian pulled the hood of the robe up over Brigit's head and then they hurried outside.

From every corner of the ringfort, people were rushing to the mounting pyre. Many were shouting, the words or their intent Brigit could not discern. The bells of the church were peeling now, as if anyone at Tara did not know there was an emergency. She could see a line of people forming at the well, buckets passing one to the other.

Best of luck with that, she thought.

Finnian grabbed her arm and led her along, beyond the monastery, to where they had a clear view of what was happening. "Dear Lord, child, it's the royal household on fire!" he said.

"Oh, Lord, save them," Brigit said in a tone that sounded like surprise and they both made the sign of the cross. The north eastern quarter of the big house was engulfed, fire spilling out of the window of Brigit's former bed chamber, licking up the wall, starting to catch on the thatch eves. Once the thatch caught, that would be the end of things.

Mesmerizing as the sight was, Brigit was ready to go. There would be no better time to slip unseen through one of the gates. But Finnian remained fixed, his eyes on the burning building.

"That's your own bed chamber, right in the middle of it, is it not?" he asked. The shock of seeing the royal household ablaze had passed, and Finnian's voice was calm.

"Yes, it is…"

"Did you know it was on fire?"

"No…I…in the fight, a candle may have been knocked over…it was all so awful, I didn't see…" Brigit stammered, the words catching in her throat. She felt the tears coming back.

Finnian looked at her for a long moment, and then in a quiet voice said, "Come along, we had better go." They turned their backs to the burning building and headed off for a gate in the north wall of the ringfort. From the light of the fire they could see there was no guard there, no one to question why they might be leaving Tara in the middle of the night.

They reached the gate and paused, looked back. No one was paying them any attention so they turned back to the wooden latch that held the oak door closed. This was not one of the chief entryways, one of the gates built to accommodate wagons, but a smaller sallyport, large enough for a single man on horseback, no more. It was a simple matter to open the crossbar and slip through. They did so, and immediately the thick wall muted the chaos from within the ringfort. They moved swiftly into the dark. They did not look back.

There was no moon, but once their eyes had recovered from watching the inferno that was the royal household there was light enough for them to see the dark scar of a road that led away to the south. They walked on, two dark-robed figures, all but invisible in the night. They did not speak.

They continued on for hours, their bare feet making no sound on the soft earth road. The walls of Tara sank below the hills, the sound of shouting and bells receded in the distance, and soon there was nothing to see of the seat of the high king but a soft glow of light on the horizon. Then even that began to fade as the fire was got under control or the building had burned to the ground, or so Brigit imagined.

As the shock of the night faded, so too did Brigit's strength, and she found herself staggering and bouncing against Finnian's shoulder. She shook her head, rubbed her eyes, forced herself to continue on. She felt a warm darkness come over her, a soothing, comfortable sensation. Then she stumbled, recovered, realized she had fallen asleep while walking. "Here, time for us to get some rest," Finnian said, softly.

The first hints of dawn were visible in the east, casting enough light to reveal a stand of oak trees a hundred feet from the road. Finnian led her over the cool, damp grass and slightly up hill until they found themselves in the midst of the grove. "I'm afraid this is the best we'll do for shelter tonight," Finnian said.

She collapsed to the ground, luxuriating in the soft earth, the blessed relief of being off her feet. "No feather bed in any palace could be more welcome than this," she said. Finnian made some reply, but through the haze of her exhaustion Brigit could not make out the words, and before she could ask him to repeat himself, she was fast asleep.

Brigit was as exhausted as she could be, in every way a person could be exhausted, physically, emotionally, and it was a blessing in this instance, because despite the horror of the night, despite the rough ground and the damp seeping through her wool robe, she slept a solid and dreamless sleep. She did not move at all, just remained fixed in the position in which she had collapsed, and for several hours was as still as if she were in her grave.

She came awake at last, but her eyes remained closed and her body remained in the position in which she had slept, but she seemed to have no control over either. She told herself to open her eyes, to move her arm, but her eyelids and her arm did not respond. It was as if she was weighted down all over by a great press of blankets. She could not move. She became aware of sounds. She could hear birds, and a rustling in the dirt beside her. She struggled to call out, was aware of a strangled yell coming from her throat, and a hand clamped over her mouth.

That seemed to break the spell. Her eyes came open. She was looking at the ground and a patch of ferns and the trunks of several oak trees. She swiveled her head and looked up, into the calm but serious face of Father Finnian. He held a finger to his lips, made a soft "shhhh" sound, softer than the breeze in the treetops. Brigit nodded her understanding and he took the hand from her mouth.

Quiet as she could she propped herself up on her arm. Her muscles were sore and stiff and protested every movement and she clenched her teeth and forced herself to remain silent because Finnian had instructed her to. Why he had, she did not know.

Father Finnian was crouched beside her with one knee on the ground. He was bending low so the bracken in the grove mostly shielded him from view from the road. His head was cocked as if he was straining to hear. Brigit did the same. She heard nothing beyond what she would expect to hear, birds and wind and insects. The overcast and the drizzling rain had blown through, and in their place were blue skies and a scattering of high, white clouds. The change lifted Brigit's spirits and gave her just a twinge of optimism.

Then she heard what Finnian heard and she felt the optimism collapse. Horses. Hooves on the road, far off but getting closer. How many riders there were she could not tell. More than two, certainly. They were riding fast, but not at a gallop. There was little chance that any rider in that part of Ireland could have come from any place but Tara.

She inched her way closer to the brush, careful not to make a sound. The patter of the horses' hooves on the dirt of the road was closer now. She peered through the tangle of green leaves and saw them at last, a mile or so away and approaching. She felt Finnian behind her, also moving to a place where he could better see.

They watched in silence. Six riders, coming on at a fast trot. They wore cloaks that blew out behind them as they rode. They drew closer, and Brigit could see tunics of rich color and swords hanging from belts and bouncing against the riders as they moved, but they were still too far away to recognize.

Her breathing was shallow and she was absolutely motionless as the riders approached. She could see they were not keeping their eyes on the road, but scanning the countryside as they rode past. She felt vulnerable and exposed and she shuffled back a few inches. From indistinct shapes on horseback they began to resolve into individuals, and then into individuals whom Brigit recognized.

Patrick, you miserable bastard, she thought. Patrick, Morrigan's man. She guessed that Donnel had been sent out with another party in the other direction, and others to cover all the roads leading from Tara. She recognized a few men-at-arms whose names she did not know, and a few of the *rí túaithe* who she would just as soon forget.

They came closer, their pace never slacking, and as they drew even with the stand of trees Patrick turned his head and looked right at her, right into her eyes, or so it seemed to her. But there was one hundred feet between them, and she saw no hint on Patrick's face that he had seen her, or anything else that caught his eye. His head turned the other way and he and the rest rode on past.

Patrick's band disappeared down a dip in the road, then reappeared up the far side before either Brigit or Finnian dared speak again.

"Morrigan," Brigit said in a soft and accusatory voice. "Patrick is Morrigan's man. She's sent them out to hunt us down."

"Perhaps…" Finnian said.

"Perhaps? What else might they be doing?"

"It's a good question. They can't know for certain you're still alive. The fire must have taken half the royal house, if it did not burn it all to the ground. They won't know yet if you were in there or not. And sure Patrick and that bunch were not making so great a search of it."

They were quiet for a moment, watching the band of horsemen growing smaller in the distance; the sound of their horses' hooves soon overwhelmed by the breeze and the song birds. Then Finnian spoke again.

"Your leine, it was quite dry."

"What?"

"Your leine. When you came into my cell. You were in a panic, but the blood on your leine was dry. Did you not come directly to me?"

"No…." She stammered, searching for words, trying to see down the verbal road here, to where Finnian was leading her. "I don't know what I was doing. I wasn't thinking…. What difference could it make?"

"None. None, I'm sure."

"And you," Brigit continued, shifting the course of the conversation, "you were dressed when I came in. I had thought to find you in bed."

"Ah, girl, you sounded like Joshua's army descending on Jericho as you came down the hall there. I knew there was something amiss."

The two of them sat in silence a while longer. Brigit could feel her stomach twisting with hunger, could feel the dull ache in her feet from the previous day's march, and she wondered how she would ever stand and continue on. Then Finnian spoke again.

"You asked me to help you get away from Tara. I know you, girl, and I know you did not run away with no thought of where you are running to. And where would that be?"

Brigit did not answer immediately. She had known, of course, that this moment would come. She had put considerable thought into it, sitting on the edge of her bed, beside the body of her dead husband, as his blood dried on her clothing.

Where can I go?

She had sat in silence, but the question had been screaming in her head. Any of the minor kingdoms which she might hope to reach on foot were either loyal to Flann, as the heir apparent to the throne of Tara, or too afraid of him to dare give her shelter. Any kingdom so far away as to be beyond Flann's sphere of influence would be too far to do her any good. They might give her shelter, might let her live out her days there, might even let her marry into the family of the *rí túaithe*, but no more. And she was not interested in any of those things. She cared about one thing alone, and that was taking her place on the throne of Tara, and her child after her.

And there was only one place where she might find an ally who could help her do that.

"There is one place I might go, Father," she said at last. "The only place. Dubh-linn."

Chapter Sixteen

If old age awaits this battle-spear
then my dreams lead me astray.
Gisli Sursson's Saga

Even before the *Black Raven* was made fast to the shore, Ornolf the Restless was there, standing in mud up to his ankles, roaring his greeting, roaring drunk. Thorgrim watched Harald approach his grandfather, arms out, watched Ornolf take the boy in a bear hug. With Ornolf, massively built, with a great hedge of gray and red beard and long hair tumbling in every direction, it was very near to being literally a bear hug.

"Thorgrim! Thorgrim!" Ornolf shouted out. "Come here and explain to me how someone so girlish as you might have sired a man such as Harald, here! I know my daughter was not disloyal, so it must be something else!"

Thorgrim looked over at Arinbjorn and Arinbjorn gave him a half smile, a cock of the eyebrows. Thorgrim nodded and a moment of understanding passed between them, a flash of a connection they had never before shared.

"I have a father-in-law, too," Arinbjorn confided. "You had best go."

Thorgrim put a foot on the gunnel and vaulted over, his soft leather shoes sinking deep in the mud of the River Liffey. He heard a soft splash behind and knew that Starri Deathless had followed. Arinbjorn, he was certain, would wait until a gangplank was rigged, which even at the moment his men were struggling to do.

"Thorgrim!" Ornolf still had Harald firmly in the grip of his left arm and he held up his right arm to hug Thorgrim, all the while keeping a grip on a half-full goblet in his hand, an impressive feat. Thorgrim held out his arms and gave Ornolf the obligatory hug, a half-hearted effort, but Ornolf did not seem to notice as he crushed father and son in return. The old man's strength and endurance never failed to astound.

"There are some impressive tales being told about my grandson's deeds at Cloyne, some mighty impressive tales!" Ornolf said, releasing his grip. His voice was louder than was quite necessary, but at least he had stopped shouting. "You were mentioned as well, Thorgrim, seems you had some part in it."

"'Tales?'" Thorgrim asked. "How could tales be told, the fleet is only now returned?"

"Ha! Don't be a fool!" Ornolf replied. "You know that word travels faster than the swiftest ship. The gods carry tales of brave deeds ahead of the men who do them."

Thorgrim nodded. It had to be true that the gods brought word ahead and whispered it in the ears of those ashore. He had seen before how tales of great deeds had spread faster than was humanly possible.

"Now who is this fellow?" Ornolf asked and the three turned to see Starri standing, silent and unmoving, a few feet away.

"This is Starri," Thorgrim said. "He played a great part in the fighting, saved my life and Harald's more than once, I should think. Starri, this is my father-in-law, Ornolf of Vik."

Starri and Ornolf clasped hands and Ornolf said, "You have a look about you. One might take you for one of those berserkers, and if so, it is no matter to me. There are some won't be civil to berserkers, until they need them to take all the risk in battle, but I'm not one of those."

To that Starri just nodded and held Ornolf's hand. Then Ornolf said, "Come, let's get us to the mead hall! They'll be drinking the health of you fellows soon, and if Ornolf is too old and tired to garner any glory for himself, at least I can gather some of the reflected glory of my grandson! And my son-in-law, of course."

And so the four of them trudged off, up the plank road, past the tight packed houses and workshops, though the low hanging smoke and the ring of hammers, the soft growl of saws, up toward the mead hall, which had been partially burned by Thorgrim and his men when Dubh-linn had been in Danish hands, but now was fully repaired by the Norwegians who held the longphort.

Thorgrim did not feel much like celebrating. He was tired, he felt the black mood setting in, and he wished only to be left alone to brood and to think of home. But in this circumstance, and with Ornolf in the lead, he had little chance for escape. Nor did he care to leave Harald unattended under the tutelage of his grandfather.

The mead hall was built in the Scandinavian style and loomed above them like a cliff as they approached, giving it an oddly menacing look in the dying light of the late afternoon. The big doors hung open, a rectangle of glowing light, as if the interior itself was on fire, and noise and smoke rolled out. Ornolf all but pushed Thorgrim and Harald in ahead of him.

For Thorgrim Night Wolf there was no sensation, save perhaps that of stepping into his own home, more familiar than that of stepping into a mead hall. The smell of roasting meat, spilled drink, of many men packed together, the roar of their shouted and drunken conversation, the occasional scream of a thrall, the banging of wooden plates and mugs, the whole scene lit by a massive fire burning in a hearth, a fire that sometimes flared and filled the hall with light and sometimes died away and threw the place into shadow, it was at once familiar and soothing and stimulating. He stepped further into the big room. The noise, loud even before their entrance, seemed to grow, to swirl upward like a flock of birds rising together.

Ornolf grabbed Thorgrim and Harald's hands, raised them up and bellowed, "Ha! They've been waiting on you!" And as he said it the rising sound burst into cheers, shouts, plates, fists and knife hilts banged on wooden tables. Up by the fire, Hoskuld Iron-skull stood with the other jarls and they raised their cups and joined in the shouting. Harald was grinning wide. There was a time, Thorgrim knew, when he too would have devoured such recognition like the most savory of meals, but now it only embarrassed him.

Starri leaned forward and spoke in Thorgrim's ear. "Thorgrim, did you storm the very gates of Asgard, and loot the treasure of the gods? I must have missed that, but sure such enthusiasm could be for nothing less." Thorgrim could hear the smile in Starri's voice, and he smiled himself, a grim smile. In his present mood, any other man who said such a thing to him would have paid a dear price for it.

The afternoon turned to evening and then nighttime with the familiar debauchery; drinking, feasting, the old songs sung with more emphasis on volume than melody or tune. The sound of rutting in the shadows. Tales were told, insults traded, toasts drunk with enthusiasm. Ornolf had not budged from Dubh-linn since returning there with Olaf the White, and he seemed to Thorgrim to have ensconced himself in the mead hall like some benevolent jarl, ordering the thralls about, summoning up more food and drink, insisting this man sit in one place, this one in another.

And to Thorgrim's surprise, the men and the thralls in the hall seemed to listen to him, and do as directed, but he suspected that this was due more to their finding the old man amusing than recognizing any authority he might have.

"Ah, Thorgrim!" Ornolf said, settling himself with care on the bench on which Thorgrim and Harald sat. To Thorgrim's annoyance he handed a fresh cup of mead to the already red-faced and unsteady boy. "This Dubh-linn is all a man could want! Women everywhere, Irish women, good and subservient! Fresh food! Every day, I tell you, the gates open and the farmers and the sheep herders and the fish mongers and what not bring their goods into town. These Irish may hate us, but damn me if they don't like selling to us for silver and gold!"

"This is not our home," Thorgrim said, taking the cup from Harald's hand and drinking deep from it.

"Exactly!" Ornolf roared. "From Vik we must cross the seas to plunder. Here, we sail down the coast, take what we wish, and use the silver to buy food and drink from the very people we took the silver from in the first place! What could be more convenient than that?"

"Ornolf has a point," Starri said, one of the few things he had said all evening, then poured mead down his throat as if the words had parched him.

"He has a point," Thorgrim agreed, "but how long it will remain true, I can't say. For all the high talk here tonight there was not much plunder to be had at Cloyne. Worse, these Irish might start helping each other. If they unite as one, we cannot defeat them."

"Ha! We won't live to see that!" Ornolf declared. "They'll keep on fighting each other like the wild dogs they are!"

Wild dogs… Thorgrim turned aside, weary of the conversation, and looked into the fire. For all the time he had been damned by the gods to spend in Ireland, he had really known only one native of that country. Morrigan, the thrall. She was beautiful, a healer, a woman who had suffered much. And she was dangerous, complicated, like one of the floating ice mountains of the northern seas, the lovely and quiet part above the surface, so much more unseen below. And that was the part that would wreck you.

Morrigan was all Thorgrim knew of Ireland, she and Almaith, the blacksmith Jokul's wife, from whom they rented a place to sleep. For Harald it was different. Harald had been to Tara, which was apparently the seat of the high king of those parts, whisked away by Morrigan and used as a pawn, though treated well enough. He told a story of a royal household as fine as any to be found in Norway, a ringfort with a church and many houses. A place worth plundering, Thorgrim imagined, though it would be no easy business, not like Cloyne.

There was a woman, too. Brageet, or some such. Thorgrim had trouble with the strange Irish names. Brigit. That was it. Harald had been circumspect in his talking about her, but Thorgrim could see there was much to the story that Harald was not saying. The boy had the subtlety of a battle-spear up the backside.

A scuffling brought his attention back, a catch in the ambient noise, a shift of tone. He looked up. There was a certain tension in the hall. Thorgrim had been aware of it, but had given it no thought. But now, looking around at the fire-lit faces, flushed and sweating, he could sense a breaking point. Those men who had not been with them at Cloyne were growing weary of the celebrations, the self-congratulatory attitude of the victors. Because they had not been part of the raiding party, they were looking to punish someone who was. And that person was Harald.

Thorgrim had not seen this play out, but still he was not surprised. Harald had managed to consume about a third of the various drinks that Ornolf had handed him, despite Thorgrim's best efforts to take the cups from his hand. The boy, unused to drinking so hard and fast, had staggered across the room, no doubt looking for a place to relieve himself, and had staggered into a big, foul-looking beast of a man with one eye sealed shut by a vicious scar that ran like a narrow valley across his face.

The hall was too loud, Harald and his antagonists too far across the room for Thorgrim to hear their words, but he did not have to. He had heard them all before, the same stupid fight played out in the same mead halls up and down the coast of Norway and in Hedeby as well.

What do you mean by running into me, huh, boy?

Nothing. I mean nothing by it. Accident.

Accident? I'll teach you a lesson about disrespecting me…

Or some variation on that tired theme. Thorgrim was on his feet as the scarred man grabbed a handful of Harald's tunic and cocked his fist. If Harald had been sober, then Thorgrim would have given even odds that the scarred son of a whore would get the worst of it, but Harald was far from sober.

"You hit the boy, you'll answer to me!" Thorgrim shouted but no one heard his words or indeed paid him any attention.

Then, with a shriek that turned every head in the hall, Starri Deathless launched himself off the bench, took three steps along the table and launched himself off that, coming down on the hard-packed dirt floor inches from the scarred man, inches from Harald. The mead hall fell silent. Motionless. Like a tapestry, a still rendering of Starri standing where he had landed, the man gripping Harald's tunic in one hand, his other hand a cocked fist, Harald's eyes wide and glistening. Then Starri twirled around and bowed deep at the waist, bowed to all who watched his performance, spread his hands as if calling for applause.

Silence. And then the hall seemed to erupt with laughter, shouts, applause. Starri bowed again.

Thorgrim pushed his way through the crowd, closed with the scarred man who still had Harald by the tunic. "Come friend," he called. "Let the boy go, let us all drink together." If Starri could so cleverly throw water on this fire, Thorgrim would not ignite it again.

But the scarred man was having none of it. He had been looking for a fight, and instead, by his lights, had received nothing but mockery. Thorgrim could see that if he had been feigning anger and insult before, he wasn't feigning it now.

"Drink with whore's bastards like you two? I think not."

The black mood, which had been lurking at the edge of Thorgrim's consciousness all night, now swept in like a fast moving fog. *This idiot could not have picked a worse man to fool with*, he thought. He took another step forward and stopped. Everything seemed held in place by opposing forces; his anger, the scarred man's anger. And then the forces let go, so fast that Thorgrim did not even see what happened, which would worry him later, as he reflected on the night. He was slowing down.

The man with the scarred face swung his fist with the speed and power of a catapult's arm, and Harald – wide-eyed, shocked, and inebriated – just stood there, motionless. It was Starri who moved first, a blur of speed, and then the scarred man was on his knees, shrieking a weird, high-pitched scream while his forearm hung at an odd angle a few inches below his elbow.

Once again the mead hall seemed to stop, the men frozen in their tapestry tableau, the space filled with the scarred man's screams of agony which were like a physical thing. And then the man's fellows launched themselves like bulls crashing a fence, fists and mugs raised, mouths open in shouts of outrage. They charged for the boisterous crowd who had been with Hoskuld Iron-skull at Cloyne, resentment boiling over, and nearest of those men were Harald, Thorgrim and Starri.

Thorgrim grabbed Harald by the collar and jerked him back just as a huge fist swung at the boy's head. The fist found only air and the man swinging it, having readied himself for the impact, stumbled when he found none. Thorgrim stepped up and the man looked at him with an expression like resignation as Thorgrim slammed a rock-hard fist of his own into his hairy temple and dropped him to the floor.

Even as the man was going down, Thorgrim felt hands grabbing his hair and the cloth of his tunic. He twisted back the other way, breaking the grip, striking with an ineffectual left. Someone's fist made solid contact with his stomach and he doubled over and turned sideways, letting his shoulder take the blow from the knee that he knew would be aimed at his face. Still in too much pain to straighten, he drove himself forward and into the man in front of him. He felt himself stumbling as the two of them headed for the floor.

A hand on his collar pulled him back and up straight, away from the man with whom he was clenched, and from behind him Harald appeared, recovered from his shock, stone sober and ready to brawl. Thorgrim's antagonist was just regaining his feet when Harald leapt clean off the floor and drove his heels right into the man's sternum, sending him flying as Harald came down with arms cocked, fists clenched for the next behind.

Thorgrim had only a fraction of a second to marvel at the loveliness of the boy's move when he sensed a motion to his larboard side, turned, deflected a fist with his left forearm and struck with his right, connecting solidly, and felt the man stagger under the blow.

He twisted the other way. A fist grazed his face. He swung with his right and felt the laceration he had received at Cloyne, which had nearly healed, open up again. He felt a warm cat's paw of blood spreading under his tunic. He grabbed the arm that had lashed at him, twisted it hard, felt the arm's owner jerk it free a fraction of a second before the bone gave way and shattered.

Starri Deathless was engaged with two of the men who had advanced on them, ducking, jabbing fast with his fist, twisting here and there. Thorgrim caught a glimpse of his face. He was smiling, nearly laughing. Thorgrim had never minded a good brawl, had even enjoyed them on occasion, but for Starri this was clearly amusement at its finest. Indeed, he seemed not to be trying to beat anyone, just sustain the combat for as long as he could.

Thorgrim turned to the sound of shouting to his right, turned in time to see a bench come sweeping at him as someone whirled it through the air like a broadsword. He pulled Harald aside and ducked as the heavy oak seat passed overhead and slammed into the men beyond, men Thorgrim was sure were on the side of the bench swinger. The fight was devolving into a free for all, with no one even recalling whom they were supposed to be fighting. But no weapons, at least no edged weapons. No one there, angry as they were, was looking for a murderous bloodbath. Tonight's violence was pure recreation.

From under a pile of thrashing arms, Nordwall the Short kicked his way to the surface. Thorgrim could see a few of Hoskuld's men coming into it, and more of Arinbjorn's with whom he had fought before. He could hear a thrall screaming in terror, someone laughing loud, the crash of tables overturned, pottery smashed. From some unseen quarter a fist made solid contact with his head, twisting him around. The open wound in his side hurt as if he was being stabbed with a knife.

He gasped and another fist caught him from the other direction and he staggered back. A blurred image of Starri Deathless' dark blue tunic swam in front of his eyes. He shook his head, willed his sight to return. He could taste blood in his mouth. Someone was taking a clumsy swing at him and he caught the fist like catching a ball, twisted the hand, and with his right leg swept the man's feet away, a move that was so ingrained in him that his muscles did it with no conscious command from his brain.

The brawl, Thorgrim could see, was winding down. Here and there men were collapsing to the ground, some beaten to unconsciousness, some finding goblets and cups of mead. The thralls, who were no strangers to this sort of thing, were already darting here and there with cups brimming with the potent brew.

Thorgrim let his fists drop to his side. There were still pockets of struggling men, but now more of the combatants were getting the tables and benches back upright or swilling mead. He staggered off and all but fell on a bench. A patch of spreading blood stained his tunic, darker even than the dark green cloth of the garment. His head was swimming. Someone handed his a cup and he drank, gratefully.

Harald sat beside him. His lip was bleeding and his hair was a wild tangle but his eyes were bright and his expression eager and enthusiastic.

"Father!" he said. "Father, are you alright?"

Thorgrim looked at the boy. It was hard to even call him a boy any more. "Yes, I'm alright," he said. "Alright. Just too damned old."

Chapter Seventeen

Men in ships, warriors with spears, without any faith,
great will be the plague,
they will inhabit half the surface of the island…
The Voyage of Snédgus and Mac Riagla

The sun rose higher and filled the grove in which Brigit and Father Finnian sat, and the bugs stirred and began their day's activities and Father Finnian made no reply to Brigit's rather remarkable statement concerning her intended destination. After some minutes he lifted himself onto his knees and examined her feet, which were bare, filthy, bruised and lacerated.

"Ah, that won't do, won't do at all," he said, and Brigit was not sure if he was referring to the state of her feet or her suggestion that they walk to the fin gall longphort. The comment hung in the air until she realized that it was in fact directed at her feet. Indeed, Brigit had been dreading the thought of putting weight on them again. "We'll find some help along the road, I shouldn't wonder," Finnian said, "but let's see what we can do now."

Finnian grabbed the hem of the oversized robe she wore and gave it a tug, pulling the folds of fabric free from the belt where he had tucked them. He tore the bottom edge of the fabric off the robe, then tore that cloth into wide and narrow strips. The wide strips he wrapped expertly around Brigit's feet, tight enough to be a comfort, not too tight as to cause pain. With the narrow strips he bound the makeshift sandals in place.

"There, that will make the walking a bit better," he said when he was done. He stood and offered Brigit a hand. She took it, and he gently pulled her to her feet. She could feel the power in his arm, the strength held in reserve, as if he was taking care to exert only as much force as was needed, and not the considerably greater force of which he was capable.

Brigit gasped as she stood, despite the wrappings. Pain shot through her feet and radiated up her legs. She had seen peasant women going barefoot all the year round, and they never seemed to have any more discomfort than if they had been wearing thick and supple deer hide shoes. But as princess of Tara, that was not a hardship she had ever endured, and her feet were in no way acclimated to the abuse to which they were now subject.

She took a tentative step forward, then another, her hand keeping a firm grasp on Finnian's arm. She was ashamed of having shown weakness, and now she kept her face expressionless, her teeth clenched, as she forced herself into an ever more determined walk.

"Here, take this, it will help a bit," Finnian said and handed her a walking stick, an oak sapling an inch thick. He had one for himself as well, though when he had cut them and from where she had no idea. She took it gratefully and thanked him.

They crossed over the grassy field they had crossed the night before and once again took to the road, once again heading south. "We'd best disguise ourselves," Finnian said and pulled the cowl of his robe up over his head. Brigit did the same. She knew the priest would not normally walk around like that, but to keep her identity hidden she would have to, and it would seem odd if only one of them had their head covered.

They walked on in silence, leaving the stand of oaks behind them. Brigit focused on her feet, tried to walk as if each step was not a knife-edge of agony, and soon the pain dulled and her feigned strength became real strength. And then she realized that Finnian still had made no comment about her desire to go to Dubh-linn.

As that realization came to her, so too did panic at what Finnian might be thinking. *Will he refuse to go?* she wondered. That would seem a perfectly reasonable response, maybe the most reasonable. She doubted that he would be afraid of the Northmen's lair, but certainly it was no place for a man of God, among those heathens, heathens who came across the water to murder the Irish people and loot the churches.

Or maybe Finnian would decide that it was no place for her. And again, he would not be wrong.

What if he does refuse to go? Could I go without him? Bold as she was, the thought of walking the roads of Ireland, alone in the lawless countryside, of sleeping out at night by herself, filled her with terror.

They continued on, the birds growing louder, a slight breeze beginning to move the branches of the trees that stood like little islands in the seas of emerald grass, and Brigit thought she might scream if Finnian did not say something soon. She was working up the courage to ask him directly when he spoke at last.

"Dubh-linn is it? And why Dubh-linn?"

For one who had been waiting for the question for the better part of an hour, Brigit was oddly unprepared to answer. "I don't know where else to go, Father," she said, the words not carrying the tone she had intended to convey. "I have nowhere else, nowhere that Morrigan could not get at me...."

They walked on a few more paces, Brigit hoping that this was explanation enough, knowing it was not. "I have friends there, in Dubh-linn," she continued. "I know that sounds odd. Morrigan...she had some of the fin gall taken hostage. To get at the Crown of the Three Kingdoms. You know of the Crown?"

"I know of it."

"The fin gall stole it. Morrigan took some of the fin gall hostage, as I said. Some of the hostages were killed...." She nearly added *by my father*, which was the case, but she stopped herself. "One of them, a young man named Harald...I helped him. He was hurt, I healed him. Made sure no harm came to him. He was grateful, and his father, and grandfather, I think they are important men among the fin gall. They will help me."

They walked on, Brigit hoping this would suffice. There was much, so very much, that she was leaving out of that story, the foremost being the fact that Harald's child was at that moment growing inside her.

It was a few moments later that Finnian spoke again. "Help you do what, girl?" he asked.

"I don't know.... Keep me safe, I suppose. Help me." She was trying to sound vague, as if she had given it no thought.

"I see. But I'll tell you true, when I think of 'safe,' I do not think of Dubh-linn."

"The fin gall are brutes and heathens, I know. But the Irish are not so much better. More Irish are robbed and killed at the hands of their own countrymen than by the fin gall, I suspect."

Father Finnian gave a grunt that might have been in part a laugh. "The fin gall are not the only vicious beasts on two legs, I'll grant you that," he said.

They trudged on, and Finnian said nothing else and Brigit found her fear turning to annoyance. *For the love of our Dear Lord,* she thought, *do you need to think every word through for half the day?*

"Well, Father," she said at last, no longer willing to wait for Finnian to speak, "will you help me? Will you take me to Dubh-linn?"

"I'll walk with you, but it's the Lord God will see you there. Or not. It's His will."

"But you will...take me there? To Dubh-linn?"

At that Father Finnian stopped, the first pause in their progress that morning, and turned to her. "Brigit, I don't know what plan you have, and I strongly suspect I don't want to know. But yes, I will take you to Dubh-linn, if it is God's will that you go."

"And how are we to know if it is God's will?" she asked. She could hear the thin edge of anger in her voice, and hoped that Finnian could not.

"He'll tell us. In his way. These fellows coming here, they may well be His instruments in this."

Brigit looked north, along the road they had already traveled. Three men were approaching, a few hundred yards away, but walking fast, faster than Brigit and Finnian, as if purposely trying to catch up with them. They had no cart, no animals, nothing to suggest they were just farmers on their way to market or someplace equally harmless. Even from that distance Brigit could see something vaguely menacing about them. She sucked in her breath.

"Who are they?" she asked. "What are they about?"

"Now, that I could not tell you," Finnian said calmly. "I'm not one of your mystics, one of these druids of the old faith."

"What will we do?"

"We'll keep walking, just like we were." Finnian turned and continued on, his pace unchanged from a moment before.

"Walk?" Brigit ran a few steps to catch up, then fell in with him. "Shouldn't we run? Hide? Something?"

"No," Finnian said. "We'll just walk in faith, and see what God has in mind for us."

They walked on, Brigit matching Finnian's pace, which had not altered; the same swing and thump of his walking stick, the steady and silent footfalls. It was only with great effort that she did not break into a run, or turn and look at the men behind them. Once she did give in to that impulse, or nearly did, started to turn her head, but Finnian said, "Don't look back, girl," before she had moved her neck even a quarter turn.

The minutes seemed to drag. Brigit had little sense for how long they had walked before she could hear the men coming up behind them, hear their feet shuffling in the drying dirt of the road, hear the soft sounds of the various things hanging from belts or from around their shoulders thumping against them.

In truth, with the breeze light and out of the north, she smelled them even before she heard them. They smelled of fish and wood smoke and old beer and unwashed skin. She felt her stomach turn and clench with fear at the thought of what they might do. A monk's robe, she realized, was a thin suit of armor, a walking stick a poor weapon.

They could not have been more than ten feet behind, Brigit guessed, when one of them finally spoke. "Hold up there, you!" he said, his voice low and ugly. Finnian stopped and Brigit stopped and they turned to face the men.

Three of them. With a few steps they closed with Finnian and Brigit. One stood square in the road while the other two took positions on either flank.

Finnian reached up and pulled the hood off his head, but Brigit guessed that he did not mean for her to do so, so she did not. Instead, from within the cowl, she considered the man in front of her. Squat and broad, with a week's worth of beard and a mop of greasy hair. He wore a filthy and patched tunic and a tattering of cloth over his shoulders that might have once been a blanket or cape or some such. His belt was a rope around his waist but there was a substantial knife hanging from it, a knife he now drew slowly, extracting every bit of menace he could from the action. He stared hard at Finnian. One eye was milky and blind, and it made the man's look even more terrifying.

Brigit felt her stomach twist again. She renewed her sweaty grip on her walking stick. This was it. In the next moments they would kill Finnian, and then they would have to kill her too because she would not let them have their way with her, not as long as the blood of Máel Sechnaill mac Ruanaid ran through her.

Then Finnian spoke. "Good day, friend," he said. There was no fear in his voice, nor was his tone either threatening or obsequious. He just spoke the words, and his manner was such that a listener might well believe the one-eyed fellow was genuinely an old friend of his.

The man looked at the priest, cocked his head as if trying to divine some deeper meaning. "Where you going?" he growled.

For a long moment Finnian did not answer, that same habit that was starting to irritate Brigit. It was apparently starting to irritate the man with the knife as well, but before he could say anything, Finnian said, "We go with God. And you?"

At that the man on Brigit's right hand snorted and gave a chuckle. "Go with God? Cronan, do we go with God?"

"Shut up," the knife wielder, named Cronan, apparently, spat at his companion. He continued to hold Finnian with the gaze of his one, sighted eye. "I asked you a question."

"And I answered it. And if you ask another, I will answer that as well."

Brigit felt a sense of ease sweep over her, as if a protective blanket had been laid around them, and she was not sure why. It was a sensation that seemed to radiate from Finnian. She recalled how, in Harald's company, three men had been confronted by in a situation much like this. Harald had killed them all and seemed not to have much trouble doing it. But she had not felt then the kind of comfort she felt now.

Will Finnian do that as well? she wondered. There seemed to be no fear in the man, as if he could rid them of these pests at any time. He had his walking stick, a useful weapon in the right hands. *Does Finnian have the skill to fight them? Will he kill them all?*

Now it was the one eyed man who stood silent, and increasingly uncomfortable, unsure how to respond. He shifted from foot to foot, and then seemed to notice Brigit for the first time.

"Here, are you too good to be seen by the likes of us?" he asked, sounding almost relieved to have something to say. His left hand shot out, reaching for Brigit's cowl, but Finnian's hand was faster still, whipping out and grabbing the man's forearm. There seemed to be no force applied, as if Finnian was just resting his hand on Cronan's arm, but Cronan's motion was completely arrested.

"Don't do that," Finnian said.

Cronan shifted his one-eyed gaze back to Finnian, and now his look was anger and outrage. "Whore's son priest," he growled and swung the knife toward Finnian's gut, but the priest caught that arm as well and held them both.

"Don't do that, either," he said. Like the pace of his walking, the tone of his voice had not altered a bit, not once since they had woken up that morning, as far as Brigit could tell.

For a long moment the two men stood there. Brigit wanted to scream, wanted to turn and see what the other two were going to do, wanted to hit Cronan with her walking stick, but instead she followed Finnian's lead and remained still. And then Finnian let go of Cronan's arms, just let them go, and dropped his own arms to his side and said, "My apologies for laying hands on you, Cronan."

Cronan grunted and again shifted foot to foot, looked down, looked at his companions, looked at the horizon. Finally he turned back and met Finnian's eyes, which had not left his face, not once. They stood there, silent, face to face. They did not speak. From somewhere far off came the rat-tat-tat of a woodpecker, and nearby the buzz of bees hard at work in the sunshine. And the two men remained silent. Half a minute. A minute.

"Well," Cronan said at last, slipping the big knife back into its sheath, "we'll be on, then."

He moved past Finnian, past Brigit. He seemed to move grudgingly, but with resignation. "Come on," he growled at his companions.

"Just a moment, friend," Finnian said and stopped them in their tracks. *Don't stop them when they are leaving!* Brigit wanted to scream, but still she remained silent. "Have you anything to eat," Finnian asked. "Anything you might share with fellow travelers?"

The three men glanced at one another, their uncertainty palpable. And then Cronan gave one of the others a quick nod. The man reached into a sack that hung at his side and withdrew a small loaf of coarse brown bread. Finnian took it gently from his hands.

"God bless you, friends," he said. He made the sign of the cross in the air and murmured "In the name of the Father, and the Son, and the Holy Spirit," and to Brigit's utter astonishment the three men bowed their heads – just a bit, but clearly a bow – and accepted the blessing without comment. They even looked relieved, like boys who are forgiven for the mischief they've caused. Then they turned quickly and once more headed off down the road, as if they were trying to get away, moving faster, it seemed to Brigit, than they had when they had been trying to catch up.

For some time she and Father Finnian watched them as they receded in the distance.

"Well, then," Finnian said at last. He broke the bread and handed the larger piece to Brigit. "There's your answer, my dear."

"My answer?"

"It seems that the good Lord means for you to reach Dubh-linn."

Chapter Eighteen

Let us go our ways silently;
though the cove-stallion's rider
be fallen, trouble is astir.
Gisli Sursson's Saga

It was well past midnight by the time Thorgrim Night Wolf was able to extricate himself and Harald Thorgrimson and Starri Deathless from the mead hall. They seemed little inclined to go, and it was only after Harald noticed the spreading wet patch of blood on the dark cloth of Thorgrim's tunic that they insisted on leaving. By then, Ornolf the Restless had found a thrall with whom he could satisfy his basest desires, but before he had even lured her off to a dark corner he had passed out in a great fleshy heap on the floor.

Harald and Starri helped Thorgrim to his feet and even attempted to support him with his arms over their shoulders, but Thorgrim, feeling more old and feeble than he cared to admit, would not submit to that indignity, and insisted on walking unaided. Instead, his two companions took up positions on either side of him, as if ready to catch him if he collapsed, and that served to only further annoy him.

They made their way down the plank road, the night dark and quiet, with only the muffled sounds of dying revelry coming from the mead hall. They found Jokul's blacksmith shop, thatch-roofed, timber-framed, tucked among the other clustered buildings. It stood out, bigger than most, with more space surrounding it, a larger patch of open ground enclosed by a wattle fence, a roofed-over workspace where Jokul could follow his trade out of doors when the weather cooperated, and not fill the house with smoke and the smell of hot steel.

The moon overhead cast blue shadows in the yard. They stepped through the gate and stumbled down the path that ran along the house. The surface was smooth and dry, made of split logs. When they had first arrived, the path had been had been made up of whole logs, treacherous and uneven, until Harald had dislodged each one, split it and set it down again with the flat side up to make a much more agreeable walking surface. Since splitting the logs had doubled their number, he had also built a path to the outdoor work area and a slightly raised platform at the forge so that even when the ground was an impenetrable mire of mud Jokul could work with feet relatively unencumbered.

That old dog will be glad to see Harald back, Thorgrim thought as he stumbled toward the door. In the corner of the yard he could see the small altar he had erected with a battered iron statue of Thor at its center, a statue he had carried many years, over many, many miles. He had first set the altar up indoors, but Almaith had insisted that there be no worship of what she called false gods in her home, so he had moved it out of doors. He would have to sacrifice to Thor for returning him safe and mostly intact.

Harald opened the latch as softly as he could and pushed the wooden door open. They stepped down, the floor of the house being dug down about a foot below the level of the street. They were greeted by smells that had become familiar in their time in Dubh-linn, the lingering smell of roast mutton and the peculiar sharp smell that Jokul's blacksmithing produced. They could hear Jokul's snoring, loud and bestial, coming from the far room.

Almaith materialized out of the dark, the linen leine that draped over her body ghost-like, her dark hair swept back. "Ah, Thorgrim! Harald!" she said, soft-voiced but enthusiastic. "There's been much high talk of your return, and I had hoped you would not shun us for another home!"

"No, never, if you'll have us," Thorgrim said, his voice thick with exhaustion and pain.

"Have you? To be sure, you're always welcome here. I made up beds for you, on hearing you were back." She steered them gently toward the open room at the far end of the house, the end opposite of where Jokul could be heard in his hibernation. A small peat fire was burning in the hearth on the floor, and against either wall there was a pile of blankets and furs.

"This is my friend, Starri Deathless," Thorgrim said, nodding toward Starri, who hung back in the shadows. "Might he sleep here as well?"

"Certainly, certainly," Almaith said. She spoke the Norse language almost to perfection, but she still carried the lilt of the Irish in her voice, and Thorgrim loved the sound. "I'll make up another bed directly."

"No, no," Starri said. "Outside, I saw a bench that looked just the thing. If I could borrow a fur or a blanket or such?"

"It's really no problem," Almaith protested. "I've no objection to another under my roof."

"No, no," Starri said again. Thorgrim could see his eyes moving around the room. "Walls, you know, walls sometimes are…bothersome to me. Hard to explain, really."

Almaith nodded. "Whatever you wish," she said. "We've blankets and furs a'plenty." She indicated a pile near the hearth. Starri grabbed up a heavy bundle that must have once belonged to some shaggy animal, nodded his thanks and was gone, as if afraid the roof was about to fall on him.

Harald and Almaith helped Thorgrim down to the bed, and he found he was too tired and hurt to protest or even snarl at them. Almaith pulled a blanket up over him. He closed his eyes as she was saying something he could not hear. Wolves were baying all around him.

It was no surprise to Thorgrim that the wolves came for him in his sleep. It was that sort of night. He was running through the woods, alone, the bracken, the trunks of the trees moving by fast as he ran, silently. Silently but not strongly, not the powerful lope he was accustom to. He was limping, favoring one leg and it hurt. He could hear other animals around him, wolves, he guessed, but he did not know. He could smell them.

And then he was in a clearing and the moonlight was illuminating the space, and it was lovely, but still he was not alone. He could see the eyes, glowing in the dark. He could hear the snarling. He knew these creatures, but they were not his friends. He wanted to cross the clearing, to reach the far side. He was not sure why, only that there would be safety there. Peace. But the wolves were in his way. His fellows, but they were in his way.

He felt a sharp stab of pain in his side. He snarled and whirled around but he was met with a soothing sound, like a breeze through trees in full leaf or the gurgle of water running down a ship's side, a ship sailing with just the right breeze on her quarter, heeling a bit, moving effortlessly, the wind warm, and strong enough to hold the sail full and immobile.

He opened his eyes. Almaith was kneeling beside him and he could see the gleam of a sharp knife in her hands. He felt his muscles tense, instinct taking hold, but Almaith set the knife down and said, "Shhhhh, shhhhh…" as if to a child. Thorgrim felt his body relax. He looked down. Almaith had slit his tunic open from the hem to the shoulder and now with long and delicate fingers she peeled it back, away from his wound. The cloth was wet and his skin was wet and warm and he realized that she must have soaked the cloth in warm water to get it free of the dried blood.

"My tunic…" he muttered. Ridiculous, but it was all he could think of to say.

"Never mind that. I'll sew you up a new one tomorrow. And we'll burn the rag you're wearing now."

Thorgrim laid his head back and looked up at the dark thatch above and felt Almaith's competent fingers swabbing the wound and the dried blood around it. "Harald told me you were hurt, just before he went to sleep," she said with her soft Irish lilt. "Foolish boy, he did not let on how bad it was. I heard you making noise in here, and then I saw the blood."

"Hmmm," Thorgrim said. He could think of nothing else to say, and the warm water and her hands felt good. "It's his age, you know. Nothing seems of any great import."

"I'm not sure I remember being that age," Almaith said. "But I have no doubt you're right." As if in agreement, Harald made a noise in his sleep and then was silent again, his snoring light and rhythmic, like the alto to Jokul's base

They were quiet for a moment as Almaith carefully washed the wound and Thorgrim considered her age. He had no idea what it might be. Certainly not as old as Jokul. He did not think she could be past her twenty-fifth summer. Not even that old, he did not think.

"There are stories in Dubh-linn about the great success you had at Cloyne," Almaith said, wiping the water and blood from Thorgrim's skin with a dry, soft cloth. "All you who sailed with Iron-skull. Was it such a great success, then?"

"Hmmm," Thorgrim said again and then realized he should elaborate. "It was a success. I could not say a great one. They fought hard, and when we finally won, there was not much to be found there."

"I see. That's a shame, indeed," she said. "Will you try for better luck elsewhere, then?"

"Not me. And not Arinbjorn. He told me that after Cloyne he was bound for Norway, and I shall sail with him. Me and Harald. It's why we agreed to go on the raid on Cloyne."

"I see," Almaith said. She stopped her work and looked in his eyes for the first time. "Jokul will certainly miss Harald," she said. "And I will miss you. Do you miss your wife?"

Thorgrim did not answer immediately. "My wife is gone," he said. "Childbirth. Two years gone, now."

"I'm sorry," Almaith said, and Thorgrim could see the genuine sympathy in her face, in her deep brown eyes that seemed to shine in the dying light of the fire. She turned back to the gash in Thorgrim's side, applied a poultice and a dressing. She worked in silence and Thorgrim closed his eyes and took comfort in her ministrations. The fire was low but he could feel its warmth, and her hands moved with the surety of a healer. Too long, too long, since he had enjoyed a woman's touch. Not carnal gratification, that was one thing, and he had not been without that, but rather the loving touch of a woman who cared.

Almaith smoothed the dressing down over Thorgrim's wound, sat more upright and shuffled closer to him. She set her hands lightly on his chest. "The poultice will help," she said, soft, nearly a whisper. "If it shows no sign of mending by morning I'll have to sew it."

Thorgrim nodded, but he was lost in her eyes, and her words, which seemed to not really be about his wound at all. She was beautiful. Even in the light of day, which hid no imperfection, she was beautiful, despite the hard years of being married to Jokul. In the glow of the fire she was the kind of vision that could send any man into a berserker's frenzy. She leaned a little closer, the fabric of her leine clinging to her and revealing the strong body beneath.

"Thank you," he said, soft, to match her tone. He reached out and stroked her arm. She reached up and gently took the silver charms around his neck in her fingers.

"You wear Thor's hammer," she whispered, "and you wear a cross. That's an odd thing."

"I am grateful for the help of any god," Thorgrim said. "In truth, the cross was given to me by a woman I knew. An Irish woman."

Almaith rubbed the thin silver cross between finger and thumb. "A friend?" she asked, but the tone of her voice suggested there was more to the question.

Thorgrim thought of Morrigan, and their time together, brief as it was. Iron-tooth had been taken from him, and she had returned it, somehow, left it stuck in the deck of his ship with the cross hanging from it. She may well have used magic to do it, he did not know, he had no notion of how she had conjured it there. "Friend?" he said. "I really don't know."

Almaith let the cross go, but her hand remained pressed against him, warm and delicate, the fingers twining through the hair of his chest.

Can I do this? he wondered. *Take another man's wife, under his roof?* She was his for the taking, he could see that, and the less cerebral parts of his body had already made their decision. He would not take a friend's wife, that he knew, but Jokul was hardly that.

In truth, Jokul was not much of a friend to Almaith, either. He treated her more like a thrall than a wife, berating her and ordering her around, giving her the back of his hand on occasion. It had always annoyed Thorgrim greatly, but he did not think it was his place to say anything, he being a guest in their house, albeit a guest who was paying a handsome rent for the privilege.

Yes, this could happen, he concluded. But not that night, not with Almaith's hands still sticky with his blood, his wound tender, his body aching. He gave her arm a light squeeze. "Thank you," he said again. "I know your hands will be quick and sure, whether sewing a tunic or a sword wound."

She gave him a touch of a smile, a wistful smile. She leaned forward and pressed her lips to his, gently, held them there. They were impossibly soft; in the hard world of men and ships and weapons and battle, he had forgotten that anything could be so soft and inviting. She stood, the bowl of bloody water in her hands, and was gone.

Thorgrim fell asleep again. He did not dream of wolves.

Chapter Nineteen

The wielder of iron must rise
early to earn the wealth from his bellows…
Egil's Saga

It was a shout, a full-throated yell that jarred Thorgrim from his sleep. He rolled over and his hand fell on Iron-tooth's grip and he all but shouted in pain as he wrenched the wound in his side. And then he heard Jokul's booming voice.

"Harald! You're back, boy! Good news, good news, that! Lots to do, you know, now that you're all rested up! Ah, Thorgrim Ulfsson! Glad to see you too, never doubt it! Good voyage, as I hear it! Lots of plunder, so they are saying! Almaith, you lazy bitch, get some breakfast for these men!"

Thorgrim rolled back slowly, sure he had pulled his wound open yet again, but he did not feel warm blood spreading under the dressing Almaith had put there. It occurred to him that the sleep he had enjoyed in camp on the field of battle had been more restful and undisturbed than that to be found in their rented quarters.

Through half opened eyes he looked up at the window that fronted the street. The first streaks of a clear dawn were visible to the east, and somewhere down the road a cock began to crow. He looked up at Jokul. The man snored like a bear and he looked like a bear, with the massive arms of a lifetime swinging a hammer, the broad stomach of an adulthood spent eating and drinking well, and a black beard that sprawled across his face like a hedge left untended for generations. Thorgrim looked over at Harald. Incredibly, Jokul's enthusiastic welcome had not caused him to stir in the least.

Jokul crossed the room, nudged Harald with his toe. "You hear me, boy? Lots to do!"

"He's pretty well done in," Thorgrim said, the words coming out in a scratchy growl. "Long night. Many long nights. I don't reckon you will get him to stir."

"Nonsense! Young boy like that, strong as a horse, they're always ready to go."

Almaith came in, a bundle of kindling and small pieces of split firewood in her arms. She dumped the wood by the hearth, poked at the coals with a thin stick. "Let the boy sleep, Jokul," she admonished. "You'll get your free work out of him, I have no doubt, but let him sleep now."

The smith glowered at her but in the end said nothing. Often enough Almaith doled out as many harsh words as she received, and that made Thorgrim happy. It always had, even before their moment, earlier, in the dark hours.

Thorgrim let his eyes linger on Jokul's face, wondering if he would see any sort of suspicion there, but there was nothing beyond the usual irritability. Then the smith grunted and turned and left the room.

Almaith stoked up the fire and hung an iron pot over the flames and soon the porridge inside was bubbling, filling the room with a warm and savory smell, and that at last got Harald stirring. He sat up, looked stupidly around until he had his bearings, then rubbed his eyes and stretched. Thorgrim was still in his bed, a rare luxury. He had no reason, none at all, to rise from his mat of furs. The realization startled him. There was not one thing that was demanded of him that day. It was comforting and unnerving, all at once.

"How is your wound?" Almaith asked in a neutral voice.

"Better. I think the bleeding has stopped," Thorgrim said.

"Good. You may be spared my needle."

"Oh, no need of that," Harald offered. "I sewed him up, back at Cloyne. Sewed him well, I don't reckon that will come free."

Thorgrim nodded. "Yes, he did sew me up," he said. Harald's fine stitching had already come apart several times, but Harald seemed to have forgotten that.

"Yes, well done," Almaith said. She ladled porridge into a shallow wooden bowl, turned to Harald and said something in Irish. She spoke slowly and Harald took a moment to puzzle it out, then replied in Irish as well. Thorgrim smiled. This interest in language was unexpected. Blacksmithing, carpentry, seafaring, any of those things Harald was eager and quick to learn, but the more academic areas of knowledge had always held little interest to him.

Almaith replied, again in Irish, and handed the bowl to Harald, who took it with a word of thanks and dug in. Thorgrim sat up. The remnants of his tunic were hanging off his shoulders and he carefully peeled them away and let them drop.

"This is Jokul's, it will certainly fit." Almaith tossed a small linen bundle, one of Jokul's leines. "I've already started in on a new tunic for you."

"Thank you," Thorgrim said. He pulled the garment over his head. The linen was fine and white. Jokul was making good money at his trade.

Jokul himself was back, his mouth opened to say something. He saw Thorgrim, scowled, opened his mouth to speak again and stopped again. From out in the yard a scraping sound was drifting in through the window, and beneath it a squeaking like a mouse, but rhythmic.

"What by Thor's hammer is that?" Jokul asked, turned and headed for the door. Harald watched him go, looked down at his porridge, looked back at Jokul, clearly torn between curiosity and hunger, but when Thorgrim stood and headed for the door, the leine flowing around him, Harald followed.

Thorgrim actually had a pretty good idea what the sound was, and he figured he had better get in the middle of it before the blood started to flow. He could tell from Jokul's bellow of outrage that he had guessed right. He walked barefoot down Harald's split-log path to the work area in the front of the house. Jokul was waving his hands in the air, trying through his fury to form a sentence. Starri Deathless was sitting at his grindstone, the heavy wheel spinning, applying the blade of one of Jokul's swords to the stone. Sparks flew in a hundred arcs of orange light.

"Who in the name of Odin are you? You miserable little…." Jokul managed to piece together. His arms came down, hands balled into fists. Thorgrim stepped up, stepped between him and Starri.

"Jokul, this is Starri Deathless. He was with us at Cloyne. He stayed the night out here. With Almaith's blessing."

"Well, what does he think he's about now?" Jokul spluttered. Spittle flew from his mouth.

"Sharpening," Starri offered. "Good blade. Yours?"

"Mine? I made it, if that's what you mean!" Jokul bellowed.

Starri nodded. "Made it? You impress me, smith. Very fine blade. Takes an edge well, as good as any I've seen."

"Of course it does!" Jokul shouted, the volume no lower but the tone softened by the compliment. "You think I'm some miserable apprentice, banging out nails and door hinges? I made the finest blades in Trondheim and now I make the finest blades in Dubh-linn!"

Starri nodded and set the grindstone spinning again. Thorgrim wondered at the truth of Jokul's words. He probably was the best smith in Dubh-linn. Trondheim? Unlikely. If he was, he would never have left Trondheim.

"And," Jokul continued, the anger mounting again, "I know damned well how to sharpen a blade!" He held out a meaty hand, a wordless demand for the return of his property. Equally wordless, Starri handed it to him, hilt-first, taking great pains to avoid cutting himself on the two-edged blade. Jokul took the weapon and Thorgrim watched him surreptitiously test with his thumb the edge Starri had put on it, saw the thin red line appear and the minor eruption of blood, which Jokul wiped on his leggings.

"Still, if you have some insane need to sharpen blades," Jokul said, calmer now, "I have some awaiting their owners that you may have a go at."

Starri nodded.

"And it's a quarter eyrir silver a week for staying here," Jokul concluded as he turned and headed back toward the house.

Almaith, true to her word and swift of finger, spent the next couple of hours stitching together a new tunic for Thorgrim, made up from a deep blue wool cloth of which she had a few ells on hand. Thorgrim assured her he would pay for the fabric and the work. She insisted there was no need for payment. He insisted he would pay anyway, repeating his insistence several times until at last she snapped at him to leave her alone.

He wandered out into the yard, watched Jokul working a length of steel into a blade, Harald working the bellows, Starri working at the grindstone, moving the blade rhythmically against the rough wheel, his body rocking slowly with the work, entranced by his task. Thorgrim wandered back inside. The luxury of idleness was not one that he actually enjoyed.

When Almaith was nearly done with the tunic, Thorgrim took it from her, despite her protests that he could not go out wearing such a thing, not a bit of decorative braid at the neck or cuffs. "You'll look like some beggar, wandering the streets," she protested.

"Then maybe some rich man will give me money enough to pay you for your work," he said, pulling off Jokul's leine. "But I could never look like a beggar in this fine piece of work, braid or no. In any event, I have important business to attend to," he added, which was not entirely true.

He faced her, wearing only his leggings which were belted around his waist, and he saw her eyes flicker over his bare chest and arms. Because he could not stand watching other men work, or fight, or do anything, and not take part himself, he had not grown soft as had many men of his age and status. Almaith seemed to appreciate this, the symmetric curves of the muscles of his arms, his broad chest and hard stomach.

"Your wound?" she said, softer than the words needed to be said. "It's not torn open again?"

"No, it seems to be mending well."

"Let me help you with your tunic," she said. She stood and took the garment. She examined the dressing on Thorgrim's wound, a hand resting softly on his chest. Outside Jokul was arguing loudly with a customer. She helped ease the tunic over Thorgrim's head, easy, so the wound did not pull open, then tugged it down and smoothed it in place.

"A fair job," she said, frowning at the tunic's fit.

"A perfect job. Fits like a man's sword fits in his hand."

"Or thrust in his scabbard," she suggested.

Thorgrim smiled. Almaith wrapped his belt around his waist and fastened it loosely, with Iron-tooth hanging at his left side. The Northmen, she knew, did not go abroad unarmed. She draped his cloak over his shoulders and fastened the corners with a bronze brooch, the stylized faces of three warriors worked into the design.

"So what is this business of yours, that's so important you must go out with clothes half made?"

"I must see Arinbjorn."

"Arinbjorn, who will take you away from us?"

"Or so he says. I'm hoping to find the truth of it." The words seemed to catch as they made their way from his throat. He was counting quite a bit on Arinbjorn, more than he ever cared to count on any man beside himself. And he knew with near certainty that Arinbjorn was not a man to be counted on.

The sun was well up and Dubh-linn in full bustle when Thorgrim left Jokul's house and headed up the plank road. Despite what he had said to Almaith, he had only a vague notion of where he was going or what he would do, beyond escaping the confines of Jokul's house.

He wandered through the market. Rickety stalls of saplings and canvas lashed together housed sellers of meat, vegetables, herbs, fish, small silver pendants, cloth, nearly everything one might look for in one of the big market towns of Scandinavia. People shouted in the Norse language and in Irish, with a few others mixed in. Dubh-linn, begun as a longphort, basically a fortification to protect the ships that overwintered there, was quickly becoming a significant market town, a center of commerce, import and export. Dubh-linn was no longer just a thorn in the side of the Irish kings, it was becoming a significant factor in the on-going struggle for power waged between those who would unite Ireland under their rule.

Thorgrim marveled at the crush of people - men, women, children. He was no stranger to crowded streets and market towns, but he had not expected to find such as this in Ireland. But here were merchants and craftsmen and farmers, brewers, even priests of the Irish faith, the Christ men, all crowded into the open market and narrow lanes of the Norwegian longphort, so many hundreds of sea-miles from Norway.

He continued up the road, knowing where he had to go. Frustration and annoyance were on the horizon, he could see that, and he did not care to head in that direction. But it had to be done.

Arinbjorn White-tooth, along with the other wealthy jarls and ship-owners, occupied rooms in the compound of Olaf the White, king of Dubh-linn. The compound was walled off from the rest of the city by a ten-foot high palisade fence, its single gate guarded by two of Olaf's men. Generally one needed a reason and an invitation to get beyond the gate, but Thorgrim was recognized on approach and allowed through without question. He found Arinbjorn in his rooms, small heaps of gold and silver piled like little burial mounds on his table. Arinbjorn was seated at the table, counting.

"Ah, Thorgrim! Welcome, welcome!" he said, standing. "You there!" he called to some unseen thrall in the adjoining room, "mead for Thorgrim! Fetch along a cup, quickly now!"

Thorgrim grasped Arinbjorn's hand. The warmth of the greeting might have pleased him, encouraged him, if it were not for the fact that Arinbjorn greeted nearly everyone, on nearly every occasion, with the same enthusiasm. He gestured toward a chair. Thorgrim sat. "Slave market was held this morning. We did well, Thorgrim, quite well. Just figuring out every man's share now, but yours will be respectable. And I have not forgotten my promise," he added, his voice dropping. "Three shares to you and Harald, two for those who went with you through the gates."

Thorgrim waved his hand, a gesture of dismissal. If Arinbjorn had said he was holding back their entire share to pay for passage home, Thorgrim would not have objected, on the condition they were leaving on the morrow. "I thank you, Arinbjorn, but I say again it is not necessary. I have come to inquire about your plans. Your plans for sailing."

"I'm making those right now. You there, where is that damned mead!" The last he shouted toward the door, and the words produced a frightened thrall with a cup in her hand. Mead sloshed on the floor as she hurried it over to Thorgrim.

"Damned idiot! It's a wonder these Irish fetch what they do at the slave markets, damned idiots. The whole nation. Where was I?"

"Making plans for sailing."

"Yes, right, right. Plans for sailing. The shipwrights are going over *Black Raven* now. We hauled her out on rollers. Might be a strake's a bit punky, they'll have a go at that. Get her ready for the sea. A week or so, I should think. And then we're underway. I don't imagine any opportunity will come along that will induce us to stay longer."

Thorgrim tried to hold his face still, but Arinbjorn was too astute an observer, and watching too closely, to miss the flash of a grimace.

"What? What is it troubles you?"

Thorgrim took a long drink, as much to compose his thoughts as to slake his thirst. "Shipwrights," he said at last. "I am well familiar with that breed. Once they find a little bit of rot they will find more and more. Soon they'd be tearing the entire vessel apart and you will have to sell your lands to pay their bill. Rotten wood is gold to them, and they will dig for every ounce they can find."

Arinbjorn nodded. "Oh, I know. Finding an honest shipwright is like finding a sober man in a mead hall. But without the work I fear *Black Raven* will fall apart half way to home, and I know I'm not up to swimming the remainder of the way. In any event, I have one of my best men overseeing the work."

Thorgrim nodded and took a long drink. He would not embarrass Arinbjorn by asking about the man overseeing the work because he was quite certain there was in truth no one overseeing the work. An awkward silence followed, and then Arinbjorn asked him how he and Harald were faring. They spoke for a few moments more about meaningless things, and then Thorgrim excused himself.

He stepped out of Arinbjorn's rooms and into the courtyard. The breeze from the ocean and the smells of the day's business wrapped around him, but the sense of despair that came from the interview just concluded was wrapped closer still. Two things that Arinbjorn had said. Two things that stuck like thorns.

The shipwrights were the first problem. Rarely did their labors not drag out for weeks, and it would be worse if some of that work were actually necessary. Arinbjorn, or his man, would need to be vigilant and demanding to avoid having *Black Raven* on the hard for weeks, if not months, but Thorgrim doubted that Arinbjorn would be vigilant or that he actually had an overseer.

He considered offering to oversee the work himself, but he knew Arinbjorn well enough by now to know that such an offer would be greeted with the sincerest sounding gratitude and then ignored. Arinbjorn already felt Thorgrim had something to hold over his head, and he would not go further into Thorgrim's debt.

The other thorn was Arinbjorn's remark about thinking no opportunity would come that would induce them to stay. Not the words of a man eager to sail for home. Not at all. The words, in fact, of a man looking for a reason to not do so.

Thorgrim walked back through the market, through the section of town where the woodworkers had their shops, then that of the comb makers and the jewelers, down toward the river front. *Black Raven* was hauled out not far from where they had beached her. She sat with her keel on the rollers, blocked up, so she was sitting perfectly upright. Some of the floorboards had been pulled up and stacked on shore to give the shipwrights access to her strakes from the inside. Soon they would begin their task of poking at the oak planks, tearing out the rotten ones like decaying teeth. Once they started, who knew where they would stop?

But there was no activity aboard her now, no one at work, which begged the question of when they would even begin their lengthy task.

He turned with something like a sigh and made his way back up the plank road, back toward Jokul's house. He thought about the mead hall, thought about drinking himself into oblivion, getting in another brawl, perhaps, but he found that none of the diversions of his younger days held much interest to him now. Maybe he would spend his hours sharpening blades with Starri Deathless.

Smoke was rolling up from Jokul's forge as Thorgrim approached the house, but there was no one in the yard, no one milling about outside. The grindstone was motionless, a sword set neatly on the seat where Starri had been. Odd. Thorgrim stepped through the break in the low wattle fence and down the split log path. He could hear voices from inside, low, excited.

He came in through the door and could see the others in the big room by the hearth, Almaith, Jokul, the rest. He stepped in and Starri was the first to see him.

"Thorgrim! Here, here, here!" The berserker seemed to dance from one foot to another and his hands were doing a weird little fluttering thing. "We've been waiting on you!"

Thorgrim stepped further in. Harald was seated by the hearth. He was smiling, but he looked confused as well, a bit shocked, like he had taken a hard blow to the head. Beside him sat a person who looked like one of the Christ men, one of these Christian priests. But the person looked up and Thorgrim could see it was not a Christ man, no man at all. A young woman, with a thick, luxurious sweep of brown hair, brown eyes that flashed like sunlight on steel. Her smile was demure, showing a hint of white teeth. She was beautiful. Thorgrim felt his heart sink, his stomach convulse. He had no idea who she was, or what she was about, but he felt a moral certainty that his neat escape from Ireland had just become much more complicated.

Chapter Twenty

Noble woman of low means,
lit by the blue wave's lands:
I fear nothing for myself.
Gisli Sursson's Saga

It was two days after her arrival in Dubh-linn, two days after her reuniting with Harald, after the jumbled, confusing introductions to the fin gall with whom he lived, fin gall and, to Brigit's surprise, Almaith, an Irishwoman, that she was able at last to move her plans forward. It was a trifling move, like pushing a pawn ahead a space, and it brought her little comfort, but it was a move.

She was seated in a big room, a fine room in the finest building she had seen in Dubh-linn, as fine as any at Tara, but built in the Norse manner out of sawn boards, not as the Irish would do it. Brigit kept her eyes on Harald as he spoke to the older man. She had asked Harald to bring her to see someone who had influence and authority with the fin gall. Harald had done as she asked, and this man did indeed seem to be the sort to whom she wished to speak. But Brigit did not know who he was.

The words flowed back and forth in the Northmen's coarse language and Brigit could follow none of it, but the way Harald moved his body in response to what the man said, those times when he met the man's eyes, or looked at the floor, or twisted his hands, told her a great deal. Almaith was there, serving as translator, but Brigit was not sure she was doing so with any great exactness.

She felt out of control, as if events were a heavy loaded wagon that had gathered too much speed going downhill. In the short time she had been in Dubh-linn, and with the great barrier of language, she did not know who had real power among the fin gall, and who simply thought they did. She had to rely on Harald. And Almaith. And that was not comforting.

In that fine room, a fire burning in an open hearth against the damp air, she explained to the man to whom Harald had brought her who she was, and listened as Almaith rendered the words into the Norse tongue and watched Harald bob his head like a dog looking to be scratched. And the man was listening, listening closely, which was good. But she still did not know who he was.

Is this Thorgrim Night Wolf? she wondered. Almaith had told her the man's name, but in the context of telling her many things, and she had not really understood and did not want to appear dim by asking for clarification. She thought that she had met Thorgrim earlier, but she could not be sure, and she could not always tell these fin gall apart.

She hoped this was Thorgrim to whom she was speaking. She had heard Thorgrim's name spoken on many occasions, and he seemed to command a great deal of respect.

This is maddening! she thought, and nearly cried out in frustration. This was her life, her fate, under discussion and her with no comprehension at all of what was being said.

Two days she had been in Dubh-linn, two days since she and Finnian had pushed their way through the crowds streaming in from the countryside. That part, the getting there, had been easier than she dared hope.

From Tara, she and Father Finnian were four days on the road. The three bandits they had encountered, the ones Finnian had somehow managed to drive off, were the worst of the lot. That night, and the following nights, they had found farmers willing to put them up in their hovels: filthy, crowded, smelling of sweat and porridge and livestock, but nonetheless warm and dry and welcome. Farmers eager for the blessings that might come from aiding two priests in their travels. The farmers had offered food, Father Finnian had offered mass, and the farmers felt they had the best of the deal.

She and Finnian knew they were nearing Dubh-linn even before they could see the mounded earthen wall that surrounded the longphort, the palisade fence that crowned it. The road grew more and more crowded with carts and small herds as the local farmers drove their produce to the biggest market to be found in that area, or indeed anywhere in Ireland. The small, rutted paths that ran into the main road fed the way like streams emptying into a river. Carts with wheat, carts with rye, carts with squealing pigs, squawking chickens, sheep and cattle on the hoof, all rolled up from the farms within a day or two of the longphort and all headed for the open market.

They fell in with this stream, often having to wait by the side of the road as various creaking, bleating or mooing traffic moved past. But there was good cheer and companionship among the people, and as often as not they were given a place to ride in a farm cart, a place on the driver's seat, not back with the animals. The heathens may have had no respect for the robe or the beads, but to the Irish they meant a great deal.

The earthwork defenses of the longphort had first appeared as a glimpse through a stand of trees, then, as they emerged from the woods, they rose up from the green land surrounding it, a long brown heap of dirt with a tall gate through which flowed the men, women and carts bound for market. Brigit and Finnian were riding on the seat of a cart loaded with wooden cages of chickens. Behind them squawked dull brownish-black hens, and roosters with magnificent tail feathers that strutted the extent of their confinement and pecked at any birds that came near them, never appreciating how soon and how completely their magnificent reigns would be brought to an end.

The farmer who had yielded his seat to the friendly priest and his silent, hooded companion walked beside the cart, using a goad to keep the oxen moving as he talked. He came to Dubh-linn often, he told them, had found so vibrant a market that he had raised himself up from a man scrambling to feed his family to one who owned such luxury as two oxen and a cart.

He knew a bit of the Norse language, had made himself learn as much as he could, knowing it would give him an advantage over those who did not. "I may hate those damned heathens," the farmer railed, "forgive my language, Father, I beg, but it's what they are. Still, the fact is, they're here to stay, and we best be used to them and get what we can from them, when they're not raiding our monasteries and making slaves of us all."

Brigit ignored his ranting. She had little interest in his opinions. But she was pleased to hear that the man could speak the language of the Northmen, or some, in any event. She hoped it would be enough to solve the most vexing problem she anticipated.

It was late morning when they were finally close enough to appreciate the full extent of the wall that protected Dubh-linn from the rest of Ireland. Columns of smoke began to rise from behind the unseen town, first one, then three, then dozens, rising up into the morning sky before dissipating in the light breeze. Brigit was surprised. So many of columns of smoke, more than she would thought there could be hearths collected together in one place. She wanted to ask the farmer about them, but she did not dare speak and risk revealing her sex, so she kept quiet and wondered.

At last they came to the gateway into the longphort, something of a bottleneck as two guards under some king's banner made a cursory search of the wagons as they rolled into the town. "Afraid of some surprise attack, they are," the farmer talked as they waited. "Ha! Us farmers take on that load of murderers and killers? And why would we? Do they not know the tale of the goose that lays the golden eggs?"

The farmer, who had kept up a steady monologue since first they accepted his offer of a ride, fell silent, and Brigit prayed he was done, but a moment later he started in again. "Things go around in a circle, Father," he said. "It's gold and silver these heathens have, and goods from across the sea they trade for the likes of my chickens. They rob the towns to the south and west, they do, and then hand the spoils back to us! So, if we're being robbed by them fin gall or the fat bastards on the throne of Tara, what's the difference, I ask?"

They reached the gate, happily for Brigit, who could feel her anger rising, and the farmer broke off his speech as he conversed with the guard. They rolled on through the gap in the high earthen walls and before them, like a curtain drawn back, Dubh-linn came into view before them.

And Brigit, despite herself, gasped.

She had, quite literally, never seen its like before. Tara, with its church and monastery, its dozens of thatched homes, smithy, stables, enclosed by the ringfort, was the largest cluster of people she had ever seen. Indeed, she had not imagined that there was or could have been a town bigger.

But here, before her, were not dozens but hundreds of buildings, houses crammed so close on one another that a tall man could put his hands on two at the same time. There were odd shaped patches of ground extending from each of the houses, each with a small garden enclosed with a wattle fence. She could hear the ring of smith's hammers and the growl of saws, the thud of some heavy work going on, the muffled sound of men shouting, too far off for the words to be distinct. Music was playing somewhere. And the whole thing was cut up into semi-regular sections by roads, some little more than muddy paths but others wide and planked over.

The farmer, quite used to the sight, made no comment as he led the oxen along the chief road through the town. Finnian also said nothing, and as usual it was impossible to guess what he was thinking. And Brigit was too shocked to speak, her impressions and thoughts, half-formed and confused, too amorphous to be formed into words.

So many buildings… she thought. *Is that a temple of some sort? The smoke…what is that?* At the bottom of the sloping town the River Liffey rolled toward the sea. More than a dozen ships of all sizes were swinging at moorings or pulled up on the shore, and even as she looked she could see three more moving slowing up river, their long oars rising and falling in such perfect unison they seemed to be controlled by a single hand.

And the people. More than Brigit could have imagined, more than she had ever see assembled in one place before, people moving everywhere, each seemingly with a place to go, a reason to be abroad. Women in Irish garb or dressed like the fin gall's women, big men with beards and heavily armed, farmers from her own country. Children.

Beneath the numbing astonishment she felt a sense of dread, and despair. Like her father, like so many Irish, she had always harbored a hope that these heathen pigs might be driven back into the sea. But how? How could that happen now? The fin gall had taken what was a toe-hold on the coast of Ireland, no more than a place to over-winter, and had built that into a trading center the likes of which the Irish could never manage. The damned farmer had said it: *the fact is, they're here to stay.*

But soon those thoughts were pushed aside as Brigit was confronted by a new problem. Even after deciding to come to Dubh-linn, she had not put a great deal of thought into how she would find Harald. She had not anticipated much difficulty because she had not imagined that Dubh-linn was anything near as big as it was. She had never imagined that any town could be as big as Dubh-linn was. But once her initial shock dissipated, it was replaced by a sense of panic. *How will we ever find him in all this?*

The farmer led the oxen down the road, rumbling along shoulder to shoulder with the hundreds of people making for the market. They came to an open place lined with rickety booths and the farmer stopped the animals in their progress. "This be the market, Father," he said, "which is far as I'm going. But maybe I can help you find him what you're looking for?"

Finnian turned to Brigit. They had never discussed whom, specifically, in Dubh-linn she was seeking, and now she saw what a terrible oversight that was. She cleared her throat, and when she spoke she tried to sound as much like a young man as she was able, giving her voice a gravely tone and lowering it as best as she could. "We're looking for one of the fin gall. A young man named Harald, middling height, but broad, with yellow hair. Perhaps seventeen or eighteen years of age."

If the farmer suspected Brigit's subterfuge he gave no indication of it, but he did laugh out loud. "You just described half these damned fin gall!" he exclaimed. "But very well, I'll see what I can make of it."

He wandered off, and for fifteen minutes or so Brigit and Finnian watched him as he asked various passers-by, or at least those who looked like they might know something, if they knew of this boy Harald. They watched as one after another shook his or her head. At last the farmer returned.

"Is there anything else you might know? Something to be of more help?"

Brigit had been digging through her memory, and she managed to come up with something. "His father was also with him," she said, tentatively. She was thinking back to a discussion, months earlier, that she had had with Morrigan. "His name is…Thorgrim. Thorgrim Night Wolf."

"Well, let me see, then," the farmer said, his tone skeptical. He walked off, approached a tall man wearing a crimson cape, a long sword at his side. The farmer spoke. Brigit could not hear the words. But she saw the light of recognition on the fin gall's face. He nodded his head. He pointed down the road. She felt the relief spread over her like the warmth from a fire.

Twenty minutes later, no more, they had found the smith's house, made their way down the path, past the big man pounding iron on his anvil, another, sinewy and powerful looking, sharpening swords. An Irish woman met them at the door. Brigit pulled the cowl off her head and, with great relief, pulled the long brown hair from the robe and shook it like a wet dog.

If the Irish woman was shocked to see a woman in a monk's robe, she hid it well. She did not recognize Brigit, but she did recognize that Brigit was no thrall or fishmonger.

"May I help you?" she asked, courteous, if a bit wary.

"My name is Brigit. Brigit nic Máel Sechnaill," Brigit replied, and the look of shock and fear and respect that came instantly to the woman's face was proof enough that she knew to whom she was speaking. She swept her arms toward the interior in a gesture of welcome, her body in a partial bow. She called out in a loud voice, speaking the Norse language, presumably to her husband. From the back room, his arms full of firewood, Harald looked up at her, his deep blue, ingenuous eyes wide, his mouth open in surprise. He did not even flinch as the pile of wood slipped from his arms.

They all crowded into the house, tiny by the standards of the royal residence of Tara but palatial compared to an average Irish peasant's home. A bustle, an awkward silence, then Brigit turned to introduce Father Finnian. But Father Finnian was gone.

Finnian's disappearance was a surprise, but it did not long distract Brigit from her desperate need to get out of the scratchy robe and the blood-encrusted leine that she had worn since leaving Tara. Once the flurry of greeting and explanations was over, she asked Almaith if she might borrow a shift of clothing, and Almaith, stuttering and apologizing that she had not thought to ask, supplied a leine and brat of wool dyed bright red.

It was not Brigit's preferred color – she liked something that set off her eyes - but she was grateful for it, and more relieved than she had expected to be rid of the cumbersome monk's robe. She twisted the brat expertly around her waist and fastened it with a leather belt. Despite being months into her pregnancy now she still had that womanly shape for which several men had already died. That was good. She would need every charm she possessed, if the next few days were to go as she hoped. The old clothing she left in a heap on the floor for Almaith to attend to.

Brigit told the tale of how she had arrived at that place to the eagerly listening Northmen in the smith's house (and it was indeed a tale, containing only a glancing similarity to the truth of the thing), and for the next twenty-four hours she rested and was waited on and met many people until names and faces all became a big blur. And then, at last, in private with Harald, she had convinced him to arrange for a meeting with someone of influence among the fin gall. Which had brought them, finally, to the fine room in the fine house with the fire burning in the hearth.

The Irish woman, Almaith, was speaking to her, translating the words of the Northman who sat behind his table, facing them. Harald smiled at her, an uncertain smile. He had reacted to her arrival just as she had imagined he would, like a big, loyal dog seeing its master return from a long voyage. And like the dog, which has no concept of the machinations of the larger world, Harald seemed not in the least surprised by her arrival. Foolishly delighted, even embarrassed, but not surprised.

"He says, your highness," Almaith was saying, "please tell him again how it could be Tara is so lacking defense? He had thought it was the seat of the high king, and that there would have been a formidable army there."

Harald was squirming, and Brigit guessed that he feared she was about to lose her temper. His fear was justified. This was taking longer than it needed, and despite how crucial the outcome might be to her, her patience was ebbing fast.

"Pray, tell him again," she said, "that most of the men-at-arms who defend Tara are the *rí túaithe* and their men. Will he know the meaning of *rí túaithe*? They have such a word?"

"I will say 'jarl,' highness, it will be close enough."

"When my husband died, the *rí túaithe* returned to their own kingdoms. There are men-at-arms at Tara, but few, far less than the fin gall…these Northmen…could gather. Flann mac Conaing who sits on the throne now is a pretender, they will not rally to him."

Almaith translated the words. Harald squirmed some more. Brigit was motionless. The man behind the desk drilled her with his eyes and tapped his fingers on the wooden surface. Brigit met his gaze, unflinching. Harald had assured her, through Almaith's translations and the bits of Irish he had picked up, that this man was a great leader among the fin gall, that he had just led the sack of Cloyne, that he enjoyed considerable respect among the others.

Brigit hoped that Harald was right. She was starting to have her doubts. This fellow asked a lot of questions, sometimes the same question put into different words. He seemed not to make decisions with the surety she expected from a real leader.

Still, she could not deny that he seemed to have wealth enough, and that must have come from somewhere. And she herself knew nothing of these people. There was little that she could do but trust Harald, trust Almaith, and hope that this fellow was the man most able to help her take the throne of Tara.

Harald was talking to the man now, his tone obsequious but not groveling. Brigit caught a name and she remembered. *Of course! This is not Thorgrim. Thorgrim was the other fellow. This is Arinbjorn. The one they call White-tooth.*

Suddenly she felt her confidence melting away. *What in God's name am I doing?* she wondered. She was all but offering her kingdom to this man, some heathen fin gall bastard, resting her future on the hope that she could trust him, even though she knew that no fin gall were to be trusted.

Then she considered her choices, and recalled that, awful as this one might be, she could think of none better.

Chapter Twenty-One

Not all my dreams bode well,
yet each of them I must tell.
That woman in my dreams
takes all my joy, it seems.
Gisli Sursson's Saga

They went at it with bare hands, and then hoes and shovels, carefully, layer by layer. The heavy, charred beams of the roof were lifted off the pile of still smoking debris, once part of the royal residence, and stacked to the side. The heaps of thatch that had somehow escaped the flames were flung in a great mound. And below that, the fired daub of the walls, hard now like pottery. Six days later and it still stunk.

The fire had consumed well over half of the big house. It had torn through Brigit's bed chamber, where it had apparently started, had knocked through a wall to the adjoining room, had reached up and grabbed the thatch roof where it found a ready source of fuel. It had been a roaring, smoke-choked, scorching bedlam, and the men, women, even the children of Tara had come to fight it like angels waging war on the depths of hell. They used whatever tools came to hand to pull away the burning material and threw buckets of water on the flames.

Flann mac Conaing had coordinated the work, issuing orders like a commander on the field of battle. Against the roaring blaze their efforts had seemed puny. The mob looked more like worshipers of the old gods, dancing around a druid's fire, than like people who might actually beat the flames into submission. But in the end they did. All night long they fought, and by dawn the flames were no longer a monstrous inferno but rather a handful of smaller fires that seemed less threatening in the growing light. Half of the big house was a smoky ruin, but half was still standing.

Morrigan had only been asleep a short while when the first voices of panic wrenched her from her bed. Not long before that, thirty minutes, maybe an hour, she had turned out to the sound of shouting from Brigit's chamber. Brigit and *Conlaed*'s chamber. The newlyweds. A few servants were already there, standing nervously outside the door, unsure of their duty. Morrigan chased them away with a few harsh words and blows.

Then she listened. They were shouting, but the thick, tapestry-draped walls muffled the words. She was certain she heard something break, something flung. Then quiet. She waited a long time. No sound. That weak-brained idiot Conlaed no doubt passed out at last. She returned to her own bed chamber.

When she did wake again, when she clawed her way up from sleep, she lay still and listened. Shouting. She heard Flann's voice, loud and commanding. She smelled the bitter smoke creeping into her room. One thought came to her, one thought alone. *The Crown!*

She threw off the bed clothes and stood and coughed in the smoke hanging in the upper part of the room. Instinctively, she dropped to her knees and crawled across the floor to where a plain wooden chest stood pushed against the wall. The last vestiges of a peat fire burning in the hearth gave her light enough to see, but she hardly needed it. She threw open the lid and tossed aside the various blankets and small rugs stacked there until her hand fell on the course linen bag at the bottom. Through the fabric she could feel the filigrees like little battlements around the edge of the crown, the smooth round jewels that studded it.

She pulled the crown from the chest and hugged it close. *Now what do I do?* she thought. She grabbed up a blanket and tossed it over her shoulders and wrapped it around herself, as much to hide the crown as to protect her from the night's cold. She half stood, and then sunk to her knees again. Her hands caressed the crown through the linen bag.

She had not looked at it for several days, and now, despite the ever louder shouting from beyond her door, the thickening smoke, she could not help herself. She was like a man who could not resist the temptation of drink, and she knew it, and like that man she did not care. She opened the bag and slowly pulled the crown into the light.

The Crown of the Three Kingdoms… She turned it over in her hands, let the weak light of the peat fire play on the gold and the jewels, reveled in the weight of it. It was the most beautiful thing she had ever beheld. And now it was hers. It would have to remain hers.

From somewhere outside the door she heard a crashing sound, like a heavy beam falling, and the shouting came louder and she knew she had no more time. She thrust the crown back in the bag and once again held it to her chest, once again wrapped the blanket around her. A long dagger was lying at the bottom of the chest and she grabbed that as well. From the sound alone she could tell that the passage from her door to the residence's main entrance was untenable, blocked by fire and debris, so she did not even try. She made the sign of the cross, and with the hand holding the dagger picked up the little silver crucifix around her neck and kissed it. She was ready to move.

Crouching low, she hurried to the window on the far wall and threw open the wooden shutters. The cool night air came rushing in and she realized that the room was more smoke-filled than she had thought. Coughing and stumbling she climbed out of the window. Her bare feet hit the cool earth and she ran.

Morrigan did not take any part in fighting the fire. Her duty, as she saw it, the duty that outweighed them all, was to preserve the crown. Since the fin gall had stolen it months before, and she had taken it back, she felt she was the crown's protector. It was her duty, given to her by God, to protect the crown and see it placed on her brother's head.

So she hung back in the shadows, holding the crown in one hand, the dagger in the other, and watched as the people fought to save what they could of the royal house. In the light of the flames she looked for Brigit. She looked for Conlaed. She did not see either of them.

She wondered if they had become trapped in their bed chamber, had failed to make it out. *Now that would be convenient.*

The night dragged on, the fire was beaten back, and still no Brigit, no Conlaed. Morrigan was all but ready to see in this the hand of God, when one of the monks, a thick, sweaty man named Cónán came huffing up to her. "Morrigan, Morrigan! There you are, by God! Have you seen Father Finnian this night?"

"Father Finnian?"

"Yes. We've not seen him at all. When we heard the alarm we all came rushing out you know, to bear a hand. And we were at it for hours before anyone realized Finnian was not among us. We've looked all over. And we've not seen him."

Morrigan was silent. The implications, the possibilities clicking away in her head. *No Brigit, no Finnian? Were they in there, in the fire? Were they fornicating in there, until God sent his wrath down on them? Or Conlaed did? Is that what the shouting was about?*

Cónán cleared his throat.

"No, I have not seen them. Him," she said.

"Well, thank you, ma'am. We'll keep up our looking." He hurried off, and Morrigan's thoughts hurried on. *Or are they not here at all? Where would they have gone?*

At first light she sent out riders. Donnel and Patrick and some few of the *rí túaithe* whom she trusted, sent them off to search all the roads leading away from Tara. They found nothing. And so the uncertainly continued.

Half of the royal residence was spared, thanks to a night of frantic labor, good luck and a shift in the wind, but it was unlivable, so Morrigan and Flann and the others who had occupied the big house moved into the monastery and the monks doubled up in their cells or took the rooms of the household staff and sent them to fend for themselves. Flann intended to have the debris cleared away as quickly as possible, to begin construction on a new and larger building. Morrigan stayed his hand. "There'll be bodies in there. Brigit and Conlaed, I have no doubt. And we don't know the whereabouts of Father Finnian."

"Finnian? What might Finnian have been doing there?"

"I'm sure I don't know," Morrigan said. "Hearing their confession, perhaps?" In truth, of the many things she suspected, she considered that the least likely.

So they cleared the debris slowly, and Morrigan kept a watchful eye on the work, to see that nothing was missed and that nothing of value – a jewel, a coin, a shapeless yellow clump that might have once been a ring or a gold arm band – went missing.

Morrigan watched nearly every moment of the excavation. She watched as the layers of debris were pulled away, starting with the highest parts of the roof, on top of the heap, down through the collapsed walls and the interiors of the rooms. It was not until the third day that they found the body.

"Don't think you'll want to look at this, Mistress," said thick, hairy Ronan of the Gate who was overseeing the work. "It ain't fit," he added as she brushed past him and through the knot of workers staring down at the blackened ruin at their feet.

It had once been a person, that much was clear. The general outline was there; arms, legs, a withered, black nob that had been a head. It was shriveled, all clothes and features gone, stiff in an unnatural way and so small that at first Morrigan thought it had to be Brigit. But the more she looked the more she realized it could have been any of them. Or none of them. There was no way to tell.

The work went on, and soon it was all cleared away, until there was nothing more than a big blackened, roughly square patch of earth. No more bodies were found.

What could this mean? Morrigan asked herself, and the answer, she knew, was, *Anything*. Or nothing. *Could a body be so burned up in a fire that there would be nothing left?* She did not know. *Could the remains of one body survive the flames, but another not?* Again, she had no answer.

And that was the thing that was driving her to distraction. She did not know. She needed information. She could not act without it. And so the relief she felt was almost beyond measure when, a week after the fire, Patrick came riding hard through the gates of Tara, leapt from his horse and informed her, *sotto voce*, that Princess Brigit had been found.

Chapter Twenty-Two

Now, folk-warder, befit thee well
the red-gold rings, and the ruler's daughter;
hale shalt, hero, hold these twain…
The First Lay of Helgi the Hunding-Slayer

Mud sucking at his shoes, Arinbjorn stepped carefully over the flats on which *Black Raven* had been drawn up. The ship was sitting proud on the rollers, propped vertical by timbers under the bilge and stripped of her rig and oars and other semi-permanent equipment. From somewhere aft he could hear the screech of a plank being ripped free of the sternpost, the clench nails that held it to its fellow plank protesting as they straightened. He picked up his pace. Beside him, Bolli Thorvaldsson tried to keep up, but with a stride a third shorter than Arinbjorn's it was a struggle.

"Hold there!" Arinbjorn called. "Hold!" He had blithely told the shipwrights to do whatever was needed to make *Black Raven* seaworthy, sure that he had wealth enough to pay. But Thorgrim's words, his observation concerning the shipwright's ability to find work equal to Arinbjorn's ability to pay, had really found their mark as Arinbjorn realized the raid on Cloyne had not been as profitable as he thought. Now he wanted to make certain that the shipwrights did not do to him what he and his fellow warriors had done to Cloyne and any number of other Irish towns.

Arinbjorn and Bolli came around the after end of the ship. One of the ship carpenters was there, a heavy iron in his hand, the butt end of the plank sticking out at an odd angle where he had levered it away from the frame. Another, big, young, not so bright looking, his apprentice no doubt, stood by a few feet away with a hammer in his hand. He looked like Thor, or, more correctly, a mockery of Thor.

"What are you about?" Arinbjorn demanded. Even as the words left his mouth he realized it was a mistake to sound so indignant before he knew if the fellow was doing needed work or not. But it was too late.

"Getting at the rot under this strake," the shipwright said. "And what concern is it of yours? Who are you?"

"Arinbjorn Thoruson," Arinbjorn replied, with as much haughty dignity as he could muster. Bolli stepped behind the shipwright, a dagger in his hand, looking for all the world as if he was going to kill the man, though in truth they would wait to get the shipwright's bill before they considered that option. Instead, Bolli began poking at the wood of the sternpost and the strake with the weapon's needle point. The apprentice did not move.

"Don't look too rotten to me," Bolli reported.

The shipwright renewed his grip on the iron bar and turned toward Bolli. "You a ship carpenter, then? Look, why don't you go back to your grave digging or cleaning privies or whatever by Thor's arse you do and leave an honest man to his work?"

This was not going as Arinbjorn wanted, and it was only getting worse, and Bolli was not helping. Arinbjorn liked to have an ally, a second. He had intended Thorgrim Night Wolf for that office, as his advisor and assistant, had guessed there was status to be had by having a man such as Night Wolf answer to him, but that had not worked out so well. Thorgrim was too independent by far. But Bolli's fortunes were on the wane, his ship *Odin's Eye* too worn out to go to sea again, his men largely deserting him. He was eager to associate himself with Arinbjorn and would do Arinbjorn's bidding. Now Arinbjorn had to hope he did not prove himself an even bigger liability that Thorgrim.

The two men, Bolli and the shipwright, stared at one another, and then Bolli grunted through his hedge of beard and stepped away. Arinbjorn saw the shipwright relax his grip on the heavy tool. The apprentice's body seemed to sag with the release of tension.

No, Bolli is not so great a problem as Thorgrim, Arinbjorn thought. Thorgrim had been a problem for Arinbjorn at Cloyne and he still was, a bigger problem than even Thorgrim himself appreciated. The Night Wolf had come out of Cloyne a great hero, but only because he had ignored Arinbjorn's direct order. A generous offer of three shares for Thorgrim and Harald, two for the others, had bought Thorgrim's discretion. But the price was high, and the take at Cloyne had not been spectacular. The number of slaves they had captured drove their price in the market down. *Black Raven* required work and others needed paying. Olaf the White would have his take. In short, Arinbjorn could not afford to pay Thorgrim what he had promised.

Thorgrim might protest that he did not care about the gold and silver, but Arinbjorn had no doubt that would change if the promise was withdrawn.

Damn him, damn him… Arinbjorn thought, his frustration mounting. Thorgrim was apparently looking only for a way home, but now this new opportunity had come up, brought to him by that shapely little Irish princess the way a thrall brings drinking horns in a mead hall, one that could change everything for Arinbjorn. Could he afford to pass it up? What would Thorgrim do when Arinbjorn informed him they would not, in fact, be sailing for Norway soon?

"So you want me to get on with this or not?" the shipwright asked.

"Huh?" Arinbjorn said. "Oh…"

He recollected himself, coughed and went on. "The situation is thus. I thought I could spare a few weeks for you to set things right, but an… opportunity has come up, and I will need the ship swimming again in three days. Four at the outside."

"Opportunity, is it?" The shipwright perked up at that. Every man in Dubh-linn, despite his professed calling, was keeping a weather eye out for that one raid that would make his fortune.

"Can't really talk about it now," Arinbjorn said. "We've only just stumbled upon it." He meant to diffuse the shipwright's interest, but he could see his vague answer was having the opposite effect. But perhaps he could use that. "I need you to just get done what you can, have her ready to sail in the next few days," Arinbjorn went on. "Just coastal sailing. Then maybe I can let you in on what we have planned."

"Two days. Three days, latest, she'll be ready for whatever you can send at her," the shipwright said with a smile.

Yesterday you said it was two weeks it would take you, you thieving bastard, Arinbjorn thought, but he just smiled and said, "Good, then."

He and Bolli trudged back through the mud, back up to the plank road and the cluster of homes and workshops. "Will you ask Iron-skull to come on this raid?" Bolli asked once he and Arinbjorn were on firmer footing.

"Iron-skull? I don't know…." It had only been a day since Harald had brought Brigit to him, a day to digest all the possibilities and implications of this new twist of his destiny. Brigit, by her account, was the true heir to the throne of Tara, but a pretender sat on it now, in a seat none too secure. If Arinbjorn and the army he assembled could topple the pretender, put her on the throne, then the wealth of Tara would be theirs. She did not care about that. Rents, taxes, she would build the kingdom's fortune back up quickly enough, as long as the throne was hers.

It was an alliance. And why not? The Northmen had been in Dubh-linn for nearly twenty years. They were not strangers to Ireland, they were part of the land now, a contending power. That woman who had translated, Almaith, was married to a Norse blacksmith, and many other men in the longphort had Irish wives, half-breed children. The Irish came every day to trade. Norse, Irish, the distinction was blurring.

Which led Arinbjorn to the next logical thought. *Why should this Brigit rule alone? If she and I conquer Tara together, should we not rule Tara together?* That part had formed slowly in his mind, like a ship coming out of a fog.

A fog. That was right. His mind had been like a fog. A fog formed by his desire for her; immediate, powerful, as impossible to ignore as thirst.

No sooner had she swept into his room then he had been her slave, her fool. She was beautiful, proud, bordering on haughty, commanding. It was laughable to see that idiot Harald Thorgrimson panting over her, as if she would have any business with a boy such as that. She had come looking for a man, and she had found one in him.

"Not Thorgrim, though?" Bolli asked.

"What?"

"Thorgrim. Night Wolf. You won't ask him on the raid?"

"Oh. Yes, certainly I'll ask him. Him and his boy. They've proved themselves good men in a fight."

Bolli grunted, said no more. *Of course Thorgrim is coming, you fool,* Arinbjorn thought. Harald was apparently Brigit's connection to the men of Dubh-linn, though how that had happened, Arinbjorn could not imagine. Harald would not be left behind, and Thorgrim would not let his son go off a-viking without him. Which was fine. Arinbjorn was moving men around like pieces on a game board. As he positioned himself to sit on Tara's throne, to lie in Brigit's bed, so he positioned Thorgrim and Harald to be on the field of battle with him, where men died brutal deaths and often times no one saw it happen, and thus Arinbjorn might be rid of them.

Not so long ago a Dane, Thorgils, set himself up as king of the Irish people, Arinbjorn reminded himself.

And the Irish people drowned him…

Thorgils was a fool, then. I am not a fool.

Thorgrim Night Wolf was angry, more angry than he could recall having ever been, blazing in red hot fury. Harald wanted to talk to him in private. He took him away from Jokul's house, led him down by the banks of the river, and now Thorgrim saw why. He understood. In fact, he understood a great deal more than he had even an hour before.

His back was turned toward his son and he was looking out at the darkening sky to the east, but he was not seeing that, or anything. He needed to speak, and he was wrestling to get command of his voice, to get to a place where he could open his mouth and trust what would come out.

He turned on Harald, his cloak making a sweeping motion as he spun around. "You went to Arinbjorn? Behind my back? Arinbjorn? Do you have any notion of what an untrustworthy snake that man is?"

Harald stood like a tree, arms at his side, not a flicker of fear in his face, and in some far off place in Thorgrim's mind he was proud.

"Arinbjorn is a snake? Well, *you* seem to have plenty of business with him!" Harald returned.

Thorgrim could hear the note of uncertainly, but only someone who knew Harald very well would have recognized it. Two years ago, even a year ago, Harald would have crumbled by now under Thorgrim's gaze, if they had every come to this point. Which they would not have done. Because Harald would never have stood up to his father in this way.

"I use Arinbjorn to my ends. Our ends. And now you've undone it all! Do not think you can play in these affairs of men. You are a boy."

"I am not a boy, by all the gods! If there's a…I can see a chance, one that's worth taking! You would never be party to this. I know enough of the affairs of men to know that. So I went to someone who might! Someone who commands men, and a ship, which you do not!"

That last hit home. Thorgrim felt the blow. But, as in a brawl with fists or weapons, he was too angry to be slowed by it. "If you are not a boy, then you are a fool of a man! Arinbjorn was our way home, and now you have distracted him with this Irish nonsense! You think there is anything to be gained staying in this wretched place? Can't you see that what you have done will keep us from our home that much longer?"

"It's you who wants to go home! Not me! Did you ever ask if I want to go with you? If I want to return to that farm, forsaken by Odin, and those stinking animals? Did you? My grandfather has chosen to stay here and maybe I do, too!"

Thorgrim staggered back a step. He shook his head. "Stay here? Why…what could possibly make you want to stay here?" But he knew the answer.

"Brigit. She wants me to stay. She loves me. And I love her."

Despite himself, Thorgrim laughed. There was nothing that Harald could have said to more perfectly demonstrate that he was indeed just a naïve boy with no understanding of the ways of the wicked world.

"Loves you? She loves you like a butcher loves his pigs, raising them up so he can slaughter them. I don't know what has gone on between you, what happened before, but any fool can see she is using you. You are but a piece, a minor piece, in whatever game she plays."

"A 'piece', is it? How would you know that? You don't even speak her language. But I do, and here is the truth, father. She means to sit on the throne of Tara, which is her right, and she means for me to rule with her. By her side. I am to be king here."

And Thorgrim laughed again.

"By the gods, father, do not laugh at me! I will not stand it."

"Oh, you won't, eh? And tell me, what proof do you have of this Irish bitch's lofty plans? Why in all Asgard would she want you to share her rule?"

"Because I am the father of the baby that grows in her belly."

In the cross-current of shocks that had come that night, this was the most powerful yet, and it knocked Thorgrim well off course. When he regained his composure, he spoke, his voice no more than a growl.

"You are a fool. I have raised a fool."

Harald took a step closer, and his tone matched Thorgrim's, the same note, a higher key, his finger pointing like a dagger. "Do not call me a fool."

Thorgrim's hand lashed out, fast as ever he delivered a thrust in battle, and his open palm caught Harald on the side of the face. The young man was knocked sideways, bent nearly double, but his feet stayed fixed where they were. He did not stagger under the impact. He straightened. In the fading light Thorgrim could see the red mark on his face where he took the blow.

"Do not call me a fool," Harald said again, his tone unwavering defiance.

Thorgrim's hand lashed out again, but this time Harald's hand was there to meet it, his right arm moving across his chest so fast that Thorgrim did not see it. He grabbed Thorgrim's wrist in a powerful grip and the two stood there, faces just inches apart, eyes holding eyes, arm pushing on hand, so that both of them, man and boy, trembled from the exertion.

Thorgrim could see the fury in Harald's eyes, a thing he had never seen before, and a stew of emotions churned in his father's heart; anger, pity, sorrow, fear. But none of that was in Harald's eyes. There, it was fury alone, a pure vein of emotion.

They stood for what seemed a long time, pushing one against the other. Thorgrim could feel the pull and tear of the wound in his side. He had expected his son's arm to fold under the pressure, once he started applying real force, but it did not, and Thorgrim could not believe the strength the young man possessed. *Harald Broad-arm…*

Then Harald, angry beyond thought, cocked his left arm for an uppercut. Thorgrim felt the slightest lapse of power in Harald's grip as his focus shifted to the other arm and Thorgrim knew it was over. He moved by instinct and muscle memory alone; there was no thought at all, no consideration of what he was doing. He twisted his arm in a tight circle, broke Harald's grip, and used the momentum to hit Harald square on the side of the head.

This time his son staggered, stumbled back two, three steps, his hand pressed against his face. Thorgrim dropped his arms to his sides. Sorrow and guilt, that was all he felt now. *How has it come to this? My boy?*

"By Thor and Odin, son, I am so sorry," he said. His hands remained at his side. He hoped Harald would hit him in return, though he knew that redemption would not come that easy, far easier than he deserved.

Harald did not hit him back. He dropped his arms to his side as well, pulled his eyes from Thorgrim's face, and walked away, walked back up the road. Thorgrim watched his back as he strode off. He wanted to say something, to call out, but there were no words in his mouth. He hoped his son would turn and come back, but he knew he would not, nor did he.

Thorgrim turned toward the river, his face into the sea breeze, and he wept.

Chapter Twenty-Three

That woman in my dreams
takes all my joy, it seems.
As I fall asleep, she appears…
Gisli Sursson's Saga

Starri Deathless let the heavy grindstone spin slowly to a stop. He sighted down the edge of the blade he was honing. It was a thing of perfection, as sharp as that particular blade could ever be. There was one tiny flaw halfway down the edge, but that could not be ground out without ruining the entire weapon. Starri said nothing to Jokul about it.

He had learned not to criticize Jokul's work, after one casual remark about the balance of one sword had led to twenty minutes of high-volume ranting. Every time he thought Jokul was winding his diatribe down, the smith would start up again, like a fire that would not go out. If Jokul had reacted with physical violence it would not have bothered Starri in the least, but Starri knew he could not endure the ranting any longer.

He set the blade aside. There were no more left to sharpen. But that was all right because he was done with sharpening blades, at least for now. He liked it. It was a prelude to battle. And even if there was no battle in the offing, sharpening a blade gave him that rise of spirit that came with the proximity to a fight. Starri had not been with a lot of women, not like many other men he knew, but he understood that the things one did prior to the final act were intended to make that ultimate release all the more intense.

So it was with the rituals before battle. But, as with lying with a woman, one could only do the preliminaries so many times without taking it to the final act before the whole thing just became tedious and frustrating.

And if he remained stuck in Dubh-linn much longer, he would be there, at the place of tedium and frustration. Sailing with Arinbjorn had been good, leading the little band of berserkers. Starri was no leader; he knew that. He had never been able to concentrate long enough to take charge of anything, himself included, but with the berserkers that had not mattered much. Not much leadership was needed or indeed possible with a group such as that. They had seen fights enough along the coast.

But meeting the Night Wolf had changed things, because he had seen, in that moment on the beach, that brilliant moment of vision, that his destiny was entwined with that man, blessed by the gods.

Starri instinctively reached for the split arrowhead that hung from his neck. *Incredible…* Incredible that Thorgrim could not see the truth that was so obvious to Starri. He was blessed, and where he went, that was where Starri Deathless would be.

At Cloyne it had been good. Going in through the secret gate. Only the Night Wolf could have known about that. The desperate fighting. Starri felt his mood improve as he reflected back on it. He had almost been slain on that field. Almost. Surely staying close to a man like Thorgrim would bring him soon to an end on the glory-field that would win the admiration of the Valkyries.

But here in Dubh-linn, that would not happen. Here, things grew worse by the moment. Why? Because there were women. Starri did not dislike women. Not at all. But he had seen often enough how their presence complicated everything. Now Almaith had some designs on Thorgrim, right under her husband's roof. And this Irish girl had arrived. Brigit. And she seemed to have some spell over Harald, so obvious that even Thorgrim recognized it, and Thorgrim was not quick where Harald was concerned. What could this mean?

Their lives were like a great sheet of ice, once solid, flawless and constant, that was now melting, melting, revealing flaws and defects long frozen in place.

This was why Starri loved battle. It was so clean, so unambiguous. The rules were straightforward and clear. As long as he let others worry about the reasons for fighting, and he focused on the fight itself, everything was good.

"Jokul? Jokul the smith?"

Starri looked up. There were two men standing there, big men, with long hair each done up in twin braids, as many of the Norsemen wore it. They wore padded tunics. Long, straight swords hung from their belts. Starri did not recognize them, but that was hardly odd. They looked like most of the men who wandered around the longphort, and Starri was not good with faces in any event.

"What?" Starri said in reply.

"Are you Jokul, the smith?" the man asked again.

Before Starri could reply, Jokul burst from the house where he had been eating his dinner. "I am Jokul, who is it who's looking for me?"

"I am Sweyn, of Hedeby. This is my brother Svein." The man in front nodded toward the one behind.

"Huh? Danes, is it? Well, what do you want?" asked Jokul at his most charming.

"We've been to see the smith Vali about swords for our men, and…"

"Vali! You can see Vali about nails and horseshoes. I am the only one in Dubh-linn who can make a decent sword. But I don't give them away, do you hear? You pay a fair price for my work, but that does not mean it's a low price."

"I understand," said Sweyn. "Can we talk about price, and how long it would take to make what we need?"

"Talk," Jokul said.

"Maybe you'll invite us in and give us a drink, so we do not have to talk on the street like this was the fish market? My brother and I are thirsty."

"Humph," Jokul said, clearly struggling between his desire for business and his unwillingness to part even with a couple of cups of beer for free. This all seemed very odd to Starri. He could see Svein was carrying a skin, and it looked quite full. But then Jokul said, "Very well, come inside."

The two men stepped through the gate and followed Jokul inside and Starri followed behind because he was curious now. They went into the big room where the table stood by the hearth and Jokul roared, "Almaith! Beer, here!"

Almaith peered into the room, surveyed the situation, and disappeared. Jokul waved toward a bench by the table and the two brothers sat, their bulk dwarfing the furniture. Jokul sat as well, and Starri took a seat on a stool in the corner. He was quiet, his movement so fluid and unobtrusive that no one seemed to notice he was there, and if they did, no one asked why he was.

In the corner, Brigit sat with her hands in a stream of dull sunlight coming in through the window. She was sewing something, but Starri had the impression that it was just for something to do. Harald and Thorgrim had left an hour or so before, Almaith had her hands full keeping up with her increasingly crowded household, and that left Brigit unoccupied. She looked up briefly, ran her eyes over the men at the table, ignored Starri, and went back to her sewing.

Sweyn and Jokul were in an animated discussion about swords, quality of steel, finish of hilts, prices. Almaith came in and set cups of beer on the table and the men picked them up without acknowledging her, as if the cups had appeared of their own volition. Starri paid no attention to the negotiations. Jokul's work was in great demand, and in the short time he had been there, Starri had heard this scene played out a dozen times.

In truth, Starri was more interested in what Svein was about, which at first glance would seem to be nothing. He did not speak, and he took one sip of beer for every three the others did. His eyes were all around the room. They lit on Brigit and stayed there for a long while. That was not unusual; Starri had noticed that few men could keep their eyes off the girl, but Svein's face did not wear the same look of desire that he had seen in others. Jokul, in particular, looked at her with something like ravenous hunger. Harald's look was different, more affection than desire. Only Thorgrim seemed to look on her with indifference.

From Brigit, Svein's eyes moved up to the ceiling and over to the door that led to the other end of the house. He shifted slightly and cocked his head, just a bit, so he could take in the hearth and the wooden chests pushed up against the wall.

Curious fellow, Starri thought.

Then they heard the sound of feet along the path and the door opened and Harald stepped in. He looked briefly around, seemed to see no one until he saw Brigit. He said something to her in the Irish language that Starri did not understand. Brigit put down her sewing and stood. She looked concerned, even a little frightened. Harald was agitated, and Starri could see on the left side of his face the unmistakable mark of a solid punch landed.

Did Thorgrim strike him? Starri wondered. That did not seem possible. Thorgrim loved the boy more than his own life. Far more. Starri could not imagine what could provoke him to hit Harald so hard as to leave a mark such as that. He watched Svein as Svein's eyes followed Brigit and Harald out the door.

"You seem to have quite a few living in your house," Sweyn observed with a laugh.

"House?" Jokul replied. "It's a damned inn, I tell you, not a house, with that Irish wife of mine letting every damned stray cat stay here. They pay me half as much as they eat! I'll be begging bread in the streets in a week, at this rate."

"Well, you've driven a hard enough bargain with me, that should keep a roof over your head for a while, anyway." Sweyn stood and extended a hand. Jokul took it and shook, but Starri could see his thoughts had already moved on to other considerations. As had those of Starri Deathless.

For some time, he did not know how long, Thorgrim stood by the edge of the water and let the cool sea breeze of late spring envelope him and let the emotions bleed out. Could he return to Vik without his son? Harald was not a boy. He was right about that. At Harald's age, Thorgrim certainly did not have his father by his side, worrying about his every move. And if Harald was being a fool, surely it was Harald's place to discover that, not Thorgrim's place to point it out.

We want the young to learn from our mistakes, Thorgrim thought, and wondered if ever in the history of all humanity such a thing had ever happened.

It was well dark when he turned at last and headed back up the hill, back toward Jokul's house, though he had no intention of going there, at least not at that hour, not while others were still awake. From the plank road he could see candles burning inside, and occasionally the bulk of Jokul eclipsed the light as he moved past the window.

"Night Wolf," a voice said. "You are prowling the roads tonight." Starri Deathless stepped out of the dark. He had been just feet away, but Thorgrim had not seen him, and that was unusual because men generally could not approach Thorgrim undetected. Starri's voice, unexpected, might have been startling, but it blended with the evening and was no more jarring than a breeze rustling through treetops.

"Starri. You are restless, too."

"I am." Starri stopped at Thorgrim's side and the two men turned and continued on up the road. No thought as to where they were going, no discussion, they just walked.

"We have to leave Dubh-linn," Starri said at last.

"Yes," Thorgrim said.

"There are things happening here. Bad things."

"Yes."

They walked on. The mead hall was loud and light leaked from around the doors and shuttered windows, but they had no interest in that place and continued past. "My only thought was to get home. I thought it was what Harald wanted, too," Thorgrim said.

"But now there is this girl?"

"Yes. She makes him her fool."

"Youth makes us all fools," Starri said. "Age only makes it worse."

Despite himself, Thorgrim smiled in the dark. "When he was a prisoner, Harald apparently laid with her. Now she tells him that she carries his child. She says she is the rightful heir to the throne of Tara, which is some Irish kingdom not far from here. She has Harald convinced they will rule it together, if he can raise an army to take this Tara from those who rule it now. So Harald has gone to Arinbjorn."

They stopped and looked out over the distant sea. The moon was rising and casting a long, textured band of gold light over the water.

"That's quite a story," Starri said at last. "Like a nursemaid might tell a child to get it to sleep. Could it be true?"

"I don't know. I suppose it could."

"If Tara is the seat of a kingdom, it sounds like it might be some hard fighting to take it. Good plunder, I would think. I am not disappointed at the thought of that," Starri said.

"I didn't reckon you would be," Thorgrim said. "That's why I didn't ask your opinion as to what to do. You would fight all the host of Asgard armed with a threshing flail, if given the choice."

"You would allow me a flail? That would hardly make it fair for the host of Asgard." They stood for a few moments more, looking out over the water, toward the horizon, black and unseen. "You'll do the right thing, Night Wolf," Starri said at last. "You'll make the right choice, as long as you don't think about it too much."

It was quite late by the time they returned to Jokul's house. The windows were shuttered and no light appeared around the edges. With all that had taken place that evening, Thorgrim would have expected the black mood to be on him, wolf dreams in the offing, but Starri seemed to have an odd, calming effect. He felt steady and even, a ship floating in a calm, flat sea.

Starri settled himself on the workbench and Thorgrim bid him good night, then followed the split log path around to the door. It occurred to him they might have already barred the door from the inside, which would require him to knock and wake someone, but when he tried it, it opened without hesitation. He eased it open as quietly as he could, stepped in and closed it behind him.

He took a few steps into the common room. It was dark, with just a handful of coals burning in the hearth, but his eyes were used to the dark and he could see well enough. Against the far wall, he could discern Harald's bulky frame under a heap of furs. Thorgrim felt a great relief to know the boy had come back, that he had not driven his son away. He felt hopeful, like things might indeed work out. He had not felt that way for a long time.

Harald was not alone. Looking at the pile of bedding Thorgrim realized there were two under the furs, and the second, he had to imagine, was Brigit. In the quiet he could hear their breathing, sometimes in sync, sometimes separate, but soft and rhythmic.

Perhaps she does love him, Thorgrim thought. He wondered if Harald was the one who saw the truth, who clearly understood the situation, and he, Thorgrim, was the one acting the fool. He stepped back to the door, dropped the bar in place, and then crossed the room to his own bed.

He unhooked the brooch that held his cloak around his shoulders, set it down and let the cloth drop soundlessly to the floor. He took the ax from his sword belt and laid it down within reach, unhooked the belt and set Iron-tooth carefully by the pallet on which he made his bed. He pulled off his shoes and leggings and crawled gratefully under the cover of furs and wool blankets.

Sleep was not long in coming, with the quiet rhythms of the house, the distant sound of Jokul's deep rumbling snores, the soft breathing of Harald and Brigit. Thorgrim felt the warm wash come over him and he settled into it, let the heavy darkness pull him down.

And soon in his unconscious mind he felt a presence, warm and pleasurable, pressed close, something beyond himself. Slowly he kicked his way back to the surface, not desperate, like a drowning man, but easy, like one who is simply done being engulfed by the warm water. He was not alone under his furs.

"Almaith?" His voice was no louder than a breath.

Almaith ran her hand over his chest. He was still wearing his tunic but he could feel the warmth of her body through the cloth. "I wanted to see how your wound was getting on," she said in a soft and sleepy voice. "But you were asleep before I could speak with you."

Thorgrim put his hand on Almaith's shoulder and let it slide down along her side. She was wearing a leine of thin cloth, so thin it was almost not there at all. Her skin underneath was soft and smooth and firm. She moved slightly under the motion of his hand and pressed herself closer.

"I was worried about you," she said in the same breathy, sleepy voice. "You and Harald. It seemed like something happened."

"Something happened," Thorgrim confirmed. "Did Harald seem much upset, when he returned?"

Thorgrim could feel Almaith shrug. "He seemed all right. He's young, their wounds heal quickly. Any sort of wound. Did you have a disagreement over Brigit?"

"Yes. He says she is the rightful heir to some kingdom called Tara."

"She is," Almaith said.

Thorgrim was quiet for some time. "She is?" he asked at length.

"Yes. She is Brigit nic Máel Sechnaill. Her father was Máel Sechnaill mac Ruanaid. His kingdom is called Brega, not Tara. Tara is the seat of the kingdom. Not far from here. Some say the king who sits on the throne of Tara is by rights the high king of all Ireland."

Tara, Brega… He had heard this before, from the thrall, Morrigan. It was coming back to him, like a dream, barely remembered.

"How do you know she is who she says? Do you recognize her?"

"I didn't at first. But when she told me who she was, I saw it was so. I grew up not far from Tara. I suppose you might say I am her subject. Or would be, if others had not taken the throne on her father's death."

They lay together, quiet, for a few moments. Thorgrim listened to the sounds of the household, listened to hear if their soft talk had pulled anyone from sleep, but he could hear no changes. Most importantly, Jokul still snored with gusto in the far room.

"Will you help her?" Almaith asked. "Harald says she hopes to get an army of you Norsemen to put her on the throne. Will that happen?"

"I don't know," Thorgrim said. He could hear the note of exasperation creep unbidden into his voice. "This is not our fight. I don't know what will happen."

Almaith seemed to hear the note as well. She did not speak again, just pressed herself closer to him and ran her hand softly up and down his chest. He in turn let his hand wander over her shoulder and down her side, let it slide along the soft curve that her waist made as it widened out to her hips. Hard work had kept her lean, but the bounty of Jokul's thriving smithy had kept her from growing thin and boney, and Thorgrim thoroughly appreciated the result.

Quietly, slowly, Almaith pushed herself up until she was draped across his chest and her lips could reach his. She kissed him and he kissed her back, both with the hunger of people who had delayed this moment until the last, until they could bear no more. Almaith slid further on top of Thorgrim, her hands running over the hard muscles of his arms, and he, with both arms free now, let his hands run the length of her body, down to her pleasantly round bottom, as far as he could reach. His fingers found the hem of her leine and he eased it up and she lifted herself off him, just a bit, just enough for the cloth to pass between them, then up over her head.

She laid on top of him, naked, the weight of the furs and blankets pressing her harder into him. He let his lips explore her neck, her shoulders, her breasts. He felt her breath coming quicker, but soft, barely audible. His hands, rough as weathered pine, moved over her skin, barely touching it, his fingers entwined themselves in her long, dark hair.

Almaith reached down and grabbed handfuls of Thorgrim's tunic and pulled it up as he had done with her leine. It was bit more of a struggle and Thorgrim could feel his wound pulling and Almaith said, "Easy, easy, easy," her voice even less than a whisper. And then the tunic was off, over his head, and Thorgrim reveled in that sensation of skin against skin, her small, soft, smooth body against his own muscled and hairy frame. He wrapped his arms around her, held her tight, pressing her harder against him. Her lips were on his, tongues exploring mouths.

Thorgrim was ready for her, more than ready. She straddled him, her knees just reaching the furs on which they lay. She moved her hips and he felt himself slide inside her, felt her body tense, her hands clench with the first sensation. She lay across his chest, moving slowly from the hips down, and he moved with her. Her long hair fell across his face and chest and she brushed it away, tossed her head back, her hair over her shoulder. Her neck was long and graceful in the dim light, her mouth open, her eyes shut. She made soft whimpering sounds, barely audible.

They moved like that for some time, a slow rhythm, steady, absorbed in the feel of one another. Then Thorgrim wrapped his arms around her again, pulled her tight to him, and rolled over. Almaith wrapped her legs around his hips and the rhythm never stopped as they shifted around, Thorgrim on top of her, propped on his elbows, draped in heavy furs, making a shelter above her.

Slowly, deliberately, Thorgrim began to move faster, jarring Almaith slightly with each thrust. Her hair was half over her face and her hand was in her mouth and she was biting down on it. Her eyes were squeezed tight. Her skin shone white against the dark fur.

Thorgrim grit his teeth. More often than not he had done this in a communal setting, a house full of people, and he was well practiced at remaining quiet despite the urge to do otherwise. His motion grew more urgent. Almaith wrapped legs and arms more tightly around him, pulled him down on her. She felt so tiny beneath him, so vulnerable. His entire body was consumed by the sensation. His eyes jammed shut, his jaw clenched. He reached under Almaith's back and grabbed her shoulders and she ran her feet up and down the backs of his legs. He felt her body under his clench tight and she gave a stifled cry, and then relaxed, like a rope under tension that is eased away, and that was enough to send him over the edge as well.

It was another minute before they stopped moving all together and lay there, quiet, wrapped in one another. Thorgrim reached up and brushed her hair aside and ran his lips along her neck. In the far room, Jokul still snored away.

Sometime later Thorgrim rolled off and lay on his back and Almaith once again draped herself over his chest. She ran her hands through the hair on his chest. Thorgrim felt sleep creeping over him again, and he thought, *We cannot fall asleep and be found like this...that would not end well...* He did not like to think about how much Jokul would charge for the rental of his wife.

"So," Almaith said, resting her hand on his chest, "Will Arinbjorn raise an army? Does he believe what Brigit says?"

Such a lot of questions... Thorgrim thought, and before he could answer, the sleep was on him and taking him down.

Then he woke with a start. How long he had been asleep, he did not know. Long enough to dream. Long enough to hear all those questions again, and to wake with a horrid realization. Almaith was still there, pressed against him.

Such a lot of questions...

At Cloyne they had known the Norsemen were coming. And not just Cloyne. Everywhere, the Irish seemed one step ahead, towns alerted to their coming, the Northman's plans laid out like runes carved in stone. *So who is the damnable fool now?*

But before Thorgrim could gather his thoughts enough to even consider the situation, he realized what had roused him from sleep. Someone was coming. Their approach was not loud, but neither was it stealthy, which meant they were coming with force enough that they were not overly worried about surprise. And such an approach, at such an hour, told Thorgrim with absolute certainty that they came to kill.

Chapter Twenty-Four

Let polished hilt-wands clash,
strike shields with brands,
test our swords' shine on shields,
redden them with blood.
Egil's Saga

Thorgrim pushed the heavy furs off him and rolled to his feet. He could see light around the edge of the door. Whoever was on the outside held a torch, and he wondered if they meant to set the house on fire, with them in it. But he could hear someone rattling the door, testing it, finding it barred. He reached for Iron-tooth, realized he was naked.

He stood for a second, a fraction of a second, caught between sleep, surprise and indecision. Then he snatched up his cloak, wrapped it around his waist and tied it off. A foot crashed against the door and Thorgrim saw it give a bit, the bar bending, but the bracket that held it, forged by Jokul, did not budge.

Thorgrim snatched Iron-tooth by the grip and swung it sideways, flipping the sheath and belt off, and heard them hit the wall in the dark. Again a foot crashed against the door and Thorgrim heard the splintering sound of the bar giving way. He bent over, felt for the battle ax he had laid on the floor, grabbed it up.

"Harald! To arms! To arms!" he shouted and looked over at the pile under which his son rested. An arm emerged, a face just visible in the dim light.

"To arms, son, we have guests tonight!" Thorgrim shouted again.

That was all he needed to say. At times it was nearly impossible to get Harald out of bed, but the call to arms always made him jump, and generally faster than anyone. He pushed the furs aside and leapt out of bed and Thorgrim was happy to note that he was clothed. In a flash Harald, too, had sword and ax in hand, because Northmen did not go to sleep without weapons at the ready.

"Who are they, father?" Harald asked. There was concern in his voice, and surprise and confusion, but not a trace of fear.

"I don't know," Thorgrim said. With a guilty flush he recalled that on first hearing the commotion he had thought it was Jokul, coming for him, but he realized now that the smith would not be kicking in his own door.

"They seem pretty determined, whoever they are," Harald said.

Another kick. The bar splintered even further. Then with a roar Jokul appeared from the other side of the house. He was dressed in a leine and held a sword in each hand.

"What in the name of all the gods is going on here!" he bellowed. Thorgrim glanced down at his bed. Almaith had withdrawn under the furs. He could just see a bit of movement and he guess she was pulling her clothes on.

Another kick and the door came open, ten inches, no more, not enough for a man to get through, but the light from the torch spilled in through the crack.

"Oh, you sorry sons of whores!" Jokul shouted and thrust his sword through the opening between the door and its frame. Thorgrim heard the sound of steel on steel as someone outside deflected the thrust. Another kick landed on the door and this time the bar gave way and the door flew open.

The shape of a man filled the door frame, but the torch was behind him and Thorgrim could see little beyond his silhouette. What he could see was not promising. He was big, and wore an iron helmet in the Norse fashion, high peaked, and a mail shirt. He held a sword in his right hand, a shield in his left. Behind him, the torch bearer was more visible in the light of the flame. He was big as well, also helmeted and mailed, his long hair done up in two long braids that hung down in front of his shirt. There were more men crowded behind. Thorgrim could not see how many. More than he could see through the single door.

The first man was through the door and Jokul, bear-like and furious, flailed at him with his swords, the kind of attack that owed more to rage than skill. The man easily turned the blades aside with his shield, stepped in and slashed with his sword at the smith's prominent stomach. Jokul in turn leapt back, and bellowed as the stranger's sword cut a rent in his leine and left a fine, shallow laceration across his flesh. Half an inch closer and the stranger would have opened Jokul up and spilled his entrails on the floor.

Thorgrim howled, a primal wolf-scream, a reflex sound, and fell on the man who had kicked in the door. He came in with ax raised, swung it hard for the man's head. The man raised his shield, an easy defense, but that was what Thorgrim intended for him to do. Thorgrim drove the ax hard into the shield, the sharp edge digging deep into the wood, giving Thorgrim a handle by which he could jerk the shield aside.

With a grunt of effort Thorgrim twisted the handle of the ax, twisting the shield and the arm that held it, jamming the man's hand in the grip so he could not let go. In the light of the torch, now just feet away, he could see the look of surprise on the man's face, the realization that his arm was about to shatter. The man shouted in pain and outrage, threw all his strength into twisting his arm back, and Thorgrim drove Iron-tooth's point straight into his throat, half an inch above the collar of the mail shirt. The man spit blood and his eyes rolled back and he went straight down, down on his knees, as if pleading for quarter.

The man behind, the one with the torch, stumbled against the unexpected obstacle. Thorgrim pulled Iron-tooth free and tried to get the torch bearer on the upswing, but the man was too fast, stepping back and swinging the blazing torch end at Thorgrim's face, forcing Thorgrim to step back as well.

Now Harald was there, trying to get the torch man while he was busy with Thorgrim, but the man was no novice. He parried Harald's blade and stepped sideways, further into the house, making way for more of the men outside to enter. The flame from his torch, dancing and guttering, cast a weird light around the room, glinting off more steel as the attackers made a rush for the door. Two more, the one in front coming low, crouched down, the one behind with ax drawn back over his head.

Thorgrim saw how it would play out. A kick to the side of the first man's head, make him stumble, trip up the second one. The best chance to stop them was in the bottle neck of the door. He lifted his foot for a well-placed heel to the side of the man's head when Jokul came charging up again, swords flailing. He slammed hard into Thorgrim and Thorgrim, at that instance balancing on one foot, was flung against the wall with an impact that made his whole body shudder, and made him grunt in pain.

Jokul swung the swords in two broad arcs and made solid contact with the second man. Thorgrim could hear the blade clang on the man's helmet, saw the man stagger sideways. But Jokul's second blade passed over the man who had come in low, and now he straightened, sword leading.

"Jokul!" Thorgrim shouted. He swiped at the man but missed. The sword caught Jokul in the side and dug deep, but the smith seemed more enraged than hurt. He roared, stepped back, knocked the sword from his flesh with one swipe of the blade in his right hand. He brought the sword in his left hand down on the man's head with all the force that thirty years of swinging a hammer could deliver. Thorgrim saw the blade cleave the man's helmet in two and keep on going until his head was all but parted down the middle.

I had no notion a sword could do that… Thorgrim thought as he pushed himself off the wall. *Maybe Jokul really is as good a smith as he thinks he is…*

Harald and the torch bearer were still engaged, Harald's sword and ax against the man's sword and flame, and as the stranger swung the torch it made the light and dark in the room dance and shift.

Two more were through the door by the time Thorgrim could get past Jokul and the man whose skull he split. The torch swung toward the door and Thorgrim caught a glimpse of long stringy hair, a beard, little rat eyes, and a battle ax swinging at his head. A clumsy bow, Thorgrim caught it with his own ax, turned the weapon aside. The momentum carried the man off balance and Thorgrim rammed Iron-tooth up under his mail shirt. He felt the point dig deep enough to kill with certainty, if not instantly, but that was good enough.

Harald was being forced back by the flailing torch. It was not a weapon he had encountered before, and the slashing light seemed to confuse him. Jokul, too, was stepping away from the door. He had dropped the sword in his right hand and was pressing that hand against the wound in his side. Blood oozed out between his massive fingers, but he was still fighting hard with the sword in his left. His eyes wide, his hair sticking out at crazy angles, his beard a great matted mess, he looked to Thorgrim like one of the giants in the ancient legends he had heard as a child.

There were just three of them defending the house, and Harald was a boy and Jokul wounded. The attackers were pushing them back, opening up fighting room, and that was bad, because having room enough meant they could bring their numbers to bear.

"Here! To me!" someone shouted and Thorgrim realized it was the man with the torch. Another, a sword and short sword in his hands, dashed through the door, stepped over to where the torch man was engaged with Harald and joined in the fight. Two against one. Thorgrim pressed himself against the wall, looked for a way to cross the room, to stand side by side with Harald, but there were three men he would have to get through first, and he would be lucky not to be killed by Jokul's wildly swinging blade.

But it was not two against one, because the torch man stepped back from the fight as soon as the other had Harald's attention. He seemed, in fact, to ignore the fight entirely as he plunged into the room, sweeping the torch through the air, lighting up the distant corners. Almaith and Brigit were huddle together by the far wall. Almaith had in her hand the three-foot iron spit that usually spanned the hearth and she held it like a club. Brigit held the small ax they used to split kindling.

"Here, here, here!" the man with the torch shouted. The next man through the door responded, rushed toward the lighted end of the room, did not even see Thorgrim in the shadow until Thorgrim's ax had all but decapitated him. He went down, but in the time it took for Thorgrim to free his ax two more were through the door and closing with the one who had called out.

How many of these sons of whores are there? Thorgrim wondered. He could see no more outside the door, but the little house was crammed with struggling men, swords and axes rising, swinging, hacking in the torchlight.

"The one with the ax! Her! Get that bitch!" the man with the torch shouted and two men advanced on the women. They advanced with care. Brigit and Almaith had the look of women who would not be taken easily.

"You dog! Coward!" Thorgrim shouted and he tried to cross the room but there were two in front of him now. He swung his ax in a wide arc, made one of them step back, thrust at the other but found only air.

Then Jokul was in front of him, a great mass like one of those floating islands of ice found in the far north seas. He was roaring and hacking, his wound forgotten, holding his sword with two hands as he flailed it at his attackers.

"Jokul, damn it, stand clear!" Thorgrim shouted. He tried to step around, then ducked as Jokul took a big wind up, backhand, with his long straight sword. But before he could even let swing Thorgrim saw a blade erupt from the big man's back, a bloody, silvery point, glinting, twisting. Jokul's roar turned to something else, something high-pitched, fury and agony all forge-welded together and he fell back with thundering force, the blade slipping free from his body as he went down.

Almaith shrieked. The man advancing on her shifted his gaze as Jokul fell and for his second's distraction took the full force of the iron spit across the side of his head. Thorgrim saw his head jerk sideways and the rest of his body follow and he went down as if the gods had taken his bones. In the same instant Brigit made a great sweeping stroke with the ax at the man who held the torch, but he stepped back and the blade missed his head by inches.

Jokul was down, dying or dead. Thorgrim was pressed against the wall, a man on his right, one on his left. In the jerky light he could see Harald across the room. He, too, had his back to a wall. It restricted his movements but kept anyone from circling behind, so it was a good thing. But they could not keep this up forever. They could not keep this up much longer.

To his right the man swung an ax and Thorgrim met it, mid-swing, with his own ax. The handles hit, wood on wood, and the attacker jerked back, caught Thorgrim's ax head in his own and pulled the weapon clean from his hand. It was a good move, and Thorgrim tried to counter with a trust from Iron-tooth, but the man dodged it and his partner lunged with his own blade.

Thorgrim twisted. The sword caught his flesh, ripped on through, and Thorgrim felt the burning pain bite into him. He swung Iron-tooth, a clumsy blow, caught the man with the flat of the blade and knocked him sideways. The blade jerked free of Thorgrim's flesh as the man stumbled, sending a second wave of agony over him.

Blood spilled.... Thorgrim knew what that meant. He would weaken. His grip would get slick with his own gore, his feet unsteady. It was the beginning of the final act.

Then, from somewhere beyond the walls, but close, a shriek rose, a death wail, a terrifying sound, but familiar to Thorgrim's ear. Suddenly the room was filled with a shower of splinters, a rush of cool air, the sound of wood shattering, metal hinges and latches wrenched free as Starri Deathless came crashing feet first through the shuttered window of Jokul's house.

Chapter Twenty-Five

Sharp from my sheath
my short sword I drew
The Saga of the Confederates

Starri had been asleep when they came, or nearly asleep, as much asleep as Starri ever was, Starri who slept like a cat, sprawled out, seemingly dead, but with an ear always listening for the mouse's scratching. Not asleep on the work bench. He had given that up. As the inactivity of Dubhlinn had preyed on him he had become more and more restless. He realized that the thatched roof over the bench, built to offer some protection to the work surface, and overbuilt like nearly everything that came from Jokul's hands, was easily strong enough to hold him.

He had crawled up there a few nights before, created something like a nest in the thatch, a bed invisible from the ground below, which was why Jokul had not flown into a rage that Starri had done that. He found some degree of comfort in his perch, hidden, looking out and down at the world at night. He was an eagle, his eyes scanning the distance for prey.

They came in the late hours, the dead hours, when the drunkard was passed out, the early riser still abed, lovers asleep after the night's activities. That last had been Thorgrim, Starri realized, the last sounds before the deep quiet had settled over the longphort. The hours of least vigilance. It was when Starri tended to be at his most alert.

He heard them coming long before he could see them, despite his eagle perch. Soft deerskin shoes on the plank road, the muted sounds of weapons thumping on legs as they walked. They were trying to be quiet and succeeding. Had there been any ambient sound at all, anything beyond the odd frog or owl, then he might have missed the sounds. Most men would not have heard them no matter how quiet the night, but Starri's hearing was acute beyond all normal measure, as it often was, he had found, with men who were quite insane.

He moved slowly, silently, because he forgot that others did not hear the way he heard. He peeked up over the edge of the thatch. He could see the glow of a torch as the group of men came up the plank road, but the men themselves were hidden behind the clustered houses. There had to be ten of them at least, he imagined, based on the sound of their footfalls. He was motionless in the thatch, and all but invisible from the ground, as he saw them emerge beyond the nearest house. They stopped and looked around. They spoke softly, so soft that even Starri could hear nothing beyond murmurs.

I know you, he thought. *Sweyn and Svein. Of Hedeby. Come to get a better price for your swords? I can just imagine.*

Sweyn held the torch and seemed to be in charge. He pointed at Jokul's house, muttered some words to the others, and they stepped silently through the gate and moved along the side of the building. Starri could feel his nerves popping and flashing like a pitch pine log tossed on a blazing fire.

Eleven. He counted eleven of them. Inside the house were Thorgrim and Harald. Jokul, too, who had the size, but Starri did not know if he could fight. And there was himself. Almost three to one odds. Starri did not much like those numbers. If Sweyn had brought a few more with him, it would have been better, a better fight, but they had who they had.

The Danes were being less stealthy as they moved along the path, as if their merely arriving at the house was enough to ensure victory. They approached in a line, Svein leading, Sweyn behind him with the torch. Starri reached down and grabbed up his battle ax and short sword. Sweyn and Svein were lost from view around the edge of the house, but he heard one of them trying the latch of the door.

That will wake them, Starri thought. Even as carnally sated as he knew both Harald and Thorgrim to be, he figured they would not sleep through that. He crept up to the edge of his nest in the roof. So many of them, their backs turned toward him. What a surprise he would make, flinging himself on them like a bird of prey. He felt giddy with anticipation.

And then he stopped. He remembered. Thorgrim Night Wolf. Starri had decided that he had to try and be more like the Night Wolf. He had to think. Where Starri Deathless would charge in, weapons moving, Thorgrim would have already thought five moves ahead, would have anticipated outcomes, made plans. Even if Thorgrim did not do that on a conscious level, even if he did not even understand that he did it, Starri did. Starri had already learned from Thorgrim that real fighting was done with the head, not with the arms. And he vowed to do the same.

So what do I do? Starri thought, and just as the words formed in his head, Svein's foot slammed against the door to Jokul's house. Starri could hear the wooden bar groan, the metal squeal, a shout of surprise from within.

What do I do? The words seemed to be screaming in Starri's brain. Every muscle and sinew in him shouted for him to leap from the roof and have at it. The last two men in line would have been dead before they knew he was there, the next two might live a few seconds more. It had all been so simple before he had vowed to think things through.

Another kick at the door, more rending wood. He heard Jokul bellow, heard steel hit steel. *All right, all right, all right…* They were outnumbered, and the Danes might have more men coming. *All right…we need more men….* he admitted to himself, a grudging admission.

Starri looked around. There were no more men. He knew enough of Dubh-linn by then to know that the mere sound of a household in a death struggle would not bring the neighbors running. It was too frequent an event, and the Norsemen kept their own council.

The light from the torch seemed to go out and Starri knew they were inside and he felt his arms and legs twitching. *Oh, let Hel and the trolls have this thinking nonsense!* He was about to leap down from the roof and launch himself into the fray when he saw a face, a small face, peering out from the doorway of the neighboring house. Starri recognized him as the youngest son of the family there, a curious boy; he often spent time watching Jokul work. He and Starri had spoken on many occasions.

Starri climbed down from the roof, moving fast and sure like a squirrel. The fight inside was fully joined. He could hear shouting, steel hitting steel. He could smell blood.

"Egil! Egil!" he said in a loud whisper, amazed that he had recalled the boy's name.

Egil emerged from the shadows, wary, half asleep, and approached the wattle fence that separated their properties. "Yes? What's happening?"

"A little fight, nothing of consequence." Starri leaned on the fence, trying to look casual and not alarm the boy. "Now, do you know my fellow, Nordwall? The Swede?"

"Nordwall the Short? The crazy one?"

"Yes, that's him…." From inside Jokul's house, a scream, the clang of weapons, the sound of a body hitting the floor. Starri turned back to Egil. Wariness had turned to fright. "Nordwall will be up in the mead hall," he continued. "Run up there and tell him I need him here, him and the others, quick as ever they can be."

Egil looked confused, a bit bewildered. He glanced at Jokul's house again, the growing sound of the fight, then back into his own house where all remained quiet.

"Your parents would want you to help, I'm sure," Starri said. "See here…." He slipped a gold armband off his arm. It was a simple design, a snake swallowing its own tail. He handed it to Egil. "Show this to Nordwall so he knows it's really me who has sent for him. Then the band shall be yours."

Egil's eyes went wide. It was an absurd price to pay for so simple an errand, but Starri cared little for such things as gold and silver. Egil snatched the armband from his fingers, nodded his understanding, and bolted like a rabbit into the dark.

Starri straightened, proud of his clever maneuvers. *I can be a thinking sort as well,* he thought. From inside the smith's house he heard a roar he took to be Jokul, then Thorgrim's voice, muffled but distinct, shouting, "Jokul, damn it, stand clear!" and Jokul's roar turned to death rage and Starri knew it was time to act. He thought of the door but it seemed an impossible distance away, and besides, surprise was one of those tools that thinking types used. He had learned that from Thorgrim.

And that was enough of thinking. In front of him, fifteen feet away, he could see the dark, square shape of the shuttered window. He knew the shutters, knew the latches well enough to judge their strength, and he was sure they were not strong enough to hold him back.

The berserker scream built in his throat, undulated in the air, built in proportion to the building speed with which he ran at the near wall. Battle ax in his left hand, short sword in his right, his scream was at full volume as he launched himself off with his right leg and hit the shutters square with both feet. He felt just a hint of resistance before they blew out under the impact and his momentum carried him straight through the opening and into the room beyond.

He might have landed on his feet, a neat trick, but he came down on what he guessed was a body, dead or knocked cold, and it threw his balance off. Instead of trying to remain upright he let his momentum carry him forward, tumbled head first, rolled on his shoulder and came up standing, crouched and ready to fight. The room was like a painting, everyone there frozen in surprise at his sudden appearance, but Starri was not surprised and he slashed at the nearest man with his short sword and that man screamed and dropped and the spell was shattered.

Harald was against the wall and Starri saw him push himself off and slam his bulky frame into the man in front of him, knocking him off balance and taking an awkward swing, but the man deflected the blow and leapt back, more fight in him.

Starri swiveled around. Thorgrim was fighting two men and Starri could see the blood running down his side. He pounced at the nearest, but the man had seen him coming, ducked quick, beneath Starri's swinging ax, lashed at Starri with his sword, a blow Starri turned aside. There was screaming now, not men's screams, but women's, a sound mostly foreign to Starri's ear.

The man in front of Starri straightened, grinned, actually grinned, and came at Starri with sword held ready. Starri took a step back. His heel hit something and he stumbled and the man swung as Starri's chest presented itself, but Starri was going down and the blade swept past. Then Starri was flat on his back and looking at the great bulk of Jokul the smith, over whom he had stumbled. He looked up. The Dane was there, sword raised, a two fisted grip that promised to cleave Starri in two. The grin was still on his lips, and Starri aimed for it as he threw the battle ax with a practiced twist of his wrist, saw the weapon turn once in the air and embed itself in the man's face.

There was a great bustling around, commotion, shouting. A woman screamed and the scream was cut short. The torch that Sweyn held fell to the floor, plunging the upper half of the room into darkness, illuminating the men strewn lifeless or dying around the room. Starri scrambled to his feet. Thorgrim was still engaged with the second man and Starri could see that his wound and the prolonged fight were telling on his strength.

Harald was still holding his own.

Starri leapt across Jokul's body, drawing back the short sword, but the man saw him coming, ducked, backed off, and then raced for the door, a move so unexpected that Starri and Thorgrim just watched him go. Right on his heels, the man who had been fighting Harald also dashed through the door and into the night.

A moment before, the room had been a noisy, shouting, clanging chaos, but now it was silent, the only real sound the gasping breath of the three men left standing. They bent nearly double, sucking in air. The coppery smell of blood was all around them. The flickering light of the torch, illuminating the room from the floor up, made the scene look even weirder than it was.

Then Harald straightened, jerked erect as if startled from sleep. His eyes were wide. He dropped his sword and raced across the room, snatched the torch from the floor. He moved to the far end of the room. Furs and blankets were mounded against the wall. A woman's body lay in shadow. Harald rolled her over and in the light they could see it was Almaith, though whether she was dead or knocked out they did not know. Harald pushed the furs aside, then tossed them aside, then straightened and looked desperately around.

"Brigit!" he shouted.

Chapter Twenty-Six

[A] race of pagans…will carry you into bondage from your own lands and will offer you up to their own gods.
9th Century Irish Prophecy

The thumping brought her around, the thumping and the motion and the pain. Quite a lot of pain. Her body was wracked with it. It was the first thing of which she became aware.

The next was that she was upside down and having a very hard time breathing. But she still did not know where she was. She opened her eyes. The night was all but black, but there was light enough for her to see feet and legs below her, a muddy plank road. She was draped over a man's shoulder. Brigit nic Máel Sechnaill was being carried off by heathen fin gall.

Her head was pounding, her thoughts disorganized, but she could recall the fight now, remembered Almaith cracking one of the bastard's head open with an iron spit, herself swinging and missing with the ax. She recalled seeing the big fist coming around at the side of her head, the frozen terror of it, her inability to move. And that was it. There was no more.

She turned her head sideways, left and right. There were four other men that she could see, moving in a tight bunch, moving toward what she believed was the waterfront where the ships were anchored or pulled up on the beach. That was not good.

No boats… she thought vaguely. *Can't let them get me on a boat…* Once they took her beyond the horizon, there was no telling what fate might befall her. She would never be heard from again. That was the thing about boats.

She balled her hand into a fist and pounded on the back of her abductor's thigh, the only place she could reach, but it seemed to have no effect. The blows felt weak and ineffectual. The man carrying her seemed not even to notice.

Damn it, damn it… She could not form a clear thought, with the thumping and jostling and gasping for breath. She let herself go limp, hoping it would make her more difficult to carry, hoping it would make the motion better, give her a chance to think.

It did not help.

The man over whose shoulder she was draped yelled something, shouted out into the dark. Brigit could not understand the words, but the tone was very much that of an order, an order, given no doubt, to men aboard a nearby ship. Orders to take up the oars. Orders to carry her off to sea.

She felt a new surge of panic and started pounding again on the man's legs, but her effort was no more effective than it had been the first time. She thought she felt the pace of the men quicken a bit. She heard another voice, from off in the distance. The man aboard the ship no doubt, reporting that all was ready.

But no. The voice was from behind them, from the direction they had come. She strained to hear. Far off, faint, but there. And the voice was one she knew.

"Brigit! Brigit!"

Harald!

The man carrying her heard it, too. He stopped short, barked an order to the men around him and they stopped as well. Together they all turned to look back up the plank road over which they had come. Brigit twisted sideways so she could see, too. It was dark, but there was a moon behind the clouds and it gave off light enough that she could see the little band of men coming after her. She could recognize Harald's broad, powerful form.

She had come to Dubh-linn with no thought beyond using him for her purposes. She had forgotten how very good looking he was. She had forgotten about his unshakable loyalty and strength. But in the short time that they had been reunited, she had been reminded of all those things, and the unfathomable attraction she had to him, the very thing that had led her into all this trouble. And once again she had been weak, and had welcomed him into her bed.

Loyalty and strength. That was Harald, at his core. And just then, seeing him charging down the plank road, calling her name, she had never been more grateful for those qualities.

"Harald! Harald! Here! I'm here!" she shouted and for her effort took a heel blow to the head. She could taste blood in her mouth, but she was willing to risk another kick if it meant increasing her chances of Harald's rescuing her. She opened her mouth to yell again but the man carrying her spun back toward the river and shouted another order in his ugly, guttural Norse language. He began to run, and the men around him ran, too.

No, no, no, no! Brigit thought. If they reached the ship before Harald reached her then she was lost. If they took her to sea, she did not think she would live to the next sunset.

Once again she pounded on the man's legs, but the proximity of rescue was clearing her mind. She abandoned that useless effort and craned her neck to look around. She could see the man running beside her, at least from the waist down. She could see his sword bouncing against his leg as he ran.

Sword… The bastard carrying her must have a sword as well. They all did. She twisted around the other way, an awkward and difficult movement, and half curled her body up at the waist. Her abdominal muscles burned from the effort, but her eyes fell on what she was looking for - the hilt of the man's sword jutting above his belt.

The man had been walking fast before, now he was running, and the jarring and bouncing was much worse than it had been. Brigit reached up with her right hand, snatched at the hilt and missed as the man's footfalls nearly knocked the breath from her. She reached again. It was so close. Inch by inch she moved her hand, tried to hold it steady against the bouncing. She could hear Harald, still calling for her, getting closer.

And in that instant the man to their left saw what she was about. He shouted, reached for her, and she lunged for the hilt. She felt her fingers wrap around the leather binding and she pulled it toward her. The sheath of the sword flipped forward like some kind of battering ram as Brigit struggled to pull the blade free.

The man beside her grabbed her arm and tried to pry her fingers from the sword. As he did, the one carrying her realized that something was going on, and he twisted around to see what it was, pulling the sword from the man's hands. With a twist of her body and a grunt of effort Brigit drew the sword clear of the sheath. The blade thumped on the road as she tried to hold it up at that odd angle. The men had stopped running. They were shouting in their foreign tongue.

Brigit, still draped over her abductor's shoulder, could see only the plank road as it swept by and the feet of the man who was carrying her. He was twisting side to side, trying to see what she was doing. Another set of feet appeared, hands reaching for her, and she slashed awkwardly at them. She tried to slash at the feet of the man carrying her, but the sword was too long and the position too awkward and she could do little more than bounce the blade off his leggings.

Slashing was a failure, so she grabbed the hilt with both hands and drew it up, then stabbed down at his heels as if she was trying to spear a fish. That worked. The point of the blade skipped off his calves and caught his shoe and she rammed it home, feeling the metal lodge in flesh and bone.

The man howled and turned again and Brigit pulled the sword free and stuck the blade between his legs. She had a thought to swing it up at his crotch, but before she could even try, his legs became tangled with the weapon and he staggered. He tried to catch himself, but between his lacerated foot and the blade between his legs and the weight of Brigit on his shoulder he could not maintain his balance. Brigit felt him going over and she braced herself. She was on his right shoulder, and as luck would have it he came down on his left, so that rather than falling on her, her hip came down on his head as they landed in a heap on the plank road.

Brigit could feel the edge of the man's helmet dig into her side as they hit the ground. The man grunted and Brigit rolled off and, miraculously, kept hold of the sword as she scrambled to her feet. She had never had any real training with weapons, as would be expected, save for sparring with wooden swords as a child with her father and the other men at Tara, but she was no stranger to the feel and use of a blade. She held it with two hands to make up for her lack of strength, and backed away slowly from the others.

She could see confusion in their eyes. The situation was changing fast, and the man who had been leading them was still sprawled out on the road, and barely moving. Then one drew his sword, and then the others did, four swords flashing out and held ready.

The man to her left took a tentative step toward her, sword leading. With a grunt of pain and exertion Brigit swung her blade in an arc, connecting hard with his and knocking it aside. Then she turned and ran.

She ran as hard as she could up the plank road. She could see Thorgrim and Harald and the crazy one whose name she could not recall running toward her and she ran toward them. Behind her she heard more shouting in Norse, and then the sound of running men coming toward her. She tried to run harder, but every muscle in her body seemed to be shouting in agony and protest. She felt a hand on her arm, a powerful grip. She tried to swing the sword at him, but she could not reach back with the blade. The fingers tightened in a crushing grip. She shouted, the one word that came to her lips, the only one that might bring any comfort and hope now.

"Harald!"

Running was not Harald Thorgrimson's strength. He was powerfully built, but that also meant heavily built, and the things at which he excelled, such as fighting or building things or rowing, tended to augment his strength of arm and not his speed of foot. He was breathing hard as he raced down the road. He had seen men who seemed to glide as they ran, but he was not one of them. Every footfall jarred his body as he careened down the hill.

But he could see her now, and that drove him on. Every step he took brought him closer to her. Every step brought the swine who had taken her that much closer to being within the arc of his swinging sword.

He and Thorgrim were pretty well matched for speed, but Thorgrim was blown from the fight and wounded and was struggling to keep up.

Starri Deathless was fast, and though he was just a few feet ahead, Harald had the distinct impression he was holding back, trying to not entirely outpace his companions.

Head jarring, heaving for breath, Harald tried to see what was happening. Five men, one carrying Brigit, making for the docks. They had stopped, just for a moment, on hearing the pursuit. But they were running again, and pulling away. Making for a ship, no doubt, and if they were able to get her aboard, get underway, then she would be lost to him.

Then, suddenly, everything changed. For no reason Harald could see, the fleeing men stopped. Brigit's hair whipped around in a wild brown tangle as the man holding her twisted left and right. And then they were down, Brigit and the man, a flailing heap on the plank road. And then Brigit was up, a sword in her hand, and running toward him.

"Harald!"

The desperation and fear in her voice was a knife to his guts. He was almost there, fifty feet, but now another of the men was grabbing her by the arm and pulling her back.

"Starri!" Harald shouted as best he could, heaving for breath, "Stop them, I beg you!"

Starri nodded and shot ahead, bounding down the road with deer-like strides, as Harald had thought he could. Ax and short sword in his hand, he let go with his berserker scream as he closed the distance. Harald could see the men freeze in place, could see swords and shields and axes held ready, the men braced like sailors holding tight as a massive wave rolls down on their ship.

The man holding Brigit seemed to expect Starri to stop and fight, not an unreasonable thought, but that was not the berserker's approach at all. Starri came in with his ax making a great circle in front of him, catching the man's sword and knocking it aside. He launched himself off the road and came at the Dane feet first, seemed to literally climb up the front of the man. Harald saw the man stagger and try to slash upward with his sword, but he was too slow. In a single motion Starri kicked him to the ground and used him as a vault to launch himself at the next man behind. He crashed into the man feet first, but that one had a shield and managed to get it up and take most of the impact of Starri's flight.

Starri came down on both feet, and the man with the shield staggered back but did not fall. He was able to meet Starri's ax blow with the shield and even took a slashing counterstroke with his sword, which Starri dodged. All this Harald saw as he closed the last few feet. He wanted nothing more than to take Brigit up in his arms, to wrap his strong arms around her and protect her and shield her, but he knew he could not do that until the threat of the armed men had been removed. And now the odds looked good.

Harald was still careening down hill, his stride less of a run than a controlled and prolonged fall. It was clear enough to him that he would not be able to stop in any meaningful way, so he did not. He set his eyes on the man to the right of where Starri and the other were fighting. He was waiting, sword and shield at the ready, and Harald charged straight at him. He came in swinging as Starri had done, knocked the man's sword aside, twisted, and hit his shield full force with his right shoulder, slamming into him with all the power behind fourteen stone of bone and muscle running full tilt downhill.

The impact effectively stopped Harald, who stumbled a few steps more but remained upright. The man with the shield flew back, his feet coming higher than his head as he lifted clean off the ground and came down again five feet from where he stood. He was still rolling when Harald recovered his step, raced over, put a foot on his shield and finished him, though from the angle of his head Harald wondered if the fall had not done him first.

Thorgrim and Starri were still fighting, but their adversaries were backing away. In a moment they would be running – Harald had seen that often enough to know the signs. He turned and looked back up the road. Brigit was there, the sword still in her hands, but drooping, as if it was suddenly too heavy for her to lift. She looked frightened and relieved and grateful all at once, and Harald felt the overwhelming urge to go to her and hold her. And then he heard the sound of the men coming up from the river.

He turned back. He saw torches and the fire glinting off helmets and swords and spear tips. They were moving fast. Ten or fifteen men. The rest of the company from the ship to which they were taking Brigit. Harald felt his heart sink, his stomach turn. So close. They had fought against such odds, had chased the sons of whores down to the water, had taken Brigit back in the final moment.

And now these bastards would take her in the end, and he and Thorgrim and Starri would die.

He turned his back on the advancing company and raced back to Brigit's side. He wrapped his arms around her and kissed her, and despite her shock and pain she kissed him back. Then he grabbed her shoulders and spun her around.

"Run!" he said in a harsh whisper, in the Irish he had learned from Almaith. "Run! There!" He pointed to a dark place, a narrow space between two houses. He and Thorgrim and Starri might be able to hold the rest off long enough for her to lose herself in the narrow streets and alleys of the longphort.

"No…" she said, but she did not sound very sure.

"Run!" he said again and gave her a little push, then turned to face the new threat. They were maybe thirty feet away, weapons drawn, spreading out in a semicircle as they advanced. The one Thorgrim had been fighting was sprawled out on the ground, and Thorgrim had found a shield somewhere and was making his stand against the advancing hoard.

I should have thought to grab that fellow's shield, Harald thought, recalling the man he had bowled over. *Too late…* Thorgrim was looking wary, his eyes everywhere, taking little steps back as the rest came on.

Starri Deathless, on the other hand, was grinning, grinning wide, and spinning his ax in his hand. His eyes were sweeping over the advancing warriors like a hungry man presented with an expansive feast and not sure where to start. He was nodding slightly to himself, and dancing from one foot to the other.

An odd quiet fell over the scene as the armed men closed with each other. The men from the ship may have felt the odds were much in their favor, but Harald imagined the limp bodies strewn around the plank road gave them pause. They would take their time, advance with caution.

Then from the dark behind them, the quiet was split by a howl, an animal howl, like a wolf, but worse than that, a high-pitched, yelping, corkscrewing sound that made Harald jump and sent a chill through him. The howl was joined by another, and then another. Harald shifted his gaze fast, back and forth, not sure where the greater threat lay.

He glanced over at Starri. The berserker also wore a confused look, and then Harald saw realization cross his face. His grin disappeared and he shouted, "No! No, no, no, no, no!"

Harald turned to face this new threat. Anything that struck fear in Starri Deathless was not something he wanted at his back. Into the light from the torches, running, leaping, screaming, came a shirtless Nordwall the Short at the head of ten fellow berserkers, most similarly dressed, some more casual. Their weapons flashed in the light. They came down the plank road like a flash flood, parted around Harald, around Thorgrim, around Starri and crashed over the Danes arrayed for a fight, and the Danes went down before them like dried reeds.

Chapter Twenty-Seven

Vikings will come across the sea,
they will mingle among the men of Ireland
there will be an abbot from among them
over every church
Berchán, Irish Prophet

Father Finnian was four days riding from Dubh-linn to Glendalough, more than thirty miles of muddy tracks called roads, rolling hills, thick woods through which he had to all but cut a path. He heard wolves often enough, but they kept their distance. Sometimes he could see the ocean from the high headlands, and he liked that.

There was a town on the coast, which the Irish called Cill Mhantáin. It was prosperous and growing, for the same reason that any other Irish town was prosperous and growing, and that was because the Northmen had taken it and turned it into a genuine trading port. The Northmen called it Vík-ló. But Finnian's brief stay in Dubh-linn had given him his fill of the Northmen and he had no wish to go there, and soon his path took him inland, onto higher ground, skirting the mountains to the west.

The horse he rode had been borrowed from a wealthy farmer whose land he had crossed a few miles south of Dubh-linn. The farmer's compound consisted of two goodly ringforts, one to enclose his home and sundry outbuildings, the other to house his animals. The man had two dozen cows and three horses, an abundance worthy of one of the more prosperous of the *rí túaithe.* Finnian suggested that the farmer might show his gratitude for the blessings the Lord had rained down on him by lending one of the horses to aid him, Finnian, in doing the Lord's work. Explained that way, the farmer seemed willing enough to comply.

When Finnian thought back on it, however, he had to admit that *willing* was not exactly the right word. *Grudging* might be closer to it. And despite Finnian's celebrating mass in his home, the man was equally grudging when it came to giving up the prodigious amount of meat, cheese, soft white bread, cakes, fresh vegetables, fruit and wine that he, Finnian, told the farmer he would need for the trip. But give he did.

Finnian assured the farmer that he would return the horse on the way back, if he could. And with that he was off, meeting with driving rain that same day. His horse, the sorriest of the three in the farmer's stable, plodded unhappily through the mud, the burden it carried on its back growing ever heavier as Finnian's robes were soaked through and through.

It was sometime after dark when the two of them, Finnian and the horse, came upon a decrepit little hovel set back from the road, a man and his wife living there with three young children of indeterminate gender. Finnian knocked and was allowed in. He bowed and introduced himself. The five in the house looked at him wide-eyed, fearful and suspicious. They seemed to take it for a near certainly he would kill them all.

Introductions over, Finnian pulled out the sack containing the food the farmer had given him and served the family what was beyond question the finest meal they had ever eaten in their hardscrabble lives. Soon after, they all went to sleep, though Finnian was quite certain one or another of them remained awake all night, keeping an eye on him.

The next morning he celebrated mass as the sun was coming up, consecrating some of the farmer's fine white bread as the host. He doubted that these people had received the Lord more than half a dozen times in their lives, and never with bread like that. The family was grateful, he could see that, and more comfortable with his presence, but still they never stopped looking at him as if he was a druid of old who might transubstantiate all of them into newts or some such creature.

And so it went for the next few nights, with families who rarely saw a stranger trying to make sense of this odd priest who rode up to their door, offering blessings, holy mass and food that seemed too good to be of this world. In the end he wondered how many tales he had spawned, to be passed down through the generations, intimate family legends of how St. Patrick himself had once appeared at the family's door.

It was late on the fourth day, well after dark, when he urged his weary horse through the gate in the stone wall surrounding the monastery at Glendalough. He found the stable boy, asleep in the straw, woke him and gave him half a loaf of bread and a large, shapeless lump of cheese. The boy's eyes went wide and his tongue all but fell out of his mouth. It was probably more food than he had ever had for himself in his life, and it bought a considerable level of care for Finnian's plodding but faithful horse.

That done, Finnian made his way into the monastery, and before removing his wet robes spent half an hour in the chapel, giving thanks for his safe delivery there. He asked the Lord for guidance, because the Lord knew that he would need guidance, and lots of it, to negotiate the epic debacle that was taking place at Tara. He had come to Glendalough to see the abbot. He did not think much guidance would be coming from that quarter.

He met with the abbot after morning prayers, in the room that he used in the front of the church, to the west of the altar. The church was small, but stone built with a small, round tower jutting from the roof. The abbot was seated behind a heavy oak table; the same place Finnian had last seen him, which was a little more than a year before. Indeed, it looked as if the abbot had not moved from his place in all that time.

"Father Finnian," he said. He was writing, the tip of his white quill making circles in the air, the black ink forming into tight little letters on the vellum parchment. He did not look up. He was very thin, very pale. He looked weary. Just as he had the year before.

At length he put down the pen and swung his face up to Finnian. He waved with his fingers toward a chair and Finnian sat. "You are well, I trust, my Lord Abbot?"

The abbot grunted. "You trust I'm well? It's four hundred years since dear Patrick and Palladius brought the Irish out of the darkness and I'm not certain the half of them know the difference between a priest and a druid. But yes, I am as well as might be expected. Though I imagine it is not good news that brings you here."

"No. Máel Sechnaill mac Ruanaid was killed before he could solidify his control over the Three Kingdoms. I wrote you about that."

The abbot nodded, which seemed to take great effort. Finnian waited for him to say something, but he did not, so Finnian continued. "Flann mac Conaing has taken the throne, but he is not secure enough yet to invoke the authority of the crown."

The abbot nodded again. Finnian waited again. Finally the abbot spoke. "Flann mac Conaing? Has he a claim to the throne?"

"He could make one. He is kin to Máel Sechnaill. But Brigit nic Máel Sechnaill still lives, and she has better claim."

"Then why is she not ruling there?"

"Flann has secured the support of the *rí túaithe*. He means to hold the throne. Or more to the point, his sister, Morrigan, means to see him hold the throne."

"And Brigit? What of her? Will they murder her?"

"They might well try. She was married…" Finnian thought back. *Three weeks ago? Four? Was that possible?* It seemed months, many months before. But no. "She was married last month. She…it seems she killed her husband. As he was trying to kill her. She has left Tara now."

"And gone where?"

"She has gone to Dubh-linn."

The abbot stared at Finnian with his red, watery eyes, a gaze that seemed to be boring into Finnian's brain and searching for his complicity in all this.

"How do you know she had gone to Dubh-linn?" he asked.

"Because I took her there."

The abbot nodded, as if Finnian had simply confirmed a thing he already knew. "And why, pray, did you do that?"

"Because she would have gone anyway. And she probably would have been killed en route."

"And why…" the abbot said next, drawing the words out, "would she go to Dubh-linn?"

"I do not know for certainty," Finnian said, which was the truth, though he only said it in hope of softening the news that would follow. "But I suspect she is planning to raise an army of the fin gall to help her get the throne of Tara back."

"Why do you not know for certainty? Were you not there?"

"I saw her safely there and then left. Dubh-linn is not a place for a man of God."

The abbot remained silent and motionless, and after half a minute he slowly closed his eyes. Finnian wondered if he might be praying. It would be a reasonable response. As the minutes passed, Finnian began to wonder if the abbot had actually died right there, but at length he opened his eyes again.

"The Crown of the Three Kingdoms was not made by Christian hands, you know," he began at last. "It was fashioned by the pagans and it carries the curse of Satan on it. Its temptation is too great for mortal men."

Finnian nodded.

"You have done a good job, Father Finnian, for the most part. You have kept an eye on things as I instructed, did what you could, though the Dear Lord knows there is little a poor man of God can do to influence these…people. Now you must return to Tara, get the Crown back. With Máel Sechnaill dead there is no one we can trust with it."

"And how many men shall I have with me? How many men-at-arms?"

"'Men-at-arms'? Oh, you choose to make merry with me, I see. You shall have none, Father Finnian. Just yourself and your God-given wits. I trust that will be sufficient."

"With God's grace it will be."

"Bring the crown back here. Throw it in the sea. Feed it to wolves, I don't care, I should be pleased to be rid of the damned thing."

"Wolves. Yes, my Lord Abbot."

"Just see that these madmen stop fighting over it, trying to use it to their own ends. May the Lord's blessings go with you, Finnian." As he spoke those last words, the abbot picked up his pen and continued his writing, the interview over. Finnian stood, nodded and left. He had considered telling the abbot that he was all but certain Brigit was with child, though whose child, he did not know, but he figured the old cleric had had enough for one day.

Chapter Twenty-Eight

West over water I fared,
bearing poetry's waves to the shore
of the war god's heart;
my course was set.
Egil's Saga

The second time the longship *Black Raven* cleared the mouth of the Liffey, Thorgrim Night Wolf was at the helm. That was quite different from the first time, months before, when the fleet had stood out for the raid on Cloyne. Then, Thorgrim had been little more than a passenger, a man with no set place, an extra sword. But not this time.

Arinbjorn had come to him, asking that he fill the role of second in command. The offer had taken Thorgrim by surprise, for more reasons than one. He had thought Arinbjorn resented him and regarded him with fear and suspicion. He had thought that Bolli Thorvaldsson had been given the dubious honor of being Arinbjorn's second. From the way Bolli had been sulking around for the past week, shooting black looks at Thorgrim whenever their eyes met, muttering to himself, yelling at anyone who got in his way, Thorgrim guessed that Bolli had thought the same thing.

But no, Arinbjorn insisted that he needed a man of Thorgrim's experience and Thorgrim, feeling that every man there would be safer if Arinbjorn was kept under close scrutiny, agreed.

Ornolf Hrafnsson, Thorgrim's father in law, had laughed out loud when Thorgrim told him this news. "Ha! You are a fool, Thorgrim! I am proud to say you are no blood kin of mine, and sorry only that my beautiful daughter was such a poor judge of men!"

The old man was holding court in the mead hall, as was his custom, sitting in his familiar seat near the back of the big open room, an oak table spread before him. It was midafternoon, and few men were there, and Thorgrim was alone at Ornolf's table.

Thorgrim took a long drink, set the cup down, nodded his head. He did not say anything. He knew that it would be pointless, that Ornolf would mock any defense he might offer. For Ornolf, mocking was like urinating, and he would continue to let it flow until he was emptied out, and then he would settle down and be sensible again.

And it was worth waiting for that, because when he wished to be, Ornolf the Restless could be sensible indeed. People dismissed the jarl as a drunken, debauched old fool, and that was a mistake. He might indeed be drunken, debauched and old, but he was no fool. It was not by accident that he had become as wealthy and powerful as he was.

"Think, Thorgrim, think. Why would such a slippery eel as Arinbjorn want you to be his second in command?"

"I *have* thought about it, you may believe that or not. I reckon he wants me there to keep him from getting into any real trouble, and to get him out of it when he does."

"Because you are such a genius? You are such a brilliant warrior? No other man on this raid is capable of rendering such service?"

Thorgrim shrugged. "Arinbjorn wants this to be his raid. He is putting it together and he has not asked Hoskuld Iron-skull or any of the jarls more powerful than him to come along. He wants no challenge to his leadership."

"*You* are a challenge to his leadership."

"Me? Everything I have is back at Vik, as you well know. I have nothing here but a small part of my share of the plunder from Cloyne. Before that, I had only what Arinbjorn was willing to lend me. I am unique among the host here at Dubh-linn. A leader with experience but no money and no men to lead. I am uniquely suited for Arinbjorn's needs."

Ornolf grunted and took a long pull from his cup. "You make sense, for once in your life. But Arinbjorn owes you money, does he not?"

"He said he would pay Harald and me three shares from the take at Cloyne but he has not. But I've told him I don't want the silver. I want only passage home to Vik."

"Yes, but the offer has been made, and that means he's given his word, and he can't back out of it without dishonor. I would not go into battle with men who owe me money. Too much chance for mischief. That is why I have grown so old and wise."

"And why I shall die a young fool," Thorgrim said.

"Too late for you to die young," Ornolf pointed out. "But not for my grandson, and he is the one who has my concern."

There was wisdom in Ornolf's words. He thought the old man was right to be skeptical. Thorgrim, in fact, had considerable doubts of his own, all of which he had no choice but ignore as he threw himself into the preparations for the raid. The raid on Tara. The attempt on Brigit's life had sealed it like a blood oath.

The commander of the Danes, the one named Sweyn, had survived the fight. He had been knocked unconscious when Brigit fell on his head and so missed being run through by Thorgrim or Starri. When the rest fled, he had been left behind, thought by his comrades to be dead. It was not hard to get him to talk. He had no particular loyalty to those who hired him, and since they were unlikely to pay him for his failure, he felt no need to suffer torture to keep their secrets.

The Danes were from Vík-ló. Hired by an Irishman who called himself Donnel and who said he spoke for very powerful people in the kingdom of Brega. Sweyn had assured Donnel he did not give a rat's ass who he spoke for, or where they came from. He was interested only in the silver they offered, which was plentiful, with more to come.

Their instructions were to sail to Dubh-linn and take the girl. They were told where she would be found. Take her and bring her to Vík-ló for Donnel to confirm their having done the job, and then they would be paid the balance of their due. As to the girl, she was theirs to do with as they wished. The only stipulation was that if she were to remain in Ireland, she could not remain alive.

Brigit insisted that this was confirmation of everything that she had told them. Harald agreed entirely, though Thorgrim suspected that Harald's reasoning was clouded by more primal urges.

Arinbjorn, however, felt as Harald did. If the people ruling Tara thought Brigit was so dangerous that it was worth paying to have her killed, then the tales she told must be true. As he discussed it with Thorgrim - the weak defenses of Tara, the lack of men-at-arms, the people rallying to Brigit - Thorgrim could see Arinbjorn's face light up with the vision of easy wealth and martial glory. There would be no talking him out of this. He would go to Tara and Harald would, too, and Thorgrim could not send his son into that maelstrom while he stayed safe behind.

The prospect of launching a full-scale attack on the seat of the high king of Brega had Starri behaving like a wolf with the taste of blood in its mouth, and more in the offing. He did not concur with any of Thorgrim's objections. That did not ease Thorgrim's mind. If Starri considered a plan to be sound and reasonable, then it probably was a seriously bad idea. That truth aside, Thorgrim understood from the first that he would be joining them, and taking his place in front of the shieldwall.

And so, a week and a day after the berserkers had overrun the Danes and taken prisoner those few they had not killed, after Starri, once again denied entrance to Valhalla even while standing at the very gates, had collapsed to the ground, weeping bitterly, Thorgrim found himself gripping the *Black Raven*'s hard oak tiller and looking down the length of a very unhappy ship.

Brigit insisted from the outset that she would be coming along and no one seemed terribly inclined to argue. As they prepared to get underway, Harald had, of course, been very solicitous of her. He had seen to her comfort, setting her up with a sea chest on which to sit, furs to protect her against the ocean wind. He had apparently been under the impression that he would be allowed to remain with her and continue to comfort her during the voyage up the coast, but Arinbjorn had other ideas. He had sent Harald forward to take his place at an oar, and Harald had obeyed, grudgingly, while Arinbjorn inserted himself into the role of Brigit's protector.

Thorgrim kept his own council. It was not his affair, and Harald would not have welcomed his interference.

Now, as the longship pulled for open water, Arinbjorn was standing beside Brigit, communicating as best he could with the few words of Irish he seemed to have picked up recently. Brigit in turn was nodding, paying just enough attention to avoid appearing rude, and doing only a tolerable job of hiding her discomfort. Harald, working his oar, was shooting dark looks aft at the little scene.

Bolli Thorvaldsson, now third in command, was standing in the bow, looking out to sea. He had spent much of the past week pissing on Thorgrim's good name, until half the ship's company now looked on Thorgrim as Loki's bastard spawn. Word got back to Thorgrim, in some cases carried by his friends, in other cases by people hoping to see Thorgrim run Iron-tooth through Bolli's guts.

Thorgrim considered doing just that, calling Bolli to answer for the things he had been saying, challenging him, and killing him. But that would only serve to solidify the divisions among the crew, those loyal to Bolli, those loyal to him. What's more, he was still aching from the fight with the Danes, and his wound, though it was healing, was painful and tight and he did not seem able to muster the energy for the task.

And then, at last, they were underway, with the green headlands at the mouth of the river falling away as the *Black Raven* cleared the estuary. Thorgrim felt the motion of the ship underfoot change as the first of the ocean rollers lifted the bow and moved along under her. It was a moment he loved, the moment when the embrace of land, and all its considerations, was left astern, and the new motion of the ship signaled a new element, and the simplicity of man, ship and sea.

Thorgrim half turned and looked astern, larboard and starboard. There were two other longships with them, Hrolleif the Stout's *Serpent* and another of similar size named *Dragon Slayer*, commanded by a man named Ingolf who was from Borgund. All told about one hundred and sixty Norse warriors. Not a particularly large force, but if Brigit was at all right in her assessment, enough to overwhelm the weak defenses of Tara.

The headlands fell astern and Thorgrim felt the fresh breeze stirring in his beard and lifting the hair that lay across his tunic. Instinctively he turned his head into it, his face like a weathervane gauging the direction from which it blew. Southwest, a good quarter to set sail for the course they would be steering, but he kept his mouth shut.

It was about five minutes later that Arinbjorn apparently gave up trying to communicate whatever it was he was trying to convey to Brigit, stood up, looked astern and then up at the weather vane at the mast head. "Thorgrim," he said, the cheerful note in his voice just a little off key, "this seems a fair breeze for setting sail. What say you?"

"As fair as we could want," Thorgrim agreed.

"Right, then," Arinbjorn said, and in a louder voice called, "Let's get some hands to set sail!"

At that, Starri Deathless, who had been sitting against the starboard side just aft of the aftermost rowing station, leapt to his feet. No one ever asked Starri to man an oar. No one thought he could keep his attention focused long enough to maintain the monotonous rhythm, and once an inattentive oarsman like Starri fell out of sync, then all was chaos. But when it came to working in the rigging, no one was Starri's equal.

The long yard was lowered and swung fore and aft, the position it generally was in when the ship was under oars. Before anyone else had even registered Arinbjorn's order, Starri was up on the yard, straddling it as if he was riding a horse and casting off the line that held the sail tightly lashed to the spar. He was already a third done before Bolli grudgingly ambled aft, took the tail end of the halyard off its cleat and laid it along the deck. On either side of the ship, the men maintained their steady pull of the oars and waited for the next order to come.

Starri finished with the lashings and hopped back down to the deck. "Ship oars! Take up the halyard!" Arinbjorn called and the men gratefully ran their long oars in, laid them on the rack on which they were stored, and moved quickly to their various stations. Thorgrim could feel the motion of the ship change as the forward momentum dropped away. A dozen men grabbed on to the halyard, ready to haul the heavy yard and sail up the mast. Others took up the braces that would swing the yard athwart ships, ninety degrees to the ship's centerline. Still others took up the tacks and sheets that would hold the lower corners of the sail down at the most efficient angle to the wind.

"Haul away!" Arinbjorn called next and the dozen men on the halyard pulled, the yard jerked up the mast a couple of feet and the sail began to billow out. Hand over hand, in the same steady rhythm they employed on the oars, the men heaved away on the halyard and the yard made its slow climb aloft.

And then it stopped.

"Haul away!" Arinbjorn called again and the men pulled, the strain clear on their faces, but the yard did not move. Thorgrim ran his eyes aloft. A stray bit of rope, frayed and twisting in the breeze, was jutting from the sheave in the mast through which the halyard passed.

"Halyard's jammed!" Thorgrim called. Arinbjorn squinted aloft, but before he could give any orders, Starri leapt into the rigging with the agility and frenetic energy of a squirrel. He pulled himself aloft hand over hand, his legs wrapped around the shroud up which he was climbing. *Black Raven* was all but stopped in the water now and starting to roll more heavily in the swell, but that seemed to have no effect on Starri's effort. He reached the masthead as quickly as if there had been a ladder to that spot, and with his legs and one arm still wrapped around the shroud he jerked on the stray bit of rope, then jerked again and it came free. He looked down at Arinbjorn and waved the bit of rope at him.

"Haul away!" Arinbjorn called and the men took up their rhythmic pull once again and the yard resumed its steady climb up the mast. The men at the braces swung it amidships as it went up. The sail flogged and snapped and Starri remained where he was, ostensibly to clear away any other jam that might occur but mostly, Thorgrim suspected, because he liked being up there.

At last the yard reached its highest point and Starri climbed onto it and settled himself into his self-appointed job as lookout. The men at the sheets hauled the lines aft and made them secure and the big square sail, checkered red and white, filled and bellied out and the ship gathered momentum once again. Even more than when she was under oars, the vessel felt like a living thing, a powerful but slightly skittish horse, a creature that was dangerous to those who could not control her, swift and agile to those who could.

Thorgrim breathed deep. He loved this, loved it with all his heart. The salt water, the tiller in his hand, the roll, pitch and yaw of the vessel, the pull of the sail. He and Brigit were alone on the little deck aft, and he thought to smile at her and nod to let her know all was well. He doubted she had been to sea very often, if ever. He pulled his eyes from the luff of the sail and looked her way, just in time to see her toss off the fur blanket, swivel around and vomit noisily over the side.

Chapter Twenty-Nine

[M]en with black keen spears
will blight the fruits of noble rule.
Irish Poem of Prophesy
attributed to Bec mac Dé

It was a fine day, sunny, warm, the wind soft from the southwest, the ugly wet spring yielding at last to summer. The sun was just a few hours from setting and the windows of the monastery were still open. The breeze drifted through the big room, which had formerly served as the sacristy but which Flann mac Conaing and Morrigan now used as their apartments from which they ran the affairs of Tara, and Brega.

Through the open windows came the sounds of the ongoing effort to rebuild the royal residence. Morrigan had been pushing the builders and laborers hard. The debris had been cleared, the new walls framed in, staves set, withies rove and ready for the fresh daub. Through the window, Morrigan could hear the creaking of ropes and blocks, the shouting of the carpenters as they raised the new roof beams in place. A couple of weeks more and the big house would be ready to receive its occupants again. Just a couple of weeks, but Morrigan genuinely did not know if she would still be alive by then.

Patrick was standing in front of her, shifting nervously though trying not to. She was not looking at him, however, but out the window, off at the hills in the distance, but she was not really seeing them, either. She had a vague thought that if she made Patrick repeat what he had just said, perhaps this time she would hear some hopeful note she had missed the first time. She wished it was Donnel here and not Patrick. Donnel was older, and steadier. But of course that was why she had sent him to Vík-ló, where she needed the utmost discretion.

She turned back to Patrick, and she tried to make her voice calm, even soothing. "Tell me again, Patrick, my dear…Segene said what, exactly?" Segene mac Ruarcc was the *rí túaithe* of a decent track of land to the west of

Tara, the fifth such minor noble to whom Morrigan had sent requesting men-at-arms to come to the defense of the throne of the high king.

"Segene says he regrets he does not have the men to send. He says he has been much plagued with the theft of his cattle by the neighboring lord and he must employ his men in putting stop to that."

No, Morrigan thought, *it did not sound any better the second time.*

"Very well, Patrick," she said. "Go get something to eat, you look as if you might fall over."

Patrick nodded and smiled his relief, relief at the thought of food and at getting out from under Morrigan's gaze. "Thank you, ma'am," he said, gave a half bow and left the room as swiftly as decorum would allow.

Morrigan let her head slump down. She considered praying for the Lord's help, but she was not sure the Lord was of a mind to help her. With the things she had done, and ordered others to do, she had been walking a cliff's edge with the solid ground of righteousness on one side and the chasm of wickedness on the other. In her mind she had not gone over the edge, but she understood that God might not employ such subtle distinctions as she did.

The door opened again and Morrigan knew it was Flann, because Flann was the only one who could open that door without knocking on it first. She looked up. Her brother was a tall man, well made, strong and handsome, a bit of grey hair showing at the temples. But he was looking tired as of late, his face thinner than she remembered, and drawn. The weight of rule did not sit so easy on him as it did on other men.

To her surprise, Flann slammed the door shut, the iron hinges screaming, the heavy oak boards hitting the frame with a thunder clap. Morrigan jumped in her seat. Her brother did not look tired. He looked angry, and that took her aback. "Brother, what news?" she said, her tone as light as she could make it.

"I hear things, various things. What of you? What news from Dubh-linn?"

"No more than the last I told you. Brigit is staying at the house of the blacksmith, Jokul. She has apparently taken up with the fin gall. I know no more than that."

"You know no more than that?"

"That's what I said. What is troubling you, brother?"

Flann crossed the room and looked out the window. His back was to Morrigan and he did not speak. The silence hung like smoke in the room. *If we turn on one another, we are finished,* Morrigan thought.

Flann wheeled around and looked at her. "You are not the only one who hears things from Dubh-linn. I have heard tales. A great row at the blacksmith's house. Men dead. A girl carried off."

Morrigan shook her head. "I know nothing of any of this," she said, which was true. She was waiting on some word from Donnel, but thus far, nothing. She had heard from Almaith, by way of her messengers who moved like ghosts through the longphort, that Brigit still lived but that the fin gall had no interest in sacking Tara. That, however, did not fit with other bits of news she heard, that an expedition was fitting out, with Tara as its object. She did not know what to believe, so, for the sake of caution, she had called for the *rí túaithe* to send men, which they had not.

"Well?" Flann demanded. "What do you know of this? Any of this?"

Morrigan shook her head, held up her hands. "Nothing, brother. I know nothing."

Flann took a step toward her, the most menacing move he had made in her direction in all their lives. "I will ask you this, sister, and you will tell me the truth. Did you order Brigit killed?"

"No," Morrigan stammered.

"The truth!"

"No! By the love of God, I swear to you I did not order her killed!" She had ordered Donnel to find men to take her, bring her to him at Vík-ló, and then do what they would with her. She had never directly ordered anyone to kill Brigit nic Máel Sechnaill.

That was one of those instances in which she feared that God, and likely Flann, might not parse the matter quite as finely as she did.

But Flann seemed to relax a bit at her vehement denial, as if all he needed was to hear her protest her innocence. He was older than she was, but had not seen, as she had, how grotesquely wicked people could be, and it made him proportionally more naïve than she.

"Well, I thank God things have not come to that," Flann said. "Though they may come to worse yet."

"Worse? What do you mean?"

Flann did not answer her directly. "What have you heard of late about the fin gall launching a raid on Tara?" he asked.

"I have heard that they would, and I have heard that they won't. I don't know what to believe."

Flann nodded. "You've sent word to the *rí túaithe* for them to send men-at-arms?"

"I have. And they won't do it. Each has his excuse, and it's usually that he must go fight his neighbor, but I say they are just cowards to a man."

Flann sighed and began to pace, not a good sign with Flann. "They are not cowards, and you know it. They won't fight to defend my place on the throne of Tara. If Brigit nic Máel Sechnaill sat on the throne, they would come."

"That's not true. They'll be cautious, see how this all plays out."

"What of Leinster? Have you had word from Ruarc mac Brain at Líamhain?"

"His wife passed away not long ago and he is in mourning. He will not bring his army here."

Flann stopped his pacing and looked at Morrigan directly. "Did you hear this from Ruarc mac Brain? Did you send word to him, at all?" The accusatory tone was back in his voice, but Morrigan had found her footing again and was ready to stand up to him.

"No, I did not send word," she said. "We do not want the Uí Dúnchada of Leinster meddling in our affairs. If Ruarc mac Brain marches an army here, he will not leave, he'll take the throne for himself."

"You would rather see the Northmen sack Tara than take the chance that Ruarc mac Brain will usurp the throne?"

"We don't need Ruarc mac Brain or any of the swine from Leinster. The *rí túaithe* will rally to your banner. I have made it known that Brigit has gone over to the fin gall, and once they see that's true, they will stand by you."

"It would be nice to think so, but in truth I don't think they will get the chance. Because, sister, I just had word. Word from the coast. Three longships were spotted at the mouth of the Boyne. That would be more than one hundred fin gall warriors. One hundred and fifty, I wouldn't doubt. And we have maybe seventy men that we can put under arms, and they are never a match for the Northmen."

Morrigan's mouth fell open. She felt as if she had been punched in the stomach. "Three longships? And you think they are coming here?" It was a stupid question, and she asked it just because she had to ask something. Of course they were coming there. If they had entered the Boyne, there was no other place they might reasonably be going.

She had expected that the fin gall would come, but she did not expect them to come so soon. A few more weeks, another month for those drunken fools to organize a raiding party. She had counted on that. But they were here now, and the main gate to Tara was wide open to them.

"Yes, of course they are coming here," Flann said. "Where else? And how we will fight them, I don't know."

Morrigan did not know either. But even as Flann said the words, she was flooded with a great determination. She would not stand idly by and see Tara snatched from her. There had been too much suffering in her life, and she had committed too many sins already to get where she was, just to see all her work undone by the filthy foreign swine, to see her brother killed and herself once again condemned to the slow death of a thrall.

"We will fight them, brother, and we will beat them," she said. "And if we can't beat them by force of arms we'll beat them by other means.

Because honestly, Flann, if we can't outwit these stupid, pagan animals, then we do not deserve to sit on the throne of the high king."

Chapter Thirty

The snake-lair's goddess,
her weeping eyes swollen
with bitter fruit, looks at me,
Odin's craftsman, for consolation
Gisli Sursson's Saga

The wind held fair from the mouth of the Liffey to the mouth of the Boyne, thirty-five miles north along the coast. The three longships kept close company, their square sails filled and holding shape in the steady wind, their long, narrow hulls heeling slightly to starboard, the seas curling around their bows and swirling aft in long, white wakes. They looked like serpents and they moved like gulls, and the heavily armed men aboard them took pleasure in the day, the rare, fine weather, and the free ride the wind provided.

Thorgrim, too, tried to enjoy the time underway. Tried, and failed. Under most circumstances he could not have asked for better. But the hostility and anger that ran through the crew and swirled and tugged like ocean currents was too distracting and worrisome for him to find any pleasure in wind and sea.

Freed from his oar, Harald came aft to sit with Brigit. This left Arinbjorn visibly displeased, and made Thorgrim realize that he might have designs beyond taking the wealth of Tara and sailing for Norway a rich and successful man. Designs that might include a lovely Irish princess. The gods alone knew how elaborate a fantasy Arinbjorn had woven around himself and Brigit. It was certainly clear that Arinbjorn did not want Harald to sit by the girl, but Arinbjorn did not speak Irish, and Harald did, to a surprising degree, and that made Harald the girl's natural companion.

But Brigit just as clearly did not wish to have a companion of any description. From the moment *Black Raven* had hit the open water she had been vomiting over the side until there was nothing left in her to vomit, and then she had slumped miserably against the strakes, wrapped in furs, her face going from pink to white to a slight greenish shade. Harald tried his best to comfort her, until Thorgrim could stand no more and called him aft.

"Son," he said in a soft voice, "I've seen this sea sickness often enough, and I can tell you, Brigit just wants to be left alone."

Harald glanced back at her. He had never been to sea in the company of women, only men who did not get sea sick or, if they did, quickly decided that comb making or blacksmithing was a trade more to their liking. "Are you sure?" he asked. "Women take it well when you tend to them, don't they?"

"Yes, they usually do. But not when they are sea sick."

"Should I offer her food? There's salt fish in the tub forward."

"If you do, she will tear your throat out with her bare hands. Or would, if she had the strength."

At that Harald nodded and seemed to accept what Thorgrim said, which was becoming increasingly rare. He squatted down beside Brigit and said something, too soft for Thorgrim to hear, not that he would have understood the words in any event. Brigit nodded, never opening her eyes, and Harald stood and sat on the aftermost sea chest, where he could remain close but not too close.

Arinbjorn, who had been standing on the after deck just forward of the tiller, striking the pose of a man in complete command of those below him, made a grunting noise but said nothing.

The little fleet cleared the headland to the north of Dubh-linn Bay and two hours later passed to the west of Lambay Island, where the first raid on Irish soil by Norsemen gone a'viking had taken place more than fifty years before. Thorgrim surveyed the island, its steep cliffs and sloping green meadows, as the *Black Raven* slipped past its shore. He could see the ruins of the monastery that had once stood there, abandoned after being sacked again and again by his own people.

Fifty years… he mused. Half a century the Northmen had been raiding that country. And now they had come to stay. They were building towns, taking sides in Irish wars, as he was now. How long before all of Ireland was half Irish, half Norse? If Brigit was telling the truth, then his own grandchild would be just that.

The breeze continued steady as they made northing, bearing off to the northwest, bracing the yards around for a larboard tack and rigging out the beiti-asses, the spars that held the corner of the sails down and forward when sailing close-hauled. The afternoon was fading into evening when they finally spotted the low banks at the mouth of the River Boyne.

For all his high talk about Thorgrim's experience and leadership, Arinbjorn did not really welcome any of Thorgrim's advice. That much Thorgrim had concluded long before. Thorgrim could not, however, resist suggesting a trick that might buy them another ten hours of surprise. Some men might be sent ashore in the boat that *Dragon Slayer* was towing astern. They could station themselves on the beach while the three ships sailed right past the mouth of the river, as if they never intended to enter the Boyne at all. Then the men on the beach would light a fire to guide them back.

They were too far from shore to see if they were being watched, but Thorgrim did not doubt they were. Any confusion they might sew in the enemy's mind could only help.

Arinbjorn pretended to consider this idea. In the end he rejected it, as Thorgrim knew he would. Unnecessary effort for a raid that would meet with little resistance, he explained with an air of patience. It might discourage the men, if they thought there was a need for such trickery. Besides, Brigit could not tolerate being underway for even a minute more than was necessary.

Thorgrim nodded. "Very well," he said. He had done his duty, given the advice he thought he should give. Arinbjorn had shown him the courtesy of explaining all the reason for why he was rejecting it. All the reasons save for the real one, which was that some personal demon drove him to reject any idea that Thorgrim had to offer.

The sun was an hour from the horizon when they lowered their yards, lashed the sails to them, then broke out the oars and set in for the long pull against the current. They covered about half a mile up the river before settling their bows into the mud banks of the southern shore. They ran lines over the water to a stand to oaks that grew there and made the ships fast. They posted watch and settled in for the night.

With the ship now steady underfoot, Brigit was much improved. She stood and shed the furs and stretched her arms. She even accepted a bowl of food from Arinbjorn and made a bold attempt at eating. Once the ship was secure, Harald came aft to see if there was anything he could do for her. But Arinbjorn was already doing everything he could think to do, and he did not care to have Harald around.

Thorgrim, leaning on the side of the ship just forward of the tiller, watched with amusement as their little power struggle played out. Arinbjorn seemed reluctant to simply order Harald forward, perhaps thinking that Brigit might want him nearby, as he was the only one who spoke Irish. Harald, in turn, was taking every opportunity to do so, conversing with Brigit and flaunting his growing fluency.

This foolish dance went on for some time before Thorgrim decided he would put an end to it. "Arinbjorn," he said, "it's only fitting the princess should have some privacy, don't you think? There's some spare sailcloth forward, we could rig her up a sort of tent easy enough. Right aft, here."

Arinbjorn pretended to consider this, but Thorgrim knew that he would have a hard time finding a reason to not follow this suggestion. Then

Harald rattled something off to Brigit in the odd tongue of the Irish and Brigit seemed to brighten and she nodded her head. "Brigit would be most pleased with a tent," Harald announced, and that settled it, to Arinbjorn's visible irritation.

The men fell to the work with a will. They lashed oars in place to form a solid wedge-shaped framework and draped the spare sailcloth over that, lashing it tight to the oars. Half an hour later there was a respectable tent standing on the after deck, its floor lined with furs and blankets, a fitting berth for a princess aboard a longship. With nods of thanks, a smile, and an unmistakable look of relief, Brigit bid her good nights and ducked into the new-made shelter.

For a moment Harald remained at the tent's entrance, and Thorgrim could see he was debated whether he should join her inside. He had, after all, been sharing a bed with her at Jokul's house, or so Thorgrim was sure he was thinking.

He's as big as a man, but he still has no more awareness than a boy, Thorgrim thought. He caught Harald's eye and gave him a barely perceptible shake of the head, and with the subtlest of gestures pointed forward with his chin. It was all he needed. He and Harald had been through enough together that they could speak volumes to one another with the slightest of gestures. And Harald, though he did not look happy, nodded as well and ambled off forward.

That night Thorgrim dreamt of wolves. He was part of a pack, and they were set upon from all sides. They were in thick woods. They could not see, but their noses alerted them to enemies in every quarter. They ran, but they did not know to where they were running. They waited to be attacked but they did not know from which direction it would come. They were wolves but they did not have the power and strength of their kind.

He woke in a sweat. There was a hint of dawn to the east, a barely perceptible lighting along the horizon. He stood and stretched his muscles then prowled up the deck, checking that all was well, trying to shake off the disturbing vestiges of his dream. He woke a couple of the men and told them they were on duty to cook breakfast. They made to protest, but one look at Thorgrim's face in the dim light of the predawn convinced them to shut their mouths and get to work.

Two hours later the men had eaten, the ships were ready to get underway, and Brigit had emerged from her tent looking considerably better than she had the day before. The food, the steady deck underfoot, the proximity to Tara, and the possibility that these men under Arinbjorn's command would take it back for her, had all worked their magic. Arinbjorn hovered and Harald shot dirty looks aft from his rowing station, but once they were underway, Brigit chose to lean against the side of the ship just a few feet forward of where Thorgrim held the tiller. She smiled at him and nodded and Thorgrim nodded back. He was the only one there who had shown not the slightest interest in her, and he guessed that she felt safe in his company for just that reason.

Women… he thought.

It was fifteen miles up the river, a slow crawl with the current working against them. With more men than rowing stations, the hands at the oars could be relieved on a regular basis. Thorgrim was happy for that. He did not want the men's strength drained getting up the river, because battle waited for them at the other end, or so he hoped. It would be a grave mistake to not attack that very day, to give the enemy another night to fortify and gather men. He hoped Arinbjorn would come to the same conclusion, so he was careful not to suggest it.

The river was familiar. Thorgrim and Ornolf and Harald and the others who had come with them from Vik had come up that way half a year before. Their ambitions had not been so great then. They hoped only to rescue Harald and their other shipmates who had been taken hostage. They had nearly all died in the trying.

But Thorgrim had a good memory for waterways and he recognized the various twists in the river, recalled where he had found sandbars and snags and back eddies, and so with *Black Raven* in the lead, the three ships made good way. On the shore he caught glimpses of horsemen trying to remain unseen in the stands of trees. He thought back to Cloyne, the horsemen on the ridge. Tara would be fully alerted to their coming, but there was nothing for it. Surprise was an impossibility when you had five leagues of river and another of land to traverse before arriving at the point of attack.

It was midafternoon when they reached the spot where Thorgrim recalled having tied up before. Brigit, realizing where they were, became more animated, pointing up the river and saying something in her undecipherable Irish tongue. Thorgrim called Harald aft because he knew Arinbjorn never would.

"What does Brigit say?"

Harald said a few words to her, and she replied, speaking slower this time. "She says there is a good place to anchor half a mile up the river, and a road from the landing that leads straight to Tara."

They continued on, and just as Brigit had said, the river widened out as it bent around, with the current carving a deep place along the western shore. There were pilings driven into the water and posts on the banks and Thorgrim guessed that the Irish made considerable use of the river. They had seen no vessels that day, but that was no surprise. On the appearance of the Norsemen, any Irish boats would have scattered like sheep before wolves.

They tied the longships to the pilings and posts, rigged gangplanks to the shore. Arinbjorn stepped off first, followed by Hrolleif the Stout and Ingolf who commanded *Dragon Slayer*, and behind them their men, carrying the shields they had unshipped from the sides of the vessels, and swords and axes and spears. They assembled on shore and the men pulled on mail shirts or padded tunics, iron helmets, strapped sword belts around their waists.

The leaders walked a dozen yards down the road, which was relatively wide and blessedly mud free, and conferred. Brigit joined them, and Harald as translator. Thorgrim was there as well, though he had no intention of adding anything beyond a nodded agreement to whatever the others came up with. Arinbjorn asked Bolli to join them, which he did, as grudgingly as he did everything else.

Brigit spoke first. Harald translated. "Tara is about five miles down this road, the Princess says."

The others turned and looked down the road, as if they might see it from there. "What does she think we'll meet for opposition?" Hrolleif asked. Harald translated, listened to Brigit's reply, asked for clarification, apparently, received it, nodded and translated back.

"She says…I didn't follow all of it…but she says she does not believe any of the…I think she means the minor jarls who have land nearby, she does not think any of them will come to the aide of Tara. She doubts there are more than one hundred men-at-arms. The walls are tall and the gates strong, but they will not be able to stand long against us."

The others nodded at this. "I say we move out now, fast as we can," said Ingolf. "Time is our enemy, not theirs."

The others nodded again, as did Thorgrim, who was coming to like Ingolf. They agreed to that plan, turned and headed back to where the rest of the men waited, now in fighting array. Arinbjorn explained the plan, if such it could be called, which was simply to march on Tara and take it by whatever means presented itself. And that was fine for the Northmen, who asked for nothing more complicated than a straight out fight.

And that was doubly true for Starri Deathless and his band of berserkers, Nordwall the short and the others. While most of the men had donned more gear in preparation for the fight, the berserkers had stripped down, removing tunics, belts, in general everything but leggings. Some wore fur capes, some wore helmets. They were well armed, the long-handled battle ax being the most common weapon of choice. They huddled to one side and made peculiar noises as if they were taking part in the worship of some long-forgotten god.

"Starri!" Thorgrim called out. "Starri!" At length Starri looked up from his huddle and Thorgrim waved him over. He jogged up, ax and short sword in hand. He was stripped to the waist and the arrowhead that had split itself on Thorgrim's sword at Cloyne was hanging around his neck on a leather thong.

"Yes, Night Wolf?" he said. There was a weird look in his eyes, a strange light Thorgrim had not seen before, and his gaze seemed to pass right through Thorgrim's head. Starri was there on the Banks of the Boyne, and he was off at some other place that only the berserkers knew.

"We move out. Some of Hrolleif's men are scouting ahead. Arinbjorn's men will take the lead on the march, and your berserkers follow. Stay behind them."

"Behind? Behind… Should we not lead?"

"No. We march to Tara, and when we see what we're up against we'll know how best to array ourselves. Now, pray, keep you men in order and in line."

Starri nodded. Thorgrim hoped that he really did understand, and was not just making some involuntary head movement. It was never easy to tell with Starri, and even more difficult in these circumstances. The truth was, Arinbjorn wished to control the berserkers for as long as he could, to deploy them thoughtfully and not in a manic rush, and for once Thorgrim agreed.

Half an hour after coming ashore they were moving again, tramping off down the brown earth road, moving as fast as they could without sapping their strength on the march. Their feet, either bare or shod in soft leather shoes, made a muted shuffling sound as they walked. Mail shirts jangled and weapons thumped against thighs. Sometimes men talked softly in the ranks, but mostly they were quiet. The berserkers did not speak, but occasionally one or another would make some kind of weird sound, a whimper or a growl, or he would bark like a dog.

Brigit was not allowed to join them. She had protested, her voice rising at one point and Harald struggling to translate the angry words, but none of the men thought her presence at the battle was a good idea, and in the end they won. She was left aboard *Black Raven* with a guard of twenty men and the ship was warped out into the river. That was ostensibly for her own protection, but also to see that she did not slip away. Thorgrim watched Harald as he fought with indecision: should he remain with her or join his shipmates in the fighting? In the end, the lure of battle outweighed even the charms that Brigit had to offer.

They walked for an hour. Thorgrim stayed mostly at the head of the column with Arinbjorn, though they had little enough to say to one another. Occasionally he would stop and let the men walk past in review, and his sharp eyes would search for any weakness, any man who looked afraid, any weapons not in fighting order, but he found nothing he could fault in that company. The country was mostly open, long green fields and stands of wood here and there. They could see smoke rising in the distance, and they guessed it came from Tara. Cooking fires, forges turning out spear and arrow heads.

From up ahead they heard the sound of running. Arinbjorn held up a hand and the column stopped and Thorgrim drew his sword. Ottar Long-legs, who had been sent ahead with the scouts, appeared around the bend in the road and pulled huffing to a stop.

"Tara lies but a mile ahead," he reported while sucking air into his lungs. "Once past this stand of trees you can see it, on a high hill across open ground."

Arinbjorn and Thorgrim waited for him to catch his breath, and Hrolleif the Stout and Ingolf joined them. "What can you see of the defenses?" Arinbjorn asked. "Are there men on the walls?"

Ottar shook his head. "None that I could see. It is a long way from the wood line to the ringfort. But it looks as if there are men on the open ground. Tents, it looked like."

Thorgrim and Arinbjorn exchanged glances, and Thorgrim wondered if Brigit had been wrong in her assumptions, or had been misleading them all along.

"Tents?" Hrolleif asked. "Men-at-arms?"

"No. They don't look to be men-at-arms."

"What then?" Arinbjorn asked. "Who are they?"

Ottar looked from Arinbjorn to the other leaders and he seemed unsure how to answer. "I don't know," he said at last. "It looked to me as if there were men, tents, banners…but no one seems to be in any formation for battle. It just…it does not look like an armed camp. And if it was, I don't know why it would be there, when they could be within the walls of Tara, fifty rods away."

At that the others nodded and took on various expressions of confusion, until Ingolf said the only sensible thing, which was, "Why don't we advance and see for ourselves?"

They moved forward again, and as Ottar had told them, once around the stand of trees they found themselves looking out over a long stretch of open ground, a field of Ireland's emerald grass broken here and there by a short hedge. The ground rose in a great, gently sloping hill and in the distance, perhaps a mile away, the great earthen ringfort of Tara, rising brown above the green. Between them and the walls of the fort, also as Ottar had described, tents, banners, men moving about. It looked more like a festival than preparations for battle.

Arinbjorn stepped to the front, turned and addressed the men. "I don't know what these Irish have in mind, but we have come to fight and we will go in fighting. We'll cross the field, and when I give the word we form a shield wall and advance that way. Thorgrim and I will be in the center, Hrolleif with your men to the west, Ingolf to the east. The berserkers in the middle with my men. Form a line!"

The men moved quickly, not a chaotic jumble but more like an elaborate dance, forming the line by their divisions, their leaders with them. It took less than two minutes, and then they were ready to go. Arinbjorn drew his sword, held it aloft and stepped off, and the Norsemen, eager for blood, ready to fight, rolled forward in his wake.

Iron-tooth was in Thorgrim's hand but he did not recall unsheathing it. He glanced to his side. Harald was there in mail shirt and helmet, his face set, determined but not frightened, and Thorgrim felt a wash of pride come over him. Harald seemed to sense that Thorgrim was looking at him and he looked back. Thorgrim smiled and to his pleasure Harald returned the smile. This was the beauty and simplicity of action. Whatever had happened before seemed meaningless when held up against the comradeship that came with facing danger together.

They marched over the soft grass, closing with Tara and with whatever awaited them outside the walls. Thorgrim squinted, trying to get a better idea of what it might be, but he could not, or more to the point, he did not believe his eyes, because what his eyes told him made no sense.

Fifty rods away, and still there was no sign of resistance or any indication that the enemy intended to fight. Thorgrim guessed there were forty or fifty men in the Irish camp, but none of them seemed even to have noticed that the Norsemen were coming. Thorgrim could hear muttering along the line and he called for quiet.

They continued on, Thorgrim expecting Arinbjorn to form up the shieldwall, but he did not. Twenty rods and Thorgrim could see what appeared to be tables.

Now a handful of people were advancing toward them. Not an armed band, no more than five or six, and they were not coming on as if they meant to fight. Thorgrim looked hard. His eyes were not what they once were, but he was all but certain that the one leading the group was a woman.

Ten rods and Arinbjorn held up his hand and the line came to a stop and they waited as the small group approached. Now Thorgrim could see that it was a woman who was leading the group toward them. He looked past her, toward the camp. But it was not a camp. It was not a shieldwall of men-at-arms, or some kind of defense of the ringfort, or a funeral party. It was a banquet.

Chapter Thirty-One

I hoodwinked those heroes,
hurling dust in their eyes.
The Saga of the Confederates

Thorgrim Night Wolf watched the small group advance toward them. He leaned toward Harald, just slightly, and said, *sotto voce*, "If they don't speak our language, you'll have to translate. If they do, then keep it a secret that you can speak theirs."

Harald nodded. Thorgrim kept his eyes on the woman. There was something familiar about her, but she was too far away yet to recognize. Arinbjorn took a step forward, and though he did not invite them to do so, Hrolleif and Ingolf left their men and joined him. Thorgrim turned to Harald and jerked his head in their direction, and he and Harald stepped up to join the other leaders. Thorgrim knew they might need Harald. More to the point, he wanted to know what was going on. He wanted to be an irritant to Arinbjorn.

Now Thorgrim could better make out the people walking toward them. A man and a woman, dressed well. Not dressed like royalty, but close. There would be no mistaking them for the scullery help. Behind them marched four soldiers, but they were lightly armed with shields and spears, as if they were more for decoration than combat.

They were just twenty feet away when the realization struck Thorgrim, struck him hard, like a slap to the face.

Morrigan!

He looked again. It was she, for certain. When last he had seen her, she had been an escaped thrall from Dubh-linn, filthy and beaten down. She had made his own escape possible, and that of Ornolf, Harald and the rest. The Crown. Harald held hostage, that had been her doing. So much of Thorgrim's brief time in Ireland was wrapped up in his memory of Morrigan.

She stopped, five feet from Arinbjorn, and the man beside her stopped as did the soldiers. Thorgrim recognized the man as well, from the fighting they had done at Tara. A good man in a battle, he recalled, though he could not remember his name.

Morrigan ran her eyes over the assembled men she was facing. There was no hint of recognition in her face, but Thorgrim and Harald were both wearing helmets, his with a nose guard and Harald's with iron rims around the eyes, so it was no surprise she did not notice them.

"Welcome," she said. Her command of Norse was so complete that Thorgrim would on occasion forget that she was Irish. "Welcome to Tara."

It may have been the voice, it may have been the warm greeting - the last thing any of them had expected - but Thorgrim felt like he was reeling, he felt like he was intoxicated, like he was watching performers acting out some bizarre play.

That voice! Soft, yet commanding, a lilting Irish tone to the Norse words, steel wrapped in velvet. Thorgrim was back in the room in Dubh-linn that had served as their prison. Harald near death from a fever that come on the heels of a battle wound, Morrigan there with her basket of herbs and medicines, the secret compartment at the bottom where she hid the daggers.

He closed his eyes, opened them, forced himself to return to the present, unworldly as it might seem.

Morrigan was gesturing to the man who stood beside her. Tall, well made, he had the air of a man in command. Or, perhaps, the air of a man trying to appear more in command than he was.

"This is Flann mac Conaing, who rules Tara. I am his sister, Morrigan nic Conaing. My brother does not speak your language, and as you can see I do, so I will serve to translate, by your leave."

Arinbjorn looked at her, glanced side to side as if searching for an answer to this odd puzzle. Finally he waved his sword in the direction of the tents and the tables and the men loading them with food. "What's the meaning of all this?" he demanded.

Thorgrim smiled. It was quite involuntary, but he had to admire how Morrigan had created this absurd situation. He wondered if Arinbjorn was now going to start whining like a petulant child. *We came here to sack this place, and now you're trying to feed us? It's not fair!*

Morrigan turned to Flann and spoke softly. Flann replied and Morrigan turned back to Arinbjorn. "My master, Flann, says that he wishes to welcome you. You are more powerful than us, by far, and he does not wish to do battle with you."

Harald leaned close to Thorgrim and whispered in his ear. "I don't think that's what Flann said."

Thorgrim nodded slightly. It would not surprise him at all if Morrigan was making the decisions here, and the man she said was her brother was as purely ornamental as the soldiers behind them. He turned his attention back to Arinbjorn, who seemed just as flummoxed by Morrigan's answer as he had been before she tried to enlighten him.

"We have not come to feast with you," he said. "We…we will not just turn and go simply because you have laid out food for us."

Morrigan pretended to confer with Flann on this. When they were done she spoke again, and her voice carried authority enough for both her and Flann. "My brother wishes for us to speak honestly. We are not children. We know why you're here. You have come to plunder Tara. Well, the truth is, we probably can't stop you. But if we can come to an agreement, we won't try."

"Agreement?" Arinbjorn said. The confusion that Morrigan was sewing stripped the note of authority from his voice.

"We'll turn over the wealth of this place if you will take it and leave, without hurting our people, or taking any as slaves. If that's acceptable to you, please join us in the feast we've set out. If not, we'll fight to the last man. We'll lose, I shouldn't wonder, but you and your men will pay a high price for what might have been yours for free."

Arinbjorn had no answer for that. He turned to the others. "What say you?" he asked in a voice too low to be heard by Morrigan and the others.

"It's a damned trick," Hrolleif growled. "I say we kill them all, now, and take what we damned well please."

Arinbjorn nodded, a gesture Thorgrim had come to recognize. "I don't think we need be so hasty," he said. "What she says has the sound of truth. They know they can't hold us off, so it stands to reason they would want to spare their people. And by Odin, if I can achieve my ends without losing any of my men, I'll be the happier for it."

Thorgrim said nothing. He scanned the faces of the others. Hrolleif looked angry, Ingolf looked skeptical. There seemed to be something vaguely dishonorable about accepting surrender in such a way, but no one could see clearly where the dishonor lay, and until they could, Morrigan's offer made sense. No one spoke.

Arinbjorn turned back to Morrigan. "How do we know this is no trick?"

"My Lord," she said, no longer pretending she was just translating Flann's words, "you fin gall are a part of Ireland now. The days are gone when there can only be fighting between Irish and Northmen. We've laid this out," she gestured toward the tables behind, "in that spirit. My people are gathering up the treasure you've come for. We can eat, and you can take what you claim. We can get more riches, but I will not see my people butchered."

Ingolf spoke up. "You still have not told us why we should trust you."

"My brother and I will join you at the feast. So will my men, unarmed. Consider us hostages, if you must. If you think you are betrayed, you may cut our throats."

She was winning them over. Thorgrim could see that. Her poise, the strength she projected, the unshakable logic of her argument, those things were working on the others. Nor could Thorgrim see the trap he was certain was there. But he knew Morrigan, and they did not. It was time to throw her off her stride and see what happened.

Morrigan spoke again. "I have no doubt that your men…" she began and Thorgrim reached up and pulled the helmet off his head, and Harald, picking up the cue, did likewise. The movement caught Morrigan's attention. Her eyes flicked over at them. Thorgrim saw her reaction in all its parts flash across her face, fast as a bolt of lightning; confusion, recognition, shock, fear, equilibrium.

"Thorgrim," she said. "Thorgrim Night Wolf. And Harald." Her composure had returned so fast that most would have missed her initial shock. But Thorgrim had not, and he could hear that the note in her voice was a little changed now.

"Morrigan," Thorgrim said, nodding. "You have done well for yourself."

"I was a thrall to the dubh gall when we met," she said, making it clear it was the Danes, not the Norwegians, whom she had reason to despise. "But my brother has always been heir to the throne of Tara."

Really? Brigit might think differently, Thorgrim thought.

"You know this Irish bitch?" Hrolleif asked, pointing with his hedge-like beard at Morrigan. Morrigan's expression did not change.

"She helped us escape the Danes in Dubh-linn, when first we arrived there," Thorgrim explained.

"And I healed your jarl, Ornolf," Morrigan added quickly. "And Harald, who nearly died of the fever."

"And you arranged for Harald to be taken hostage."

"I did what needed to be done, as any of you would have. And Harald, I see, is fine."

"He is. Not so Giant-Bjorn and Olvir Yellowbeard who were also taken hostage. They were beaten to death."

"That," Morrigan said, "was the work of Máel Sechnaill mac Ruanaid, the last king of Tara. Not my brother Flann. Máel Sechnaill was an enemy of the fin gall. We are not."

Thorgrim smiled. *You are a smooth one, with your answers to everything*, he thought.

"Very well," Arinbjorn said in a loud voice, reasserting his authority. Most of the men there belonged to the *Black Raven*, and Hrolleif and Ingolf, in exchange for some largess, had sworn loyalty to Arinbjorn, so in the end, it was his decision alone. He turned back to Thorgrim and the rest. "We cannot show indecision here," he said in his emphatic whisper. "We must decide."

"I know this woman, Morrigan," Thorgrim said. "She speaks well, as you can see, but she's clever. Very clever. I don't think she's to be trusted."

The others made sounds of agreement, but even as the words left Thorgrim's mouth he realized his mistake. If he suggested a thing, Arinbjorn was bound to do the opposite. Proof of that mistake came with the next words Arinbjorn spoke.

"I hear truth in her words, and reckon myself to be a decent judge of such things. We'll accept their offer, and if there are any tricks, then, Hrolleif, we will indeed kill them all."

"But what of Brigit?" Harald protested, though in that company he had no right to speak at all. "We came here to restore her to the throne, that was why she sought you out."

But Arinbjorn turned even before Harald had finished, and if he had heard Harald's protests, he did not indicate as much. "Very well, Morrigan," he said. "You make your case…your brother's case…very well. If you and your men will set their arms aside and join us, then we will feast with you. On the morrow we will accept your…gifts, and if there are any tricks, or if you try to cheat us, it will go hard on you. Very hard on all of Tara."

Morrigan, recalling her role, translated this to Flann and Flann made reply, then Morrigan nodded and said, "You have made a wise choice." Thorgrim watched her close for any sign of triumph or relief or amusement, but there was nothing. Her face was a river stone, featureless and unmoving.

"Father," Harald said in a tone that was more pleading than he had heard from the boy in some time. "What of Brigit, and the throne?"

"Arinbjorn has made his decision," Thorgrim said, his voice soft, his tone final. "All we can do is see how the gods will toy with us next." Then, in a slightly more encouraging tone added, "But we will keep our eyes open, and keep a sharp lookout for any lucky chance."

"And what do we do until then? What do we do now?" Harald asked.

"We do the very thing that comes most naturally to you, son," Thorgrim said. "We eat."

Chapter Thirty-Two

"[F]ain would I see that feast;
brawls and bickering I bring the gods,
their ale I shall mix with evil."
The Flyting of Loki

It was one of the oddest feasts that Thorgrim had ever attended, perhaps the oddest ever. Everything was laid out for a grand banquet; suckling pig and lamb, bread and heaping bowls of butter, spring vegetables, dried fruits, porridge and honey. The mead was flowing, as was the beer and the wine. There were the hosts and the guests, and between them, mutual loathing and distrust.

For all Morrigan's high talk about Irishmen and Norsemen occupying that island in peace, it was pretty clear that the Irish regarded their guests with undisguised hatred. The Norse, in turn, looked on their hosts as pathetic and weak. For a successful party, the circumstances were not ideal.

It played out as Morrigan had promised it would, no tricks, no betrayal. But Thorgrim had some experience with the depth of Morrigan's cunning, and he kept his eyes open, his guard up. The Irishmen who joined them at the feast were the ones whom they would have met in combat if things had gone differently. By their expressions, the way they held themselves, Thorgrim guessed that they would have preferred combat, even a greatly uneven fight, to the humiliation they were suffering, feeding their enemies while others gathered up tribute to pay them to leave.

Thorgrim watched the Irish as they talked among themselves, even as he feigned a lack of interest. He was looking for some sign of treachery, but saw instead impotent anger. He could not understand the words that they muttered to one another, but he did not need to understand them to know their nature.

Even the one who Morrigan introduced as her brother, the one called Flann, did not look happy about this arrangement. At first Thorgrim had dismissed him as some effete pretender to the throne, but a closer look told him that was wrong. Flann had the look of strength about him, strength of arm, strength of leadership. Not the strength of ultimate command, like one who wears a crown easily, but the strength of one used to leading men, and that included leading them in battle. Thorgrim recalled seeing this Flann on the field when they had last fought the warriors of Tara. Such a man would not be happy about the capitulation Morrigan had arranged, and indeed Flann did not look happy.

The rest of the Northmen seemed oblivious to the angry looks and muttering directed at them. The food was good and plentiful and they tore into it with gusto. The berserkers in particular, denied the climax of battle, vented their frustration on the food, as if they could sate their blood lust with gluttony and intoxication. Which, Thorgrim realized, they just might be able to do.

He moved among the men, skirted the tables, whispered in their ears. "Don't drink yourself to insensibility," he warned. "Keep your wits about you." It occurred to him that Morrigan might intend to let the Norsemen drink themselves into oblivion and then fall on them. It was the only treachery he could envision.

But if that was her plan, it was not a very good one. It was damned hard to get a Northman so drunk he could not fight, and if he were only partially insensible with drink, then he would fight harder still. Morrigan had been many years among them, she had to have known as much.

So the men of Arinbjorn's hird, and Hrolleif's and Ingolf's, drank deep but they did not drink until they fell to the ground, and they ate well of all that was put in front of them, and they largely ignored their Irish hosts whom they had already dismissed as weaklings. Thorgrim ate little. Between his suspicion-driven vigilance, his worries over Harald, his concern that his men not drink themselves to unconsciousness, he all but forgot about eating, save for a half a loaf of bread which he snatched up and gnawed at as he patrolled.

Night fell and the feast wound down and the Irish retreated back into the walls of Tara, leaving only a dozen slaves behind to clean up the mess and pack away that which had not been consumed. Morrigan called to the men in command, waved her arm toward the tents. There were a dozen or so, and blankets and furs, though the night was not cold.

"These tents are for your use," she said to Arinbjorn and the others. "I fear we do not have enough for all your men, but we have blankets and such for them to make their beds where they will."

"Arinbjorn," Hrolleif said, louder than necessary. "My men will take the first watch. I have posted a dozen near to the gate of this place, and have more watching the north side, and still others encircling the camp."

Good man, Thorgrim thought. Hrolleif did not want to inform Arinbjorn of what he had done so much as he wanted Morrigan and Flann to know that they would not be taken by surprise.

"A wise move, Hrolleif," Morrigan said. "But not necessary. You shall see. Flann and I bid you good night. We will talk more in the morning." With that, she and Flann made shallow bows, and with their small, lightly armed bodyguard, they turned and strolled back to the gate of Tara.

It was later that evening, after the rest had gone off to sleep, after he had fended off Harald's questions about what would become of Brigit, that Thorgrim replayed the night in his mind. *So very odd…* The Irish on one side of the tables, the Norsemen on the other. Eating together, with all that hatred hanging like smoke between them. Each to his own preferences. The Irish drank mostly beer, the Northmen mead. Even the meat; the lamb was on the Irish side, the suckling pigs, so loved by the Norse, on their side, and the Irish showed no interest in it at all.

Thorgrim opened his eyes in the dark. He pictured the feast in his mind. The Irish did not touch the suckling pig. He could recall a few instances when one of his men had reached over the table and cut off a chunk of lamb, as much to provoke the Irish as from a love of that meat, but the Irish did not touch the pigs.

"Harald?" Thorgrim said. He waited. Silence. "Harald?"

At last he heard a grunt in reply.

"Harald, do the Irish not eat pig?" he asked. Harald was as close to an authority on the ways of the Irish as he was going to find in Arinbjorn's hird.

There was another pause, long enough that Thorgrim thought Harald had fallen back asleep, but at length he answered. "They eat it like anyone does, I think." The tone of his voice was not right, and it was not sleep affecting it.

"What's wrong?" Thorgrim asked. He sat up.

"I don't know… It's my stomach."

"Did you eat too much?" Thorgrim asked, and then thought, *stupid question…there is not enough food in Ireland for Harald to eat too much.*

"No…" Harald replied, sounding more miserable than Thorgrim had heard him sound since he was a child. "But what I did eat, I think I'm about to lose…."

And as he said that, another sound reached Thorgrim's ears, from beyond the tent, from out in the dark. Retching. Groaning. Those sounds were not foreign to a Norse encampment, but not like this. Not so many.

Thorgrim was out of his bed, Iron-tooth in hand, and out through the flaps of the tent. The night was cool and there was a dampness in the air, and the thick smell of earth and grass such as he had come to associate with

Ireland. The sky was unusually clear, the pinpoint fire of stars casting a soft light over the camp.

It was light enough to see by, and Thorgrim did not like what he saw. Men were staggering out of their tents, crawling from under piles of furs. Men were doubled over and vomiting up the prodigious meal they had eaten. Men were laying curled on the ground, hands clamped on their stomachs, groaning in agony.

Starri Deathless had dragged a heap of furs over by Thorgrim's tent and Thorgrim could just make out his head jutting out from under the pile. He knelt down beside him. "Starri? Starri, how goes it with you?"

Starri looked up at him, his eyes half closed, his mouth hanging open. "I am run through the gut, Night Wolf," he whispered. "Run through from within…"

Thorgrim stood. "Oh, you damnable bitch!" he cried out into the night, but his real fury was directed not at Morrigan but himself. "Idiot, idiot!" he shouted next. If Starri Deathless met his end in this manner, lying helpless as a baby, and not with a sword in his hand, Thorgrim swore he would have her head on a pike. But how he would ever live with himself, for the part he played in this, he did not know.

He headed off though the line of tents, calling out as he did, "Turn out! Turn out! To arms!" He was met with a chorus of groans. No one moved, save for those staggering aimlessly, bent nearly double.

There was a candle burning in Arinbjorn's tent, as Thorgrim had come to expect, and a guard outside, as was also Arinbjorn's custom. The guard, however, was down on one knee, swaying and trying to stay upright as Thorgrim approached, sword in hand. Such a thing would surely have warranted a challenge, but now the guard did no more than raise one hand, make a sound that might have been a word, and fall sideways onto the ground. Thorgrim pushed the tent flap aside and stepped inside.

Arinbjorn had his camp bed with him and he was sitting on the edge, bent over, his weight supported by one arm. He looked up as Thorgrim burst in. His eyes were wide, his face white and waxy in the light of the single candle. Thorgrim could see beads of sweat on his forehead, a sheen on his cheeks.

"You…" was all that Arinbjorn managed to say. Only his eyes moved, shifting from Thorgrim's face to his sword and back.

"We are betrayed," Thorgrim said. "Morrigan. I told you she was not to be trusted."

But Arinbjorn just stared at him, as if he had not heard. At last he spoke, and his voice was weak. "What have you done? Are you here to kill me now?"

"What?" Thorgrim said. "Kill you?" He followed Arinbjorn's eyes down to Iron-tooth. "No! Not me. Morrigan. You are poisoned. If that doesn't kill you, her men will."

"How are you…how are you not sick?" Arinbjorn asked. Fear and suspicion seemed to be giving him strength.

"The food was poisoned, but I didn't eat. See here, we must rally those who can still fight. Maybe we can get back to the ships…"

Arinbjorn forced himself up until he was no longer leaning on his arm. "Who told you not to eat? How did you know?"

Thorgrim looked into Arinbjorn's wide, watery eyes, and through the man's pain and the waves of nausea he saw only hatred and suspicion. Arinbjorn was lost to him. Even if Arinbjorn had been in his right mind, in full health, Thorgrim understood there was no trust there, and never would be again. Something had happened. Arinbjorn may not have ever been a friend, but he had never been an enemy. Until now.

"I will do what I can," Thorgrim said. "I'll see if there are men enough to fight, if it comes to that." He turned and ducked out of the tent. The guard was lying in a pool of vomit. He was not moving.

Thorgrim strode quickly down the row of tents, hoping to find even a knot of men who could make a stand when the killers came from Tara, but he could see no one left standing.

Hrolleif, he thought. *Maybe Hrolleif still stands.* It was hard to imagine any poison, or anything else, that could fell that human oak. But which tent was his? As he looked left and right his eye caught a flare of light, off beyond the camp, a dull glow rising up from the ground. And with it a sound, a jingling sound, like a series of tiny bells. It was a sound that Thorgrim could not mistake. It was the sound of mail shirts on marching men. Men holding torches that lit up the dark. Men coming for a stricken enemy.

Thorgrim shook his head. Any idea of organizing a resistance was dismissed; futile, pointless and it probably always was.

Chapter Thirty-Three

Let the gods banish the king,
pay him for stealing my wealth,
let him incur the wrath
of Odin and the gods.
Egil's Saga

"This is a damned business," Flann said. "A damned, dishonorable business." His mail shirt was making the particular sound that mail shirts made, like small surf on a shingle beach. The two of them, Flann and Morrigan, were on top of the earthen wall that surrounded Tara. The evening breeze was lifting his long, fine hair and flicking it off to leeward.

Morrigan sighed. *Again? We discuss this again?*

The night was quiet, and by her orders there was no sound coming from within the ringfort, despite the seventy armed men standing ready to do their business once the gates were thrown open. The breeze carried on it a sound she longed to hear, a sound that would not generally have held so musical a quality to her; one hundred and fifty or so Norsemen retching and puking and falling groaning to the earth. One hundred and fifty filthy rapists, murderers and thieves feeling the full effect of dining on suckling pig, spit roasted and spiced with cowbane. It was a recipe she saved for very special guests.

"You practice your arts," Flann continued when Morrigan did not respond, "because you do not concern yourself with honor. Not the way a man thinks of honor. Honor on the field of battle, which is how we should have met them."

Morrigan pulled her eyes from the Norsemen's camp and regarded her brother in the light of the torches that flickered up from the ground below, hidden from the enemy by the walls of Tara.

Honor? she thought. *The honor of having your head on a fin gall pike? The honor of having all the women of Tara raped, the men butchered, me a thrall again, to be used like a dog by these Godless bastards?* But she did not say it, because she had said it all before and she was sick of saying it.

"Maybe you value your honor above the lives of everyone in Tara," she said instead, "but I do not. In any event, we've not murdered them. They'll live. Most of them, I should think." The cowbane, a short, hollow root that could easily be mistaken for parsley, would have been fatal if given in a sufficient dose. But that was not the intent. Instead, Morrigan had added just enough to the other spices in the rub to see their guests debilitated with nausea. Once that happened, they could be gathered up like fish in a weir, but they would not die.

It was mostly for Flann's sake that she agreed to let them live. Her brother was not at all happy about their present treachery, the false good will, the tainted food, and had agreed, in the end, because truly the only other choice was to see the Northmen visit their particular brand of horror on Tara. But Flann would not allow Morrigan to simply murder the Norsemen. His honor, absurd by Morrigan's way of thinking, could not tolerate such a thing. It was why Morrigan worried that Flann would never make a decent high king. Máel Sechnaill mac Ruanaid, she was certain, would have had no qualms about poisoning them all and watching with delight as they died in agony.

So they would make prisoners of the fin gall, and not carrion. And Morrigan knew that in some small way she was relieved by Flann's intransigence on that point. The fin gall were pagans; they were killers, cursed by God, but still the thought of simply murdering them all made Morrigan uneasy.

Despite all the wicked things that she had done, and often done and not confessed, things for which she had not been absolved, she still held out hope that she might reach heaven. It was a hope that was growing more remote as she struggled to hold onto the throne. If she caused all these men, God's creatures, supposedly, to die in agony, it would put salvation that much further out of reach. So she agreed to sicken them instead, and once sick, they would be taken prisoner. Some would be ransomed, some would be sold as slaves, but they would live, mostly.

Morrigan turned her eyes back to the fin gall camp spread out on the ground beyond the walls. It was dark and she could not see anything of the men in the camp, but the chorus of retching and groans and wails of agony had grown appreciably in the past few minutes. The timing on this had to be just right. If her men sallied forth too soon, the fin gall might still have some fight in them. If she waited too long, the Northmen might find the strength of stagger off into hiding. And then she would have to call up the hounds.

"It's time, brother," she said, softly.

Flann made a grunting noise. "Very well," he said. He turned and found the crude ladder that led down to the ground, and Morrigan followed behind. By the time she stepped off, Flann had taken his place at the head of the column of men-at-arms who stood ready to advance. These were not the lightly-armed guard that had accompanied them, just for show, when they went out to meet the invaders. These were men ready to fight, armed with swords, spears, shields, mail, helmets.

Behind them, teams of horses stood in their traces, nervously shaking their heads and stomping the earth. They were not accustomed to work at that late hour and they knew something was amiss. Hitched behind them were empty hay wagons, which would be used to haul men who could not walk. Leg irons, and leather thongs for binding wrists, were piled on the wagons' floors.

"Go!" Flann shouted, and his voice had the ring of authority that Morrigan liked to hear. This was what Flann loved, Morrigan knew, the field on which he excelled. The plotting, the maneuvering, the manipulating one against another, that was what he could not do. Between them, Flann and Morrigan, they made a fully competent ruler.

On Flann's command the big oak doors at Tara's main gate are swung open and the column moved forward, seventy pairs of feet making a dull sound on the soft ground, and with it the creak and groan of the crude wagons, the jingle of horses in their tack. Morrigan wanted to walk at the head of the column, side by side with Flann, but she knew that would never do, so she stayed back, walking beside the first of the empty wagons. It might not be her place to lead, but neither would she be left out of this affair. She knew the fin gall better than anyone at Tara, and she knew what had to be done to secure this lot.

Donnel and Patrick were waiting for her, back at the end of the column, and they fell in on either side and a few paces back as the men advanced. They, too, were armed with swords and knives and mail shirts, but they were not a part of Flann's column, not men-at-arms. They had spent most of their brief lives as sheep herders and their skill with weapons was rudimentary at best. They were Morrigan's men, and she knew well how to exploit their God-given talents.

They covered the ground quickly. The guards whom the fat, bearded one had so ostentatiously posted near the gates of the ringfort were lying on the ground, doubled over. Some had managed to crawl a little distance, but most were right where they had fallen. On Morrigan's order, their wrists were bound and they were tossed into the rearmost wagon, the first of the catch.

There was no alarm, no shouts, no sound of men taking up arms to meet them. Even the groaning and retching had dropped off, so there was little to be heard over the sound of the wagons and marching Irishmen. The smell of vomit was in the air.

Flann brought the column to a halt. "Very well, you men," he called back to the troops. "Round them up. Drag them here if need be and we'll manacle them and bind them." There was a tinge of disgust in his voice.

Morrigan hurried to the front of the column, Donnel and Patrick keeping pace. "Flann! Thorgrim must be secured quickly, he is a danger. Please, may I have four of the men-at-arms with me?"

Flann looked around, which is what he did, she knew, when he required a second to make a decision. He looked at Donnel and Patrick as if to say, *you have men, are they not enough?* But he did not say it, because he knew the two young brothers were not fighting men. "Very well. You four," he gestured to the four men directly behind them, one of whom carried a gutting torch. "You go with Morrigan. Follow her orders."

Morrigan stepped off without looking back, but she was gratified to hear the sound of the men following. Donnel moved past her and she followed him down the row of tents. He and Patrick had been among the slaves cleaning after the feast, but their work had involved watching and taking note and only pretending to clean.

Donnel stopped outside the tent that Thorgrim and Harald had occupied. Morrigan turned to the four men-at-arms behind her. "Go in here and secure any you find within," she ordered. If Thorgrim or Harald had any strength left, then taking them prisoner was a task for real soldiers.

Four swords scraped out of four sheathes and the first of the men-at-arms threw the tent flap back and plunged in, followed by the man holding the torch and then the others. Morrigan waited and listened. She heard bedding being rifled, saw the weird shadows of the men inside cast by the torch against the tent walls. Half a minute and they were out again.

"No one in there," the man with the torch reported.

Damn it, Morrigan thought. "Very well. Follow me." The seven of them, the four men-at-arms, Donnel and Patrick and Morrigan, began a sweep of the camp. They looked in each of the tents, rolled over the groaning figures of the fin gall strewn around the field and held the torches close to their faces. No Thorgrim. No Harald.

As they searched, Flann and his men-at-arms methodically rounded up the rest of the fin gall, dragging those who could not walk to the place where the banquet tables had been set up earlier, clapping leg irons on them, binding their wrists with leather cords. There was no resistance from the Northmen, not so much as a half-hearted slash with a knife, or the feeble swing of a fist. Cowbane was proving to be the most effective warrior Morrigan had ever known.

Midnight was an hour gone when Flann called for one last sweep of the camp, but no more of the fin gall were found. Any who had been in camp were now bound in the back of the wagons. The victory was bloodless, and it was complete. Or nearly so.

Morrigan grabbed up a torch and went from wagon to wagon. She looked in the face of every man there. No Thorgrim. No Harald.

"Flann," she said, her voice low, her tone urgent. "Thorgrim is not here. He's escaped somehow."

Flann shrugged. "He's one man. One more or less will make no difference."

"His son is with him. And the Lord knows how many others."

"Even if he has a dozen it makes no difference. We have all but the entire fin gall army. The other *rí túaithe* will rally to us now, now that they see we've prevailed."

Morrigan shook her head. "We cannot allow Thorgrim to remain free. He is too dangerous."

Flann looked at her, and Morrigan did not like his expression. "What is it about Thorgrim?" he asked. "Why are you worried so about one man?"

Morrigan felt her face flush at the question, and hoped the dark would hide it. She had, in a moment of weakness, given herself to Thorgrim, back aboard his ship. He had a strength that she found comforting, and she sensed a decency about him, something she would never have thought to find in a Norseman, but there it was. Thorgrim loved his son very much, she could see that he cared far more for Harald's life than he did for his own, and that told her a great deal about what sort of man he was.

And there was no denying that he was attractive. Very attractive. She remembered the thrill that had run through her when he pulled his helmet off that afternoon and she saw him again after all that time. She remembered it, and she was embarrassed.

But those things, she assured herself, were not influencing her thinking now. "I know Thorgrim well enough to know he's a danger if he's loose," she said, a new hardness in her voice. "We must find him. We must call out the hounds."

Chapter Thirty-Four

Let us make our drawn swords glitter,
you who stain wolf's teeth with blood.
Egil's Saga

They moved across the open country, Thorgrim and the small band with him. The road would have been better. It would have led them directly to where Thorgrim wanted to go. But they could not take the road. That much was clear. In open country they stood a chance of escape. If the Irish did not have dogs.

Harald's right arm was draped over Thorgrim's left shoulder, and a man named Osvif, who was of Arinbjorn's hird and took the oar opposite Harald aboard *Black Raven*, had his arm over Thorgrim's right. Twenty paces behind, Starri Deathless staggered along, as did four others, the sum total of those whom Thorgrim could get moving.

He had ordered them all, all the men in the camp, to rise, to take up arms. He had yelled at them, kicked them, cajoled them, pleaded, but those seven were all that he could get to respond.

Harald was so accustomed to following Thorgrim's orders that he turned to with never a complaint, even though he could hardly walk. Starri, too, had moved at Thorgrim's command, rising to his knees, which he insisted was as far as he could go. Thorgrim squatted beside him and talked to him softly. He planted an image in Starri's mind of the death he now faced, kneeling before his enemy, a pool of vomit on the grass, too weak to even hold a sword, let alone fight.

"This is how the Valkyries will find you, Starri. Starri Poordeath they will call you. They'll leave you to be eaten by pigs." It was cruel, but it was effective, and it was sincere. Thorgrim did not like the thought of Starri killed, but he could not tolerate the thought of him butchered with never a weapon in his hand. A man who had so courted a noble death, a man who so deserved his time in Valhalla. His friend.

And those words were enough to convince Starri to stand, with Thorgrim's help, and stagger off.

The others, Osvif and a man named Halldor, another of Arinbjorn's hird, a man from Ingolf's hird whose name Thorgrim did not know, and Nordwall the Short, were all the men Thorgrim could manage to rally. There seemed to be no reason for it; what they ate, perhaps, or a natural resistance or pure determination; but whatever it was, these few were the only ones of the men who had sailed from Dubh-linn who could still stand and stagger forward.

Thorgrim's first impulse was to fight, but when he saw the well-armed column marching from Tara, eighty men at least, with spears and swords and shields and perfect health, and then looked at his own men, who could barely walk, let alone wield a sword, he decided that a hasty departure was the strategy of the day.

"Come along," he said and headed off across the open ground, toward where he remembered the edge of the wood began. His men shuffled after him, and he quickly realized that they would never be able to move fast enough to put sufficient distance between themselves and the Irish soldiers. So he took Starri's arm and Nordwall's over each shoulder and half supported them, half dragged them a hundred yards toward the wood. There he left them to stagger on and went back for Halldor and Ingolf's man, and then for Harald and Osvif. And then he took Starri and Nordwall's arms and began the whole process again. In that way he managed to get his band to a place where they were swallowed up by the dark before Morrigan's men even reached the camp they had left behind.

As he moved back and forth, ferrying his men to safety, Thorgrim kept careful eye on the camp, trying to divine what was happening. The torches swirled like flying embers in the dark, and Thorgrim expected to see them sweep across the field as the Irish slaughtered the Norse who lay curled on the ground. The men from Tara would move fast, not because the Northern host represented any threat, but because the work was distasteful, shameful to real soldiers, and they would want to be done with it. But that was not what Thorgrim was seeing.

Instead, he saw the torches move back and forth, out into the camp and then back to where they had started. And finally in the flickering light he saw wagons.

Wagons? That could only mean one of two things. Either the Irish had brought wagons to haul the bodies away, or they had brought wagons to haul their prisoners into Tara. And if the latter was the case, then that meant the poison they had been given was not fatal. Morrigan, he knew, was skilled at the use of plants and herbs and he imagined she could get whatever result she wished, be it sickness or death.

By the time they reached the woods, the wagons were starting to move. Thorgrim hustled his men in through the bracken and into the trees. The cover gave him comfort, though in truth the night had hidden their escape entirely.

"We'll pause here a moment," Thorgrim said. His words earned no response, just the sound of crunching brush as one by one the men crumpled to the ground. Thorgrim peered out through the trees. The wagons were ringed by the torch bearers and rolling away from the camp. Thorgrim watched them swing away from the line of tents. He saw the light from the torches illuminate the gates of Tara and the high earthen walls, saw the gates swing open and the wagons move on through.

By all the gods, what is this? Thorgrim thought. Morrigan had taken them prisoner, all of them. It was the only explanation. The Irish would never have taken the bodies of the slain, or men who were dying of poison, into Tara. So that meant they were being kept alive. He did not think that Morrigan had any pleasant fate in mind for them, but as long as they lived there was hope.

And that meant his men would live, too. The poison was not fatal. Harald and Starri would live.

But only if he could keep them safe. Morrigan would soon realize that he and Harald were not among the prisoners. Would she care? How much of a threat did she think they were? Enough to hunt them down? He had to assume she would send men after him.

"I have good news," Thorgrim said in a loud whisper. No response. "The poison, it has made you sick, but I am fairly certain it will not kill you." He waited. No response. "Is that not good news?" Harald managed a groan. From the others there was nothing.

"The bad news is that we cannot remain here," Thorgrim said next. He reached down and grabbed an arm, Halldor's as it happened, and pulled the man to his feet. Halldor swayed and groaned, but he remained upright. One by one he pulled the others to a stand. "Come on," he said, and plunged further into the woods. Behind him he heard the shuffling, agonizing, stumbling steps of the small handful he had led to freedom. Freedom that might be temporary indeed.

The woods were thick in places, the undergrowth dense and the night dark. In any circumstances it would have been tough going, but with men who could barely walk, progress was all but impossible. They staggered along for half an hour or more, and Thorgrim did not like to think of how little a distance they had covered. In truth he had no idea, but he did not think it was much. He did not even know if they were going in the right direction.

The woods were too dense for him to continue hauling the men forward two at a time, and he could not risk letting them get separated.

Once they lost sight of one another there would be no joining up again. So they hobbled on in a single file, moving at the pace of the slowest man, which happened to be Osvif, who swayed and stumbled and heaved for breath.

It did not take too much of that for Thorgrim to realize it was a waste of time. They might get another half mile if they shuffled on through the night, at which point there would be little they could do beyond lying down and letting death take them. Better to stop now, to rest, and hope they could find strength enough to save themselves.

"We'll stop here," Thorgrim said when he had found a thick clump of trees that would offer some shelter and hiding. "In here, among the trees. We must rest, and see if that will make us well enough to reach the ship in the morning." That was all Thorgrim could think to do – reach the ship. The ship was sanctuary, the ship was escape, it was a familiar thing in a strange land. Even if that sanctuary was an illusion, it still drew him like a lodestone.

He heard no protests from the others, no suggestions, no comments at all. Once again freed from the force of Thorgrim's authority, which alone had been driving them, they collapsed to the ground and did not move again.

Thorgrim stood absolutely motionless and let the night settle around him. He heard the rustle of little creatures in the underbrush, the swish of the trees' upper branches as they caught the soft breeze. He could smell the pungent soil and the dried leaves underfoot. He could make out the dark bulk of trees and brush in the tiny light of the stars that crept in through the dense growth overhead. There was nothing out of place there, save for himself and his men, and the forest was already ignoring them.

He found a thick tree and sat, leaned back against it. He was weary in such a way as he had not been in a long time, a weariness that went well beyond the physical. He told himself to stay awake, keep alert, keep his senses tuned to the forest. He knew he should not sit. He told himself to stand. He assured himself he would, in a minute. Five minutes. Surely he deserved five minutes rest?

The next thing he knew he was shuttering into wakefulness, and things had changed. How long he had slept he did not know. It was still black night and he was still in the clump of trees, but his senses were sharper now. His men were in the same positions in which they had collapsed, they had not moved. He could see the trees and the brush, dim but visible in a way they had not been before. His nose picked up and pulled apart every scent that drifted toward him from the forest. He thought vaguely that it was the sleep, that the little rest he had enjoyed had sharpened him, but that was not right.

He leaned forward from where he sat, tense, alert, and in his belly a growing fury, an anger he could feel running though him in the way one feels a hot drink running down one's throat. He wondered what it was that sparked that anger, though the question came not as words in his head, but rather as feelings, instincts more powerful than words.

And then he heard it, far off, and the smell came to him on the night air.

Dogs!

They were coming after him, him and his men. They had dogs. He could hear the baying, far off, but even in the seconds it took for him to understand, he heard them getting closer. But they would not reach him there. They would not find his men, they would not lead men-at-arms with swords and spears and leg irons to where his people slept.

With no thought at all, no plan, Thorgrim was off, running through the woods, running toward the sound of the dogs. The brush whipped past him, the ground seemed to fly by as he ran, the weariness replaced by the drive of his rage. He thought he could taste blood, like a distant memory, in his mouth.

The hounds were closer now, he could hear them coming, and behind them the clumsy tread of the men who held their leashes. A dozen men at least, and a dozen dogs, crashing along the trail of scent left by him and his men in their stumbling escape. Thorgrim was following the same trail, following it back the way they had come, he and the Irish hounds converging on some unseen point.

Then he stopped. The trail of scent was broken where it ran over a narrow stream. Thorgrim recalled having passed it before. It formed a natural break in the path that led right to Harald and the others. He could smell the water, and smell the approaching dogs and the men. He could smell the acrid scent of burning wood and cloth. The men had torches. He could see pinpricks of dancing light flickering through the trees, far off.

Thorgrim crossed the water and found where the trail took up again. He paused there, moved around in the brush, breaking branches, leaving his scent, making his presence there as obvious as it could be. He stopped, listened, his ears picking out the sounds of pursuit, his nose filled with the stink of men and dogs. They were close now. He felt his teeth press together. But this was not the time. Not now. He had to lead them away from this place, away from the real trail.

He bolted to his left, into the thick brush, felt the saplings and tree branches whip against him as he ran. He followed the bank of the stream for a little way and then plunged into the woods again. He stopped. He could hear the whine of the hounds, a confused baying as they came to the place where the trail seemed to take off in another direction. The smell would be different, because it was just him on the new trail, and he did not know if the hounds would be fooled.

He could hear the sound of the men shouting one to the other but he could not make out the words. He tensed. If he had to go back and fight them there, he would, but he wanted to choose the ground himself.

And then he heard them move again. The hounds set up a yelping and howling as they picked up the new trail. They pulled at leashes and sniffed the ground and bounded along, once again following Thorgrim's scent through the woods, down trails that were hardly trails at all.

Thorgrim ran on. He marveled at the power in his legs, the strength that he felt in his body as he raced through the woods. This might be his night to die, he knew, but he knew he would die well, and he would not die alone.

The trees opened up in a small meadow, one hundred rods across, and beyond it a steep and wooded hill, like a natural wall. The starlight illuminated the open ground, but still Thorgrim was surprised at how clearly he could see in the dark night. He bounded across the field. The hounds were close, he could hear them, but he could not see them and so he knew they could not see him. He reached the far side of the meadow. A small stand of oaks backed up against the steep ground and he plunged into it. There was little underbrush, and the trees stood some distance apart. The hill behind was eroded away so it formed a sheer face, like an earthen wall. This was good. This was the place to stop and fight. Thorgrim knew he would not find better.

He pulled to a stop and turned. His breath was coming hard and fast but he did not feel winded. He could see the hounds and men emerge from the trees on the far side of the field. Three torches cast a strange, undulating light on the scene. The hounds straining at their leashes, howling and baying and standing on hind legs as they pulled at their collars. They knew he was there, and they were desperate to get at him. And he was ready to let them come.

The men were talking again, but still Thorgrim could not make out the words. He saw arms pointing in his direction. There seemed to be some sort of discussion. And then the men holding the leashes stepped forward and grabbed the collars of the hounds and jerked the leashes free. With a great howling and baying and barking the pack took off like stags across the open ground, tongues lolling out of mouths as they whipped across the meadow. Thorgrim watched them come. He waited. He was ready.

Chapter Thirty-Five

Odin's wife, the earth,
I clad in a cloak of blood.
Egil's Saga

Donnel was not happy about this, any of it, and had not been for some time. Morrigan had charged him with leading the search for Thorgrim and whoever else was with him. He was no stranger to this sort of thing, but he knew little of dogs and less of battle. He felt like a man riding a bull, thinking he was in control, knowing in the back of his mind that he really was not.

The master of the hounds and his four men had brought the dogs into camp, straining on their leashes. Thorgrim's bedding and his cloak, left behind in the tent, were shoved in their noses. It was all they needed. A quick swing around the edge of the camp allowed them to pick up the scent of the escaping fin gall, and they were off.

Donnel had no doubt that the hounds were following a band of men, half a dozen, by his guess. He had been tracking lost sheep through every kind of countryside since he was a little boy, and he knew well how to read a trail. Indeed, he was often called upon by other sheep herders to find lost animals when they could not. And so, even though he could not say for certain that they were following Thorgrim, he knew the dogs were on the scent of men.

They came to the woods where the escaping band had entered. In the light of the torches Donnel could see the broken branches where they had entered the tree line and various patches of disturbed earth where they had apparently fallen to the ground before standing again and moving on.

"The hounds are on their trail, this way," the master said, his arm pulled out straight by the straining animals on his leash, as if he was pointing down the trail. Donnel looked around him. Their war party consisted of himself and Patrick, the master of the hounds and his men, and five men-at-arms whom Morrigan had sent with them. They did not know how many of the fin gall they were tracking, but however many there were they would likely be deathly ill, and if they were not, the dogs could do most of the work of subduing them.

Still, Donnel wanted more than anything to send the men-at-arms in first, right behind the dog handlers. Though he and Patrick had engaged in a bit of weapons training since coming to Tara, they were not fighting men, not by any means, and certainly not men to take on the fin gall. But he was also the leader of this little expedition, and that meant he had to lead, so he took his place right behind the master of the hounds. "Very well," he said with as much authority as he could gather, "Let them take up the trail."

The small group plunged on through the wood, the torches casting weird, frightening shadows. Donnel cursed the dogs and their howling and yelping. He wanted to hear, to let his ears tell him what was out there. Eyes, even with torches to aid them, were all but useless in the thick woods. But they did not dare let the dogs off their leads, not yet. They would disappear into the forest and the men would have no hope of keeping up with them.

The branches whipped their faces and grabbed their clothes as they tumbled after the frenetic dogs, deeper into the woods. He heard Patrick muttering a prayer to the Blessed Virgin and would have loved to do the same, but he did not think the men-at-arms would take it well. They did not seem to him a very pious bunch.

They came at last to a place where the trees opened up a bit and the dogs stopped their headlong pursuit, milling about, sniffing the brush, whining. Donnel stopped before he ran into the master of the hounds, who had also stopped.

"What is it?" Donnel asked.

"Stream," the master said, jerking his chin in the direction of a small stream that crossed the trail just ahead of them. "Dogs lost the scent."

"Do you think they took to the stream, might be walking in it?" Donnel asked. It would have been a smart move if they suspected their pursuers would have dogs.

"Don't know," the master of the hounds said, and just then one of the dogs took up his baying again, not the confused whimper of the dogs searching for the scent, but the confident call of a hound on the trail. The others converged on it and soon they, too were baying loudly and once more dragging their handlers though the trees.

The chase seemed to Donnel to go on for a long time, and he was a little surprised that men as sick as these - for he assumed they were as bad off as those they had found in camp - had managed to drag themselves so far. He wondered if perhaps they had split up, because the few glimpses of the trail that he saw in the light of the torches did not look to him like the track of half a dozen sick men staggering along. It looked, indeed, more like an animal's track than that of a man.

Stupid dogs, they've likely picked up the scent of a fox or some such, Donnel thought, but he kept his mouth shut. The master of the hounds knew his business.

The trees grew thinner as they plunged on, then yielded to open ground, a meadow of some size that ended in a stand of trees and a steep hillside. Donnel could clearly see the parted grass where someone or something had passed over the ground not long before them. The trail ran straight and true like the frozen wake of a ship right to the trees at the far side of the field.

The dogs seemed to have lost their minds. They were barking and howling and straining at the leads, but there seemed to Donnel's inexpert ear something odd about the sound, some note to their chorus that was a little off key.

"Are the hounds all right?" he asked the master. "Is there something wrong?"

"They're fine, fine. Nothing wrong, nothing wrong," the master said but his tone, too, seemed to belie the words. "Shall we let 'em go, eh? Let 'em soften up them fin gall sons of whores a bit?"

Donnel looked at Patrick, but his younger brother just looked frightened. He looked at the men-at-arms who looked tense but unafraid. One of them gave Donnel a small nod. "Very well, master, let 'em go!" Donnel said.

The handlers pulled the leashes short and deftly released the knots from the collars. Each dog as it was freed shot away like an arrow from a bowstring, bolting across the grass that was belly high to them, charging for the stand of oaks and whatever lay within. The last of them was released and the handlers, the master of the hounds, Donnel, Patrick and the men-at-arms charged off in their wake, racing across the open ground, ready to drag the dogs off the bleeding, shrieking Northmen, bind them and march them back.

They were half way across the field when they saw, in the light cast from the torches, the last of the hounds disappear into the stand of trees. The barking and howling and snarling was terrific, a great chaos of sound. The men came panting to the edge of the wood and stopped, weapons drawn, and listened.

The hounds were in a fury, their barking filled the night. And then suddenly the cry of a wounded animal, a mortally wounded hound, pierced through the sound of the others, and that was followed by another. Donnel caught the master of the hound's eye. The man looked frightened.

"Voices," Patrick said, almost too soft to hear. "There are no voices, no one's crying out. Are we sure they've caught the fin gall?"

"They've caught the damned, bloody fin gall!" the master snapped. "The dogs ain't stupid, they can follow a scent." Another cry of pain was cut short in the middle, just stopped, like a flame snuffed out. The barking was noticeably diminished, as if the number of dogs had been cut in half, but it was still loud, and under it a deep throated snarling and the snapping of jaws.

A hound burst from the underbrush, bounding away in full retreat. Its head, its chest, its forelegs appeared and then it stopped in midflight, grabbed by something unseen in the brush and dragged howling in panic back into the trees. They heard the animal's desperate cry and then it stopped, as suddenly as the last.

"Jesus, Mary and Joseph…" Donnel uttered. His hand, unbidden, made the sign of the cross and he saw he was not the only one to do so.

It was hard to separate out the sounds, but it did not seem as if there were more than two dogs still fighting. A whimper, a crunching sound like a foot on dried twigs, and then there was one.

The men outside the tree line took a step back. The torches were held a little higher. Donnel wiped his palms, wet with perspiration, on his mail shirt, a useless gesture. They heard a cracking of the brush, something coming through the undergrowth, moving slowly. Swords scraped out of sheaths. The last of the hounds staggered into the open, limping, its flanks a mass of blood. It made a whimpering noise and fell over dead in the grass.

For a few seconds no one moved. All eyes were on the dog, which was all but torn apart. Then, as one, they turned and fled back across the field.

It was not an orderly retreat but a panicked rout, a mindless, terror induced race for the dubious safety of the far tree line. They plunged through the grass, stumbled on unseen obstacles, pushed each other out of the way in their flight. When they reached the trees they continued on ten feet or so, until they were fully away from the open ground. Then they stopped, heaved for breath, let the trembling subside and the humiliation set in.

Donnel was the first to react, and his reaction surprised even him. He straightened, took a step forward and shoved the master of the hounds hard, sending him stumbling. "You stupid son of a bitch!" he hissed. "Your damned dogs were on the trail of a wolf or a bear or some damnable thing! Those were not the fin gall in there!"

The master of the hounds straightened and took on a defensive look. "You don't know that. I seen men take on hounds. Man who's quick with a sword, he can stand his ground against dogs. Those were my dogs was killed there!" That last he said as if just then realizing the great loss he had suffered, and his expression changed as he spoke the words.

Donnel turned away. He did not want to engage the man any more. "See here," he said to the others, "back at the stream, when the hounds took off on this trail, I could see on the other side of the water that men had passed there. If the dogs didn't take off after a wolf, then mayhap the fin gall fooled us. Anyway, we go back and we follow the trail across the stream."

The others grunted their agreement. Donnel grabbed one of the torches and headed back into the woods, back the way they had come. He moved quickly down the trail, well blazed by the passage of the men and the half-wild dogs. He felt a sense of relief to be leaving behind whatever it was that killed the dogs, and a sense of dread to be leading the way back into the forest, with the fin gall waiting at the other end.

They came at last to the edge of the stream. Donnel held the torch aloft and examined the far side. He could see where the low growth had been trampled, branches broken or swept aside. He could even see the print of a leather shoe in the soft ground. He stepped closer to Patrick and the men-at-arms, who were right behind him. The master of the hounds and his men, now having nothing to do, were hanging toward the back of the column.

"Whatever trail the damned dogs were on, I say the fin gall went that way." He spoke just above a whisper and pointed across the stream into the blackness of the woods. He swallowed hard, braced himself to say the rest of what he had to say in an even and commanding tone. "We go after them. Let us draw our weapons now. We don't know how far off they are, how many or what shape they are in. My guess is half a dozen and I think they'll be near dead with the sickness Morrigan gave them, but let's be on our guard."

The others just nodded. No one had anything to add. Donnel pulled his sword and the others did the same. The dog handlers had knives, and they drew those, though they looked even less certain about all of this than Donnel felt.

Donnel turned and stepped into the stream, cold water filling his shoe. Two steps and he was across and moving along the trail of the fin gall, which was as easy to follow as if it had been a road. These men were not trying to hide their escape, and Donnel hoped it was because they were too sick to do so. Had he been alone, he would have been able to move silently enough that he could have heard all the sounds of the forest, and his quarry as well. But, with the exception of Patrick, the stumbling fools behind him were making as much noise as an army on the march.

He held up his hand and the column stopped and he listened close. Nothing. There was no sound that he could hear, save for the soft gurgling of the stream they had left behind and the wind in the branches. He continued on, taking his steps slowly and softly, and the men behind him did the same, but it was a pointless gesture, with the shaking of the mail shirts and the various thumping and cracking and stumbling sounds they made.

Another five rods and Donnel held them up again. This was it. The end of the trail. He could see quite clearly where a dozen feet had trampled, kicked and shuffled the ground right up to a thick stand of trees, a natural shelter. It was not where men would go who meant to stagger on, it was where they would go if they were looking for concealment, a place to collapse, to let their bodies recover from some debilitating affliction.

Donnel turned again to the others. When he spoke, it was hardly louder than a breath. "They are in there, I'll warrant," he said. He held his sword in his right hand, the torch in his left, and with the sword he pointed at the trees. If the fin gall were not unconscious, the torches would have warned them of the Irishmen's presence, but there was nothing for it. With luck they would be too sick to resist, forewarned or no.

"Softly, now," he said and stepped off in the direction of the trees. The others followed behind, trying their best to move silently, though with little success. Donnel closed the distance quickly, sword and torch held in front of him. The sweat was slick on his palms but he had no way to wipe them, so he gripped the hilt of the sword and the handle of the torch harder still.

The underbrush was trampled going into the stand of trees, and Donnel was certain there would be a bit of open ground beyond, where the tall oaks had deprived any younger ones of light and stopped their springing up. He pictured in his mind what he would find; Thorgrim and half a dozen fin gall sprawled in the dirt and leaves, oblivious to everything. The Northmen would be outnumbered. If he and his men-at-arms moved fast, their enemies would be bound by the wrists before they were even fully awake.

At the edge of the trees he stopped, just for a second. He took a deep breath and uttered a quick prayer, then plunged in through the bracken, through the trees, into the hidden place beyond. And there it was, almost as he pictured it; the open ground, broken by roots and saplings, the leaves and dirt kicked up and trampled. But no men.

Donnel swung the torch around. No one. He could see where they had been lying on the ground, like animals bedding down. But there was no one there now.

He stepped further in and heard the rest follow. The other torches poked here and there, shedding light on the dark places. "Where are they, Donnel?" Patrick asked. He could see the signs of their having been there as well.

"I don't know," Donnel said, looking up from the ground at last, trying to see through the trees. "Do any of you see anything?" he asked the men in general. He was answered by a series of noncommittal grunts.

"Dogs were chasing a wolf, were they?" the master of the hounds said as he and his men came into the shelter of the trees. His tone was more than a little triumphant. "I reckon they know their business, and me mine."

"*Knew* their business," Donnel corrected. "The dogs *knew* their business. They're all dead now."

The master of the hounds squinted and frowned and was clearly about to make some unpleasant reply when one of the men-at-arms called out. It was one word, or perhaps not even a full word. It sounded to Donnel something like, "Here…" and then the night seemed to come apart around them.

Chapter Thirty-Six

My foes sought me out,
swinging their swords,
but I did not fall then.
Gisli Sursson's Saga

Harald had had the good fortune, the damned good fortune, to fall to the ground with a root jabbing him in the back. At first it had made no difference. Indeed, he was not even aware of it. His body, sick, exhausted, drained from having purged itself for hours in every way a body could purge itself, passed into the dream world so completely that he appeared to have left the earthly one for good. And thus he remained for hours, mouth open, limbs flung out, root in his back.

As he lay there, motionless, his guts did epic battle with the forces of the cowbane, and though it was an enemy unknown, and an enemy to be feared, Harald was young and strong and in the end he prevailed. Not a complete and unqualified victory – he was still weak and battered – but he had won and the cowbane was in retreat.

The sleep fell away, bit by bit, like snow cover in the rain, and as it did it revealed the root. He became aware of the pain and he moved a little, but that only made it worse. He grunted. He was far from well and his body cried out to sleep again, but the root, like an insistent, prodding finger, continued to jab.

He rolled onto his side, clear of the offending woody protrusion, and opened his eyes. It was dark and he had no idea where he was. He tried to walk his dulled thoughts back. The banquet. The nightmare stumble through the woods, the power of his father's urging pushing him on when all he wanted to do was fall to the ground. He remembered now.

He pushed himself up on one arm. All around him, men were strewn on the ground like the victims of a battle, heaps of cloth and hair and furs. The light was meager in the stand of trees and he could see little beyond shapes, but he could hear breathing and see some slight motion among the heaps so he knew he was not the only one who had lived.

Father…? Harald thought. He looked around at the men on the ground, but could not identify any of them as Thorgrim. He pushed himself to a sitting position, then closed his eyes and clenched his teeth and let everything settle again. The worst of the poisoning had passed, but still the motion required to sit up left him sick and dizzy. He waited as his churning stomach calmed and the spinning in his head slowed to a stop.

As he waited, perfectly still, he let his ears take in the sounds of the night and pull them apart, the way his father had taught him to do while hunting and tracking in the forests of Norway. He heard the breathing of the men, the tree branches moving high up. Something moved through the dried leaves, something small, Harald could tell, but making a sound quite out of proportion to its size.

And then Harald's ears picked out something that did not belong to the forest. He sat a little straighter and his eyes shot open, though he was only staring into the dark. He listened. There were feet moving toward them, trying and failing to be stealthy, and the only reason they were not more obvious was because they were still a far way off. He focused his mind and his hearing. More than a couple of men. He could hear a low, murmuring sound, like a brook, but he was fairly certain it was the men talking to one another in low tones.

Harald leapt to his feet, forgetting the condition he was in, but he did not forget it for long. His head whirled and a wave of nausea washed over him and he staggered back a few steps looking for his footing. He caught himself and once again remained still as his equilibrium returned. Then he moved slowly, careful to make no sound or any movement violent enough to start his head spinning again. He picked his way through the sleeping men around him. One or two he pushed over with his foot so he could see their faces. No Thorgrim.

He listened again and could hear the men coming closer. He looked out through the tangle of brush and the low branches. Far off he could see three tiny pricks of light, bobbing through the forest. *Torches…* he thought. That told him a few things. There were at least three men, but undoubtedly more. They were searching for something, and that thing was most likely the Norsemen who had escaped the camp. And they came in sufficient strength that they did not feel the need for stealth.

Harald made a circuit of all the men sleeping in the shelter of the trees and Thorgrim was not there. This both worried Harald and gave him hope. If men were approaching, then Thorgrim would no doubt have been the first to become aware of them. Not because he had his health, but because he was Thorgrim, and Harald had come to expect such things from his father. So perhaps Thorgrim had slipped away and had some trap ready for those coming toward them. Perhaps he would lead them away.

Why did he not wake me? Harald wondered. *Let me know what he was about….*

For whatever reason, Thorgrim had not shared his plans, and Harald knew that he had better make plans of his own. He crouched low and moved quickly to where Starri lay slumped on the ground. With his left hand he shook him gently, then shook him again. His right hand hovered above Starri's mouth, and when Starri snapped awake, Harald's hand clamped down fast so that Starri's manic shout of alarm was muffled and all but silent.

"Starri, Starri, it's me, Harald…" he whispered, and when he saw a look that passed for recognition on Starri's face he took his hand off Starri's mouth. In the best of times Starri never seemed to be entirely cognizant of his surroundings, and this was far from the best of times.

"Listen, Starri," Harald continued, "there are men approaching. Hunting us, no doubt."

At this, Starri looked around, and the familiar signs of agitation set in immediately, the jerking arms, fingers clasping and unclasping. He reached for his sword. They all had their weapons, all the Northmen, because, sick as they had been, they were no more likely to leave camp without their weapons than they were to leave without their arms or legs.

"Wait, wait!" Harald said, his whisper harsh and emphatic. "We don't know how many they are, and we are few, and weak. They'll have no problem following our trail. We'll hide in the brush, let them come in, and then fall on them, take them by surprise."

Starri looked at him.

"Do you understand my meaning?" Harald asked.

Starri nodded.

"Good. Wait here, I'll rouse the others." Harald moved quickly from man to man, waking each, explaining what was happening, ordering him to retreat into the brush, stand silent and ready, move when he moved. It took some doing to make the sick, exhausted, half dead men understand, but in the end each stood, let his head clear, and moved into the darkness of the tree line.

No one asked by what authority Harald was now giving orders. Indeed, Harald himself never thought to question why he had assumed command. He just did, and everyone obeyed. He was Harald Thorgrimson, son of Thorgrim Ulfsson. Son of the Night Wolf.

It took less than a minute for the men to stagger into the trees, conceal themselves and fall silent. Harald remained in the open, and when he looked around and could see no one, when he listened and could hear none of his own men, just their pursuers drawing closer, he ducked into the bit of wood where he had seen Starri go. If they were to hold fast and spring the trap at the right moment, Harald figured the berserker might need some steadying.

The darkness wrapped around them. Harald could smell Starri, just inches away, and could hear the soft sound of his tunic rustling with the jerking of his arms and legs.

"Steady…steady…move when I do…" Harald whispered.

The sound of the approaching men was clearly audible now, and the light from their torches licked and flickered into the stand of trees where they had been hiding. Harald shook his head in amazement. He could not believe how clumsy the Irish were, approaching an unseen enemy in this way.

If we were not all sick, these fools would already be dead men, he thought.

A foot came down on a twig and it cracked, loud, and everyone froze, the Irish and the Northmen. Silence. The branches overhead moved in the breeze and then the hunting party began its slow approach once more. The light spilled into the open place where the Norsemen had slept. Those spots where the leaves and dirt had been disturbed would be obvious to the most obtuse tracker, and Harald had to admit, as loud as their approach might be, whoever was following their trail was doing a good job.

Starri Deathless was quivering now and making the leaves around him shake and Harald hoped the sound would be mistaken for the wind. "Steady, now…" he said, the words merely a breath.

A man stepped into the ring of trees, not ten feet away from where Harald and Starri stood concealed. He held a torch in one hand, a sword in the other, though he did not hold the sword with the ease of one very familiar with its use. He wore a mail shirt. Starri was making tiny whimpering sounds now, and Harald did not know how much longer he could hold him back. Springing traps, he could see, was not the berserkers' forte.

Others came in, torches in hand. They exchanged words and Harald was able to pick out a few here and there. Something about dogs, and he thought one was asking the other where the men whom they had expected to find there had gone. They could see the Northmen had been sleeping there.

More men came in, six or seven all together, and they began to spread out, apparently searching for some clue as to where their prey had gone. *Ready, ready…* Harald thought. He wanted them spread out, and he wanted to know how many they were facing. Two seconds more, one second…

With a scream Nordwall the Short burst from the tree line fifteen feet away, his hair and eyes wild, a battle ax held overhead. He looked like some kind of mad troll of ancient legend.

"Damn!" Harald shouted. A few seconds more and the moment would have been perfect, but there was no changing things now. "Go!" he shouted, his command rising up in volume and pitch until it had changed into a piercing war cry. He plunged forward out of the trees, but Starri was already clear of the brush and swinging his sword and ax.

Right ahead of him, Harald saw Nordwall make a shrieking, running attack on the man with the torch, the one who had first come into the stand of trees. That man took a panicked step back and Nordwall began a full-bodied stroke of the ax. Then Nordwall's foot caught a root and he stumbled and from his left side another of the hunters lunged forward with his spear and caught Nordwall in the pit of his arm and drove the iron point in.

Nordwall was knocked sideways, the spurting blood visible in the light of the torch. His ax came down in a great arc but the force of the spear thrust had knocked him sideways. The blade met only air and Nordwall hit the ground, the spear like a ship's mast standing straight out of him. He shrieked and clawed at the shaft, and his legs kicked pathetically as if he was still trying to run.

And that was all the attention Harald could spare for Nordwall as he sensed a motion on his right. He turned, sword up. A spear came at him, a man in mail trusting as if he was hunting boar. But Harald was no berserker, he was not blind with fighting rage, and with a deft turn of his wrist he used his sword to knock the spear aside.

The move was easy enough, one he had practiced a thousand times and performed in combat dozens. Turn the spear aside, step in past the point, let the momentum of the sword carry the blade around for the counterstroke. It was as ingrained in his muscles as walking, and yet now his body would not do it. He found himself past the point of the spear and then his arm seemed to lose strength, the momentum was not there to bring his blade around and fell his opponent. He could only look on dumbly as the man in mail punched him hard in the face.

Harald staggered back, vaguely aware of the point of the spear coming up again, and him with no shield, no mail. The spear was heading for his gut and he seemed unable to do anything but watch it come, when some bizarre creature materialized out of the dark, whirling toward them. It came into the light and Harald had a vague realization that it was Osvif and one of the men-at-arms, clenched together and flailing with fists as they stumbled forward. They hit the man threatening Harald with the spear and the three went down in a heap.

Harald staggered forward. An arm came up, dagger in hand, clad in mail, so he knew it was not Osvif's. Harald slashed at it and saw the dagger drop. He tried to jab at the struggling men, but found he could not move fast enough to hit one of the Irishmen and be certain he did not hit Osvif as well, so he straightened and staggered back and looked for another fight.

Two of the torches had dropped to the ground, but they continued to gutter and burn and in their light Harald could see that the uneven fight was not going their way. The Norsemen may have had surprise, and it bought them some advantage, but the Irish had numbers, and mail, and shields, and they were not weakened by exhaustion and poison.

Nordwall was down, and if he was not dead he soon would be. Osvif had managed to extract himself, but he was bloodied and limping and facing two men. Another man was down as well, but Harald could not see who it was. Starri was fighting like the madman he was, but not with his accustomed exuberance. It was as if he was moving underwater – the same frenetic, wild, heedless fighting, but slowed down. Slowed down enough that an enemy who was fast might get a blade on him.

Harald stumbled forward where Osvif was confronting the two mail-clad men-at-arms. He raised his sword, but even that took surprising effort. He was breathing hard and his head was spinning. A spear was thrust at him and he twisted to the side, but slowly, and he felt the iron tip rip the flesh of his upper arm and he gasped in pain.

Osvif was staggering back, making a weak defense with his sword against the sword and shield of the man he faced. *Not good, not good…* Harald thought. His mind flailed around for an order to give, a course of action to try beyond remaining in this confined place and watching as they were all systematically hacked to the ground.

Then, from beyond the ring of trees in which they were fighting, came a scream like none that had been heard that night, and rarely on any other night, a scream of such piercing terror that all of them, every man locked in the battle, Norse and Irish, stopped, frozen where they stood.

The scream came again, and with it a terrible snarling sound, a snapping like dried branches breaking, and then silence. And then another voice, shouting this time. Words, Irish words that Harald could not understand. They heard a man or an animal crashing through the bracken, and then another scream, as shrill and awful as the first, and then silence again.

And the fight was over. The Irish to a man flung their weapons away, torches away, and raced for the narrow path they had followed into the trees. The last of them, his mail shirt whipping around his thighs, disappeared from the circle of light cast off by the torches and was gone. Harald and the others listened but all they could hear was the sound of the panicked men crashing through the woods. Another shriek cut through the dark but that did not seem to slow the running feet, the terror-stricken Irish fleeing through the undergrowth.

Harald stood looking out into the black forest, his sword held before him, ready for what might come through the trees, but the light of the torches had ruined his night vision. He thought about ordering them extinguished but he was not comfortable with the notion of being plunged into the dark. Around him, some of the others stood in a similar posture, weapons at the ready, and some slumped to the ground, wounded and spent.

The sound of the running men faded off into the distance and soon it was swallowed up by the quiet of the forest night. Harald had no idea how long he remained standing, sword held before him, but the ache in his arms and legs told him it had been some time. He moved back slowly, sank to his knees and then sat and rested his back against a tree, sword across his lap. Some of the others men were already asleep. He could hear them snoring.

I will keep watch, he thought. *Let the others sleep.* It is what Thorgrim would have done, and with Thorgrim still gone, Harald took it upon himself. He let his body relax as he settled in for the long night vigil, let the quiet of the forest surround him. He would keep awake and alert for danger while the others rested and regained their strength. He felt himself relax and drift away on that comforting thought.

The sun was an hour up when Harald woke again from a heavy sleep, back against the tree, sword across his knees. He looked quickly around. The others remained where they had fallen, sleeping or dead. Nothing had come in the night.

He stood slowly, carefully, in case his head began to spin again. He felt a little dizzy, but his equilibrium was much improved from the night before. From his new vantage point he looked around again. Though it felt as if they had been hiding in that stand of trees for months, he had never seen it in the daylight. He looked behind him. Starri Deathless was not there.

Harald moved toward the beaten trail out of the trees. He moved slowly, not sure what might be out there, beyond their dubious shelter. He pushed the branches aside and saw, twenty feet away, Starri and his father squatting on their heels, talking in low tones. Starri was doing that thing he did, grabbing the split arrowhead that hung from his neck and rubbing it.

The two men looked up and smiled at him and he smiled as well, and a great sense of relief came over him. He walked toward them and they stood and met him halfway. Thorgrim extended a hand, shook Harald's and gripped Harald's arm with his other hand. "Starri was telling me of how you led the men last night, son," he said. "I'm proud. Very proud."

"Thank you," Harald said. He felt the blush spread over his face. He opened his mouth to ask Thorgrim where he had been, then stopped. There was mud on his father's shoes, and spatters of blood on his clothes. *Wolf dream*, Harald thought. He did not want to know any more.

"We must bury the dead and be off," Thorgrim said. Harald nodded. And so for the next hour they struggled to dig graves of adequate depth to give their dead a proper burial. Two men had been killed in the brawl, Nordwall and the man from Ingolf's hird whose name they never did know. Once they were interred, with weapons at their sides, for surely after their long and valiant struggle they would have need of weapons in Valhalla, the remaining men limped off toward the River Boyne.

With the sun rising but still low in the east, it was not hard to navigate through the woods. After twenty minutes they stumbled onto the road that had taken them to Tara the day before. They paused in the cover of the trees and listened for some sound of pursuit, but they heard nothing, so they left the trees and continued on along the dirt road, shuffling, limping and staggering toward the water and the ships.

The landing was close, but not yet in sight, when they heard the sound of men through the trees. They had left a small guard behind, to watch over the ships and Brigit, but what they were hearing sounded like a larger crowd than that. Harald felt a flush of panic. Had Morrigan sent men from Tara to capture the ships? It would make sense. Was Brigit a prisoner now?

"Father," he said in a harsh whisper but Thorgrim put up a hand to silence them. He turned to the others.

"Hide yourselves in the trees," he said, whispering as Harald had. "Starri and Harald and I will get to a place where we can see what's acting. The Irish may have captured the ships."

That news prompted worried glances from the others, but they moved off the road and into the cover of the woods. Thorgrim led Harald and Starri forward. The three men kept to the edge of the trees, ready to disappear into the brush at the first sign of a patrol. They moved quietly, but with the degree of noise coming from the landing, Harald did not think such a precaution was entirely necessary.

Ten rods down the road and they could make out words, and the words were not Irish. They were Norse. They moved on, still not willing to be seen until they knew what was going on. The road began to widen out into the landing at the river's edge and the three men moved into the trees, working their way to a place where they could see and not be seen. They dropped to hands and knees and crawled the last ten feet, until they could peer out from the bracken at the forest's edge.

There were seventy or so men on the river bank. Norsemen. They were armed, but they were not organized in any fashion, not readying themselves to move. They were talking, drinking, some running sharpening stones over the long blades of their swords. Plumes of gray smoke rolled up from several fire pits where pigs were roasting on spits above them, the sight of which made Harald hungry and sick at the same time.

Then he heard a voice, a voice he knew well, but one which, in that context, he could not identify. He looked past the crowd of men to his right. There, louder than the rest, bigger, the center of all the activity, a cup held high, his long red and gray hair bound behind, his great beard jutting from his chin, enveloping his face, a leather belt containing his ample girth, stood Harald's grandfather, Ornolf the Restless.

Chapter Thirty-Seven

The first prey was taken by the heathens from southern Brega…
and they carried off many prisoners,
and killed many and led away very many captives.
The Annals of Ulster

When the high, brown walls of the ringfort at last came into view, Father Finnian felt a great sense of relief, in his soul and in his aching feet. He had assured the wealthy landowner from whom he had borrowed the horse he rode to Glendalough that he would return the animal if he could. But in the end he had taken a different route back, so instead he gave the horse to a poor farmer with whom he had stayed the night, a man who could not have been more shocked and grateful for the gift than if a wee little *luchrupán* had presented him with a pot of gold.

And so is born another legend of the return of St. Patrick, Finnian thought as he headed down the road on foot, leaving the farmer's little hut behind. He smiled to himself. *It will do the faithful no harm…*

Finnian had covered the past fifteen miles on foot, and they were starting to tell. *I am growing soft and fat in that fine monastery at Tara,* he thought, but he made no resolution to change things. In his experience, God was good to intervene when he found his circumstances becoming too comfortable.

He was only half a mile from the gate when he met a woman and her child coming down the road in the opposite direction. They were both barefoot, their clothes worn and well-patched. He stopped them. "My dear," he asked the woman, "do you know if the master is within?" He nodded toward the ringfort.

"Yes, Father, I hear he is," she said. "But I did not see him. They say he is in mourning still."

Finnian nodded. "Very well, my child. And one other thing. Would you do me the great favor of taking this from me? Keep it for yourself?" He removed the sack that was draped over his shoulders and handed it to her.

She looked inside. There was a quantity of bread and smoked meat and cheese and, unseen in the bottom, a couple of silver coins, all of which he had picked up along the way of his travels.

The woman's eyes went wide. "Take this…?"

"Please. You would be relieving me of this burden, which has grown so heavy."

"Oh, yes. Oh, thank you, Father," she said, and made a bow. He gave them a blessing and sent them on their way and continued on to the main gate, which, in the light of day, was open to allow the traffic to pass. Finnian joined the flow of farmers and apprentices and carters making their way into the ringfort. Inside was a bustle, and Finnian guessed it was some sort of market day.

He ran his eyes over the various working men and women until he found one whose clothes were not mud-stained, course and patched, a prosperous looking man giving instructions to a servant.

"Excuse me, good sir," Finnian interrupted the man's discourse. The man turned and looked at Finnian, his face a picture of irritation, but as his eyes flickered over the monk's robes and the tonsure, the look of annoyance faded to one of confusion and a touch of guilt. It was a transformation Finnian had seen many times.

"Yes, Brother?"

"Father."

"Yes, Father," the man said and Finnian admonished himself to confess that want of humility.

"Could you tell me where I might find Ruarc mac Brain?"

The man half turned and pointed across the wide expanse of ground contained by the walls of the ringfort of Líamhain, a quarter of a mile at least from one side to the other. "My Lord Ruarc resides in the big house there," he said. "But he's taking no visitors. He's in mourning for his wife."

"I see. Thank you, my good sir." Finnian gave him a bow and headed off through the crowds, toward the big timber frame house at the far end of the fort.

Ruarc mac Brain was indeed not taking visitors, just as Father Finnian had been warned, and so it took more persuading than he was accustomed to, along with the judicious mention of the name of the Abbot of Glendalough, before he was granted an audience.

It was a big room into which Finnian was ushered, twenty by thirty feet, perhaps, with a high ceiling and a big fireplace, which stood unused in the warmth of the early summer day. Ruarc sat in a tall oak chair at the end of the room, flanked by two men who had the unmistakable air of advisors and lackeys. This gave Finnian pause. A man who surrounded himself with lickspittles was not a man to be trusted.

"Father…?" Ruarc said.

"Finnian. Father Finnian."

"Yes, of course, Father Finnian. What business brings you here? I am in mourning, you know."

"Yes, forgive me," Finnian said. Ruarc did not, in truth, appear to be in mourning. He was a handsome man, perhaps as old as thirty-five, but Finnian doubted any older. His expression was grave, but his clothes had the look of one who had dressed with care, and his manner was of a man who was attending to business.

Finnian was about to continue but Ruarc cut him off. "You are thinking, 'Here is a man who does not appear to be in mourning,' am I right?"

Finnian was taken aback by the question, but before he could answer, Ruarc spoke again. "I loved my wife very much, Father, and I grieve her loss. But her death was a long time coming, and so shock does not add its burden to my grief. What's more, the duty I owe my people is not lessened by my own weakness and pain. So I continue on, despite what I might wish."

"Of course, my Lord Ruarc," Finnian said, his opinion of the man much improved by those words. "I am sent here by the Abbot of Glendalough. On a…delicate matter." This, of course, was not entirely true. The abbot had instructed Finnian to retrieve the Crown of the Three Kingdoms. He had given no instructions as to how it should be done or what should be done with it. Finnian had taken it upon himself to try and bring some relief to beleaguered Tara.

"So I am given to understand," Ruarc said.

"The situation at Tara is not good," Finnian continued, feeling his way along. "Since the death of Máel Sechnaill mac Ruanaid, the devil has been on the loose."

"One moment, please," Ruarc interrupted. He turned to the two advisors who flanked him and made a gesture of dismissal. They each gave a shallow bow and disappeared quickly from the room.

There is another mark in your favor, Finnian thought. Advisors or no, Ruarc was apparently a man who would keep his own council, and made his own decisions.

"Please, Father Finnian, continue."

"Flann mac Conaing, who is cousin to Máel Sechnaill, has taken the throne at Tara. But I suspect you know this already."

Ruarc nodded his head in acknowledgement.

"Flann is a good man. But Máel Sechnaill's daughter also makes claim to the throne, and I fear that this will lead to some unfortunate results. Bloodshed. Indeed, it already has."

"Flann is a good man," Ruarc agreed, "but it is his sister, Morrigan, who wields the power there. Since she escaped the fin gall she has done much to strengthen her brother's position. And hers."

"That is certainly true, my lord. And it makes things even more complicated."

"I have heard," Ruarc continued, "that Brigit has gone to the fin gall. That she seeks their aide against Flann, that she has allied with the Northmen in some sort of devil's bargain to regain the throne of Tara."

"That is also true, my lord Ruarc," Finnian acknowledged. "It was not a wise decision, but the young woman is desperate, and quite lacking in support."

For some time Ruarc said nothing, just regarded Finnian. Another man might have begun to fidget under that relentless gaze, but Finnian did not. He just waited.

"Very well," Ruarc said at last. "I think I can see what road we are on here. But please tell me what this has to do with me. Or you."

"My part is simple. The Abbot of Glendalough, as you are aware, has charge of the Crown of the Three Kingdoms. That crown he gave to Máel Sechnaill mac Ruanaid for the purpose of uniting the three kingdoms and driving the heathen invaders into the sea. But Máel Sechnaill died before he could wear the crown. Now my lord abbot charges me with overseeing the crown's administration."

Is that true? Finnian wondered. Probably not. He had hoped the abbot might give him some sort of proof that he had been ordered to retrieve the crown, written instructions or at least some mark of authority over the matter. But he realized, as he rode empty handed from Glendalough, that the abbot was not fool enough to do any such thing. If Finnian made a mess of it, which he might well do, there would be no official link to Glendalough.

In any event, Finnian could see that mention of the crown had gained Ruarc's attention, though, careful negotiator that he was, he was trying hard to hide it. "The crown is of no matter to me," he said. "I may be of the Uí Dúnchada, but I am not high king of Leinster. I cannot wear the crown."

"The crown may be no matter to you, but the fin gall are. They grow stronger every year, their hold on Ireland more powerful. Dubh-linn stands in direct threat to Líamhain." Finnian sat more upright and locked eyes with Ruarc. "We are in a battle for all the souls of this country. When Irish fight Irish, we do the fin gall's work - the devil's work – for them."

"You wish me to march my army to Tara and save it from the heathen host that Brigit has so improvidently raised? She and Morrigan scratch at each other's eyes and so my men must die to stop them?"

Now it was Finnian's turn to remain silent and hold Ruarc in his gaze, but Ruarc did not flinch any more than Finnian had. He waited, patiently, for the priest to reply.

"There needs a strong ruler at Tara, because the one who rules Tara may wear the Crown of the Three Kingdoms. The abbot will not give the crown to the high kings of Leinster or Mide. Forgive me, but he does not trust them. Brigit nic Máel Sechnaill is the rightful heir to the throne, but the *rí túaithe* are not yet willing to support her."

"The *rí túaithe* are whores who will sell themselves to whoever wields the most power," Ruarc observed, "and they will not do a thing, and certainly will not risk their precious necks, until they can see clearly who that is."

"I would agree with that assessment," Finnian said. Most men were more circumspect in their speech when talking to a priest, but Finnian could see that Ruarc was not most men. "Brigit needs an ally," Finnian continued. "She is young. She is, to be frank, very beautiful, as you well know. She is a widow. You are a widower…."

At that, Ruarc sat bolt upright. "Dear God, sir, what are you suggesting? My wife is not a month in her grave."

Finnian nodded. *Good, good….* Ruarc's thoughts went first to his late wife, and not to the extraordinary power that he, Finnian, was dangling before his imagination. He felt more confident still that he had guessed right about the man.

"Never would I suggest any disrespect to your late wife's memory, God rest her soul," Finnian said. He crossed himself and Ruarc did likewise. "Nor am I suggesting any immediate plans be made. But if Flann mac Conaing solidifies his control of Tara, or, worse yet, the fin gall take it from him, then any possibilities for the future are lost. As you yourself so correctly said, you owe a duty to your people that is greater than yourself. And your people are not just the Uí Dúnchada, or the people of Líamhain. The Irish, they are your people."

For some time the two men sat in silence, and Finnian had no doubt that Ruarc was carefully considering every possible nuance, every stroke and counter stroke. Then, without warning, Ruarc clapped his hands loud, which made Finnian start. Seconds later the two advisors, earlier dismissed, returned at a near run.

"I want word sent to all the *rí túaithe* within two hours ride that they are to turn out with their men-at-arms and any foot soldiers they can muster," Ruarc said, giving the orders as if he had been considering them for days. "We march tomorrow for Tara. Any of my people who still owe their military service for the year, they are to turn out as well. Set the bakers to work, as much as they can bake in a night, that will have to do. And tell my servants to get my horse and armor in readiness."

The advisors said nothing beyond "Very well, my lord," and hurried off. Ruarc looked at Finnian.

"You'll ride with us?" he asked.

"It would be an honor, my lord."

"You know," Ruarc said, "one hears many things. I heard a rumor, just a rumor, mind you, that a priest was the one who accompanied Brigit to Dubh-linn so that she might sell Tara to the fin gall."

"One hears many things. Next the country people will be saying that Saint Patrick himself has come again, I shouldn't wonder. But I do not think that Brigit ever intended to sell Tara to the heathens, not for any price."

Ruarc nodded. He said nothing.

"My Lord, does Father Senan still serve at your pleasure?"

"He does," Ruarc said. "He is old, but he is hale. You will find him at the monastery, I should think."

"I have not seen him in many a year. By your leave, I would like to pay him my respects."

"Of course. I'm sure the brothers will find accommodation for you. And after supper we must talk more. I'll wish to know all I can about how things stand at Tara before I risk the lives of my men."

"Yes, my lord, of course." Finnian stood, made a shallow bow and turned and left the room. He was eager to see Father Senan. He had a great deal to confess.

Chapter Thirty-Eight

Let whoever opens a door
make certain there are no
enemies hiding behind it.
Old Norse Saying

If Thorgrim, or especially Harald, had been injured or killed by Morrigan's men, then Ornolf Hrafnsson would have single-handedly ripped Tara apart with his teeth. But since neither of them had suffered any permanent damage, and since Ornolf did not give a rat's turd about any of the men who had, he roared with laughter and soundly mocked the two of them as they told their tale.

"Ha! That's my courageous, brilliant son-in-law! Beaten by a pig!" he proclaimed. "Now, if the pig had actually been alive I might have called it a fair fight, but by all the gods Morrigan even did you the courtesy of killing the thing first!"

Thorgrim smiled grimly and took another deep drink of his mead, which Ornolf had brought by the barrel-full, along with beer, ale, and even some food. He knew better than to offer any defense of his actions. The fact that he had not been in command of the raid, that he had warned Arinbjorn, that he had personally saved the handful of men who got away, none of that made any difference to Ornolf. Not when there was fun to be had.

Nor did Thorgrim have to make any arguments in his own defense, because Harald, who was too young and naïve to realize how pointless it was, was making them for him, raising objections to each of his grandfather's jibes, just to see them tossed aside like chicken bones. But if anyone was going to argue with Ornolf, Harald was the obvious choice, because there was no one on whom the old man would go easier.

They drank more and tore into the roast pig once it was done. "Careful, there, Thorgrim, don't let this one best you, too," Ornolf warned as Thorgrim used his dagger to cut a chunk of meat free. Harald was unsure at first if he could stomach roast pig any more, but his youthful appetite soon got the better of his associations and he tore into it like the ravenous young man that he was.

Thorgrim was more than eager to ask the obvious question – how did Ornolf happen to be there? But he knew he would never get an answer until Ornolf had heard everything he wanted to hear. So, when the tale of their escape from Tara was finally exhausted, Thorgrim asked.

"Why am I here? To save your sorry skins, obviously," Ornolf explained. "It was clear to me this was a fool's quest you were on, I said so back in Dubh-linn."

"So why didn't you sail with us? You might have played the role of all-father from the onset, and not waited until Arinbjorn's stupidity led to so much trouble."

"It was Arinbjorn's raid. If I had sailed with you, then I would have been putting myself under Arinbjorn's authority. I reckoned that if I just happened to show up some time later, then I was my own man."

"That's another thing," Thorgrim said. "I can't help but notice you seem to have a ship. Where, pray, did you get a ship?"

"Why, that's the ship that was owned by the Danes who tried to kidnap the Irish girl. Remember, you and your berserker friend there nearly killed them all. I reckoned the ship was your prize, and since you are still my hirdman, despite how puffed up you have gotten, I figured that gave me the right to use it."

Thorgrim nodded. It was dubious logic, but arguably correct. It had not occurred to him that the Dane's ship would be his property. And if it was - and Ornolf's sailing off with it would only strengthen his claim - then that meant he now had the means to return to Vik without making himself beholden to another. And that in turn sparked a cascading series of notions, crowding together, one after another.

"I came as fast as I thought decently possible," Ornolf continued, interrupting Thorgrim's river of thought, "but I'll be honest, I didn't think you would lose your entire army within half a day of your arrival!"

"You underestimate Arinbjorn White-tooth's capacity for foolishness."

"Perhaps I do. But I think part of the problem is there." He pointed with his massive beard at Brigit, seated demurely on a barrel of ale. Harald had excused himself and joined her. Thorgrim and Ornolf could see him talking in an animated way to her, and they could see her making a pretense of listening.

"Harald," Ornolf continued, "is thinking with that part of his body that young men think with, and it is not his brain."

"You're right about that. No question. But the princess seems to have worked her wiles on Arinbjorn as well. It was she who talked him into this raid on Tara, not Harald. You should have seen him when we sailed up the coast. I thought he might start humping her leg."

Ornolf laughed loud and long at that. When he stopped he turned to Thorgrim, and his mood was more serious. "So, what do we do now? Between my men, the guard you left behind and the men you dragged from Tara, we have around ninety under arms."

"I don't think they have more men-at-arms than that at Tara, and if they do, then not very many more," Thorgrim said. "We should be able to make a good show of it, if they come out and fight."

"Do you think they'll come out and fight?"

"No. Why would they?"

Ornolf nodded. Why, indeed? Morrigan had defeated the entire Norse army without a man of hers lifting a weapon. Why would she risk it now by meeting an enemy outside the walls of the ringfort?

Whatever Ornolf might have said in reply was cut off by the sound of raised voices nearby. The two men swiveled around. Brigit was standing now, speaking to Harald in a loud and harsh tone, a finger wagging for emphasis. Harald, in turn, looked confused, in part by the rapid-fire Irish but mostly the sudden and unfamiliar anger. He looked more than a little frightened as well.

"Ha!" Ornolf cried. "The boy knows nothing of women! Look at him, he gets a tongue lashing and he has no idea what to do. Hasn't he seen his shrew of a grandmother in full fury often enough, and me handling her like a man should handle a woman?"

"You handle your wife the way a squirrel handles a dog, racing up the nearest tree as fast as its furry legs will take it."

"The pretty girls love my furry legs, they swoon at the sight," Ornolf said, but their attention was on the young couple. Harald stood, shrinking a bit as if he thought he might be struck, and then he and Brigit walked over to where Thorgrim and Ornolf sat. Or, more correctly, Brigit stormed over and Harald trailed behind.

"Father, Grandfather," Harald began. "Brigit has a question…"

Thorgrim smiled. He could not stop himself. Brigit seemed well beyond the point of questions. Ornolf, also unable to stop himself, doubled over with laughter. "A question?" he shouted. "She looks like she has a damned sight more than a question! She looks like she has a wolverine up her ass!"

Despite himself, Thorgrim chuckled. Harald blushed. Brigit, unable to understand the words but understanding clearly that she was the butt of whatever Ornolf had said, just looked madder still.

"Grandfather, please," Harald pleaded. "This is Brigit's very life! She wishes to know what you are planning."

"Yes, Ornolf," Thorgrim asked, "what are you planning?"

"Me? I came here to lend a hand if I could, not to rescue Arinbjorn's whole damned army, or to secure a throne for her. Tell her she picked the wrong damned errand boy when she asked for Arinbjorn's help."

Harald made what appeared to be a stumbling translation. Brigit listened, arms folded, her mouth in a tight line, eyes slightly narrowed. When she replied, the words were harsh, fast, and much louder than they needed to be for Harald, standing two feet away, to hear. Harald asked for clarification on some points, or so Thorgrim guessed, and when Brigit spoke again her word were slow and clipped, but softer now, and carrying true menace.

"Ah…Princess Brigit says Arinbjorn was a fool, and…she said…I think…she was a fool to let him leave her behind. She…ah…demands we march on Tara again, and this time she will…I believe she said that she would…lead. I think."

At that the humor dropped away from Ornolf's face. He stood and turned slowly, anger growing like storm clouds. "'She demands'?" he said. "'She demands?' You tell this little Irish bitch that she doesn't demand anything, not a thing! We do not serve at her pleasure, and if we so choose we'll sail away and leave her standing here alone to be eaten by wolves!" He was ostensibly speaking to Harald, but his eyes were on Brigit, and he was pointing a sausage-like finger at her face.

But Brigit was not in the least intimidated. She put her balled fists on her hips and leaned her face toward Ornolf and let out a stream of Irish, which if it was not obscenity-laden invective, certainly sounded like it. Harald, trying to follow the words, was looking more confused, more uncomfortable, more shocked by the second.

"She says…." Harald began, verbally stepping between them, "she says she appreciates the fact that these men are yours, and you are free to command them as you will…" he began, but Thorgrim cut him off.

"I'm sure she's the picture of reason, just like your grandfather is," he said. He grabbed Ornolf by his massive arm and half led, half dragged him away from the furious Irish princess.

"See here, Ornolf," he said when they were out of earshot. "Clearly neither you nor me nor anyone but Harald cares if the little princess sits on the throne of Tara, and I think he will soon find out that she does not adore him quite as much as he thinks." He considered telling Ornolf the part about Brigit carrying Harald's child, but decided against it. It only complicated matters, and he did not entirely believe it himself.

"However, there are seventy or so men who sailed with us who are now prisoner of the Irish. Some are our countrymen. We should at least try to do something for them. If you succeed, they'll be beholden to you." Ornolf frowned and said nothing, so Thorgrim brought out his weightiest argument. "If Brigit does regain the throne, or if at least we can take possession of Tara, even for a few hours, then the plundering might be such as we have never seen yet in this land, forsaken by the gods."

At that notion Ornolf brightened, and his former anger seemed to subside. "Sure, we can use the little princess to our ends," he said, thinking it through as he spoke, "and maybe even get that fool Arinbjorn to pay a ransom to us. Very well, we'll march to Tara and see what damage we can do!"

Ornolf's enthusiasm, however, did not translate into swift action. He had already eaten and drank enough that day that any thought of marching down the road was out of the question. In fact, as the day wore on, the Northmen seemed to become even more entrenched. Tents were brought ashore and set up, more fire pits dug, logs for seats rolled into the spreading camp. The wood smoke hung above the clearing, the smell of roast meat and strong drink with it, the laughter of men, the clatter of gear as it was stacked here and there, it all gave an air of permanency to the place.

The next day saw more drinking and eating. Ornolf called together the leading men of his ad hoc hird to make plans for the upcoming campaign. That was followed by more eating and drinking, then more plan making, then loud, boisterous and tuneless singing. Finally, as the afternoon yielded to evening, and no one had left the camp for any reason other than to relieve himself, Thorgrim understood that Ornolf was purposely delaying, in part to make it clear to Brigit that the men moved on his schedule, not hers, and in part, he believed, simply to annoy her.

Thorgrim could not tell if the first purpose was working on her, but the second clearly was. She spent the day far removed from the others, pouting, or taking her frustration out on Harald when he foolishly tried to mollify her. Ornolf was enjoying himself, and made certain that Brigit knew he was enjoying himself, and took pains to look like a man who did not intend to go anywhere soon.

The following day they woke to a lowering, dark sky and a cool wind moving the branches of the trees and making a sound like a soft warning. Thorgrim had been in Ireland long enough to know that the spell of good weather they had enjoyed was unprecedented, and now it looked as if the gods would make them pay double for that indulgence.

Thorgrim knelt before the small altar he had built of stones from the river, the much battered iron Thor resting behind the sputtering flame, and he asked his god that the men be protected, Harald foremost, and that they all be allowed to die a man's death if it came to that. He realized that even as he was saying that he was rubbing between his thumb and forefinger the silver cross that Morrigan had given him so long before.

He stood. Starri Deathless was standing there. Thorgrim had not heard him approach. He looked agitated. The thick weather and the proximity of an enemy, an enemy he did not know when or if he would fight, were working on his nerves.

"Thorgrim?" he asked. He was rubbing the split arrowhead just as Thorgrim had been rubbing the cross. "Do you think Ornolf will move today? This is not good, this is not good, this waiting."

"No, it is not good," Thorgrim agreed, though his reasoning, he suspected, was not the same as Starri's. Starri wanted only to fight. Thorgrim wanted to win. And every minute they allowed their enemy to send to the other kings for help, to grow stronger in their defense, to do what only the all-father knew to their captives, put the chances of victory further from hand. "I will talk to Ornolf," Thorgrim assured Starri. "This morning."

But in the end he did not have to use his influence to get Ornolf moving. The big man's sense for timing bordered on the theatrical, and he had judged, correctly, that he had played his game for as long as he could. It was not Brigit's patience that worried him, of that Thorgrim was certain. But Ornolf was not blind to the growing frustration among the men, the frequency with which they drew their weapons, sharpened them, put them back in leather sheathes, their muttering and quiet conversations. Even Norsemen could only eat and drink for so long before they required more diverting action.

It was just after dawn when Ornolf burst from his tent, his massive body swathed in the yards of fabric that made up his tunic, and fastened around his neck a great bear skin that he wore whenever a fight was in the offing. He had killed the bear himself, in his youth, or so he claimed. At first he had killed it with just a knife, but as the years passed and the story became more elaborate the knife became teeth and then the teeth became his bare hands.

"Very well, you pathetic pack of housewives and whores!" he roared to the assembled company. "Make ready to leave in an hour's time! We march to Tara, to show these damned Irish what real men are! Harald, come and buckle your grandfather's sword belt on, there's a good boy!"

A palpable sense of relief swept through the camp as men ate and drank in preparation for the march, and gathered up weapons against the possibility of a fight. No guard was left behind. Every man would be needed. And there would be no need to watch over Brigit, because there would be no possibility of leaving her behind this time.

When everything was in readiness, the men and Brigit gathered in a loose formation and headed off along the road, a road that was now quite familiar to Thorgrim. Some of the swifter men were sent ahead as a guard against ambush, and the rest trudged down the rutted, soft way that ran through open ground and wood.

They had been walking for twenty minutes when the heavens opened up on them, rain like water dumped from buckets. One second the ground was dry, as dry as Irish ground ever got, and the next it was standing water and rain dancing on the dirt road as it fell. The mud grabbed at leather shoes and water ran down the backs of tunics and soaked through hoods and furs and anything else held over head in a useless attempt to keep the rain off.

They continued on through that netherworld of falling rain and sucking mud, and finally the scouts who had been sent ahead met them on the road and told them the woods opened up just ahead and they could see across the fields to the ringfort.

"Do you see anyone? Anyone about?" Thorgrim asked, the rain running into his mouth as he spoke.

"Yes, a great many," the scout said.

"What?"

"Yes, there are many. There is an army at Tara, isn't that what you said? Men-at-arms?"

Thorgrim did not answer. Yes, he had said there were men-at-arms, but he would not have expected that the scout should see them. He would have reckoned they would all be snug and dry within the walls and buildings.

"Show us," Thorgrim said and he and the scout and Ornolf hurried on, and the rest of the men followed behind.

They came soon to where the road ran clear of the woods and yielded to the open ground rolling away up the long, high hill to the walls of Tara. It was only a few days since Thorgrim had seen this same view for the first time, standing at Arinbjorn's side. It looked much different under the dark sky, seen through the driving rain. He wiped water from his eyes.

"There!" the scout said, talking loud over the downpour. He pointed not at the ringfort but in nearly the opposite direction, on the other side of the open ground. And there they were, just as the man had said. Tents of all sizes. Banners snapping in the wind. Thorgrim could see horses and men moving about.

"Are those Morrigan's men?" Ornolf asked.

"No," Thorgrim said. Morrigan's men would not be in the field when they had a perfectly sound fort.

"So who are they?" Ornolf asked.

"I have no idea," Thorgrim said, and he didn't. In truth, looking at that camp, which he could see sheltered a considerable force of men, he realized that he knew only one thing. He and Ornolf were too damned late.

Chapter Thirty-Nine

Devastation of all the islands of Britain by heathens.
The Annals of Ulster, 794 AD.

Brigit nic Máel Sechnaill could not believe how stupid these people were. She had known Norsemen, Harald most intimately, and so her expectations were not high. She had not expected to find philosophers and sages among the great filthy beasts who had turned the little town of Dubh-linn into a reeking, depraved longphort. But she had expected better than this.

Not from Harald, of course. She understood Harald, could play him better than she could play the lyre, and she played the lyre most excellently. Harald did not act, he reacted. Eating, fornicating, fighting, those were the things that set him in motion. That and his wildly unshakable love for her. If she whistled, Harald came bounding, tongue lolling from his mouth. She had never owned a dog that was better trained than Harald.

The others were the same as far as what stimulated them to action, but unlike Harald she could not control them. Perhaps if they spoke her language, as Harald did, to a surprising degree, then she could have played on them as well. But they did not, and so Brigit could only hope the Northmen did nothing irreversibly stupid, and then suffer disappointment when they did.

She looked out over the rain soaked field at the distant camp, the cluster of tents at which Thorgrim and Ornolf and the rest were pointing and jabbering away in their barbaric language. *They are accustomed to matching swords with other heathens*, she thought, *not matching wits with the Irish.* As much as she loathed Morrigan, she recognized that the bitch possessed considerable skill in the art of trickery, manipulation and the use of herbs.

Or magic. Black magic. It would come as no shock to Brigit to discover Morrigan had summoned up the forces of the devil, and that she had unleashed them on the idiot Arinbjorn and defeated his entire army. With a pig, apparently.

Except Thorgrim, she reminded herself. *She did not beat Thorgrim.* And Brigit was sorry for that. There was something frightening about Thorgrim, something she did not understand. She had no influence on him. He seemed hardly to notice her. Whatever she had to do to regain her throne, she knew it would be harder if Thorgrim was there.

The water was running in streams down her hair and face as she looked out over the dull green fields, up the long sloping hill at the curved walls of Tara. It was not so far away, but it seemed to Brigit just then that it might as well have been on the moon, and the sight of it created all at once a desperate longing in her, a sense of despair, and a spark of renewed determination that even the rain could not quench.

Tara.... It was hers, by right. It would be hers again.

The heathens were still jabbering, pointing in one direction and another, from the ringfort to the cluster of tents and flags. Brigit could see horses, and men walking about, but she did not know what it meant. *Why would Morrigan have men in the field,* she thought, *when they might be perfectly safe within the walls?*

After some time of listening to the Northmen's talk, which sounded to her like just so much porcine grunting, Brigit turned to Harald. "What is going on?" she demanded. "What are they...you...discussing?"

Harald pointed across the field. "That...Tara," he said in his broken Irish.

I know it's bloody Tara! Brigit thought, and clenched her teeth to cut off the biting retort forming in her gut. She forced herself to remain silent. Harald's arm swung around until he was pointing at the cluster of tents. "And there...men-at-arms in camp." He paused as he figured how to express the next bit in the Irish tongue. "We...don't know... how many. Big army, maybe. Many."

"Are they not Morrigan's men?" Brigit asked. "The men-at-arms from Tara?"

Harald shook his head. "Morrigan, her men...in Tara."

Brigit nodded. There was her answer as to why Morrigan would send her men beyond the walls of the ringfort. She hadn't. These were someone else's men.

But whose? Brigit's mind started sorting through the possibilities. They were Irish, of that she was certain. She had seen enough Irish camps, and enough Norse, to recognize the difference. If they were not inside the walls of Tara, then they were not Morrigan's friends. And if they were Morrigan's enemies, then perhaps they were friends of hers, or at least potential allies.

She wiped the rain from her eyes and peered across the open ground. It was three quarters of a mile at least, maybe more, and she could not make out any details of the camp. There were banners flogging around in the wind-driven rain, and she felt certain that if she could get a good look at them then she would know whose camp that was. There was no *rí túaithe* or any other minor king within marching distance whose colors she would not recognize.

"We must get closer," she said to Harald.

"What?"

"Closer. We must get closer. You and me. We must see who this is. How many. What they want."

Harald looked a bit bewildered at the thought, but he turned to Thorgrim and Ornolf and spoke fast. The two older men looked out over the field at the distant camp, and then back at Brigit. Ornolf spoke. Harald translated.

"Ornolf…says he will send his man. See. What army?"

Brigit shook her head. *Idiots*, she thought. "You will not know who it is. Friend or enemy. I will. We'll go, you and me. Come back and tell Ornolf."

Harald nodded as she spoke, confirming that he understood. He turned and related the words to Thorgrim and Ornolf, which led in turn to more gibberish from them. Harald turned back to Brigit.

"Ornolf says good, we go. You and me."

"Good," Brigit said, though in truth she was annoyed by their apparent lack of concern for her safety. She was sure that the drunken old buggerer Ornolf did not care if she lived or died, but Thorgrim might have expressed a stronger objection to her putting herself in danger, or at least insisted that she take a bigger guard than just Harald. But instead they seemed ready to let her expose herself to unknown risks, with no effort made to stop her. Indeed, they were no longer even paying her any attention.

Fine, she thought, *you will most assuredly be sorry.*

Harald led the way, taking Brigit a few rods back down the road they had come, then plunging into the tree line and circling around the open ground under the cover of the woods. The branches sprayed them with water as they brushed past, but the canopy above offered some relief from the relentless drumming of the driving rain, which made the going slightly more pleasant. Harald moved like a fox or a wolf through the woods. His feet seemed to find the clearest path and his passing seemed not to disturb a thing, no branches broken, no leaves kicked over. Brigit, in contrast, felt as if she was crashing along like a wounded bear, despite the solicitous help that Harald insisted on offering.

It took them twenty minutes to work their way around the open ground. Occasionally their path would bring them close enough to the fields that they could see Tara and the camp and the few of Ornolf's men who had revealed themselves. But mostly they were in the thick woods, lost in a maze of trees and bracken. And when they were, Brigit would become convinced that Harald was lost, only to have the tree line thin out and reveal that he was still following the edge of the fields as if the way was marked with signs and arrows.

It was tiring, dodging branches and catching herself as she stumbled, dragging the extra weight of her soaked clothing, and Brigit was about to suggest a rest when Harald stopped short and made a shushing sound, finger held to his lips. He gestured for her to follow, then turned and crept forward, parting the undergrowth with care, bending low as he advanced.

Brigit did the same, moving to a place by Harald's side, carefully pushing aside the thin branches of the saplings at the edge of the wood. And then they were there, at the tree line, the open ground stretching away at their feet. The closest parts of the Irish camp, the tents and the banners and the men-at-arms, were no more than fifty feet away. Brigit felt suddenly exposed, but she realized that they were still well hidden by the foliage, and even if anyone was looking, his sight would be much impeded by the merciless downpour.

Besides, these are my people. These are Irishmen. They won't kill me or sell me as a slave, she reminded herself, knowing even as the thought came to her that it was not true. The Irish were at least as brutal to one another as the Northmen were to them.

They stood in silence, looking out from their cover. Brigit's eyes went to the banners, wet and heavy and hanging from poles driven into the ground near the largest of the tents. The most prominent of them looked brownish gray, but she knew that could not be right. No one chose that sort of color for his banner.

A gust of wind rolled across the field, shaking the trees, dumping water on Brigit's head, and lifting the banner and holding it straight out. Brigit gasped from the deluge of water and the sight of the banner all at once. It was not gray, it was gold, the color dulled by the soaking rain. Splayed across the gold field was a red eagle, its wings outstretched. She knew that flag, though she had not seen it in a long time and she could not immediately place it.

"You…know?" Harald asked in a soft voice, nodding toward the distant camp.

"I think…" Brigit said. She pictured the banner, tried to imagine it dry and waving in the sunlight. And then she remembered.

Ruarc mac Brain of Líamhain! His wife had been ill, he had not come to her wedding. Her second wedding. She remembered him from her first. He was ten or fifteen years her senior, well-made, with a commanding presence but not one that was overbearing. She remembered the flush of guilt she had felt when she caught herself admiring him on the very day of her wedding to another.

He's of the family Uí Dúnchada of Leinster... she thought. *What does Leinster want of Brega?* But that was a foolish question and she knew it. The Crown of the Three Kingdoms was at Tara, the royal seat of Brega, and Ruarc mac Brain would want it as much as any of the nobles in Brega, Leinster or Mide.

Taking the crown by force of arms, however, would not bestow on Ruarc the authority over the kingdoms. Only the Abbot of Glendalough could do that. But even if Ruarc could not wear the crown, he likely had his eye on the throne of Tara, for he would never be averse to holding power over Brega as well as Leinster.

Or perhaps he is looking for an alliance with the true heir to the Throne of Tara and the Crown of the Three Kingdoms.... Brigit knew that her father had never considered Ruarc mac Brain one of those men intoxicated with power, eager to fight anyone if doing so might expand their kingdom. So why was he here? If Ruarc had been willing to recognize Flan and Morrigan's authority, then he and his men would have likely been within the walls of Tara now, and not hunkered down in an armed camp outside.

"You know...flag?" Harald prompted and Brigit realized that she had been lost in her thoughts, caught in the labyrinth of this Irish struggle for power.

"Oh...yes. Yes, I believe I do," she said and in that instant she came to a decision. She straightened, took a step toward the open ground. She heard Harald draw a sharp breath. "Let us go and speak to them," she said over her shoulder, with no attempt to keep her voice low.

Before Harald could object, or physically restrain her, which she thought him quite capable of doing, she stepped boldly out of the tree line and headed directly toward the camp. She heard the rustle of Harald coming behind her, then his frantic whisper, "Stop! Wait!" but she did not look back or slow in the least.

At first, no one in Ruarc mac Brain's camp seemed to notice. The few men who Brigit could see were standing miserable and hunch-shouldered in the rain, looking out toward Tara or across the rolling fields toward Ornolf's band. She and Harald were no more than twenty feet away when one of the guards finally turned enough to notice her approach. She could see him visibly start and lower his spear in her direction and call something over his shoulder, which sent another guard scurrying away. Harald was still whispering something, his tone becoming increasingly frantic, but she did not bother to try and decipher the broken and heavily accented words.

Ten feet from the wicked iron point of the guard's spear Brigit stopped and drew herself up, mustering all the royal dignity she was able to in her soaked and filthy condition. "Is this the camp of Ruarc mac Brain?" she demanded.

The guard cocked his head at her, and then glanced over her shoulder at Harald, but her imperious tone and clear assumption of superiority had their intended effect. "Yes, ma'am...yes..." the guard said, and then, recollecting his duty, added, "And who might you be? And what your business?"

Brigit ignored the question. "Please inform your master Ruarc that the princess Brigit nic Máel Sechnaill is here and would speak with him."

The guard, clearly impressed, made to comply without hesitation, but before he could even turn, the man who had first run off returned. "Lord Ruarc says...." he began, but the guard cut him off.

"This here's the princess Brigit nic Máel Sechnaill," he said, proud to possess such knowledge.

"Oh," the other man said. "Well, pray, your highness, would you follow me?"

Brigit headed off after the guard, hoping that Harald would have the good sense not to follow but knowing that he would not. They walked through rows of tents, flies strung from poles with fires struggling and smoking beneath them, toward the gold banner with the red eagle and the large marquee that rose up behind it. The tent seemed to glow from within, candles lit against the gloom of the day, and it held a promise of warmth and shelter which Brigit suddenly found unendurably alluring. She picked up her pace. She heard Harald do the same.

At the door of the marquee the guard stopped, lifted the flap, and called, "My Lord? The princess Brigit nic Máel Sechnaill."

"Come, come!" Brigit heard a voice, vaguely familiar but not intimately so. She stepped through, into the blessed dryness and the warmth generated by the profusion of candles set around the interior.

Ruarc mac Brain was standing in the center of the space, a mail shirt over his tunic, which told Brigit right off that it was not a social function that brought him to Tara. "Dear Lord!" he said as he saw her. He nodded to a servant and the young man hurried over and put a blanket around her shoulders.

"Thank you, my Lord Ruarc," Brigit said with a little nod of her head. He was older than she remembered him, a bit of gray at the temples, which did his looks no harm. His face was a bit more lined, but again, the signs of being careworn did not detract from his physical gifts.

Brigit pulled her eyes from Ruarc because she realized that there was someone else in the marquee, standing off to the side. His clothes were dark and he had not moved or spoken so she did not notice him at first. Now she looked. And drew in a breath.

"Father Finnian?"

"Yes, my dear." The priest stepped closer to her. His presence alone filled her with a sense of peace and hope. "And you can't know how glad I am to see you here," he said, extending his hands, which she took.

There was a shuffling behind her, a throat cleared, and Brigit was surprised to realize that Harald was still there. She turned to him. He was just inside the door of the tent, his eyes wide as he looked around, his expression confused as he tried to grasp what was happening right in front of him.

"Harald?" Brigit said. She pronounced the words slowly and clearly so he would understand. Her tone was kind, more kind than it had been in some time, but there was a finality to her words. "Thank you for taking me here," she said. "And now you may go."

Chapter Forty

I thought I felt how the Valkyrie's hands,
dripping with sword-rain, placed a bloody cap
upon my thickly grown, straight-cut locks of hair.
Gisli Sursson's Saga

That morning, with the first hints of dawn creeping in around the shuttered windows, Morrigan's maidservant, a clever girl named Mugain, had shaken her out of sleep. As she came awake she knew something was wrong. Morrigan was in the habit of rising early, but not that early, and she generally woke of her own accord.

"What is it?" she asked. Mugain had brought a candle that cast a sphere of yellow light around her and Morrigan and the bed.

"The men are up on the wall," Mugain said. "Something is happening, ma'am. I know not what."

Morrigan frowned. "Someone sent you?"

"No, ma'am. Your brother and some of the others, the lead men, they were up on the wall, and there seemed to be something happening beyond the walls, but they did not say what. I thought you should know, ma'am."

Morrigan nodded and swung her feet out of bed. "Smart girl, you were right to fetch me," she said. This was why she kept Mugain close. Like Donnell and Patrick, she was useful and she understood how power was wielded at Tara. "Fetch my clothes."

Mugain set the candle down and was gone into the semi-dark of the room, then back with Morrigan's brat, which she arranged over her shoulders. She took up the candle and led the way through the darkened hall of the royal household, which they had re-occupied the week before. At the end of the hall Morrigan pushed open the big oak door and stepped out into the morning air.

It was not as early as she had thought, but the low, heavy clouds made the morning darker than it would normally be at that hour. Soon the rain would set in, she could see that, and then they would pay in full for the fine weather they had enjoyed over the past week. The sky had all the look of divine retribution about to be visited upon them, and she felt a twinge of apprehension as she walked quickly toward the main gate of Tara. Beside the gate, a ladder rested against the wall.

In the gray light she could see them, the outline of her brother, Flann, and a handful of others, standing on the top of the ringfort's chief defensive works. Something was going on and Flann had not called her. That, too, made her uneasy. Flann was still angry about the trick they had played on the Northmen, even though it had worked out as well as Morrigan might have hoped. Better, in truth. They had rounded all the bastards up like so many sheep and marched them into the great hall, which was now, and for the past few days had been, their prison. How they would ever get the stink out of the place, Morrigan did not know.

It had worked very well indeed, with the one exception of Thorgrim's having escaped. Donnel and Patrick had returned in the morning and told her the tale of the night's hunting, how the dogs had accidentally cornered a bear or a wolf in the stand of trees. But Morrigan knew Thorgrim, knew the stories that were told about him, and the brothers could not hide their surprise when she made the sign of the cross and, wide-eyed, whispered, "Holy Mary, protect us…."

But Flann had not been so delighted. It was, by his lights, a dishonorable victory, a victory won through trickery rather than bloodshed. The fact that it had worked so well actually made Flann angrier still, or so Morrigan divined.

Men! Morrigan thought as she crossed the open ground. *Men and their honor and fighting…* Such things were fine for them. They had victory or they had death, and with the latter a hope of heaven. They did not think about the women left behind to be raped, the children to be sold into slavery. *Men and their damned, damned honor.*

She reached the foot of the ladder and climbed and at the top she stepped onto the earthen wall. From there she looked off in the direction in which the others were gazing and pointing, and she could see right off the focus of their attention. The irregular gray shapes and the spots of light might have been meaningless to many, but Morrigan recognized it immediately for what it was – tents, cooking fires. A camp. And though she could not see much detail with the dull light and the distance, she had no doubt it was an armed camp. They had come in the night, set up in the dark.

Morrigan moved along the wall until she was standing at Flann's side. "Brother, who is this?" she asked. Flann looked over at her and then back at the new arrivals. He did not speak. But she knew he would. She would let him have his little victory, let him make it clear he spoke when he felt like it. At length he did.

"We're not sure. They arrived in the dark, we never even knew they were there until first light. They came from the north, so I do not think they are fin gall."

For a minute they were silent, looking out over the fields growing more distinct in the gathering light. Then one of the men with Flann spoke. "Here, My Lord." He pointed to a place somewhere between the wall and the distant camp. They could just make out a figure running across the field.

"I sent a man out to see who this was," Flann explained.

It was five minutes before the runner had come through the gate and climbed the ladder to the top of the wall. He was breathing hard and Flann gave him a moment to collect himself. When his breathing had subsided to the point where he could speak, he did.

"It's an armed camp, my Lord Flann. Two hundred and fifty, three hundred men at least, I should think. Horses. Well equipped."

The men and Morrigan considered this. Morrigan was aching to ask the obvious question, but she held her tongue. Finally her brother asked it. "Do you know who they are?"

"I do not. I could not find out. But I think I could make out their banner. It was tan or light brown, it seemed, and had a bird with wings spread. An eagle, perhaps."

"Ruarc mac Brain," Flann said.

Oh, you son of a whore, Morrigan thought. *Why don't you just mind your own affairs?*

An hour later the riders appeared, five men mounted on horseback, trotting at an easy pace across the open ground between the camp and Tara's front gate. Two of them held aloft banners on poles, and as they drew near Morrigan, who was still standing with Flann atop the wall, could clearly make out the gold field and red eagle, the colors of Ruarc mac Brain from Líamhain, scion of the Uí Dúnchada of Leinster.

"This will be a delegation," Flann said to no one in particular. "I had better go see what they want." He brushed past Morrigan and headed for the ladder and Morrigan followed. But then Flann stopped and looked back at her, and they held one another's eyes, the silent words loud in their thoughts. Flann was angry still, and he had lost patience with Morrigan and her trickery.

But this was not fighting he was going to, now. It was talking, negotiation, and they both knew that Morrigan was the more formidable one in that arena. They looked at one another, and all that wordless debate flew between them, brother and sister. And then Flann turned, defeated, and headed for the ladder, with Morrigan following right behind.

They would normally have welcomed the delegation into the great hall, the most impressive of all the rooms at Tara, but that place was crammed with angry Norsemen, so instead they met in one of the larger rooms of the royal household. The king's throne had been brought over so that Flann might be seated in regal style, and smaller chairs for the others were arranged in front of it. Morrigan stood just behind and to one side of Flann, her hand resting on the ornately carved back of the big oak chair.

Ruarc mac Brain did not come himself. The man he sent to head up the delegation was older than Ruarc, in his late forties, perhaps, and appeared to be no one's fool. He bowed and said, "My Lord Flann, I am Breandan mac Aidan. My Lord Ruarc mac Brain sends his regards and…"

"Does he?" Flann interrupted. "Sends his regards? An odd way to do it, arriving unannounced with an army in tow, setting up a camp just an arrow shot from my walls."

Well done, brother, Morrigan thought. Flann was taking the initiative, hoping to put this man off guard, though it truth he seemed not in the least flustered.

"My Lord Ruarc regrets the manner in which he has arrived," Breandan continued, "but he feared he might not be so welcome if he announced his intention of coming."

"Whether he is welcome or not remains to be seen. It will depend much on the reason for his coming." Flann gestured toward the seats in front of him and the delegation sat.

"Yes," Breandan said, taking a seat with the others. "His reason, indeed. It is thus. The Abbot of Glendalough has sent word to my Lord Ruarc that he would see the rightful heir seated on the throne of Tara."

"The Abbot of Glendalough?" Flann demanded. "What business is it of his?"

"It is well known that the Crown of the Three Kingdoms was sent to Tara. The Abbot is commanded by God to see that it is used as it should be."

Brigit has gone to him, to see Ruarc," Morrigan thought. *Why else would he concern himself with these affairs? 'Abbot of Glendalough' indeed. Perhaps she did not go to the heathens at all.* And then Morrigan had another thought.

Finnian! What part is he was playing in all this?

"God may command the Abbot as he wishes," Flann was saying now, "but the Abbot does not command at Tara. Neither do the Uí Dúnchada of Leinster."

Breandan bowed his head as if in acknowledgement of this truth. "My Lord Ruarc understands that this would seem to be beyond his sphere," he began, but Morrigan decided to take a chance and interrupted.

"Is Father Finnian behind this?" she asked, her tone sharp. That question did elicit a reaction from Breandan, just a trace of surprise, but enough for her to know that she was right.

"I don't believe I know a Father Finnian," Breandan said, but the lie came too late, and Morrigan continued, addressing her brother as if Breandan had not spoken, or, indeed, as if he was not even there.

"If Finnian is behind this, Lord Flann, then that means Brigit is behind him," Morrigan continued. "The Lord knows what they have promised Ruarc, but they have clearly enlisted him in their effort to remove you, the rightful king of Tara, from the throne."

"Is this true?" Flann demanded of Breandan.

Breandan cleared his throat and sat up straighter. "I am commanded simply to tell you that my Lord Ruarc is here to enforce the wishes of the Abbot of Glendalough, and to see put in place the rightful heir to the throne of Tara. The peace of the Three Kingdoms and the safety of our people against the heathen invaders demand this. That is why it is of interest to him."

"The Abbot of Glendalough?" Morrigan said, stepping around from behind Flann's throne. "You invoke his name much, sir. You must have some written command from him, something that spells out his wishes to Lord Ruarc, and to my Lord Flann. May we see it?" She held out her hand, knowing full well that he had no such thing. He would have revealed it by now if he had. Breandan, for the first time since their meeting, looked unsure of himself.

"The Abbot sent no written word," he explained, his voice carrying less surety than it had before. "His desires were related to us by a messenger, sent direct from Glendalough."

Finnian, Morrigan thought.

"And on that," Flann took up the discussion, "Does Ruarc expect us to fling open the gates and welcome him in? To stand aside and let Leinster determine who shall rule Brega?"

Breandan stood, no doubt sensing, correctly, that the impasse had been reached. The rest of the delegation stood as well. "My Lord Ruarc does not wish for bloodshed, nor does the Abbot. We would suggest that you do indeed open the gates and allow us, and all the parties concerned, to come to some sort of mutual agreement."

Flann stood as well, putting as much aggression as he could behind the move, and when he spoke his voice was loud, his anger palpable. "There will be no agreement as long as that grasping villain will dare keep his army on the soil of Brega. You may tell your Lord Ruarc that we will not be cowed by his threats. He may fling his men against our walls as much as he wishes, he will find no quarter here. By God, if he wants bloodshed, sir, then he shall have it!"

With that Flann turned his back to Breandan and stormed out of the room, a servant frantically pulling the door open for him so that he did not have to break stride. Breandan kept his eyes on Morrigan; he did not watch

Flann exit. "Well?" he said, as if sensing that Flann's word was not the last on any subject.

"You have heard my Lord Flann's words, Breandan mac Aidan. You may take them back to your master, and may God have mercy on us all."

Breandan did not argue. He could see that they were done. He bowed and the rest of his delegation bowed and they turned and made for the door through which they had come.

Morrigan remained motionless, alone in the room, staring at the door long after the men had gone. The whole thing had played out pretty much as she had imagined it would. Flann had done well, he had shown only strength and fearlessness, and that was a good message for Breandan to bring back to Ruarc. But it did not change the underlying truth of the situation.

If Ruarc chose to take Tara by force, then he could. The walls and gate would not hold out for long. For that matter, the people within the ringfort might be starved out in a matter of a week or so, if Ruarc chose to lay siege to the town rather than risk the lives of his men. The *rí túaithe* would most certainly not involve themselves in this affair. They would not pick sides, and if they did, they would likely go with Ruarc, because Ruarc had the stronger position.

We need an army, we need to deliver a wound to Ruarc, she thought, but she knew that the men-at-arms at Tara were outnumbered three to one. If they went beyond the gates of the ringfort they would be butchered.

And then she saw the spark of an idea. She caressed it, blew on it gently, let it flicker and grow and burst into life. *Yes*, she thought. *Yes, here is a notion…* If it did not play out as she envisioned, then they were no worse off, and if it did, then half a dozen problems were solved with a single stroke. A faint smile played over her lips. The hardest part, she realized, would be making Flann see the wisdom that was so clear to her.

Chapter Forty-One

Let us make our drawn swords glitter,
you who would stain wolf's teeth with blood...
Egil's Saga

Arinbjorn White-tooth stood on the raised dais of the great hall, the place that he reckoned was reserved for the king of Tara and his retinue. The hall was much as he had imagined, and this was the place that he had imagined as his place, above the heads of the rest, in the king's seat at the center of the table. But of course there was no table, no seats, nothing but a big, empty room in which, far from being feasted, they were being held prisoner.

One hundred and fifty men, scattered over the packed dirt floor, gathered in little groups according to old friendships. It was dark, with only a little daylight sneaking in around the edges of barred shutters and rendering the whitewashed wattle walls gray. The upper reaches of the ceiling, the heavy wooden beams, the tight thatch, were all but lost in the gloom.

There *had* been a feast, of course, and Arinbjorn had allowed himself to believe the Irish had gratefully served it up in tribute, so terrified were they of him. And that in turn had landed him and his men there, shuttered up in the great hall, prisoners, the most shameful of conditions, and all his earlier fantasies of ruling Tara and bedding Brigit served only to mock him now. They had been played for fools, he and all his men, and now they were stripped of their weapons, their freedom and their manhood.

All but Thorgrim. Thorgrim Night Wolf.

Thorgrim, Thorgrim... Arinbjorn thought, the name coming to mind frequently and unbidden. It was certainly no coincidence that Thorgrim and his son and the lunatic Starri, whom Thorgrim counted as a friend, were the only ones to have escaped. This had all been Thorgrim's doing, all this treachery.

Arinbjorn had figured that out once the effects of the poison had passed, once he realized that Thorgrim was not among the prisoners. It was Harald Thorgrimson who had brought that traitorous bitch Brigit to him, with her tales of the riches to be had at Tara, and Harald was too dim witted to think of such a plot on his own. He did not act without Thorgrim's explicit instructions.

Damn him, may he end as carrion for crows and vultures! Arinbjorn thought as the frustration got the better of him. He had insulted Bolli by putting Thorgrim in his place, just so that he might go into battle side by side with Thorgrim and run a sword through him when the chance presented itself. Thus would he use Thorgrim to help him gain Tara and free himself from being in Thorgrim's debt, all with a single thrust. *And now see how it has turned out!*

Not everyone could see Thorgrim's part in this. For a day and a half, Hrolleif, who had consumed a superhuman amount of the roast pork, was too sick to speak, and when he had partially recovered, and found himself a prisoner of the Irish, he was too furious to make a reasonable reply to anything. Indeed, he seemed to blame Arinbjorn for their situation.

Ingolf was skeptical as well. "Why would Thorgrim do this? What has he to gain?" he asked when Arinbjorn had laid out his suspicions.

"He's in league with the Irish whore, don't you see?" Arinbjorn explained.

"Which one? The one we brought with us from Dubh-linn, or the one who poisoned us?"

"Both! I don't know. It is just clear to me this is his doing. He knew the one who poisoned us of old. Why is it that he alone and his son and the other one, Starri, they alone escaped?"

"The gods favored him?" Ingolf suggested. "He was smarter than us? I don't know, but I don't see how any of this would have been in his favor. If I find that Thorgrim is befriended by the Irish, if they have done him honor, then I will find truth in your words. But for all we know, he and his son were killed by the Irish and fed to the dogs."

Ingolf's words did nothing to allay Arinbjorn's suspicions about Thorgrim, but they did convince him that Ingolf, too, was part of the plot in some way and that he, like Thorgrim, must die once the chance presented itself. This he relayed to Bolli Thorvaldsson, who was the only one of them whom he still trusted completely. And Bolli made certain that word spread throughout the company of prisoners, word of Thorgrim's treachery, of how he had sold out Arinbjorn's men for his own gain.

It was a message that the men heard, and were inclined to believe. Surely it made more sense that they had been betrayed by one of their own than that they had been played for fools by some Irish wench. If the latter was true, it might suggest that they were not as clever as the Irish, and that was a thought to be dismissed out of hand.

For all of Arinbjorn's insights into the circumstances of their imprisonment, however, there was not much that could be done as long as they remained locked up in the great hall. So Arinbjorn, alone with Bolli on the dais, made plans. "We will escape this prison, Bolli," Arinbjorn said, his voice low and conspiratorial. "Either by tricking these Irish or…."

He got no further than that. A key turned in the lock of the small door to the side, the door through which food and drink was passed, though it was not above an hour since they had been given the tough bread and weak beer that constituted their breakfast. This was some other business. Heads turned at the sound; some men stood and faced the door. A good turn of events or bad, either way this promised to be a break in the unbearable monotony of the days past.

Arinbjorn, too, faced the door. He watched it swing open to reveal a pair of guards, well-armed, spears held ready to impale any who might rush them. None of the Norsemen moved, so the guards took steps aside and Morrigan passed between them. She cast an inquisitive look around the great hall, as if assessing the condition of the men inside, like a farmer looking over his herd. Finally her eyes moved to the raised area on which Arinbjorn stood.

"Arinbjorn," she called out in her clear, strong voice. Once again Arinbjorn could not help but notice what a beauty she was, her long, dark hair tumbling around her shoulders, her strong, slim body obvious even under the loose fabric of leine and brat. "Arinbjorn, would you accompany me? I would have a word with you."

A bit of a smile played over Arinbjorn's lips. Morrigan, he imagined, had finally realized the great danger she had brought to all of Tara, trying to fool him, bringing him and his men within the walls of the ringfort. Now she would try to back her way out of the trap in which she had put herself.

"Very well," he said, trying to sound as if she was interrupting some important business. He hopped down from the dais and strolled toward her. Morrigan's face remained unreadable, but he could see on the faces of the guards the frustration that his unhurried pace was causing.

That's good, he thought. *They should know I do not hurry for them.* But once he was within arm's length of the door, one of the guards reached in and grabbed a handful of his tunic and jerked him through while the other slammed the heavy oak door and locked it behind. Arinbjorn found himself in the passage outside the great hall. There were four guards in all with spears at the ready. Morrigan stood before him. She was a foot shorter than he was, at least, but with her posture and her air of confidence she did not seem in the least diminutive.

"Lord Arinbjorn, first, please let me apologize for what we have done," Morrigan began, her words reinforcing what Arinbjorn had already come to understand about her fears. "It was an unkind thing, true, but, pray, try to see our position. An army of Northmen descending on us. We quite unable to defend against you. It is no secret what your people have done to other towns and monasteries in this country."

Arinbjorn nodded his head in gracious acknowledgement. "I understand, of course," he said. "It was Thorgrim who put you up to this, is that not right?"

"Thorgrim…?"

"Thorgrim Ulfsson. The one they call Night Wolf. I know that he put you up to this, that this treachery was his doing, it is no secret." Arinbjorn saw the look of understanding sweep over Morrigan's face and he knew that this thrust had found its mark, more confirmation that he was correct in his assessment of the situation.

"Yes," Morrigan said. "Exactly so. Thorgrim was the one who came up with this entire scheme. To undermine you."

"Of course. He's not nearly so clever as he thinks. Is he with you now, in Tara?"

"No, no. Nothing of the sort," Morrigan said, shaking her head, her expression now distraught. "A man like that, he'll betray anyone. I should have known that. I should have spoken with you, then I would have met with an honest man. Thorgrim has abandoned us and joined with our enemies. They are camped just outside our walls. We need you, Arinbjorn. We need you and your men to join with us in battle, to defeat Thorgrim and the men with him, so that the riches of Tara will be ours."

Arinbjorn nodded, but in truth this was sounding a little less promising. "'To defeat Thorgrim', you say?"

"Yes," Morrigan said, her tone brightening now. "They are but seventy men or so with Thorgrim, but my men-at-arms are afraid to take them on. If you join with us, however, we will outnumber them two men to one. My men will fight if you will lead them, and then victory will be certain."

This made sense to Arinbjorn, but there was still one significant problem. "We have no weapons," he pointed out. "They were…we lost them when…" he stammered, then stopped. They both knew perfectly well what had become of the Norsemen's weapons, but Arinbjorn did not care to say it out loud.

"We have your weapons," Morrigan said. "They will be returned, all of them. With our thanks and apologies."

"You will return our weapons? Just like that?" Arinbjorn felt a little flame of suspicion kindling in his head. "You fooled us once, and I don't care to let it happen again."

"We did what we had to do," Morrigan said. "I've told you before, the safety of my people, of Tara, is all I care about, and I will do what I have to do. And if that means fighting with the fin gall, then that is what I will do. I am not offering to give you your weapons, your freedom, for nothing. Fight with us, against Thorgrim, and those things will be yours."

Arinbjorn nodded. Put that way, Morrigan's offer seemed reasonable. Had she been trying to trick him, she would have offered anything. But here she was making it clear that her offer was good only if they joined in the fight against Thorgrim and his new band. That made the offer seem far less suspicious. And, as it happened, far more tempting to Arinbjorn.

"I must discuss this with the lead men," Arinbjorn said.

"We do not have much time. Thorgrim and his men are at the gate. I will give you half an hour and then I will come for your answer. You must let me know then."

With that, Arinbjorn was returned to the great hall in as rough a manner as he had been withdrawn. He recovered himself and called for Bolli and Ingolf and Hrolleif. They gathered on the dais and Arinbjorn explained the situation, and Morrigan's offer.

"Lying bitch!" Hrolleif exploded. "Are we to believe her again? Hasn't she played us for fools enough?"

"She explained why she did what she did," Arinbjorn replied, "and I for one am satisfied with her explanation. As I suspected, this was mostly Thorgrim's doing. She wants revenge as much as we do. She offers us the chance."

"It is not clear to me just how Thorgrim is involved here," Ingolf said. "Did she tell you what part he played?"

"She didn't have to," Arinbjorn said. "She told me Thorgrim was part of this, which I already knew and told you, and that is all we need to know." He hoped Ingolf would drop this line of questioning, because he realized when he tried to explain Thorgrim's part, that he really did not know at all what it was, only that he had done something, and that their captivity had been the result.

"Here is the matter, boiled down," Bolli said. "We stay in here, like swine ready for the slaughter, or we take Morrigan's offer and gain the chance for freedom. If she puts weapons in our hands, we cannot lose. Even if we die, it is a better death than that of prisoners or slaves."

Heads nodded at that sentiment, the first inarguably true thing any of them had said. If they were let out of their prison, they could die fighting, fighting someone, and such a death would certainly be preferable to rotting behind locked doors.

Twenty minutes later, Morrigan was back. Ten minutes after that, the Northmen marched from the great hall, free for the first time since the night they had feasted on Irish pork.

It was raining, they discovered, as they left the confines of the hall and stepped out into the open ground of the ringfort. The sky was dark and brooding and the rain was coming down in torrents. Wide puddles, their surfaces dancing and roiling in the downpour, were spread across the trampled ground. But the rain did not bother Arinbjorn or his men. They were filthy and stinking after their sickness and captivity, and this fresh water from the gods, on a morning that was not overly cold, seemed more a blessing than a torment.

The marched across the grounds in a loose file, flanked by a few dozen guards with lowered spears.

"I had thought we were supposed to be allies, now," Hrolleif growled.

"Morrigan is being cautious, that's all," Arinbjorn said. "Think of it from her side. We could easily overpower all the men-at-arms here at Tara, even without our weapons, and we have reason to do it. These precautions are insufficient, of course, but she must take them."

At that Hrolleif grunted but said nothing.

They came at last to the big oak gate, fifteen feet in height, the main way in and out of Tara. It, too, was flanked with guards, and to one side, a pile of swords, spears, mail shirts, battle axes. All the weapons that had been taken from them when they had been taken captive after the feast.

"Welcome, Lord Arinbjorn!"

Arinbjorn looked up, shielding his eyes against the driving rain. Standing on the wall, above the gate and a little to the side, was Morrigan, a cape around her shoulders, a hood pulled over her head. Beside her, in mail and a helmet, sword hanging at his side, stood the man she had introduced as her brother, Flann. Arinbjorn wondered if he was indeed a brother to her.

"Morrigan!" Arinbjorn called back. "You have been true to your word."

"Of course I have!" she called back. "You see your weapons there. Pray, let every man take what is his and arm himself. Then we go forth, fin gall and Irish, and we will fight these enemies of ours."

Arinbjorn turned to give the order, but the men were already swarming over the pile of weapons, pulling mail shirts over their shoulders, strapping sword belts around their waists, settling helmets on their heads. Behind them, the men-at-arms of Tara formed up, their lines more neatly dressed than the Northmen were wont to be. They were ready to go, and a moment later Arinbjorn's men were as well.

"We will open the gates," Morrigan called from the wall above, and Arinbjorn looked up again. "But the enemy is hard by and we do not wish to keep them open long. My brother instructs me to tell you that you men, you fin gall, will sally forth, and the men-at-arms of Tara are behind you." She pointed to a place beyond the walls, lost to Arinbjorn's sight. "We can see the enemy, they are still in camp, they have not taken the field. You will have time enough to form up, and then you can sweep them away."

Arinbjorn pulled his sword from its sheath and raised it in a dramatic gesture. "We are ready to fight, and we are ready to kill, or to die, by the will of Odin, all-father!" he shouted.

"By the will of the Father, the Son and the Holy Spirit!" Morrigan shouted back, to Arinbjorn's discomfort, but before he could even think of anything to say the bar was lifted from its brackets and the big oak gate swung ponderously open, revealing the fields and the distant wood that Arinbjorn remembered. He turned, raised his sword higher.

"You men, follow me! To victory or death!" He stepped forward, moving faster with each stride, and the host of Northmen flowed behind him. He could see smiles on their faces, faces that had been twisted with fury just hours before. They were free and they had weapons in their hands, and that was the most that any of their kind might desire.

They poured through the gate and onto the well-trod ground beyond, the hundred and fifty or so men under Arinbjorn's command. He stepped aside and with his sword directed them to form up to the north of the open gate. Behind them, fifty or sixty feet behind, was the head of the column of Irishmen from Tara. Arinbjorn smiled to himself. Those Irish, with all their spears and mail and helmets, were not as eager as the Northmen to get into the fight. They were not rushing forward as he and his men had done, but marching at a more slow and regular pace.

I will send them in first, Arinbjorn thought. Why throw away the lives of his men, men who would be the most effective on the battlefield? He would order the men-at-arms in first, to take the shock of the attack, and then his men would sweep in and finish the enemy off.

He turned to wait for the men-at-arms to come through the gate so that he could direct them to where he wanted them. The Irish were still within the ringfort, ten feet from the gate, and then he heard Flann shout something and to Arinbjorn's surprise they came suddenly to a stop.

"Get out here, you cowardly bastards!" Arinbjorn shouted, but he had not even completed the sentence before the ponderous gates swung shut again and he heard the sound of the bar dropping in place.

Chapter Forty-Two

You battle-windswept warriors,
I wish you'd suffer
loss of giant's laughter
and good fame both
The Saga of the Confederates

The drumming of the rain on the roof of the marquee made it hard to hear the hushed conversation. It also made Father Finnian grateful to not be plodding along some miserable excuse for a road or huddled in some peasant's pathetic, leaky hut. Ruarc mac Brain's tent was roomier, better furnished and more comfortable than the homes of many of the poor farmers with whom he had stayed in his travels.

"My only wish is to bring stability to Brega," Brigit was explaining. "My father longed for the Crown of the Three Kingdoms, but I am not so eager to wear it. Until we are at peace within our own kingdom, I don't see how we can hope to unite the three and defeat the fin gall."

Ruarc, who was seated across the small table from Brigit, nodded in agreement. The three of them, Ruarc, Brigit and Finnian, were the only occupants of the marquee. The servants had been sent away. Outside, two guards flanked the entryway, visible whenever the canvas that covered the door flogged in the wind.

This has the blessings of God, Finnian thought. It was he, Finnian, who had arranged for Ruarc mac Brain and his troops to be here, but God had delivered up Brigit just when she was needed. Finnian had been staggering in the dark, feeling his way, unsure if any of what he was doing was right. And then like Abraham's ram in the thicket, Brigit had appeared. The sense of relief he felt was like nothing he had experienced before.

"As long as Flann sits on the throne, there will be no peace in Brega," Ruarc said. "The *rí túaithe* will not rally to him, and soon they will be fighting one another. And Flann made it clear to Breandan mac Aidan that he would not willingly give the throne up."

"When I am on the throne, secure on the throne, then the *rí túaithe* will come together," Brigit said. "And then I can begin to strengthen the alliance with the Uí Dúnchada of Leinster."

Something in the way she said that pulled Finnian from his musings. He looked over at her. But she was not looking at him. She was looking at Ruarc mac Brain and Ruarc was looking at her in a way that suggested to Finnian something deeper going on. There were undercurrents in their talk that went beyond simply discussing who would rule what.

He was just wondering if he should excuse himself when a voice, loud and urgent, ended the discussion. "My Lord Ruarc! Something is happening at Tara!"

Ruarc was out of his seat and out of the marquee before Finnian and Brigit had even quite understood the implications of this. They both leapt to their feet, but Finnian put a hand on Brigit's arm. "One moment," he said. He grabbed a cloak that was tossed onto Ruarc's camp bed and draped it over her shoulders, pulling the hood up over her head. "I am sure my Lord Ruarc would not mind," he said, and the two of them ducked out of the tent and into the hard rain and what appeared to be total chaos.

Men were rushing in every direction, snatching up swords, spears and shields, fitting helmets on their heads. "To arms! To arms!" they could hear someone cry and the cry was taken up around the camp as men stumbled to grab their weapons and stand ready for action.

They found Ruarc beyond the tents, looking out over the long stretch of open ground between them and the ringfort. He was flanked by Breandan mac Aidan and a few of his senior men, and they were talking in low voices and pointing here and there, seemingly oblivious to the madness behind them.

"Princess Brigit, Father Finnian, pray join us," Ruarc called, welcoming them in among the others. "See here." He pointed toward Tara. "Men have come out, do you see them, before the gate?"

Finnian squinted through the rain. He saw them at last. Quite a few men. More than a hundred, certainly. Distance and weather made it hard to see, but it appeared that they wore helmets and mail, or most did, the armor shining dull gray in the rain and low clouds. Finnian could see spots of color, which he guessed were painted shields.

"Are they men from Tara?" he asked.

"I would imagine so," Ruarc said, "though why they have left the safety of the ringfort and taken the field I can't imagine. I would not, if I was in Flann's position, and I didn't think he would. That's why we weren't ready for this."

They may not have been ready a few minutes before, but they were nearly so now, the men forming up behind and to either side of Ruarc and the other lead men. Ruarc's men-at-arms were not a bunch of farmers filling out their military obligations to their lord, they were professionals and it showed.

"What will you do, my Lord Ruarc," Brigit said, "if I may make so bold as to ask?"

"I'm not entirely sure," Ruarc said. His words were slow and measured, as if he was working out his options as he spoke. "Once we're formed up we'll advance into the open, get some fighting room. But I won't attack them, I'll let them make the first move so I can see what they have in mind. I'm tempted to think they've made a terrible blunder, but I know Flann better than that. There's something acting here that I have yet to see."

Finnian felt his stomach knot up. He had hoped that this might all be accomplished without bloodshed. Both he and Ruarc had thought the show of force would be enough to make Flann and Morrigan see the benefits of a negotiated peace. But now it looked as if they meant to fight, and it would be a bloody affair if they did. And that in turn meant he had precious little chance to make anyone see reason. Once steel met steel, that chance would be gone for good.

"They're making a shieldwall," Breandan mac Aidan said. In the distance Finnian could see the men rushing here and there, organizing themselves, moving from an amorphous cluster into a line, an unbroken line with shields held chest high, dull colored dots against the brown walls of Tara.

"Form our men up!" Ruarc called, loud but calm. There was no edge of excitement or alarm in his voice; he might have been calling across a yard for his groom to bring his horse. But behind them the men-at-arms fell into a line of their own, ready to counter any move the enemy might make. Finnian was impressed and heartbroken all at once. Irish fighting Irish. It was not right, and no wonder that the Northmen had so easy a time setting themselves up in that country. It made him ill.

He turned his eyes from the men before Tara and swept the field, and was surprised to see a lone figure, one man, walking across the open ground. No one else seemed to have noticed him, or if they did, they did not think he was worthy of comment. One man. Not even walking so much as staggering, seemingly oblivious to the great machinations around him.

And then Finnian realized who he was. It was the young Norseman who had escorted Brigit nic Máel Sechnaill to Ruarc's camp.

Now, I wonder what he's about, Finnian thought.

Arinbjorn felt the panic rising like a fast moving tide and he struggled to keep above it. It was not fear of the enemy or the possibility of injury or death, it was fear that Morrigan had once again played him for a fool. That, he did not think he could endure.

"What by the name of Thor is the meaning of this?" Hrolleif the Stout roared out as the big doors shut behind them. It was the very same question that was shrieking in Arinbjorn's brain. The buzz of conversation, the talk of the confused men around him grew louder, louder even than the rain drumming on Arinbjorn's helmet, louder than the screaming questions in his head. He wanted to tell them all to shut their mouths, but he did not dare because he was afraid they would not listen.

"There, look!" Ingolf called and pointed downhill and across the wide expanse of open, grassy field. There was a camp in the distance, about three quarters of a mile off, the camp that Morrigan had been pointing toward. Presumably that was the enemy with whom Thorgrim had joined up. Then, suddenly, Arinbjorn was struck by the truth, coming like a cowardly punch from the blind side.

Oh, you cunning bitch… he thought, then, speaking loud so the others could hear over the driving rain, he said, "This is what the Irish are about. They know we'll do anything to have our revenge on Thorgrim and those other traitors, so they've sent us out alone to fight their battle for them!"

He was pleased with those words, the sound of them, so he continued on in his most inspirational tone. "Very well, then, if they won't fight like men, then I say we kill them all, all those yonder with Thorgrim, and then we come back and kill every one of the miserable, lying bastards at Tara as well!"

He had expected a rousing cheer to follow this bold statement, but he received only bewildered looks. To Arinbjorn's further discomfort, though not his surprise, Hrolleif was the first to speak, prefacing his remarks with a great clearing of his throat, followed by a great glob of spit hurled in the direction of the distant camp.

"Thorgrim?" he roared, which seemed pretty much the only volume at which he was capable of speaking. "No one but you cares a turd about Thorgrim! How do you even know he is over there? Who told you that?"

Arinbjorn did not answer, because he realized how stupid the answer would make him appear. Unfortunately, the truth was not hard to guess, and Hrolleif did, and guessed correctly.

"By Odin's one festering eye!" he roared. "Was it that Irish bitch, Morrigan? Thor's hammer, is there anything she could say that you wouldn't believe? If she told you she could squat down and shit silver ingots you'd stand there with your hands under her arse!"

Arinbjorn could feel his face flush and flailed around looking for a suitable reply, but there was none at hand. Happily, Ingolf saved him. "Look there!" he cried. "They are going to arms!"

All eyes turned from Arinbjorn and Hrolleif to the distant camp, where the men seemed to be racing around like ants on an overturned hill. There was something rushed and disorderly about their actions, as if they had been taken by surprise, and it was no wonder if they had been. Whoever they were, if they had come to fight, they probably did not think the men at Tara would leave a perfectly intact ringfort and meet them on the open ground. Arinbjorn knew that he certainly would not have done so, given a choice.

"It appears they are well armed and their numbers are great," Ingolf continued. "We have no dog in this fight. We have our weapons, we have our freedom. Our ships are likely still where we left them. Let the Irish kill the Irish, I say, and let us return to Dubh-linn."

This met with considerable approval among the others, heads nodding, voices murmuring ascent. Arinbjorn pressed his lips together. Desperate as he was to do so, he did not dare order them to prepare to attack the enemy across the field. He was all but certain he would be ignored, and that would be more humiliation than he could endure.

Thorgrim!

"We can't just turn our backs and walk away," Hrolleif said, giving Arinbjorn a faint glimpse of hope, until the big man added, "If they do attack, and we're unprepared, they'll murder us all. We need to form a shield wall and back away across the field, keep our faces and our shields toward the enemy as we retreat."

This, too, was met with general agreement. No orders were given or needed. The Norsemen knew well how to form a shieldwall and they did so, quick and neat. Arinbjorn could see the effect that the move had on the enemy in the far camp. The men who had been rushing chaotically about tumbled into place, making a formidable line of troops, mail-clad, helmeted, stretching from one end of the camp to another. In numbers and equipment and discipline they made the Norsemen look weak and puny.

"Very well," Hrolleif shouted. "Stand ready to move back. Nice and easy, we'll be ready for these bastards if they charge, but if they stay put it's back to the ships for us." All eyes were locked on the distant men-at-arms, waiting, waiting for them to make a move, to roll forward and charge the shieldwall and turn the standoff into a bloody fray.

All but Arinbjorn. Something had caught his eye and he half turned and looked across the field, right in line with the flank of the shieldwall. A single man, walking slowly along, as if he was out for a stroll, except that he seemed to be all but staggering as he plodded through the driving rain.

Who by Loki could that be? Arinbjorn wondered. The man looked like he might be drunk. Indeed, he would have to be, to be wandering around in the open like that, with two armies facing off and him seeming to not even notice.

There was something familiar about him, his size and shape and the way he moved. Arinbjorn squinted through the rain. And then it hit him. *Harald?* he thought. *Harald Thorgrimson?*

*   *   *

They had slipped back into their familiar roles as easily as pulling on a worn pair of shoes; Ornolf loud, commanding and outrageous, Thorgrim doing the actual leading, making the decisions that were really Ornolf's to make when Ornolf could not be bothered to make them. It was not an arrangement that was meant to fool anyone, and it didn't. It was simply the most pragmatic division of labor, each man acting as his strengths dictated.

Thorgrim did not want their presence revealed. He understood that surprise was the most precious of weapons, and like so many precious things, once it was lost it could not be had again. So, by his command, only he and Ornolf and a few others stepped from the tree line to the place where the road ran out of the woods and the ground opened up and rolled away to the walls of Tara, standing proud on the crest of its hill. There was little chance that the small knot of men would be seen from as far away as the ringfort, or the cluster of tents at the other end of the open ground, but even still they hung toward the edge of the wood, standing in the bracken that lined the road, lost against the trees behind them.

He had meant for the rest of the men to remain back and out of sight, but that was as likely to happen as the tide was to stop flowing at his command. So, like the tide, the men had inexorably crept forward, inching closer, seeping into the open places at the edge of the trees. But they knew what Thorgrim wanted, and they kept hidden by the arboreal cover, never exposing themselves as they maneuvered to a place where they could see what was going on. And since they did not threaten to ruin the gift of surprise, Thorgrim did not try to order them back.

"See here," he said, pointing toward the ringfort. Across the distance Thorgrim could see some movement, which he interpreted as the big oak door swinging open, and a moment later men emerging, marching out in a something akin to a military fashion, but not so disciplined as good and experienced troops would be.

"What do you make of them?" Ornolf asked.

"I can make out little at this distance," Thorgrim said.

"Ha! Your eyes dim with your advancing age, Thorgrim Night Wolf!" Ornolf said. Thorgrim smiled. He knew that Ornolf, his senior by nearly two decades, would reckon himself lucky if he could distinguish the fort from the hill on which it sat. Instead of pointing that out, however, he turned to Starri Deathless, who was with them in the bracken.

"Starri, what do you make of this?" All of Starri's senses - hearing, sight, touch, smell - seemed preternaturally acute. He took a step forward and held his hand up to his forehead to shield his eyes from the rain, the way someone who did not live in Ireland might shield his eyes from the sun.

"Armed men," Starri said at last. "More than one hundred, sure. But I don't think they're Irish. Their armor, shields, the way they organize themselves, they look more like Norsemen." He swiveled and looked off in the other direction. "Whoever they are, they have the attention of the men in that camp. Look at them, racing around like chickens when a fox is among them!"

Starri found that all very amusing, though Thorgrim could not really see anything in the distant camp beyond the suggestion of movement, or, at Tara's gate, the shuffling of the men clustered there. For some time no one spoke as they watched the two distant armies and waited to see what would happen, to see who would do what. It seemed to be a standoff, the two forces holding each other in check, neither one willing or able to make a move. It had a brittle feeling, like standing on new frozen ice, knowing it might break underfoot at any second.

Who are they? Thorgrim wondered, looking at the men who had just come out of Tara. *If not Irish, then who?* If they were Norsemen, then the most likely answer was that they were Arinbjorn's men. But he could not imagine why Morrigan would go to the trouble of poisoning them all and taking them prisoner just to hand them back their weapons and let them go.

Something to do with this armed camp? he wondered. Might Arinbjorn have made a pact with Morrigan, freedom for him and his men in exchange for fighting this new host? That made sense. Thorgrim could well picture Arinbjorn's desperate negotiations to free himself from an Irish prison. There was very little he would not promise, Thorgrim guessed.

"Now what?" Ornolf asked, pointing toward Tara.

"They are forming a shieldwall," Starri said.

Thorgrim could see they were moving again, the cluster of men at the gate, but as to their forming a shieldwall, he would have to take Starri's word on that. He could not make out that sort of detail.

"Only the Irish could take a simple thing like a battle and turn it into such a damnable mess!" Ornolf roared. "What by Thor's ass are they doing, and what are we going to do about it?"

"We'll know more once Harald and Brigit are back," Thorgrim said. "But this looks like their fight, no business of ours." There were two things working on Thorgrim now. The first was that he could see the chance for plunder had dropped off precipitously with the appearance of not one but two armies. The second was the realization that the ship in which Ornolf had come was in fact his ship, taken by him from the Danes. He had a ship, and that meant he now had the means of returning to Vik without putting himself in debt to some whore's bastard like Arinbjorn.

"So where is the boy?" Ornolf demanded. "Been gone a long time. I hope he and his princess didn't stop to rut like wild boars in the woods.

He's my grandson, you know, so if that's what they're about we might be hours waiting for his return."

Ornolf's voice was like the rain - a near constant sound and nearly devoid of meaning. So, like the rain, Thorgrim hardly even heard it after a while. His eyes ran over the storm-swept field, from the ringfort to the camp, trying to imagine what the next move would be. Whatever it was, he did not think it would involve them. Once Harald was back, they would return to the river. To his ship.

It was then that Thorgrim saw the man walking toward them, far off but headed in their direction. He was walking slowly, with no apparent purpose, not strolling so much as staggering, as if he might have been drinking. He was still fairly far off, and the rain made it more difficult to see, but there was something very familiar about his shape and the way he moved.

"Starri," Thorgrim said.

"Yes. It's him."

"Harald?"

"Harald Broadarm. Your son. Yes, that's him. He's alone."

Thorgrim nodded. *Alone*.... That spoke volumes. And then another thought occurred to him. "Is he wounded?"

Starri shielded his eyes and for a moment did not speak. "I can't see that he is," he said at last. "But I can't see that he isn't. He's walking along fully exposed in the face of two armies and doesn't seem too concerned."

"I'm going after him," Thorgrim said.

"I'm going with you," Starri said.

"No," Thorgrim said. "This whole thing hangs in the balance. If we tip it too far it will all go."

"Two will not tip it. More will, but not two."

Thorgrim considered this. Two might tip it, or they might not. But Starri was a good man to have when he could be kept in control. What's more, if Harald had to be carried back across the field, Thorgrim was not at all certain he could manage by himself.

"Very well, let's go," he said, and the two of them stepped from the brush, stepped into the ankle high grass and headed off across the green, green fields and through the driving Irish rain.

Harald was walking because that was what his legs seemed to be doing, though not through any conscious decision that he had made. Each step appeared to be taking him back to the place from which he had come, but he was not really sure and certainly did not care. He did not care about any of it. There really was no place he wanted to be.

And now you may go... That was what she had said. *And now you may go*... He heard the words sounding over and over in his mind, like the constant peal of a bell. Standing in the tent, free of the rain for the first time in hours. The candlelight had played off her wet skin. Her clothes clung to her body, which was still lithe and strong, though the soaked fabric, tight over her belly, made her… condition…more obvious than it had ever been. She had that haughty look that she could get. It made her more beautiful than ever.

And now you may go… As if he was some servant, some stable hand to be dismissed. He walked along. He heard her voice.

"You are carrying our child!" he shouted into the rain, but the words came out as more of a protracted groan than as real communication.

Harald had no idea whose tent they had been in, but clearly Brigit did. Her words had stunned him like a club to the side of the head. If they had not, if he had been able to think, he would have pulled his sword from his sheath and killed them all, save for Brigit. Killed them all and taken Brigit back to where she belonged. He would have killed them or he would have died in the attempt.

Instead, he had been so dumbfounded by her casual dismissal that he could do nothing but obey. He was halfway back to his own people before it dawned on him what he should have done.

"How could you do this?" he cried. The depth of this betrayal was more than he could wrap his mind around. He thought of those times when they had sailed out of sight of land, when he had looked down into the sea below the ship and wondered how many miles deep the water ran. It gave him an unsettled feeling, bordering on panic, to think on it. This feeling was akin, but now he had no ship below him; now he was sinking down, down into the darkness.

He was pretty sure that he was crying, but with the rain he could not tell, which was something of a blessing. Water ran down his face, into his eyes, which were not really focused anyway, so at first he did not see the two men moving toward him. When he did, he stopped in his tracks and blinked the rain away. He reached for the hilt of his sword, but he realized he did not have the will or the strength to even defend himself, so he let his hand drop to his side once again.

They drew nearer, and Harald could see there was something undeniably familiar about them. He wiped more rain from his eyes and watched them approach. And then he recognized them.

Father? Starri? Of course… he thought. He had been walking back to them, back to his people, without even thinking about it.

The sight of the two men coming for him filled him with hope and comfort, like stepping out of a cold night into a home with a fire blazing. That was what his father had always meant to him.

He was right… The realization dawned on Harald. *About Brigit, about all of it, he was right….* And with that thought, all of the good feelings were gone, and in their place, humiliation, despair. He, Harald Thorgrimson, Harald Broadarm, had been so certain. He had learned to speak the Irish language. He had insisted he did not want to return to Vik, that his new life was in Ireland. He had defied his father on that point, had actually fought with him. He had envisioned himself on the throne of Tara.

And Thorgrim had been right all along. It was more than Harald could stand.

No, no, no... he thought. His father would not gloat or hold it over him, but that would make it worse, in its own way. His grandfather would laugh. He could hear it.

No, he could not stand it, any of it. He would do what he should have done. He would take Brigit back or he would die in the attempt. Now, of course, that second option was all but certain, but that was no matter. He could not go back to his people, not after having been played for such a fool.

His father and Starri were close enough now that he could see them clearly. His father was waving, and through the constant drum of the rain he could hear him calling his name. Harald felt his determination wavering, but he clenched his teeth and forced himself to recall the agony he had been feeling an instant before.

His hand reached across his waist and his fingers wrapped around the familiar grip of his sword. He pulled the blade from its sheath, the weapon nicely balanced in his hand.

I have never named you, he thought, his eyes running over the long, double-edged blade. He had often cast around for a good name, but none had ever come to him.

Vengeance Seeker, he thought. *Yes, that's good. Vengeance Seeker.* He looked at the sword. "You shall be Vengeance Seeker, for as long as we are together," he said. "But I don't think it will be long, not on this earth." With that he turned and faced the camp from which he had come.

He could see the soldiers standing in a loose line, not a shieldwall, but something like. He started walking toward them, his pace purposeful and determined now. He moved faster.

The walk became a jog, then a flat out run. He held Vengeance Seeker over his head. A battle cry formed in his chest and then burst from his mouth, a wild undulating howl of pure mindless bloodlust. It echoed around the field as he plunged, single handed, into the fight.

Chapter Forty-Three

In fury we fought battles,
fire swept through men's homes,
we made bloody bodies
slump dead by city gates.
Egil's Saga

Thorgrim and Starri stopped in their tracks, drawn up short by Harald's utterly unexpected move. "What by Thor's hammer does he think he's doing?" Thorgrim asked.

For a moment they just watched him as his pace increased, as he raised his sword above his head and shouting out across the field. "What, by the gods…" Thorgrim said. He looked over at Starri, but Starri's eyes were fixed on Harald and he was rubbing the arrowhead hanging around his neck. He was grinning.

"He's taking the fight to the enemy," Starri said. "None of us old women standing around would do it, but he will."

"The enemy?" Thorgrim said, nodding toward the camp. "We don't even know who they are. Anyway, he can't fight them all, not all by himself. What do we do now?"

Starri turned his gaze from Harald and met Thorgrim's eyes. He had that crazed look that Thorgrim had seen before, when there was fighting to be done and Starri ready to do it. "Thorgrim Night Wolf has to ask this?" he said. "What to do? We join him!"

With that, Starri dropped the arrowhead, pulled his short sword from its sheath, his battle ax from his belt and leapt forward, bolting like a startled deer, going from dead still to a flat out run in the blink of an eye. And not just running. Running and waving his weapons and howling like the mad berserker he was.

Thorgrim felt suddenly very alone, his friend and his son racing off to join a battle that had not yet begun, his men back at the tree line and himself standing alone in the middle of the open ground, the rain pouring down. For a second, no more, he looked back and forth, lost in indecision. Then, with a howl of disgust, disgust with himself, mainly, he pulled his sword and turned to the men in the woods behind him. "To arms! To arms! Follow me! Rally to me!" he shouted, as loud as his formidable voice could shout. "To me!"

The men came out of the trees like a breaking wave. One moment there was nothing, just the still and motionless woods, and then the Norsemen burst screaming from the trees, weapons raised, cresting and roiling and charging forward. Thorgrim waited one second, two seconds, until he was sure that they were all on the move, that their momentum would carry them across the length of open ground without his having to urge them on. And when he was satisfied that they were moving forward, that they would join in the fight as quickly as they humanly could, he turned and raised Iron-tooth and ran after Harald and Starri and the distant enemy he did not even know.

Ruarc mac Brain saw them first. The others, Breandan mac Aidan, his officers, Brigit, were looking toward Tara when Ruarc noticed the movement to their right.

"Here they come," he said. "Bloody fools."

At that distance, the better part of a mile away, he could not make out much in the way of detail, but the sight of a hoard of men making a disordered attack was unmistakable. They came rushing out from what had been the effective cover of the trees – Ruarc had not even known they were there. But they had tossed that advantage away. Even from Norsemen he might have expected a more orderly approach, a shieldwall or what they called a swine array, but this was just a headlong rush. Suicide, really.

"Is this a reason to be concerned?" Brigit asked. She did not sound very concerned.

"No, I think not," Ruarc said. "It was clever of them, hiding the right wing of their force in the trees. Might have been put to good effect. They would have done well to make an approach through the woods, the way that young Northman brought you here. Never saw you coming. If they'd done that, and timed their attack well, they might have had our right flank, rolled it right up. As it is, they will exhaust themselves running across the field, and we're not just forewarned, we practically have time for a nap before they get here."

The others grunted with amusement at that. "These fellows here," Breandan said, pointing toward Tara and taking up the narrative for his lord, "will make an attack as well, hope to catch us between two armies, as it were."

"They *will* catch you between two armies, will they not?" Finnian asked. "After all, they have two armies, and you but one."

"We'll divide our force, left wing and right wing. We've men enough, and these are only heathens, here," Ruarc said, "or so it appears. We'll advance a few hundred yards and meet them on the field, no need to fight with our arses resting on the camp."

He said that for the benefit of Brigit and Father Finnian. He had no need to explain his thinking to Breandan mac Aidan and his other officers. They were skilled enough, and they had all fought together long enough, that such elementary orders were unnecessary. Indeed, Ruarc was still explaining the situation when Breandan and the others made quick bows in his direction then hurried off to form the men up.

So who are you? Ruarc wondered. These men coming from the woods, they were the fin gall who had accompanied Brigit from Dubh-linn. Or so she said. But what of the men who had come through Tara's gate? They seemed to be working with Brigit's men, or they probably would have retreated in the face of his army. Did Morrigan have her own fin gall army? Was Brigit playing a double game here?

Ruarc shook his head. "Father Finnian," he said, "why does everything in Ireland have to be so damnably complicated?"

A shieldwall was meant as a stationary defense, or a line moving forward. It was not intended as a formation for retreat, which is why the men under Arinbjorn's command had covered no more than twenty yards when the others burst from the woods, three quarters of a mile away, coming from the exact direction in which Arinbjorn's men were going. Arinbjorn did not even notice them until Hrolleif the Stout bellowed, "Now who's this? By the gods, these people are dropping out of the sky!"

Arinbjorn turned. He saw a hundred or so men, emerging from the woods on a run, following Harald Thorgrimson, who was now running back in the direction in which he had come. Arinbjorn frowned and shook his head and tried to imagine what all of this could mean. Who were these men? Was Thorgrim with them, or in that distant camp? Or nowhere at all nearby?

Hrolleif was shouting again. "The gods don't think much of our retreating, and come to think on it, neither do I!"

"See here, Arinbjorn," Ingolf said. Arinbjorn pulled his eyes from this new host and looked where Ingolf was pointing with his sword. A moment before, the men-at-arms in the distant camp had been standing in a loose and undisciplined line, taking little interest in Arinbjorn's retrograde motion. But they were taking interest now. Down the long length of the hill they could see the armed men forming in two divisions, one to meet the threat from the men from the woods, one to advance against Arinbjorn's shieldwall.

"Those men, they must think these fellows who've come from the wood are part of our force," Arinbjorn said.

"Of course they think that, you god-forsaken idiot!" Hrolleif shouted.

"Very well, then, Hrolleif, who is so wise," called Bolli Thorvaldsson, who was standing at Arinbjorn's side and pointing toward the men from the wood line, "who are these men?"

"I don't know! How by Thor's arse should I know? Ingolf, do you know?"

Ingolf shook his head. "I don't know and I don't much care, right now. These men-at-arms yonder are making ready to attack. We can either turn and flee back to the ships like a bunch of girls, or we can advance like men. What will it be?"

The rest apparently felt as Hrolleif did, that they were done with retreating, and their fighting spirit was bolstered by the sight of the hundred or so screaming Northmen on their left flank, now a half a mile away and racing headlong for the enemy. A cheer rippled along the line and built in strength, swords were held high or beaten against shields, cheers turned into battle shouts, and with never an order given, the shieldwall, which had stopped in its retreat, now rolled forward, down the long hill, down at the enemy advancing toward them.

Thorgrim's left foot snagged on something hidden by the grass. He stumbled for a few steps, caught himself before he fell, and ran on. He had nearly gone down, and worse, he realized that he had nearly allowed himself to go down. His chest was burning, his legs were aching, his breath was coming in gasps. He actually longed to stumble and collapse into the soft green grass, to lie motionless in the rain. To stop. Just stop.

He staggered on for a few more yards and then he did stop, because he could not physically go any further. The old wound in his side throbbed, but it was too far healed now to open up again without significant help. He bent nearly double, hands on his knees, gasping. He looked up. Harald and Starri had been drawing away from him since he had first gone after them. He had envisioned catching up with them, ordering them to stop, making them join the others. They would be slaughtered if they charged the enemy's line, just the two of them.

But he soon realized that he could not catch them, and then he realized he could not even run all the way across the open ground. There had been a time, a decade or so earlier, that he would have kept up with them and likely beaten them, but those days were gone. So he had called out for them to stop, but by then he was so winded that he could not make his voice heard over the rain. And then he was done.

He was still heaving for breath when he straightened and turned to see where the others were. He had started with a lead of a quarter mile on them, but now they were only a few dozen yards behind. And behind them, quite far behind, Ornolf the Restless was stumbling and staggering after.

At least I am not the most pathetic old man here, Thorgrim thought. He straightened and, as the men grew closer, he held up his hands to stop them. He could not prevent Harald and Starri from making their death run, but he could prevent these men from being butchered for want of discipline. And maybe they could reach Harald and Starri in time.

"Swine array!" he shouted, his words coming out more like a gasp than the powerful command he was trying for. "I'll take the lead, form up on me!" He ran his eyes over them, men he did not really know, until he found the one he was looking for. He was more bear than man, over six feet in height and broad and solid as an old oak. His sword was like a toy in his hand, his shield like a dinner plate.

"You there, what's your name?"

"Godi."

"Godi, with me. The rest of you get in order, quickly now." The swine array, Odin's arrow, was designed to break shieldwalls. Two men took the lead, with three behind them, and then four and then five, creating a great human arrowhead that could break through the wall of interlocking shields and reduce the fight to a massive brawl, to the great advantage of the Viking horde.

"Thorgrim, take my shield," one of the men – Thorgrim did not know his name – stepped up and handed him a bright painted red and white wooden disk.

"Thank you," Thorgrim said. He had left his own shield behind, because when he had gone after Harald he had not expected to be racing into battle, and in the agony of running it had slipped his mind entirely.

Harald does not have a shield, he thought, *nor does Starri.* Starri, of course, never carried a shield because he did not want anything that might interfere with his being killed on the field of battle. But Thorgrim did not like to think about Harald hitting the shieldwall with no shield of his own.

"Let us go!" he shouted, his voice coming back. "Let us go and let us bring bloody murder to these sons of whores!" A cheer went up, loud and gratifying, because the men were charged with fighting spirit and it had not occurred to them that they did not know who this enemy was, or why they were doing battle with him.

Thorgrim turned and headed off across the field once more, his breathing restored, his sense of purpose renewed, because he, at least, knew why he was fighting. The enemy was closer than he had thought, and that too gave him hope. He could see Harald and Starri ahead of them, halfway between them and the enemy line.

Maybe they won't be such fools, Thorgrim thought. *Maybe they'll stop before they are cut down.* He knew, however, that it was too much to hope that Starri would do the reasonable thing, and he could only hope that Harald would. And so he ran, shield thumping against his side, his soft leather shoes parting the wet grass, ran to get into the fight before any hurt came to his son, his boy, his boy whose feelings he had so callously, thoughtlessly brushed aside.

There was nothing, Harald realized, that cleared the mind and honed it razor sharp quite as effectively as a mile run through driving rain at an enemy that outnumbered you two hundred to one.

His breath was starting to come hard as he and Starri closed the last ten rods. Running across the field, he had watched the enemy forming from a loose line into a real shieldwall, and he was pleased that they considered Starri and him as threat enough that they needed to take such measures. But as the physical exertion drained the fury away, and Harald considered the solid shieldwall before him, he began to see that they were not quite the threat he hoped, and that they would be lucky to take even a few of them out before they were cut down.

"Starri! Starri, hold up!" Harald shouted, and Starri came to a stop a few feet ahead of Harald. He turned, and his eyes had that weird look that Harald had seen before, and he knew he could not hold Starri back for long.

"Let us at least catch our breath," Harald gasped. The odds were enough against them without their going into the fight gasping for air, though he noticed that Starri was not breathing nearly as hard as he was. Seventy feet from the enemy and Starri began to make low animal noises and spin slowly around like a leaf in a whirlpool.

"Just a moment, Starri, just a moment," Harald said, sucking in air as hard as he could and spitting out rainwater. He straightened and some sound from behind caught his attention. He turned. Two hundred feet behind, his father and the huge fellow, Godi, were charging at them in a swine array.

So that's why they formed a shieldwall, Harald thought, embarrassed by his mistake, and glad that he had not mentioned to Starri that he thought the preparations were for them.

Starri Deathless saw them as well, and the expression on his face took on a veneer of panic at the thought of missing his chance to attack the shieldwall single-handed. "Come along, Harald, come along, they will be up with us!" he shouted, and then, unable to wait a second longer, turned and raced on toward the line of soldiers ahead.

Harald also took a step forward, and then another, building his pace back to a run. He had made the decision to charge the line, even if it had not been made with the clearest mind, and he could not now stop and wait for the others. That would be as much as admitting that his actions had been a mistake, and he would not admit that. Even if they were.

Starri was now thirty feet ahead, closing fast with the line of soldiers. Harald lifted Vengeance Seeker above his head and reflexively twisted his forearm to re-adjust the grip on his shield when he had an unsettling realization. *I have no shield…*

This would take some change of tactics, and he looked up to see how Starri dealt with the problem, since Starri did not have a shield either and never did. The berserker was charging hard at a point in the shieldwall, and Harald could see the men there ready for him, no doubt baffled by this madman charging straight at them, and all alone. Spears emerged from behind the line of shields, wicked iron points reaching out ahead of the men, ready to impale Starri as he flung himself at the line.

Starri was ten feet from the shieldwall when he went down. Harald pulled to a stop and gasped, certain, in that second, that Starri had tripped and fallen and would now be run through by half a dozen spears. But Starri had not tripped. He went down head first and hit the ground with his shoulder, rolled once, completely over, and sprung back onto his feet, inches from the shieldwall, well past the line of spear tips that were now too far extended to reach him.

He let his momentum carry him into the line of men, hitting the round wooden shields with his shoulder. The men who held them were trained to stand fast and hold back the press of an attacking shieldwall, but Starri's onslaught took them completely by surprise. Harald could see the looks of shock on their faces as Starri was suddenly on them, smashing a hole in the line, flailing with ax and sword with such maniacal fury that the soldiers within the arc of his weapons could do nothing but hold their shields up and cower.

Harald saw a shield splinter under a blow from Starri's battle ax, saw the short sword drive through the opening that was created, and then a spray of blood and the man fell away as Starri wrenched the ax free and swung on the next man. And Harald realized, to his disgust, that he had stopped running and was gaping like a little boy witnessing his first fight. He raised Vengeance Seeker over his head, let a shout build as he regained the momentum he had lost, charged the last few rods toward the enemy, eager to get in the fight ahead of his father, eager that everyone should know the truth, that he was no more hesitant than Starri Deathless to plunge into so mad a battle.

He was fifteen feet away, heading for the edge of the hole Starri had driven in the shieldwall, when the men there saw him coming. A second before, all eyes had been on Starri, but in that last instant they saw Harald coming and the spears came out, the black dagger points. Harald thought of

Starri's rolling attack but he doubted he could pull that off, and he did not care to die sprawled at the feet of these men, stabbed like a wild boar.

Harald could not roll, but from a dead run he could make himself stop in his tracks. It was a trick he had practiced often and found quite handy indeed: the heels dig in, the body leans back to check the momentum and he would render himself motionless when the instant before he had been at a full run. He was now just feet away from the nearest spear point and he could see the look on the faces of the men bearing the spears, the certainty that he would run right on to them. But then he slammed to a stop, so close the nearest spear tip was touching his chainmail, and just as the surprised soldier tried to thrust further, Harald swung Vengeance Seeker around in a great arc, knocking the spears aside, then leaped forward, past the spear points, right at the men in the line.

The men in the shieldwall had been shocked once by Starri's attack and now Harald's threw them off balance again. Harald reached out with his left hand, grabbed the upper edge of the shield nearest to him and jerked it close, pulling the man who held it along too. To his right someone tried to drive a sword into his gut, but Harald twisted the shield in the way of the thrust. He swept Vengeance Seeker down between the two shields, felt the blade hit steel as he indiscriminately knocked weapons aside.

The one whose shield Harald held was tugging it back, trying to break it free from Harald's iron grip. He drew his sword back as if to cleave Harald's head in two, but before he could bring it down, Harald lashed out with his fist, his sword still clamped in his hand, and punched the man full in the face. His nose crumpled under the blow and his helmet went askew and he staggered away. Harald deftly twisted the shield out of his grip as he fell, then held it up, wrong side to, as a spear struck out though the press of men, aimed square at his heart.

The shield took the thrust and Harald twisted it free, flipped it over, thrust his arm though the leather strap and took hold of the iron grip behind the boss, even as he raised Vengeance Seeker and warded off another blow.

Very well, I have a shield... he thought. Now he was ready to join the battle in a serious way. To his right Starri was unleashing his berserker rage on the Irish. Harald could not actually see the man, just flailing weapons, and bleeding men-at-arms crawling across the grass or lying still. The screaming was constant, some Starri's, some the soldiers, and under it, the snapping of weapons, the renting of wood, and a crunching sound that Harald did not like to think on.

Harald Broadarm slammed against the shieldwall again, but this time it did not move, and he reached out with Vengeance Seeker for a target, thrust and parried. He was in a bad place. It took a shieldwall to fight a shieldwall, not one man, no matter how good he was. Even Starri would soon be overwhelmed, and these men, these men-at-arms, knew their business. Harald could see them starting to step out to his right and left, extending that portion of the shieldwall around, and soon he would be fighting men on three sides, and he could not do that for long.

Go back, go back! The thought rang in his head, but it was a hateful thought. Retreat, disgrace, it was not what he had been trained to do, it was not their way, the Northmen, so he parried another blow and thrust again. He caught a movement to his left, someone advancing from the shieldwall, and he swung his shield around to deflect the thrust of his sword. But now he was exposed on the front. A spear tip like a snake strike whipped out and he just managed to knock it aside with his sword.

Shield back in front, but now there was someone to his right and before he could react something unyielding as stone struck him on the side of the head. He stumbled, saw the ground whirl past, the men in front of him strangely indistinct. He tried to make the images clear in his eyes but he could not. And suddenly, through the blur of rain and muted colors, he thought he saw his father, and the big man, the one called Godi, charging past on either side.

Chapter Forty-Four

I raise the ring, the clasp that is worn
on the shield-splitting arm,
on to my rod of the battle-storm
in praise of the feeder of ravens.
Egil's Saga

That brief moment when Thorgrim had stopped and set the men in the swine array made the difference. It allowed him to catch his breath, allowed him to go on again, but the revivification did not last long. Running in mail was never an easy task, and the mail shirt he had borrowed from one of Ornolf's men was not particularly light, and so he soon found himself once again gasping for breath. To make matters worse, he had to keep pace with Godi who, with each step, covered half again as much distance as Thorgrim did.

In his favor was the fact that a swine array did not want to go into battle at a full out run. Better to hit the shieldwall at a fast but controlled pace. Thus, it was not entirely for his own benefit that he called for Godi and the men in the front ranks to slow to a jog.

Thirty feet from the line, and he could see Harald fighting for his life, and doing a very credible job of it. But there was only so much one man could do against a shieldwall, only so long he could hold out.

A minute more, Harald, stand fast a minute more…

To the right of where Harald was making his stand there was a great whirl of activity, a chaotic, wild fighting like two packs of wolves tearing into one another. Thorgrim guessed that in the middle of all that he would find Starri Deathless. He changed the angle of his advance a bit so that he and Godi would hit the shieldwall just to Harald's left side. Fifteen feet now, the faces of the men-at-arms behind the shields clear and sharp, the grunt and clang and rent of battle loud in his ears. It all worked on Thorgrim's spirit and he felt a new energy surge through him and he felt the battle cry build and then burst out as if it was not something that came from him at all, but some other living thing desperate for escape.

He saw the concentration on the faces of his enemy, he saw the fear, and then he and Godi slammed into the shieldwall like a breaking wave, and behind them he sensed, more than saw, the rest of the Northmen hitting the wall, spreading down its length as surge after surge slammed into the enemy's defense.

The men-at-arms staggered and stepped back under the power of the impact. The Norsemen's weapons rose and fell, reaching beyond the edge of the shields, or thrusting in those gaps that could be found between the overlapping disks. To Thorgrim's right, one of the Northmen tried too late to deflect a spear thrust. The weapon caught him under the chin and the combined force of the thrust and his forward momentum drove the point home until it erupted from the back of his skull in a welter of blood and bone. The man flailed but he did not scream because he was dead before the reflex to scream even hit him, and he went down, the spear still through his skull, an Irishman disarmed.

Iron-tooth was a thing of beautiful balance; a long, straight, double-edged blade with a leather and wire bound grip and a heavy pommel to counterbalance the weight of the steel. Thorgrim used that to good advantage, not hacking as if his weapon was a battle ax but thrusting over and between the shields, looking for his targets and lashing out with a skill honed by long practice on straw men.

The Irish shieldwall wavered. The men took half a step back, Thorgrim could feel them giving. Somewhere to his left he heard one of the Irishmen scream, a scream of terror, like a woman. He saw the man turn and run, deserting his comrades, flinging his weapons away. He made it ten feet before one of the Irish officers put a sword through his gut. The wall where he had left a hole closed up again, the disciplined move of well-trained men.

"Push them back! Push them back!" Thorgrim shouted. Godi at his side was fighting like a fury, his shield like a battering ram, his massive body exerting tremendous force against the line as his sword slashed at anything within his substantial reach. Thorgrim caught a glimpse of Harald. The boy was bleeding from a laceration to his face, but it did not look too bad, and with the effort he was putting into the fight, Thorgrim guessed he did not even know the cut was there.

Some commotion on his right, and Thorgrim stole a glance, enough to see the great bulk of Ornolf the restless pushing his way through his own men to get at the shieldwall and the Irish beyond. He had reached the line at last, after the great effort of humping it over nearly a mile of open ground, but the fight was in him now, and like Thorgrim he seemed to forget age and exhaustion as he thrust his shield against the Irish wall and wielded his battle ax as Thorgrim had seen him do a hundred times before, in a hundred different fights in a dozen lands in more than twenty years of going a'viking.

Again the shieldwall shifted, just a bit, the Irishmen taking a half a step back, but that was a start, a weakening, and Thorgrim knew it meant they would break soon. But as he lashed out with Iron-tooth, he saw something he did not expect – more men, fresh men, coming to that weak spot in the shield wall, rushing to shore it up.

Reinforcements...the buggers have held men back... Thorgrim thought and he knew for certain now that they were not fighting a bunch of farmers, but soldiers who knew their business.

And why are we fighting? he thought, and he realized he did not have an answer for that, not really.

And then a horn sounded, loud, cutting like a sharp sword through the noise of the battle, the drumming of rain. It sounded again and was joined by another and then another, and whatever it meant, the Irish at least understood. The shieldwall stepped back and back again, not a retreat, really, but a disciplined disengagement, a coordinated move. The shields were held chest high and the weapons held back, ready to strike, but they did not strike. Up and down the line the sound of the fighting fell away as the Irish backed off, not yielding, but not fighting either, and the Northmen, not understanding what was going on, stepped back as well, and let weary arms hang at their sides, weapons in hand.

There was a bustling to Thorgrim's right and he saw four of the Norsemen haul a frantic, flailing Starri Deathless out of the mass of Irishmen. His eyes were wide and he seemed to be foaming at the mouth and he was as covered in blood as if he had painted himself.

Thorgrim rushed over to where, with great difficulty, the four were holding Starri down while Starri in turn lashed out and kicked and twisted.

"Starri, Starri!" Thorgrim knelt beside the berserker and yelled in his face. Starri's wild eyes rolled over and caught Thorgrim's and held them. Thorgrim put his hand on Starri's shoulder and he felt the man relax under his touch. "Let him go," Thorgrim said to the four and they released him, then leapt to their feet and backed off quick, eager to get out of the way.

"What is it? What's happening?" Starri asked.

"I don't know," Thorgrim said. The horns were still sounding but now no one was moving. Up and down the line, Irishmen and Norsemen stood, a few yards between them, and they waited for what would come next.

"Are we dead?" Starri asked.

"More or less," Thorgrim said. He stood and Starri sat up and looked around. There was some movement off to the right, the shieldwall swinging back, opening up. Then to Thorgrim's astonishment a tall white horse appeared through the parted men, and on its back, in a robe edged with gold trim, sat Princess Brigit. She held a sword in her hands, and she held it with surprising authority; not the timid, unfamiliar grip with which he had seen other women - women not from his homeland - hold weapons. Brigit held the sword like a woman accustom to holding swords, and from her high perch she searched the faces of the men who were now silent and looking up at her.

"Harald!" she shouted, when she finally saw Harald Thorgrimson among the Northmen, "Harald!"

Harald stepped forward, a curious look on his face – anger, confusion, uncertainty. Brigit called out more words in her Irish tongue. Harald nodded, said a few words back, then in a commanding voice, a voice that carried over the length of the field, he called, "Princess Brigit nic Máel Sechnaill has asked that I translate her words. It is her you see before you."

He nodded to Brigit, and Brigit went on again in her odd language, Harald listening close and nodding. "She says that we Northmen came with her to help restore her to the throne of Tara. That we were promised gold and silver for our efforts…." He paused as Brigit added more. "She says that has not changed. That we should not fight her. That we should join with her and these men to defeat the army at Tara, and then the gold and silver will be ours."

If Brigit had expected shouts of agreement, a rousing cheer of excitement at this alliance, then Thorgrim figured she must have been disappointed. The Norsemen made no sound, just stood their ground and stared at her. Silence hung over the field, making the rain sound louder still.

"Night Wolf," Starri said, standing. "I don't think this is Valhalla." The rain was washing the blood away, not evenly, but in patches, and it made Starri look even more nightmarish then before. "By the gods," he said, looking around, "Valhalla had damned well be better than this."

Brigit spoke again, her voice loud, a tone of command. Harald translated. "What say you?"

A voice came rolling down from the far end of the line, and Thorgrim recognized it as belonging to Hrolleif the Stout. "I say, we've had enough of these lying Irishmen," he shouted. Men stepped aside and Hrolleif came stamping down toward the break in the line, pointing at Brigit. "And worse, these lying Irish wenches!" That elicited a murmur from the men. Thorgrim looked at Harald and he could see the boy was struggling with how, or if, to translate those words.

But then another voice came through the rain, a voice that made Thorgrim flush with anger at the mere sound of it, a voice that brought equal measures loathing and revulsion. Arinbjorn White-tooth pushed his way to the center of the line in Hrolleif's wake, hurrying as if to catch up, a "me, too" quality to his actions.

"You do not speak for the men, Hrolleif," he shouted. Thorgrim shook his head. This was pathetic. If Arinbjorn had ever held any position of command, it was clearly gone now. He sounded more like a nagging housewife than a jarl commanding hirdmen.

"Nor do you, Arinbjorn!" Hrolleif bellowed back. "I would not follow you to the privy if I had to puke!"

Ingolf stepped up. "We will meet on this in council. All the lead men must discuss this!" he shouted and that met with a murmur of approval because it was the first sensible thing anyone had said. Harald's eyes met Thorgrim's and Thorgrim could see in them a plea for guidance. Thorgrim nodded and Harald translated Ingolf's words to Brigit. Brigit answered, and Harald called out, "The Princess sees the wisdom of this, but she begs you hurry as we must attack soon. Every minute we delay, the defenses of Tara will grow stronger."

The lead men broke from the line of Norsemen and retreated to a spot a dozen yards away: Arinbjorn and Bolli Thorvaldsson, Hrolleif, Ingolf, Ornolf. Thorgrim slid Iron-tooth into his scabbard and headed toward the group, then stopped and turned. "Harald!" he called. "Join us!"

Harald hurried over, looking surprised and uneasy. "Why, father? I'm no jarl, or even hirdman."

"No," Thorgrim agreed. "But you are the only one who has any idea of what is going on here."

Ruarc mac Brain sat on his chestnut mare and watched as Brigit expertly swung her horse around and walked it back to where he and Breandan mac Aidan and the others waited. This had been her idea, and he had been more than a little skeptical at first, but now he was starting to think she was right. The sharp note of the horns sounding *disengage*, the men-at-arms stepping the shieldwall back, had been enough to stop the Northmen from fighting. Now, they might be swayed to change allegiances. Or change them back. Or some accursed thing. He could hardly keep it straight.

"They are talking, Lord Ruarc," Brigit said. From his horse, Ruarc could see that a horde of them had gone off for a private conference. These he took to be their leaders, though with the heathen swine one could not tell leaders from stable hands.

"Very well. Let us hope they come to the right decision."

Ruarc mac Brain did not mind fighting, in fact he rather liked a good battle. But he could not tolerate pointless violence, could not stand to see men's lives thrown away for nothing, and that was exactly what had been happening just minutes before. Why these men, who had come with Brigit from Dubh-linn and had been tricked and nearly killed by Flann mac Conaing, had then turned on *him*, whom they did not know, he could not imagine.

Brigit was quick to ascribe it to animal stupidity. Ruarc would not generally be satisfied with so simple an answer, but try as he might he could think of no other.

"Do you have a feel for their mood? Will they join us in arms?" Ruarc asked.

"I don't know," Brigit said. The rain had turned her wavy hair into straight tendrils and her formerly ruddy complexion was white, making her look as if she had drowned. But the rain, at last, was starting to ease. "I don't know," Brigit said again, looking not at Ruarc but at the fin gall leaders gathered some ways off. "They are animals, you know, and they are governed by their appetites alone. Appetites for silver and gold, food, women. If they can conjure up one intelligent thought between the lot of them, they'll realize that those things will not be had fighting you, only by taking Tara."

"And if we take Tara? What then?" Ruarc asked. "We round up what gold and silver is there and hand it to them?"

Brigit turned to him quick, as if surprised by his words. "Dear God, no," she said, and there was a hardness to her voice that he would not have expected from one so young and lovely as Brigit nic Máel Sechnaill. "They cannot be suffered to live. We send them in first, against Flann's men, and any who live through that, we kill them like the rabid dogs they are."

"Indeed," Ruarc said. He looked off at the gathering of leaders. He could see arms waving, an animated discussion. He was not certain how comfortable he was with this. To form an alliance with these men, and then butcher them? He was not sure.

"My Lord Ruarc," Brigit said, as if he had voiced his doubts out loud. "These are not Irishmen and they are not Christians. They come to our land, take what they wish, plunder our churches, rape and enslave our women. They try to crush the true faith under foot. And they will not stop. If there was a pack of wolves on your lands, killing your sheep, you would hunt them down and kill them all, by whatever means available. Well, sir, there *is* a pack of wolves on your lands."

Ruarc nodded. Every word she spoke was true, and the threat from the Northmen was real and it was here. She was right. They could not be suffered to live.

Before he could reply he saw that the council of leaders was breaking up, that the men had come to some sort of decision. They approached the line. Leading the way was an older man, a huge man with a massive beard and long hair who seemed to roll as he walked.

"This old sodomite is the one they call Ornolf," Brigit said, her contempt clear as the purest water.

"He is their leader? Lord over these men?"

"I don't know the extent of his authority," Brigit said, "but he is a drunkard and a fool, so that would put him in good stead to command the others."

The shieldwall opened up wider and the one called Ornolf stepped through and the others followed behind like geese in flight. They stopped ten feet from where Ruarc, Brigit and the others waited, looking down at them from their mounts. A young man, much younger than the others, came and stood by Ornolf's side. Ruarc recognized him as the boy who had brought Brigit to their camp.

Ornolf spoke in a voice to match his frame. The young man translated the words into a broken but passable Irish. "I am Ornolf Hrafnsson, jarl in East Agder, in Vik,"

"Have you come to a decision?" Ruarc called before the old man could continue with his titles.

The boy translated, listened to Ornolf's reply, and then said, "We have. We will join you. We will fight to conquer this place you call Tara. In exchange for the plunder of that place."

Ruarc nodded. "I honor your decision, and I welcome your friendship," he said and the boy translated. "We will advance in a line of battle. We have a battering ram and we will use it to knock the gate open. My men and your men will use their shields to protect those wielding the ram from arrows. Then, when the gate is broken down, your men will advance through and engage the enemy there, and we shall follow behind and join with you."

He waited while the boy stumbled through the translation. When he got to the end, the old man named Ornolf threw back his head and roared with laughter. When he was done he wiped his eyes and said something to the boy, which the boy translated as, "Ornolf says…he says, the fight is for the Irish…Norsemen and Irish will go in together…"

Ruarc had the sense that the boy was softening the words, but it did not matter. "Very well," he called, "We go in together. Let your men form up there." He pointed to the right wing on his line.

The boy translated. Ornolf shouted orders, and then others shouted orders, and the Northmen began forming up in a surprisingly coordinated manner. Ruarc swung his horse around so he was addressing Breandan mac Aidan and the others, his back to the line of men. "Pass the word to your officers," he said. "Once the main gate is battered open, we enter, Irish and Norsemen, and we engage Flann's troops. They are not many, and it should not be any great task to defeat them. Then we turn immediately on the Norsemen, cut them down where they stand. They are a threat, not to be trusted, and we must eliminate them. No quarter."

Heads nodded. These men understood. They had been in Ruarc mac Brain's service for some time, many years in some instances. They knew he spoke plain and his judgment was good, and they would do as he instructed.

Ten minutes later the line was formed, and ready. Ruarc mac Brain called an order in a voice that carried over the wet field and with an answering shout they rolled forward, Irish and Norsemen, a battle line three hundred or more strong, moving inexorably up the hill to Tara.

Chapter Forty-Five

They will tunnel beneath God's oratories;
churches will be burned...
Irish Poem of Prophesy
attributed to Bec mac Dé

It was all visible from the walls of Tara. They could see it, but they could not understand it.

Morrigan, Flan mac Conaing and a few others watched it play out as if they were Romans of old watching a battle in the Coliseum, staged for their amusement. In this instance, however, the outcome mattered far more to them than a few coins they might have bet on one side or the other.

They watched Ruarc mac Brain's men assemble as Arinbjorn and the Norse army rushed from the gate of Tara. For a moment it looked as if Arinbjorn was going to retreat, but then, as if conjured up from thin air, came another horde of Norsemen appeared, racing across the far end of the field and falling on Ruarc's left flank. No doubt greatly encouraged by this, Arinbjorn's men immediately advanced against Ruarc's right.

Morrigan stood by her brother and said nothing. But in mind and spirit she was near ecstasy as she watched her plan play out just as she had imagined. Better, in fact, than she had imagined. Her hope had been only for Arinbjorn to inflict some debilitating hurt on Ruarc mac Brain before Ruarc killed the Norsemen to a man. She had not known about this other army. And now it looked as if Ruarc mac Brain's army would be the one destroyed, and the Northmen left crippled. And that was good, because the Northmen were not interested in sitting on the throne of Tara, as Ruarc no doubt was.

Once Arinbjorn's troops stopped their cowardly retreat and advanced, the fighting quickly enveloped the whole line, a great, bloody struggle, which Morrigan was privileged to witness from her high, safe vantage. And then the horns sounded, their clear note easily heard from the walls of Tara, and, inexplicably, the fighting stopped.

What had happened she could not imagine, and when she asked, Flann admitted that he, too, had no notion of what was taking place on the far field. The fighting stopped, the two lines, Irish and Norse, separated. For long minutes no one seemed to be doing anything. And then the Vikings were moving again, but rather than renewing their attack they fell into the Irish battle line. Facing Tara. All of them, shields making a long row of bright dots in the wet, gray afternoon, all of them facing Tara. And then they began to move.

"They have made a peace," Flann said, soft, with resignation. "They have made a peace and joined together to fall on Tara." They watched in silence for a minute more while the long line moved forward as one, building momentum as it came.

"What Ruarc mac Brain might have said to those heathens, I cannot imagine," Flann said at last. "What he promised them, once they have taken Tara, I do not like to think on."

"What will you do, brother?" Morrigan asked.

"There is not much we can do. We will have our men on the walls, defending with spears and arrows. But they will have a battering ram, I have no doubt, and they will beat the doors of the gate down. It will not take them long. Then we'll fight them as they come."

"No!" Morrigan said, frightened by what he was suggesting. "No!" she said again. "There must be something else." Her mind was flailing like someone thrown into the sea, someone who could not swim. "Let me think!"

"Sister," Flann said, and his voice did not carry the harsh tone that it had these past days. It was soft, almost tender. "You're a very clever girl, and you've done a great deal. You nearly saved us before. But the time for tricks is past. Now is the time to stand like men."

He turned and headed for the ladder.

"No, brother, wait!" she said and Flann stopped and turned. She ran to him, stood very close and spoke softly. "You need not do this. There is a back way out, you know that. We can take horses, we'll take Donnel and Patrick and we'll ride hard. We can be miles gone before the gate is battered down."

Flann did not say anything, he just smiled a thin smile. Then he did something he had not done in a long time. He took her in his arms and hugged her, softly, and kissed the top of her head, the way he used to when she was a little girl and she had scraped her knee and he was the only one to comfort her.

"God go with you, sister," he said, "and pray for me, because I have put my soul in great peril." Then he turned and hurried down the ladder, his officers following behind.

Morrigan stood on the wall and watched him. She watched him as he crossed the open ground with bold strides, his arms waving as he issued orders and the men falling in, making two lines, one behind the other, facing the gate that would be battered down, forming a human wall against the tide that would rush in. This was when Flann was at his best, she knew, when he most felt he was doing what God had made him to do. Leading men into battle. Not ordering them into battle. Leading them.

She turned and looked out at the line moving up the hill, the impossibly long line of men, more visible now as they grew closer, the shields distinct as individual circles, the helmets gleaming dull and wet in the slacking rain. Then she looked back at her brother. He was talking with his officers now, putting a reassuring hand on their shoulders, gripping their arms.

All my clever manipulations, she thought. She had done this, all of it. Since she first conceived of setting the lineage of Flann mac Conaing on the throne of Tara, this had all, in one way or another, come about because of her plans and her tricks and her damned pride. And now she had killed Flann, her beloved brother, the only person in all the world she really loved. She had killed him as sure as if she had driven a dagger through his heart.

The tears came with that realization. She could feel them welling up in her eyes and she could feel them rolling warm down her cold, wet cheeks. She ran along the wall and down the ladder, her feet slipping on the rungs, finding their place again. For her sins her brother would die and the heathens would rape Tara and unleash their horrible vengeance on her people.

She did not consider what might happen to her; she didn't care and in truth would have been happy for any torment that might help erase the pain of what she had done, any horror that could be visited on her that might distract from the anguish she was suffering now.

She stumbled blindly across the open ground, past the lines of men readying for the moment when Tara's gate would be battered down, and those being deployed to the top of the wall with spears and arrows. She ran through the ankle deep puddles and the mud that sucked at her shoes and grabbed at her feet as if trying to stop her flight, to drag her down to some place of torment beneath the earth.

She ran past the royal residence with its new-build section, the fresh, clean daub and new thatch clearly delineating the border between it and the original house. She had ordered the new section to be built bigger, grander than it had been, a monument to her hubris and greed.

At last she came to the lovely church, the sanctuary, the place she loved above all others within the walls of Tara. She pulled the doors open. The space was in twilight with the rain outside and no candles lit, the house of worship now a scene of frantic confusion, the monks rushing about with an urgency that bordered on panic. In the northern corner of the church a grave was open, the flat, heavy stone that marked the resting place of Blessed Cummian, fifth abbot of Tara, moved aside and settled on wooden blocks.

Unknown to all but the monks and a select few others, there was no Blessed Cummian, fifth abbot of Tara, and never had been. The grave was a hiding place, and the monks were now carrying armfuls of gold and silver chalices and incensors, plates, bowls, reliquaries, bibles and prayer books with gold and jewel encrusted covers, wine ladles, monstrances, gold chains and crosiers, all the considerable wealth of the monastery at Tara, and placing it all in the hole in the floor that ostensibly housed an innocuous abbot one hundred and fifty years dead.

Morrigan paid no attention to any of this activity. She could not think of it, or of protecting Tara, or hiding its wealth or anything at all beyond the spreading and perhaps irremovable stain on her soul. She knelt before the altar, the tears now running down her cheeks with abandon. She made the sign of the cross and began to pray and then, aware of how insufficient that gesture was, laid herself out, face down, arms outspread on the mat of rushes on the floor. In that position of supplication she began to pray, for her brother, for the people of Tara, for her enemies, and lastly for her own damaged soul.

She prayed as she had not prayed in years, the way she had prayed when she was a little girl, the way she had prayed when she had been first taken by the Norsemen, all those years before. Before her life had become one nightmare of pain and humiliation built on another, and she had abandoned prayer in any meaningful way and let hate and doubt and ambition take its place.

Soon Morrigan was lost in her prayers, oblivious to the world beyond the spiritual world in which she had entered, and it was only when a sound intruded on her prayers, a sound so rhythmic and insistent that she could not ignore it, that she returned from that place where she had gone. She had no notion of how much time had passed. The monks had left and Blessed Cummian's stone was back in place. She cocked her head and listened. *Boom…boom…boom…* She did not recognize the sound, had never heard the like before. It was like a hand knocking on a door, a giant hand on a giant door.

Yes… she thought, understanding at last what she was hearing. *That is exactly what it is.* It was a battering ram and it was knocking down the gates of Tara.

* * *

I am glad they are not all like this, these Irishmen, Thorgrim thought as he watched the men-at-arms deploying the battering ram. The ram itself was no great marvel, just a substantial tree trunk with an iron cap and smaller cross pieces lashed beneath at regular intervals to serve as handles for the men wielding the device. What impressed him was the ease with which they had brought it into place, manned the grips while the others spread out and held their shields aloft to protect against a potential rain of spears or arrows. There had been few orders given. The men simply knew what to do and they did it.

If every Irish army were disciplined like these, and if they did not all fight one another, we would be driven from this land in a week…Thorgrim thought.

But that was not quite true, and he knew it. The Northmen represented a potent military force which, for a price, one Irish king could deploy against another, as was happening now. The Norse with their raids represented a redistribution of riches, which worked to the benefit of many Irish. Norse trade brought Irish goods to the world, and the world's goods to Ireland in a way that the land-bound natives of this island never could. The Irish might bemoan the Norse sacking their Christ-God temples and monasteries, but Thorgrim knew for a fact that the Irish plundered their rivals' temples as frequently as ever the Vikings did.

No, for all their hatred of the *fin gall* and the *dubh gall*, the Irish found the Norsemen useful in a hundred ways.

Perhaps we are *here to stay*, Thorgrim thought. *But not me.*

All this he considered as he watched the Irish take hold of the battering ram and with a rhythmic shout slam its iron-tipped end against the great oak gates of Tara. The doors shuddered and moved a bit, but held, and the men with the ram drew it back and slammed it into the doors again. On either side of them, more men-at-arms held shields aloft to defend against the occasional spear that darted down from the wall above, but there was little threat from that direction.

Twenty feet behind the battering ram, Norse archers stood poised with arrows nocked in bows, ready to pick off any of the defenders of Tara who showed themselves on the wall. After the first three or four Irishmen had been flung back, screaming, arrows jutting from their bodies, the people on the other side had come to understand the deadly accuracy of the Norse bowmen, and the number of men who mounted the wall to interfere with the battering had dropped precipitously. Behind the archers, and spread out in a loose V formation, the rest of them, Norsemen and Irish, waited for the big door to break down, for their moment to rush in.

The battering ram hit again and the doors moved a bit more. It hit again and a gap opened up between them, and splinters appeared where the ram had struck. The men at the handholds swung it back, swung it forward again and again in a regular rhythm that made the door gape and jump with each blow.

The Northmen around Thorgrim took a small step forward, as if drawn by the sound of the splintering wood. He could see hands readjusting their grips on weapons, men shrugging their shoulders and working the kinks out of their arms. Starri was doing that weird, whirling thing he did when he was having trouble containing himself.

And then another crash of the ram against the gate, and this one sounded different. Thorgrim looked up in time to see the big doors crash open, a gap of several feet appearing between them as the bar holding them closed gave way under the relentless pounding. A shout rose up from the waiting men. The ram was tossed aside and the men in the front ranks pushed the doors more open still, the main gate wide enough to let a dozen men enter abreast.

They began to crowd forward, every man eager to get in through the gap, to get at the enemy. Then suddenly the space beyond the doors bloomed with light as a great column of flame rose up just within the walls. There was shrieking from the front, and orders shouted in the Irish language that Thorgrim could not understand, but Thorgrim smiled and thought, *Smart…these Irish can be smart when they wish.*

Tara's defenders had stacked flammables just inside the gate. Thorgrim guessed it was straw, no doubt soaked with some sort of oil, since nothing would burn otherwise on a day such as that. They had waited until the doors had been smashed open, the enemy surging through before touching it off. Where the walls of dirt and oak could not keep this attacking army back, they had set a wall of flames. But that would not hold their enemy back, either, not for long.

The men in the front ranks, Irish men-at-arms and Norsemen, charged forward, shields held high to deflect the flames as they would any other weapons. They kicked the burning material aside, but as they did, the real defense, arrows and spears from the Irish ranks within, came ripping through the columns of flame, fired by men hidden behind the fire.

Thorgrim pushed forward, Harald at his side. He was eager as any to get into the fight, but experienced enough to know it did no one any good for them to crowd and jam into the relatively narrow gate. He reached over and put a hand on Harald, restraining the boy. "Do not forget what we are about!" he shouted over the din and Harald nodded.

Thorgrim looked to his right, where Starri had been, but the berserker was no longer there, which was no surprise. Thorgrim looked ahead, just in time to see Starri literally climb over another man's back and launch himself off the man's shoulders at something unseen beyond the press of struggling warriors.

Just inside the gate a line of men-at-arms kicked at the burning material and batted it with their shields, fighting to make a hole. Two of them were flung back like they had been gored by bulls, arrows buried in their chests, and two more stepped up to take their place.

The fire and the arrows and spears were taking their toll, but it was clear to Thorgrim and must have been clear to all that the defenders could do nothing to hold the attacking army back for more than a minute or so. *I wonder what other surprises they have waiting for us?* Thorgrim thought. *Morrigan, what have you conjured up? We shall know directly…*

There was a gap now in what had been a solid wall of flame, the front ranks had managed to knock the burning straw aside and made a passage through the fire. Now Irish and Norse were pushing through, pouring through the gap. Thorgrim could see the ranks of men beyond the flames, two ranks, shields ready, and archers and men with spears in the front, taking down the enemy as they came. But the gap in the flames grew wider as more and more men pushed through, and the archers tossed their bows aside and drew swords, readying themselves for the bloody hand to hand fighting that would come.

The Irish troops, Brigit's troops, charged the line, a semi-organized attack that drove the defenders back a step, but they did not break or yield. All along the line the swords rose and fell, the sound of shouting and metal on metal, metal on wooden shield and the links of mail shirts rolled around the ringfort.

But the Norsemen were holding back. The very men who would otherwise have been in the front ranks of the bloody fighting were three paces behind, and they did not look eager to take part. Because it was, in truth, not their fight.

Thorgrim and Harald were through the gate, through the last of the burning straw and the choking smoke, and the great inner grounds of Tara lay before them, the many buildings, round and wattle built, or tall and square and framed with heavy beams. It was an impressive sight.

"There, Father, there!" Harald pointed with his sword and Thorgrim followed the direction of the blade. Two hundred rods away stood a building framed with black timbers, its daub walls whitewashed, a tall, proud looking structure, not the largest within the walls but set off from the rest in a way that gave it an air of importance. It had a tall spire, and on top of it, a great wooden cross, a massive version of the tiny silver one Thorgrim had strung around his neck, along with the silver hammer of Thor.

"This way! Northmen, with me!" Thorgrim shouted, Iron-tooth above his head, waving and pointing in the direction of the church. The others; Ornolf, Hrolleif, Ingolf, even Arinbjorn took up the call, shouting in words that Thorgrim knew would be as unintelligible to the Irish as the Irish tongue was to him.

"This way! This way!" The Norsemen who had come with Arinbjorn, and who had come with Ornolf, began to peel away from the line and fall in with Thorgrim and the other leaders. The men whom Thorgrim had designated to bring Starri along dragged him out of the fight, shrieking and flailing, and pulled him after the others. Soon they had their backs to the Irishmen, still fighting in two lines of battle, contending for the throne of Tara, while the men from Dubh-linn, the men from across the sea, raced through the mud and standing water toward the church and the riches to be found there.

Because in the council of the jarls, held back on the rain soaked field, Harald had assured them all that they could not believe a single promise made by these Irish, that the Irish would betray the Norsemen every time. This advice had fallen on ears quite ready to believe it. If they wanted the wealth of Tara, Harald suggested, then they had better go in and take it themselves, because it would not be offered up, no matter what they were told.

The others agreed. But how, they wondered, might they gather up the plunder and escape, when the Irish army would be at the gate? But Harald had an answer to that as well. There was a back way, he told them. Another way out of Tara. And he knew where it was.

Chapter Forty-Six

I felt blood spilled
over my shoulders
by a corpse- net's wielder
with his sharp sword
Gisli Sursson's Saga

They covered the ground quickly. The one time that Thorgrim looked back at the Irishmen still struggling for ground by the gate, it seemed to him they had not even noticed the Norsemen had deserted them, or if they had they were far too busy to protest. Either way it was of no concern. Plunder the church and be gone, leave these ridiculous struggles for control of Ireland to the Irish; that was all they were thinking of now.

Hrolleif was the first to reach the door. He threw his massive shoulder against the solid oak, and grunted as he bounced off. "More of you, come on, bear a hand here!" he shouted and eager men leapt forward and began to drive their shoulders against the unyielding door.

Then Ingolf spoke. "Are you certain it's bolted?"

Hrolleif grabbed the iron latch and lifted. The door swung open and Hrolleif made a grunting sound, said something unintelligible, and stepped in. The rest followed behind.

The interior of the church was dimly lit by the gray daylight coming in through the tall, narrow windows. There were no candles burning, no one inside the church that they could see. The Norsemen spread out slowly in the big space and no one spoke. The quiet of the church seemed to infect them, and the possible presence of spirits, spirits of the Christ-God whose power they could not judge, made them wary and afraid in ways no human could.

"Very well," Ornolf said, louder than was necessary, and Thorgrim saw several men start with surprise. "We have very little time if we don't want to fight our way out of here. Godi, stand by the door, keep watch on the battle by the gate, give warning if they come this way." Godi nodded and went back to the door, still ajar, and peeked out through the narrow gap.

"There'll be gold and silver here somewhere," Ingolf said, "all these churches, they all have gold and silver. Let us find it, quick."

The loud voices, the harsh orders helped break the spell cast by the quiet of the church and the men began to fan out, tossing chairs and small tables aside, kicking up the rushes that covered the floor to look for hidden places below. They were moving toward the altar when one of them, one of Ingolf's men, gave a stifled scream, not a particularly manly sound, which made the others freeze and look up.

The man was pointing toward the altar, and by the sheepish look on his face Thorgrim guessed that he now saw the threat was not as terrible as his reaction suggested. "There's someone here," he said.

Thorgrim pushed through the men and walked quickly toward the altar. A woman was lying on the floor, flat out, arms spread, and Thorgrim was certain on seeing her that she was dead. And as he stepped closer, he was equally certain that he knew who she was.

"Morrigan?" he said, his voice low. He was not really expecting an answer, but to his surprise she turned over and sat up, staring up at him. Her face was wet with tears, her eyes rimmed in red, and she looked at him with an expression such as he had never seen her wear: confusion, dismay, a lost and distant look.

Ornolf stepped up by Thorgrim's side. "I know you!" he exclaimed. "Why, you are that thrall, Morrigan!"

"We all know her," Thorgrim reminded him. "And we are the worse for it." But Morrigan still looked at them, with an expression like a stunned bird, and said nothing.

"Well, this is a bit of luck," Ornolf declared. "This thrall will know where the churchmen hid their treasure. Come there, Morrigan, tell us where it is."

But Morrigan just continued to stare, and after some seconds of silence she slowly shook her head.

Arinbjorn pushed his way through the press of men. He had a dagger in his hand, and his face was red, his jaw working. "I will make this bitch talk, by the gods, see if I don't," he said, and he advanced on Morrigan, but Thorgrim put a hand on his arm and held him back.

"No," he said, tightening his grip as Arinbjorn tried to shake it off. "That will do nothing, you will get nothing from her." Thorgrim had spent time enough with Morrigan to know what she was made of, and he guessed that he knew what would loosen her tongue, and what would not.

"See here, Morrigan," he said, "we are done with fighting you Irish. We mean to plunder this church and be gone, but we do not have much time. If you won't help us find the silver and gold, we'll tear the church apart, and as a diversion we will set it on fire when we go."

He held her eyes and she held his and neither spoke, neither moved. Half a minute swept past and Thorgrim said, loud, still looking at Morrigan but addressing the others, "Very well, she will not speak. Tear this place apart." He pointed with Iron-tooth toward the altar. "Start there."

Half a dozen men had moved passed Thorgrim, past Morrigan, toward the altar when Morrigan finally spoke. "No. Wait." Everyone stopped and the church was silent, completely silent. Then Morrigan pointed toward the final resting place of Blessed Cummian, fifth abbot of Tara.

With their numbers substantial and their motivation high, it took the Norsemen little time to move the stone and empty out the hoard of treasure hidden in the floor of the church. The sight of all that gold and silver put them in a generous mood, and they were willing even to do as Morrigan asked, removing the relics from the reliquaries before tossing them in the makeshift sacks made from altar clothes, tearing the bejeweled covers off the bibles and tossing them in the pile but leaving the illuminated manuscripts behind.

Five minutes and they had cleaned out the false grave and Godi had called no warning from the door. They could still hear the shout and clash of battle, but it was becoming less frenetic as the combatants grew weary or collapsed from wounds received.

"Let us go," Ornolf said in a commanding voice. "Harald, show us the way." The alter clothes were gathered up, the men headed toward the altar and a small door behind it. Morrigan stood by the open grave, the relics and torn manuscripts at her feet. Arinbjorn grabbed her arm, squeezed it and dragged her along.

Thorgrim stopped and turned to him. "What are you doing?"

"She comes with me. After all the tricks she has played, the deaths of my men on her head, she will come with me and she will pay it back in full."

"No," Thorgrim said. "She did us a good turn. In Dubh-linn. She saved Harald's life. And she spared yours. Leave her be."

"I care not what she might have done for you. I only care what she did to me. And my men."

"She was defending her home, her people," Thorgrim said. "Who here would not have done as much? Would you kill her because she outwitted us?"

The two men stared at one another, their hatred like a physical presence. Neither spoke. But Thorgrim was aware of the seconds slipping past, and each one lost lessened the chance of their escape. "Leave her," he said with finality. "If you try to take her, by Odin you will answer to me."

He saw Arinbjorn release his grip. He turned to follow the rest to the door when he heard the motion behind, and before he could turn back he felt the needle point of the dagger pierce his mail shirt and drive in deep, felt the point deflect off his shoulder bone and bury itself in the muscle under his left arm.

He whirled around but Arinbjorn did not let go of the handle, and the action pulled the knife free. Thorgrim could feel the blood running down inside his tunic. A half a second later the pain came, like forked lighting tearing through his shoulder, his back, his neck. He staggered sideways his eyes on the knife, dripping blood, still gripped in Arinbjorn's hand.

And then they came for Arinbjorn, Harald from one direction, Ornolf from another, swords raised, and Arinbjorn looked left and right in panic.

"No!" Thorgrim ordered, surprised at the strength he found in his voice. This had been coming for a long time, and he could not allow Arinbjorn to simply be cut down by half a dozen swords. His right arm still worked, and neither he nor Arinbjorn carried shields, so he had no need for his left. Fair enough.

"Arinbjorn and I will settle this," Thorgrim said, raising Iron-tooth and feeling the shaft of pain as he did, realizing he may have just made his last mistake. "Let no man interfere here."

Arinbjorn wiped the blade of his knife on his trouser leg, sheathed it and drew his sword. Their attacks were simultaneous, the blades coming together, the ring of steel loud in the now silent church, the men forming a circle around the combatants like some sort of human amphitheater. Thorgrim stood sideways to Arinbjorn, his wounded shoulder well back, lunged and missed. Arinbjorn swept his blade down in an arc, looking for Iron-tooth, but Thorgrim twisted his sword aside and Arinbjorn found only air.

Thorgrim renewed the attack and Arinbjorn backed away. The blood was spreading, warm and wet, down Thorgrim's back. The pain in his shoulder was such as he had not endured in a long, long time.

Arinbjorn swung his blade again, but this time Thorgrim was not fast enough and Arinbjorn connected with Iron-tooth and swept it aside. He stepped in and lunged and, lacking a shield, Thorgrim could do nothing but use his left arm, mail-clad, to parry the thrust. But his arm would barely respond, and as it struck Arinbjorn's sword and pushed it aside the pain was redoubled. Arinbjorn stepped closer still, too close to use his sword, but with his right hand gripping the hilt he punched Thorgrim hard in his wounded shoulder.

Thorgrim shouted with agony, something he could not recall ever having done. He lashed out at Arinbjorn with his fist, connected with the side of his head and sent him stumbling back, but the punch was weak and he knew it, and he could see Arinbjorn had moved more from surprise than from the impact of the blow.

There was no sound save for the two men gasping for breath, and then Godi's voice came echoing down the length of the nave. "They've left off fighting!" he called. "I see men pointing this way!"

Arinbjorn attacked again, driven by anger and a desperate need that Thorgrim could see in his eyes. And Thorgrim, growing weaker with each pulse of blood flowing from his wound, could do nothing but step back and step back again and try to keep Arinbjorn's blade from getting past his defense. He was a leaking cask; the strength was flowing out of him now, and soon he would die because he could no longer hope to do anything but fend off Arinbjorn's attack, and even that he could not do much longer.

"Here they come!" Godi shouted and Thorgrim was vaguely aware of a murmur running through the watching Northmen and then his foot tangled in an overturned chair and he went down, falling back, straight back. There was something inevitable, even comforting in the fall, as if he was free from the terrible burden of fighting now, as if he would just fall and keep falling until he had fallen clear into oblivion.

And then he hit, and the shuddering impact brought another scream of agony to his throat, but he clenched his teeth this time and held it back. Arinbjorn was above him, sword raised, and then the man's throat seemed to explode in a shower of blood. His eyes went wide and his head snapped back and he made some weird noise, a liquid noise, and he collapsed, missing Thorgrim by inches, his arm falling across Thorgrim's chest like a lover.

Morrigan was standing there now, behind where Arinbjorn had been, a blood-tipped sword in her hand. "There," she said. "No *man* has interfered with your ritual of pagan vengeance. Now take your plunder and go. Perhaps you will trade it all with Lucifer for a cup of water, but I think not."

And they went. Thorgrim, supported by Harald on one side, Starri on the other, was half-dragged, half carried through the door in the back, the others following behind, so that the church was between them and the Irish men-at-arms whom Godi reported cautiously advancing toward them. They crossed the open ground, made for the door, which Harald remembered well, the door that Brigit had led him through so many months before when she helped him escape from her father's fatal designs. There were no guards this time. Every man who could carry a weapon had been fighting.

If they were seen by the Irish, they had no knowledge of it. No shouts, no pursuit. They swung the door open, poured through that opening in the ringfort walls, made for the woods at the base of the long Hill of Tara. The Irish did not come after them. Any lust for combat they may have felt that morning had been sated long before.

* * *

Morrigan sat amid the ruins of the church, the nave, like her life, torn apart, a tumble of broken bits, the damage the Northmen had inflicted before they discovered her prostrate on the floor. They had left through the back door, and soon after Ruarc mac Brain's men had come in the front, and they had been none too gentle either, and with less excuse because they were not looking for plunder. They were just looking to destroy something that was not theirs.

Through it all Morrigan had sat on the edge of an unturned chair, the heavy oak seat that the priest used when he was not at the altar, her eyes fixed on a crucifix lying on the floor. It was made of wood, not silver or gold, and so it had been left behind. Morrigan stared at the carving of her Lord in agony on the cross and she felt one with him, and she understood that it was not the physical pain, not the pain of nails through hands and feet, which gave him the hurt that consumed him so. She might have wept, but she was far beyond that now.

After a while Ruarc's men had left and still Morrigan sat, unmoving, unsure what she would do, other than simply remain where she was until she died of hunger and thirst. That would be fine. Would it be suicide? Did it matter? Was there any hope left for her stained and tattered soul?

She heard the door open softly. Not flung open, but eased, just a crack, and she sensed rather than heard someone moving toward her.

"Morrigan?"

For the first time since the Norsemen had carried Thorgrim out the back door Morrigan lifted her eyes from the crucifix. "Father Finnian," she said. It was a simple statement. She was not surprised to see him, because she was far too drained to feel surprise.

Finnian walked further into the church, looking at the debris left in the wake of the pillaging warriors. He stopped just a few feet from Morrigan. "Your brother Flann is dead," he said, his voice soft and compassionate. Morrigan just nodded her head. She already knew that, knew it in her soul.

"Ruarc mac Brain has taken Tara," Finnian continued. "He will put Brigit on the throne. But no harm will come to you, I've seen to that."

Morrigan looked at him for a moment, then looked away. "It does not matter," she said.

Finnian came closer still, until he was inches away. He reached out and gently pressed his palm against her cheek and turned her face so she was looking up at him. She saw in his eyes an empathy and a tenderness that she had not seen in many years, and even then had seen only in her brother's eyes, when they were children, before Flann had come into the service of Máel Sechnaill mac Ruanaid, before he had learned how to kill men.

"You have suffered greatly, Morrigan," Finnian said. "I know that."

"And now I am to suffer more?"

"That I do not know. I can absolve you of your sins. Beyond that, it is not up to me."

Morrigan looked back at the wooden Christ on the cross. Genuine repentance, confession, absolution, these were things she believed were as true as the sunrise, but she no longer believed that they could be hers. Not after all this.

"I can see the repentance in your eyes, my child," Finnian said. "Let me hear your confession, and absolution is yours. And then you will help me to remove a great evil, and we will see you off to another place. And I pray, sincerely I do, that it is a better place."

Epilogue

The haughty unshaven horde
Began to traverse the harbours;
Birds' bills with bearded heads were seen
Coming from the churches of Ulaid.
The Annals of Ulster

From the ship's afterdeck, Thorgrim cursed it all: the Liffey, the thick cluster of homes and shops, the earthen walls of the outer defenses, the hills rolling away green from the edge of the sea, ugly Dubh-linn, huddled against the gray river, the smoke hanging low over the thatched roofs. The deck was his deck, the ship his own ship, and he was a richer man now for all the plunder they had taken from Tara, but none of that could ease the bitterness he felt at being here again, once more crawling up the river to Dubh-linn, that cursed Dubh-linn, from which the gods seemed unwilling to release him.

It was one week since the fighting at Tara. They had half carried Thorgrim to the edge of the woods and there had paused long enough to rig up a stretcher and carry him back to the ships that lay at anchor in the river Boyne. They kept a sharp lookout behind, waiting for the Irish, enraged and hungry for revenge, to burst like a flock of ravens from the ringfort and tear into them, but they never came, and the only impediments that the Northmen encountered on their march to the river were their own weariness and the wounds they had suffered.

They removed Thorgrim's mail shirt while he forced himself to remain silent, despite the agony. They cut the blood-encrusted tunic away. It was now that they wanted for Morrigan and her healing ways, but there were men among the Norsemen who had considerable experience in treating battle wounds, and they attended to Thorgrim with skill. The wound was deep, but Arinbjorn's dagger had been thin and sharp and had not ripped up the muscle in its passing. The dried blood was washed away; a poultice was put in place, bandages wrapped around the ugly laceration. Harald hovered and made himself conspicuously helpful until Thorgrim, biting back the irritation, commanded him to stop.

They were underway the next morning, but little wind, and then contrary wind and racing currents made their voyage back to the longphort a long, wearisome and frustrating endeavor. Six days underway before they raised Dubh-linn, and then for eight hours the mouth of the Liffey remained in sight as the fleet pulled against the tide with their long oars, the carved heads at the bows removed so as not to frighten any spirits ashore, and to signal to those watching from the longphort that they did not come with the intent to do harm.

The ships were hauled up on the beach and once again Thorgrim was eased into the stretcher and with Harald and Starri at his head and Godi and Ingolf at his feet, Ornolf at his side keeping up a running soliloquy, they carried him swaying and cursing up the plank road to Almaith's house.

The forge was cold, and the house quiet, the constant hammering and the hiss of the bellow now gone, but Almaith was there and she gasped in surprise to see Thorgrim and the condition he was in. She ordered him brought inside and laid out on the bedding in the big room while she stoked up the fire under the iron pot and gathered up her medicines: dried nettles, dandelion, St. John's wort.

Thorgrim did not doubt they would find a welcome at Almaith's hearth. Almaith cared about him, he could see that. He could see past everything she was and see that at her very core the affection she had for him was real. And on a more practical level, she needed him and the other men, Harald, Starri, Ornolf. She needed them there because she, an Irish woman alone in the Norwegian longphort, was in a precarious way without them. And Thorgrim knew her secret. He knew the treachery of which she was guilty, he knew that it had led to many needless deaths among the Norsemen. He knew and he kept it to himself. She would be grateful for that, and she would be wary of him.

But mostly, he was welcome because she cared for him. It was as simple as that.

And so Thorgrim lay back on the thick furs and tried to ignore the extraordinary pain in his shoulder and the bustle around him, the voices of the people as they shuffled in and out, and noise from the town crowded around the house, the ring of the hammers and the sounds of labor and commerce, the call of gulls fighting for scraps and men and women and children living out their lives. He closed his eyes and he thought of the sea, and he thought of his ship cleaving the dark blue waves and sending the water curling white down the long run of the hull. He pictured himself at the tiller, shifting the steering board a bit to larboard, a bit to starboard to keep her track straight and true.

The track led east. It led away from this accursed Dubh-linn, this Ireland with its fighting and treachery and pain. It led back to his farm in Vik, his grandchildren, his home. He would heal and he would take his son, and his father-in-law if he would go, and he would gather a crew and he would steer his ship that way, north and east, straight and true.

It was six months after Ruarc mac Brain had taken Tara from the pretender Flann and reestablished the line of Máel Sechnaill mac Ruanaid on the throne, half a year during which the rains of spring had yielded to summer and Ireland bloomed with the glorious abundance of that place, the cattle and sheep grew fat, and the brown earth was lost from sight under the great blooms of wheat and barley before Father Finnian had the chance to ride north.

And when he did, the rains had come again, bitter cold and driving hard with the advent of autumn, and the harvest was brought in and the stores laid up for gray winter and he stood huddled before a peat fire in the scribe's room at the Abbey of Kells, ten day's ride from Tara.

The abbey had stood where it stood for nearly three hundred years, and though generations before it had been all but abandoned, it flourished again during the lifetime of Finnian's father, when an order of Columban monks had fled there from the edge of the sea, the sea that brought the heathen raiders again and again. But even that had not spared the monks from the wrath of the Northmen, who spread like rushes across Ireland, because proximity to the sea was no longer necessary to invite their depredations.

Finnian held his hands up to the inadequate flame, and then with a flush of guilt he tossed another peat brick onto the fire. It flared and caught. The flame blossomed and a wave of heat rose up to Finnian's numb hands. He had just made some extra work for some peasant, some poor soul who would toil in the peat bog to cut one more brick because he, Finnian, felt the need for more warmth.

His particular friend, Father Ainmire, sat at the tall writing desk behind him. Ainmire would not mind the extra peat; it would not even occur to him that Finnian was being wasteful, because Ainmire was, in Finnian's opinion, the most generous of souls. Here indeed was yet another example of that generosity. Ainmire was desperately eager to hear what Finnian had to say, and Finnian knew it well, but his friend was willing to wait with admirable patience as Finnian regained his circulation.

The wind whipped around the stone walls and worked its way into the cracks and the windows and made a whistling and moaning sound. The fire danced in the fireplace and the flame of the candle on Ainmire's desk danced and the two men enjoyed the moment of companionable silence.

"The devil has been loose in Brega this year, or so I hear from those few travelers who pass this way," Ainmire said at last.

"The devil has been there, my friend, but the angels, too, I'm pleased to say." Finnian turned to face Ainmire and to give his backside a chance to enjoy the delicious warmth of the fire. Ainmire's face was all yellow light and shadow from the flame of the candle. He reached up and drew a quill from an inkpot, feigning all the indifference he was able to feign.

Gossip was a sin, and such eagerness for news unseemly, but Ainmire's interest in the goings-on was more than mere curiosity. Before him lay a scrap of vellum on which he would record those things that Finnian told him. Later he would transcribe those words into the great volume of annals that was his sacred duty, and that of his fellow monks, to keep. The annals comprised the history of the land of Ireland, a record of the events of great importance and a way to mark the passing of the days and months that allowed them to calculate the proper date for their moveable feasts.

"We heard here that Brigit nic Máel Sechnaill was wed," Ainmire prompted.

"Wed this past spring, to Conlaed uí Chennselaigh of Ardsallagh, but it was not a fortunate union. Not a week or more after, there was a fire in the royal house. Half the building in ashes. Brigit managed to get out, but Conlaed did not."

"How did she escape and not him?" Ainmire asked.

"I don't know. Brigit did not know, she seems to have forgotten all that took place that night. She reckoned Conlaed died in saving her."

Ainmire's quill scratched at the vellum.

"That was when the devil came to Tara," Finnian went on. "Flann was already on the throne, and his sister, Morrigan, held much of the power and did not seem inclined to give it up. Brigit feared for her life. So she fled."

Scratch, scratch, scratch. "To where, brother?"

"To Dubh-linn at first, I believe," Finnian said. "She told me after, she thought there was no place among the Irish where she would be safe. But later she realized the heathens were worse than any Irish might be, so she sought out Ruarc mac Brain, who she knew to be a good man, and it was he who restored her to the throne of Tara."

"And is it true they are to wed?"

Finnian smiled. "Yes, it's true. Ruarc is a brave man. Brigit has been married twice thus far, and twice have her husbands come to bad ends."

Scratch, scratch, scratch. "So there might yet be an heir to the throne at Tara?"

"There is already," Finnian said. Ainmire looked up from his vellum with a quizzical look in which Finnian took a secret delight. "A son was born to Brigit about three months back."

"How…?"

"He is the child of Brigit and Conlaed uí Chennselaigh. They were married but a week, it's true, but a week is time enough. A wedding night is time enough." By the light of the candle Finnian saw Ainmire blush and turn back to his writing.

"And Flann?" Ainmire asked. "And Morrigan?"

"Flann was killed in fighting Ruarc mac Brain," Finnian said. "As to Morrigan, I'll admit to stepping in there and seeing no harm came to her. She did a bad thing, but she was repentant, truly, and forgiven in the eyes of God. And she has suffered a great deal in this life."

Ainmire wrote. "So, where is she?" he asked.

"She has joined a holy order. Her life will be spent bringing glory to God."

Ainmire wrote. *And thus is history created*, Finnian thought.

"There is one more thing…" Ainmire said, and his tone was slightly embarrassed. "I would not mention it, but we have heard rumors, you know, more than one."

"Yes?"

"There are some that say St. Patrick himself has come back, and has visited poor farmers to the south. Have you heard such? I ask because of the annals…."

Finnian smiled. "Yes, I've heard such," he said. "But I think I would not put that in your book. Who can tell from where such stories come?"

It was just over a year after Ruarc mac Brain set Brigit nic Máel Sechnaill on the throne of Tara that a certain beamy, squat merchant ship moved listlessly in the light air blowing over the Sea of Marmara. It may have been a distant cousin to the Viking longships, with its single square sail and the smooth run of its sheer, but there the similarities ended. Where the longship was narrow and fast, the merchantman was wide and slow, with a deep and heavy hull, decked over as the longships were not, providing safe storage below for the considerable cargo she carried; silks and amphora jugs of wine and olive oil, sacks of grain, all the varied commerce that had moved for centuries around the Mediterranean world.

The sun beat down on the deck, oppressively hot, like a hand pressing down on the passengers and crew who moved slowly when they moved at all. And there was not much need to move. With that light breeze it would be an hour at least before they were close enough to the waterfront to think about getting the anchor out or warping the ship alongside the stone quay.

At the after end of the ship, on the raised quarterdeck where the master and the steersman stood, a small knot of passengers had gathered to watch the approach to the city, their destination after a very long journey. They were silent, almost unwilling to speak, as if their voices might make it all vanish, as if any noise might render it all a dream, because after all those months, all the hardship, the suffering, the depredation, it did not seem at all possible that they could at last be there.

Constantinople was spread out along the larboard side of the ship, a great city of towers and grand stone edifices, churches, flags, great houses, surrounded by massive stone walls. Even from that distance they could see the people, so many people. They reckoned in one glance they had laid eyes on more souls than they had seen cumulatively in their lifetimes. And such people! White people and brown and black, in flowing gowns and rich silks, with turbans and veils and helmets and straw hats, some walking, some carried in chairs, some peaking from gilt coaches pushing through the jammed streets.

That much they were able to see from the deck of the ship, and it made them wonder what they would find when they finally set foot ashore, and it made them a bit afraid. In all the things they had seen in the year past, things they could not have imagined, the countries through which they had traveled, the cities of Europe, the lands of the Mediterranean, there was nothing that compared to the sight of the Queen of Cities.

Morrigan reached for the purse that hung from her belt, concealed under the linin cloak draped over her shoulders. She fingered the soft leather, gauging the contents, and, satisfied, she pulled the knot loose and took the purse in her hands. She crossed the deck, feeling the melting pitch in the seams tugging at the bottom of her shoes. She approached the master who stood, bored, by the steersman.

"Sir?" she said. They had no common language, she and this fat, swarthy man. He had told her once from which country he came, but the name was meaningless to her. They had no language in common, but by stumbling through Norse and Latin and some of the Gaulish she had picked up they managed to communicate. They had sailed from Barcelona, which was once more a Christian stronghold after being wrested from the Moors two generations earlier. They had not been far from port before the master managed to communicate that passage might be free in exchange for certain services, and Morrigan in turn communicated that the passage would be paid for in the traditional way.

Now she wished to settle that matter, before they were alongside the quay. The master looked at her, annoyed. "Yes?"

She opened the purse and withdrew three rubies and three emeralds, and held them up for his inspection. They were large and perfect and if he hoped to play coy with her his bulging eyes had already given him away. "They are all I have. For us?" She indicated the two with her.

The master collected himself, pretended to consider this, then said, "Very well." He held out his leathery palm and Morrigan dropped the jewels in the cupped hand and the fingers wrapped around them.

It was not entirely true that the six jewels were all she had, but she had no qualms about misleading the likes of the ship's master, who was likely no sort of Christian. She had other jewels, and she had silver and gold. It had been enough to get them that far, and still a fortune remained.

The jewels had been pried from the rim of the Crown of the Three Kingdoms, the silver filigree as well, the massive gold crown itself cut and weighed and melted down. The crown for whom so many had died, for which Morrigan had committed so many sins against God, and now its gold and silver were cast into small ingots and its jewels scooped into a leather purse and only she and Finnian and Ruarc mac Brain knew it, because they alone had been there when it was done in the blacksmith's shop at Tara.

They had traveled to the town of Cill Mhantáin, which the Northmen called Vík-ló, and there had found a ship, a beamy knarr, bound for the Gaulish countries. Finnian had negotiated the passage and they had sailed aboard her, Morrigan and Patrick and Donnel. They had reached Paris, a city of great churches which, like Ireland, had fallen victim to Norsemen's depredations again and again. But, also like the Irish, the Gauls were not adverse to some honest trade with the Northmen, and so the knarr reached the quays of the Seine unmolested, and Morrigan and her two companions began the long overland journey to Barcelona.

It had cost money, but they had money, and they found charity with Christians along the way, who were pleased to hear of their mission and happy to aide them on their journey. Through bitter cold, withering heat, over mountain passes and across interminable plains the pilgrims had traveled; they had seen sights they could not have imagined, met people of every possible stripe. They had feared for their lives and they had thanked their God for their deliverance and they had never wavered in their determination.

And now, at last, from the deck of that stubby ship, the great city of Constantinople was spread out before them. Down below, secreted in a hidden place in her trunk, Morrigan still held a small fortune in ingots from the crown and gold and silver that had been donated by those along the way, money for her travels which thanks to her frugality and the kindness of others she had not spent. She had volumes of manuscripts, copied out and illuminated by the monks of Ireland, the great learning of Western civilization, preserved, and now sent back to the countries from which it had come.

Somewhere out there, in that city, amid the grand edifices to the Christian God, there was a small monastery, a gathering of Columban monks, charged with disseminating the work of the Irish monasteries and the great troves of literature that had been preserved by them in their far-flung land. And here was Morrigan, who, by Finnian's orders, would arrive like an angel from heaven with the treasure needed to keep that monastery, those monks and their mission alive. Morrigan nic Conaing, ready to start life anew, her pale skin turned brown, her sins washed away, her life resurrected as if bleached white and clean by the sun of the ancient world.

To sign up for our (occasional) newsletter with announcements of upcoming titles, exclusive short stories, sample chapters and lots of other good stuff free, please visit our web site:

www.JamesLNelson.com

The story of Thorgrim Night Wolf, Harald, *et al* continues in:

The Lord of Vík-ló
Book III

Glendalough Fair
Book IV
(January 2, 2016)

Glossary

Asgard - the dwelling place of the Norse gods and goddesses, essentially the Norse heaven.

berserker - a Viking warrior able to work himself up into a frenzy of blood lust before a battle. The berserkers, near psychopathic killers in battle, were the fiercest of the Viking soldiers. The word berserker comes from the Norse for "bear shirt" and is the origin of the modern English "berserk".

boss - the round, iron centerpiece of a wooden shield. The boss formed an iron cup protruding from the front of the shield, providing a hollow in the back across which ran the hand grip.

brace - line used for hauling a **yard** side to side on a horizontal plane. Used to adjust the angle of the sail to the wind.

brat – a rectangular cloth worn in various configurations as an outer garment over a *leine.*

bride-price - money paid by the family of the groom to the family of the bride.

byrdingr - A smaller ocean-going cargo vessel used by the Norsemen for trade and transportation. Generally about 40 feet in length, the byrdingr was a smaller version of the more well-known *knarr.*

curragh - a boat, unique to Ireland, made of a wood frame covered in hide. They ranged in size, the largest propelled by sail and capable of carrying several tons. The most common sea-going craft of mediaeval Ireland.

derbfine – In Irish law, a family of four generations, including a man, his sons, grandsons and great grandsons.

dragon ship - the largest of the Viking warships, upwards of 160 feet long and able to carry as many as 300 men. Dragon ships were the flagships of the fleet, the ships of kings.

dubh gall - Gaelic term for Vikings of Danish descent. It means Black Strangers, a reference to the mail armor they wore, made dark by the oil used to preserve it. *See* ***fin gall****.*

ell – a unit of length, a little more than a yard.

eyrir – Scandinavian unit of measurement, approximately an ounce.

félag – a fellowship of men who owed each other a mutual obligation, such as multiple owners of a ship, or a band of warriors who had sworn allegiance to one another.

fin gall - Gaelic term for Vikings of Norwegian descent. It means White Strangers. *See* ***dubh gall****.*

Freya - Norse goddess of beauty and love, she was also associated with warriors, as many of the Norse deities were. Freya often led the **Valkyrie** to the battlefield.

halyard - a line by which a sail or a yard is raised.
Hel - in Norse mythology, the daughter of Loki and the ruler of the underworld where those who are not raised up to Valhalla are sent to suffer. The same name, Hel, is given to the realm over which she rules, the Norse hell.
hird - an elite corps of Viking warriors hired and maintained by a king or powerful **jarl**. Unlike most Viking warrior groups, which would assemble and disperse at will, the hird was retained as a semi-permanent force which formed the core of a Viking army.
hirdsman - a warrior who is a member of the **hird**.
jarl - title given to a man of high rank. A jarl might be an independent ruler or subordinate to a king. Jarl is the origin of the English word *earl*.
knarr - a Norse merchant vessel. Smaller, wider and more sturdy than the longship, knarrs were the workhorse of Norse trade, carrying cargo and settlers wherever the Norsemen traveled.
leine – a long, loose-fitting smock worn by men and women under other clothing. Similar to the shift of a later period.
Loki - Norse god of fire and free spirits. Loki was mischievous and his tricks caused great trouble for the gods, for which he was punished.
longphort - literally, a ship fortress. A small, fortified port to protect shipping and serve as a center of commerce and a launching off point for raiding.
luchrupán – middle Irish word that became the modern-day Leprechaun.
Odin - foremost of the Norse gods. Odin was the god of wisdom and war, protector of both chieftains and poets.
perch - a unit of measure equal to 16½ feet. The same as a rod.
Ragnarok - the mythical final battle when most humans and gods would be killed by the forces of evil and the earth destroyed, only to rise again, purified.
ringfort - common Irish homestead, consisting of houses protected by circular earthwork and palisade walls.
rí túaithe – Gaelic term for a minor king, who would owe allegiance to a high king.
shieldwall - a defensive wall formed by soldiers standing in line with shields overlapping.
skald - a Viking-era poet, generally one attached to a royal court. The skalds wrote a very stylized type of verse particular to the medieval Scandinavians. Poetry was an important part of Viking culture and the ability to write it a highly-regarded skill.
sling - the center portion of the **yard**.
strake – one of the wooden planks that make up the hull of a ship. The construction technique, used by the Norsemen, in which one strake overlaps the one below it is called *lapstrake construction*.

swine array - a viking battle formation consisting of a wedge-shaped arrangement of men used to attack a shield wall or other defensive position.
tánaise ríg – Gaelic term for heir apparent, the man assumed to be next in line for a kingship.
thing - a communal assembly
Thor - Norse god of storms and wind, but also the protector of humans and the other gods. Thor's chosen weapon was a hammer. Hammer amulets were popular with Norsemen in the same way that crosses are popular with Christians.
thrall - Norse term for a slave. Origin of the English word "enthrall".
thwart - a rower's seat in a boat. From the old Norse term meaning "across".
Valhalla - a great hall in **Asgard** where slain warriors would go to feast, drink and fight until the coming of **Ragnarok**.
Valkyrie - female spirits of Norse mythology who gathered the spirits of the dead from the battle field and escorted them to **Valhalla**. They were the Choosers of the Slain, and though later romantically portrayed as Odin's warrior handmaidens, they were originally viewed more demonically, as spirits who devoured the corpses of the dead.
Vik - An area of Norway south of modern-day Oslo. The name is possibly the origin of the term *Viking.*
wattle and daub - common medieval technique for building walls. Small sticks were woven through larger uprights to form the wattle, and the structure was plastered with mud or plaster, the daub.
yard - a long, tapered timber from which a sail was suspended. When a Viking ship was not under sail, the yard was turned lengthwise and lowered to near the deck with the sail lashed to it.

ACKNOWLEDGMENTS

With thanks to Steve Cromwell, whose excellent work on the cover of *Fin Gall* aided so greatly in that book's success, and who kindly worked his magic on this volume as well. Thanks to Kathy Lynn Emerson, author of the terrific *Face Down...* series and many other wonderful works of historical fiction for sharing her knowledge of the use of herbs in medieval times, and to Nathaniel Nelson whose love and knowledge of Norse mythology have been invaluable. A big thanks to David Bellows and his uncanny ability to spot errors in the text. Thanks to Edmund Jorgensen for the terrific help he's given me in navigating the strange seas of internet publishing.

And, as always, to Lisa for more than two decades of love and support.

Other Books by James L. Nelson:

Fiction:

The Norsemen Saga - Novels of Viking Age Ireland
Fin Gall
Dubh-linn
The Lord of Vík-ló
Glendalough Fair (January 2, 2016)

The Brethren of the Coast - Piracy in Colonial America
The Guardship
The Blackbirder
The Pirate Round

The Revolution at Sea Saga – Naval Action of the American Revolution
By Force of Arms
The Maddest Idea
The Continental Risque
Lords of the Ocean
All the Brave Fellows

The Samuel Bowater Novels - Stories of the Confederate Navy
Glory in the Name
Thieves of Mercy

The Only Life that Mattered – The Short and Merry Lives of Ann Bonny, Mary Read and Calico Jack Rackham

Nonfiction:

Reign of Iron: the Story of the First Battling Ironclads, the Monitor *and* Merrimack

Benedict Arnold's Navy: How a Rag Tag Fleet Lost the Battle of Lake Champlain and Won the American Revolution

George Washington's Secret Navy: How the American Revolution Went to Sea

George Washington's Great Gamble: And the Sea Battle that Won the American Revolution

With Fire and Sword: The Battle of Bunker Hill and the Beginning of the American Revolution

Made in the USA
Las Vegas, NV
01 May 2022

48260979R00179